NINE LIARS

NINE
LIARS

MAUREEN JOHNSON

 KATHERINE TEGEN BOOKS
An Imprint of HarperCollins Publishers

Katherine Tegen Books is an imprint of HarperCollins Publishers.

Nine Liars
Copyright © 2022 by HarperCollins Publishers
Map art by Charlotte Tegen

Library of Congress Control Number: 2022941990
ISBN 978-0-06-303265-1 — ISBN 978-0-06-329318-2 (intl ed)

Typography by Carla Weise
10 9 8 7 6 5 4 3 2 1
❖
First Edition

For Gillian Pensavalle and Patrick Hinds,
who would never go to the murder
mansion in the countryside

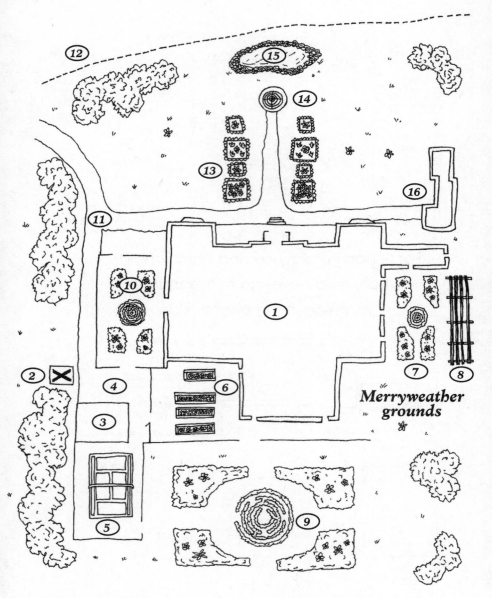

1. House
2. Woodshed
3. Garage
4. Parking area
5. Tennis court
6. Kitchen garden
7. Formal garden
8. Pergola
9. Sprawling back gardens with a circular labyrinth
10. Formal garden
11. Road
12. Ha-ha
13. Front gardens
14. Folly
15. Small pond
16. Stables

Merryweather grounds

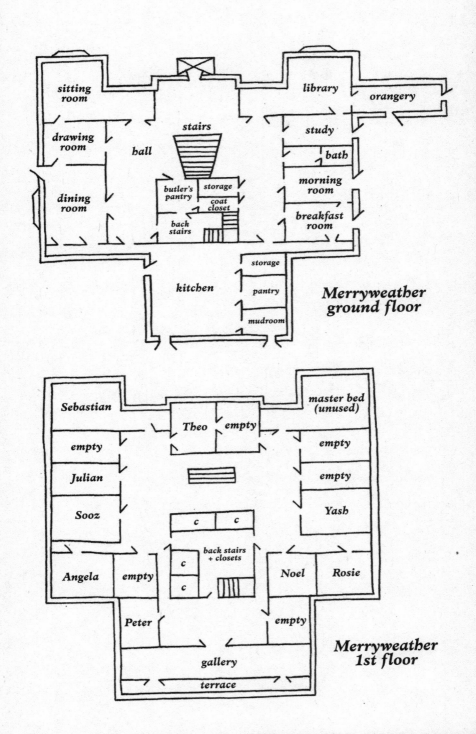

sitting room

library

orangery

drawing room

hall

stairs

study

bath

dining room

butler's pantry

storage

coat closet

morning room

back stairs

breakfast room

kitchen

storage

pantry

mudroom

Merryweather ground floor

Sebastian

Theo

empty

master bed (unused)

empty

empty

Julian

empty

Sooz

Yash

c   **c**

Angela

empty

c

back stairs + closets

Noel

Rosie

c

Peter

empty

gallery

terrace

Merryweather 1st floor

June 23, 1995
9:30 p.m.

"JULIAN IS AN ARSE," SOOZ SAID. "A WORLD-CLASS, UNMITIGATED arse."

Sooz Rillingon took full advantage of her spot in the front seat of the Volvo. She stretched out her six-foot-tall frame, allowing the world at large to behold her abs, which were neatly exposed by a sports bra she pretended was a shirt. There wasn't much of an audience at present, aside from maybe a few sparrows or wood pigeons in the trees along the road, but if they were interested in human abs, they were in for a treat.

They had gotten a late start from Cambridge, but English summer days stretch on for miles. There was still plenty of golden light spilling down on the country lane in Gloucester even at this late hour. The sky was clear now, but there was a vertical line of gunmetal clouds in the distance. It would rain soon.

This was England. There was always rain in the future.

"A *Titanic* arse," Sooz continued, "that sinks all who ride it."

The remarks were directed at Rosie Mortimer, who was paying no attention. She was looking through the open window of the car, reaching out her fingers to gently brush the hedgerows. Her blond pigtails flapped in the breeze, slapping her face. She didn't seem to notice or care. Rosie was not the quiet type, so this distracted silence of hers threw off the usual chemistry.

"We know," Yash said. Yash Varma was about as tall as Sooz, but also had unfailing good manners and had ceded the front seat to her. "Why were you with him for the better part of two years if he's such an arse, Sooz?"

"Because he also *has* a world-class arse."

From the driver's seat, Sebastian Holt-Carey nodded at this.

"Undeniably true on all counts," he said. "Our Julian is in all ways arse."

Sebastian checked the rearview mirror to make sure he hadn't lost the beat-up Volkswagen Golf that was following them. It had vanished from view for a moment, but soon reappeared. There were five people in this car, the Volvo, and another four in the Golf, weaving their way through the hedgerows. Nine in total. Not just any nine. The Nine. Greater than the sum of their parts. Sebastian, Theodora, Yash, Peter, Sooz, Angela, Julian, Rosie, and Noel.

They require introduction. They were:

Sebastian Holt-Carey: future sixth Viscount Holt-Carey. The lord of the manor. Quick-witted and bighearted, with a taste for glam and goth and boys who liked glam and goth.

He slid through Cambridge on a trail of red wine, charm, and a title. Squeaked by with a third in chemistry, and missed out on last place in the exams, which bothered him. You'd think he was passed out or not paying attention, and then he'd bring the house down with a single comment. Tremendously good at playing intense people and improving scenes. Never at a loss for words.

Rosie Mortimer: A pocket-sized Irish student, barely five feet tall, but with the voice and personality of someone five times that size, and a laugh that made the walls shake. An unstoppable force. A bit dramatic, perhaps, but that's what's called for in a drama group. Always willing to take things to the maximum level. Once threw a mug of tea at a policeman.

Sooz Rillington: Big doe-like eyes, legs for miles, and the confidence of ten mediocre men. A brilliant mind for Shakespeare and masterful impressionist. The one who would take off all her clothes on the slightest provocation and run down the road, laughing. Go on. Give her a reason.

Noel Butler: Tall and thin—all angles and nerves and cigarette smoke. He favored vintage 70s clothes—not fancy ones, but proper charity shop ones. Big glasses. Wide-collared shirts. Wide-gauge corduroy jackets. The best straight man a comedy group could have.

Peter Elmore: The natural athlete who had no interest in rowing or chasing a ball. Lanky, with reddish-blond hair that was always an inch longer than he wanted it and heavy-lidded eyes. Technically he was a student of modern political theory; in reality he was a walking database of jokes and gags and

3

the history of comedy. Perhaps the most determined of the group to break into the business. Most likely to burn down the kitchen trying to make toast.

Yash Varma: The other comedy nerd. Obsessed since childhood with all things funny. Sat in front of the TV, transcribing shows by hand to study the patterns and learn how to write. The only person in the group who could possibly take on Peter in terms of comedy knowledge, which was why the two had decided to merge their brains and form a writing pair. The most romantic of the group, with an easily broken heart.

Julian Reynolds: The beautiful one with the soulful eyes and the long lashes. The trouble. Tourists asked him to stand with them in pictures, for no reason aside from the fact that he was a Cambridge student or English or simply there. Irritatingly gifted as a performer. The full package—could act, could sing, could play the guitar. The one who never raised his voice, ever. He never had to—everyone leaned forward to hear what he had to say. His little town up north couldn't contain him. Most of the Nine would grudgingly admit he was often the only reason people came to their shows.

Angela Gill: The history student from Leeds. The quiet one, until she wasn't. Cried with homesickness for the first three nights at Cambridge until she met Sooz at a mixer. She wrote her sketches alone, often with a gin and tonic in a mug on her desk and a cigarette dangling from her lips. Detail oriented, conscientious, and the only one who ever used the washing machine properly.

Theodora Bailey: Without question, the academic of the group. A medical student from Notting Hill in London. The one who planned on using her degree. The one who fixed you up after a long night. The director. The one who figured it all out. As a Black woman at Cambridge, the one who had to deal with the looks, the muttered remarks, and the remarks said right to her face about the color of her skin. Usually locked hip to hip with Sebastian.

The Nine. Going off on a final adventure in two cars down a country road late on a June night.

"The trouble with Julian . . . ," Sooz went on.

"Oh God." Yash put his hands over his face. "Enough. We've talked about Julian nonstop for three years. Let's call a moratorium this week, all right?"

"How do we not talk about him when he's right there?"

"He's not here *now*, in this car."

"I just want Rosie to know she did the right thing. You know that, don't you, Rose? I did the same myself when he did it to me. He's a cheat. He's rotten. One of us should have killed him a long time ago."

Rosie maintained her distracted silence, her brow furrowed in thought.

"We're close, aren't we?" Theo said. Theo was the fifth passenger in the car, squeezed between Yash and Rosie. In the middle of everything, as usual. This attempt to redirect the conversation fooled no one, but it had an effect.

"About ten minutes away, darlings," Sebastian replied.

Sooz accepted that the topic had been adjourned and

reached into a bag of cheese and onion crisps. She found that there was nothing but crumbs left and crushed the empty bag into the pocket of her tracksuit bottoms. Or someone's tracksuit bottoms. Possibly Peter's, as they were long, and Peter was both tall and one of the few people in the house with any sportswear. In their house at Cambridge, the laundry would get mixed together, and clothes slowly became communal property. If you didn't take your shirt off the drying rack fast enough, it would be claimed by someone else.

"Here," Sooz said, reaching into her purse and producing five large black sleeves of photographs. "Forgot to show you these. Pictures from the last two weeks. I picked them up yesterday."

She passed the photos to the passengers in the back seat.

"Are you still getting free developing from that guy at Boots?" Theo asked.

"Is that what they're calling it these days?" Sebastian said.

Sooz playfully swatted him, almost causing him to drive the car into a hedge.

"I can't help it if he likes me. And it saved me almost twenty quid."

The photos roused Rosie from her reverie. She reached for one of the packs. For a few minutes, conversation ceased as the passengers in the back looked at the photos, Sebastian steered the massive Volvo through the twisting lanes, and Sooz fiddled with the radio. There was music, there was sunset birdsong, there were probably more crisps somewhere in the car, and all was right in the world. Sebastian turned through an opening in the hedgerow that was barely wide enough to accommodate the car, then made his way down a pitted dirt path through the trees. They had reached a tall iron gate, the only break in an ivy-covered brick wall.

"Who's going to get out and open it?" Sebastian said.

"I'll do it," Yash said, popping open his door.

"The code is 19387. Pull the right gate toward you a bit. It sticks. Hold it for the others. It closes quickly."

Yash did so, holding the gate so both the Volvo and the Golf could pass. They proceeded onward, down a peaceful drive arched by trees that created a lush hall of greenery, with slender beams of late-day sun poking through. This was England at its finest—the Hundred Acre Wood, the magical forest, the green and pleasant land of yore.

"Have to go slow," Sebastian said. "Chester is hard of hearing. It would be a bad start to the week if I ran over our beloved gardener while he was standing on the drive."

"Might make a good sketch," Yash said. "You run over the gardener but then still keep trying to have a weekend party like nothing happened."

"That's not a good sketch," Theo said.

Yash considered for a moment.

"No," he said. "It's not. Well, maybe with some polish on the idea. Remind me to mention it to Peter. We still have one sketch to write for Edinburgh . . ."

"You are *not* working this week," Sooz said.

"We have to," Yash replied. "At least a little. This is the Fringe Festival we're writing for, Sooz, not the usual knobheads at the pub. Peter thinks that—"

"I don't care what Peter thinks. No. Working. This. Week. Sebastian, do something."

"If you think I can stop Peter and Yash on their quest for comedy glory," Sebastian said to her, "you have more faith in me than I deserve."

"Theo?"

"I am but one woman," Theo replied. "I cannot perform miracles."

They made the final turn of the drive, breaking out of the woods. Suddenly they were surrounded by walls of hydrangeas in hypnotic shades of electric blue and violet. Around them there were pergolas and paths wound with wisteria, and rosebushes with peach-colored blooms that stood on point. The air was full of the smell of lilacs that trapped the raindrops and released their perfume into the air.

Merryweather was before them. A sprawling creation of sand-colored stone, flat-fronted and hip-roofed, with a columned portico. Ivy and flowering vines crept up the house, an organic coat to soften the solidness of the building. A stone terrace wrapped around the house, lined with urns and statuary. A glass orangery jutted from the far side of the building, filled with potted trees. Out the front, a long apron of green rolled down to an ornamental pond with a folly. The rest of the grounds were quilted in a pattern of walled brick gardens and paths.

"It's always absurd to me that this is your house," Sooz said.

"Well, I'm an absurd person," Sebastian replied. "Half of it is falling down anyway. We use the lesser staff to hold up the roof."

The journey ended on the gravel drive, next to a garage on the side of the house. Rosie bolted from the car, walking off a few paces. Sooz and Sebastian got out to stretch and have a cigarette, while Theo and Yash set about unpacking the car.

"Rosie's having a hard time of it," Sebastian said quietly.

"Yes," Sooz said, accepting a cigarette that was offered. "Also, did you see the way Yash elbowed Peter out of the way to ride with us?"

"Hard to miss. Do you think this will be the week one of them finally makes a move? It's now or never. Maybe we need to take action. Lock them in the attic together."

"I like that," Sooz said, watching as Yash almost fell over himself trying to lift the heaviest of the bags, even though Theo was more than capable. "Too bad you don't have a dungeon."

"The dungeon is for my private use, darling. But perhaps I could make an exception for a good cause."

"If Yash was busy shagging, he couldn't be working."

"Don't bet on that," Sebastian said. "Anyway, Peter would carry on. You know our ambitious boy can't be stopped. He'd sit by the bedroom door with a notebook and write down any awkward sexual remarks Yash made."

"Oh God. That could actually happen. They would turn it into a sketch."

"Are you two planning on helping at any point?" Yash

called out as he pulled Sooz's suitcase from the car.

"No," Sooz and Sebastian said in unison.

"Just checking," Yash said, nodding.

The Golf pootled up and parked. Four more people extracted themselves from it, far more crushed and rumpled than the passengers of the commodious Volvo. Peter, who had been riding in the passenger seat with a map in case the group got lost, popped out, beating a happy rhythm on the roof of the car. Noel, the driver, unfolded himself from the driver's seat. He placed another in an endless series of cigarettes between his lips, lit it, and stretched his arms above his head.

"Bloody hell," he said. He didn't elaborate. The remark might have been about the drive, the mansion and grounds spread out around them, or life in general.

Angela and Julian had to be released from the back seat, where they had been packed in with suitcases and assorted bags. Angela crawled out from the space, clinging to her bag, her clothes sweaty and wrinkled. Julian emerged from the other side, looking just as warm and sweat-glazed, but he wore sweat well and the warmth only loosed his gait. Nature had gifted him pool-water blue eyes, a tiny gap between his two front teeth that rendered every smile a heartwarming aw-shucks vibe, and an overall symmetry in every feature that resonated deeply and pleasingly with all who looked upon him. No amount of time crushed into the back of a Volkswagen under a pile of luggage diminished his appearance.

"We made good time," Julian said. "It didn't take that long."

Angela, who had dropped down onto the gravel of the drive and was flapping her shirt to air out her chest, groaned in reply.

"Picture!" Sooz said. "Picture, now! We'll do it here."

There were several protests from the group, but Sooz waved them away.

"I want pictures of this whole week. Every moment. This is our arrival picture. Come on. Everyone over here."

She motioned for her friends to come over to join her at the edge of the gravel drive, by a nondescript outbuilding.

"In front of the woodshed?" Sebastian asked. "Very scenic."

"I can put the camera on the car if we do it here. Quick, before we lose all the light!"

While the others got into position, Sooz set the camera on the roof of the car and hit the timer button. She ran to get into frame. Once the photo was taken, they lugged their bags through the gate into the kitchen garden, down the outside passage that was built so that the servants could lug wood and coal and supplies without disturbing the tranquility of the back garden. Great estates are like Disney World—designed to look effortless, with the labor going on behind a bit of decoration. When they reached the back door, Sebastian unlocked it, admitting them to a capacious mudroom filled with wellies and rain slickers.

"Rooms, then game!" Sebastian shouted.

Yash dropped his bags first and took off running. The race for rooms was on. Angela, Peter, Julian, Sooz, and Theo ripped through the kitchen and the maze of small back rooms. Some took the back stairs, while others headed for the main hall. From there, they scrambled up the grand staircase, ignoring the looks from the Holt-Careys of the past, who stared at them from paintings on the wall. Merryweather had sixteen bedrooms—but some had four-posters, and others their own bathrooms. They were all good in their own way, but everything was a game and a competition, so they slid down the hallways, slipping on the highly polished wood, pressing each other good-naturedly out of the way to claim rooms they might not even have wanted.

Sebastian did not run; it was his house, and his room was fixed. After setting down his things in the mudroom and stretching for a moment, he went to the kitchen, removed the bottle of champagne that was always chilling in the refrigerator, and popped it open. He poured the contents into a pint glass and gazed out the window over the sink. This one had a view into the kitchen garden, which was lush with shaggy clusters of mint, blue-flowering borage, and strawberry plants, heavy with bright red fruit. There was something else in the garden, along with the bountiful plants and the cold frames. Over by the wall, Rosie and Noel were conferring. They had not yet come inside, and were pressed close together, tall Noel leaning down to bend his ear to Rosie's lips. He was leaning low enough that he kept having to slide his massive glasses back up on his nose. Whatever they were talking about, it was intensely private, and Rosie occasionally turned to look up at the windows above.

This was an interesting development, Sebastian thought. Something to be watched.

Upstairs, Sebastian heard something large fall over. There was no cacophony of falling objects, so not a cabinet. A side table, then, possibly the little mahogany one with the marble inlay. It was sturdy. It would survive.

Besides, he thought, sipping his pint of champagne contently, things were bound to be broken this weekend. There was no getting around it.

I

Dear Miss Bell,
I have been reading about your recent success in solving cold
cases, like the ones at Ellingham Academy and at Camp Sunny
Pines. There is something going on in my town and I need your
help getting to the bottom of it. My neighbor has been killing
people in an industrial dryer and putting their remains in our
community garden. I have tried to dig up the garden myself but
I am not permitted inside due to a legal matter, and it is very
hard to do with a small shovel. Can you come here and help me
to . . .

Stevie Bell stopped reading.

It was a quiet October night in Minerva House. At the farmhouse table in its cozy common room, she sat with her friends. Janelle Franklin and Vi Harper-Tomo were side by side working on their laptops.

"You finished your Stanford essay, right?" Janelle asked Vi.

"Almost," Vi replied.

"Are you using that same one for Tufts?"

Vi looked up. They had gotten a new pair of white glasses over the summer and had cropped their hair and bleached it to almost the same shade, with a fade of blue down the back of their head. They were wearing a massive blue-and-silver fuzzy sweater that sort of matched their hair. Janelle had embraced the fall palate in an orange sweater and a vibrant kente cloth head wrap in gold, red, and green.

"No," Vi said. "I'm writing one in Japanese for Tufts, and I'm not done with that one either."

"Let me know when you're finished so I can input it into the spreadsheet."

Janelle and Vi had become a couple from the moment they'd met at the start of last year. They had decided that they didn't want to go to the same school, probably, but they wanted to go to schools that were close to each other. In true crime talk, they had done a geographical profile of the unsub—worked out exactly what they wanted from their schools, and targeted the regions, then the programs. Every night, Janelle updated the spreadsheet that tracked where they were in their mutual application process.

Next to this, Nate Fisher was also typing away furiously, his face a scowl of concentration. Nate was one of Stevie's closest friends—lanky, the kind of pale the Victorians would have classified as consumptive, with his never cool T-shirts and his wrong-sized pants hiding an athletic build. A fringe of overgrown brown hair half-shaded his eyes as he bent over his computer. He was usually her companion in avoiding things, but tonight he was letting her down. His fingers hadn't stopped moving all night.

Stevie was supposed to be working. She had six articles to read tonight for Modern American Political History. When your class only had five people in it, you couldn't get away with not doing the reading. You can only vamp so long about the media in general until your teacher raises a practiced eyebrow and puts the imaginary cone of shame on your head.

She looked at the article on her screen: "Defining Bias: How We Interpret What We Read."

The sound of Nate's typing echoed in her ears. He had headphones on and his fingers were flying. She had never seen him work this hard. Nate was a writer—he had gotten into Ellingham on the strength of a novel he wrote and published in his early teens. Since that time, he had been running from deadlines and the concept of writing in general like it was an angry bear on an electric bike. Where had he found all this *focus*?

Maybe from the fact that it was October. Senior year. How had she gotten here?

Well, time does that. The clock ticks steadily on.

Time was ticking right now. She had to read. This was the shortest of the six articles. She knew that because for the last hour, she had scrolled through all six, looking at how long they were and figuring out what to read first. Then she would go to the little kitchen off to the side of the common room and get some more water, or a hot chocolate, or she went to pee, or she walked to her room to get a hoodie, or she walked to her room to get her slippers, or she just stared at the moose head with the holiday lights on it that was mounted above the fireplace.

The rest of her time she looked at her phone, which was how she'd found this new message about the shovel and the industrial dryer.

Time to work. Okay. She would do it this time. She would read. Her sightless gaze dribbled down the first paragraph. . . .

She tapped Nate under the table with her foot.

"What?" Nate said, pulling off his headphones.

"Do you want to go for a walk?" Stevie said. "Go over to the dining hall and get some cake?"

Nate glanced at his screen, looked back at his friend, and sighed.

"Fine," he said. "But only because I love cake."

Stevie sagged with relief when he agreed. She had been dangerously close to almost reading three entire sentences.

Fall nights in Vermont were crisp. The air had an edge to it that snapped you awake. There was a general crunchiness to everything—leaves, frosted grass, cold gravel pathways. When you stepped on a stick, it sounded like a firecracker going off under your foot, and every pile of organic detritus rustled with some life-form. The moon tonight was full and huge—a massive yellow eye suspended overhead, casting its gaze down on the mountaintop.

"You get any new ones today?" Nate asked.

"Visions. Industrial dryer. Community garden."

"It's been a while since you got a vision."

"It's a nice change from everyone who has a neighbor who gets a boat and an oversized cooler," Stevie said. "A lot of people buy boats and coolers. Only, like, half of them are serial killers."

"How many of these messages are you getting now?"

"Just a few a week," she said. "Maybe ten."

"That's still a lot of people who want you to solve their weird crap."

"They don't want me to solve anything," Stevie replied. "They want to tell me about something they saw. And everyone sees stuff. There's nothing to *do*. I'm just . . . itchy."

"I'm aware. This is what you're like when you don't have something to work on. It's not great. Once it gets dark and you've already talked to David, you basically turn into a zombie. Which is why I'm out here walking with you now, to keep you from eating the sheep."

"I'm not going to eat a sheep," Stevie replied. "Maybe an owl, though."

"Crunchy, hollow owl bones. Delicious owl meat."

"Or a moose. If I ever see one."

They reached the central green, in front of the Great House—the school's administrative heart. The green was the wide oval of pristine lawn that rolled out in front of the building, with a marble fountain depicting the god Neptune at the top and a cupola at the bottom. Normally, there was nothing but open space in the middle, but one of the new students, a girl improbably named Valve, who'd grown up on a farm sanctuary and wore at least seven crystals at all times, had introduced three sheep to the school. They meandered around the grounds but preferred the green. They noodled around under the moonlight, largely in the vicinity of the little wooden structure that had been erected for them.

Free-range sheep might be a strange sight at most schools, but this was not most schools. This was Ellingham Academy.

Ellingham was in the mountains of Vermont. Its story was the stuff of legend, its reputation gold-plated, its illustrious graduates legion. Its story was long but can best be summarized thusly: Famous rich guy Albert Ellingham climbs a mountain in the roaring 1920s, gets loopy from the limited oxygen, decides to build his dream school—a place where learning is a game. He even decides to build himself a massive mansion in the middle of said school so he can be a part of the whole process. He dynamites the face off the mountain and empties his bottomless pocketbook, building the most elaborate and fantastic campus. Yale and Princeton would bite their ivy-covered knuckles in jealousy over the red and gold bricks; tree-lined paths; sculptures; twee, twisting pathways; and Gothic spires.

Albert Ellingham declared that his school would have no admissions criteria; students applied in whatever way they thought was right and expressed their passion. If the school chose you, the experience was free for two years, which was the length of the program. The school would design bespoke learning experiences for each student. Only fifty students were accepted each year. It was competitive. It was egalitarian. It was forward-thinking. It was perfect in all ways except for the murders.

Murders. Plural.

Some had occurred in 1936, when Ellingham's wife and daughter were kidnapped and a student killed. This turned into one of the great crimes of the twentieth century. Stevie had gotten into Ellingham with the stated purpose of solving this case. The other murders had been more recent—just one year ago. Last year at Ellingham had been, as the administration called it, "a time of challenges." That was a polite way of saying, "we had a minor murder spree and a mass evacuation." (This explained why the incoming class all seemed a bit on the nervous or excited side. They were *jumpy*.)

Stevie topped off this experience by working on another cold case on her summer break, this one in Massachusetts and dating from the 1970s. This should have gotten her a pass on reading something like "Defining Bias: How We Interpret What We Read." But that is not the way the world works, because the world didn't care what she did last year, or last month, or even earlier tonight when she had bravely tried to read three sentences. If the world is feeling super charitable, it might take a passing glance at what you are doing now. What matters is what you are doing next. And high school was nothing if not about the next box you had to check.

"You hate it when Vi and Janelle work on their spreadsheet," Nate said. "It freaks you out every time."

This was true. It was October in her last year of high

school, and Stevie's entire college plan so far consisted of seven bookmarked pictures on Instagram, three browser windows she never closed, and a notebook page that contained insights such as "science?" and "where is it?"

Because college meant majors. It meant knowing who you were and where you wanted to go in life. It meant figuring out how smart you *really* were, and would you be as smart as everyone else at your imaginary school? Should you go somewhere you were the smartest? Should you go somewhere tiny or to a huge university that filled a city? College also meant money, and money was confusing. She had a little now, enough for small things, and maybe a semester somewhere if she used it all at once. The rest would have to come from somewhere. Loans. Scholarships. Her parents didn't have it, that was for sure. The only reason she could go to Ellingham was because it was free.

So, to counter Nate's entirely justified remark, she responded with a question.

"You never mention where you're applying," she said. "What have you been doing for college stuff?"

"I'm working on it," he said. "I've done some applications."

"Where to?"

"Different places. I'm still working it out. But you have to start and I know you haven't even really looked yet. You can't avoid it forever."

"What are you, the college police?" she asked.

"I'm just saying," he went on, "you've been genuinely spaced, and that shit is going to be due soon. You have to pick

21

some places. Any places. Start filling out applications. There are first years here who have some of that stuff ready to go. Even *David* did it."

He had invoked Stevie's far-off boyfriend a second time. This was a direct jab at her.

"Sounded like you were getting a lot of writing done," Stevie replied.

"Yeah, I am."

This confident *yeah* was both direct and squirrelly, and it attracted Stevie's interest.

"Yeah?"

"Yeah," he replied. "I am. I'm writing. I write."

"No you don't," Stevie said. "I mean, you do, but mostly you don't. Are you working on the second book? Is it . . . going well?"

"It's fine," he said dismissively. "We're not talking about my book."

"We kind of are."

"Stevie," he said. "You're turning into that person. The one with the long-distance partner. Do you want to be a *girlfriend*?"

These were fighting words.

"Work on one of these dumb cases," he went on. "Why not look into this thing with the dryer and the garden. Do *something*."

Stevie had no defense. They mutually decided to stop talking and went to the dining hall in silence, filled their reusable, Ellingham-issued takeout containers with cake and other sustenance, and walked back out under the big yellow moon.

Nate was right. All she needed, really, was a little murder. Not a big one. A little something to take the edge off. And not a neighbor with a dryer and a shovel. A real one. There were so many murders out there. Surely, she could have one.

June 23, 1995
10:30 p.m.

IN THE LILAC ROOM (NO FOUR-POSTER, BUT A PRIVATE BATH WITH A claw-foot tub and climbing roses all around the window), Angela Gill unpacked her things—and they were actually *her* things. Unlike the other Nine, Angela was always careful not to take things that were not hers, or if she did, to give them back washed and folded. She set her reading on her bedside stand. Just because she had graduated didn't mean there was any less to do. She was about to start work at the Victoria and Albert Museum, and she had to become an expert in Tudor textiles and clothing as quickly as possible.

Somewhere down the hall, someone was already blasting music—Blur. That was probably Noel. The response came at once from another room, louder. That was Sooz, replying with Oasis. There was constant debate in their house about which was the better band. The battle had been brought to Merryweather, turning it into a Britpop echo chamber.

Angela opened the window, sticking her face out to smell the fresh country air and the flowers outside. The view wasn't as grand as that from some of the other rooms—it overlooked a walled kitchen garden—but it was pleasant enough, and the air was sweet. The cloud cover had caught up with them, and the first grumblings of a summer thunderstorm shook the sky.

This was it. This was really, really it. The last week together. Her friends. How would she live without them? The rest of the world was going to be so lonely.

Cambridge University is made up of a collection of colleges under the umbrella of a university, and the Nine came from different ones and varied fields of study. They would not have met at all if not for a shared love of theater and a series of auditions in their first weeks. They had varied levels of success at these auditions, but they recognized something in each other immediately. Group friendships are products of the right time—the chemistry of season, activity, emotion, and random occurrence. They coalesced over a series of long nights at the pub, in rehearsal spaces, cafés, and bedrooms. It was Yash who first proposed that they form a sketch comedy group; Theo kept the topic going and made it all come together. By the end of the first term, the decision was made and the lineup solidified.

They had gone through a series of names in those first weeks: DangerGran, Basket of Rats, the Toastkillers, No Fun Before Bedtime . . . Those kinds of names were popular for student comedy groups—some kind of weird phrase. Right before their first show, it was time to come to a decision, which meant a trip to the pub, many bags of crisps, and hours of discussion. Over the last round, Rosie was sober enough to count and find that there were nine of them.

"We should be the Nine . . . ," she said, clearly having had enough of the meandering debate.

"The Nine what?" Yash had asked.

"Just . . ." Rosie considered her empty pint glass. "The Nine. That's it. It's different from all these other names. It's simple. *Monolithic*. Like Blur or Pulp or Suede."

It was late, they were all a bit drunk, and they needed something for the flyer by morning. The Nine it was.

From that point on, you never saw one of the Nine without at least one of the others. In the summer before their final year, Angela found the perfect house—a student rental with nine minuscule bedrooms, three bathrooms with questionable plumbing, a kitchen with only two working burners on the stove, and signs of recent fire damage in the lounge. It was farther out from town, so getting to lectures required long bike rides, bus trips, or perhaps a ride in one of the two cars owned by members of the group.

But it fit nine people—even if that fit was snug, and there seemed a small but not impossible chance of the whole structure going up in flames. Best of all, it had a muddy walled garden out the back that led down to the river. This became the featured spot at their house parties, and the saggy and half-rotted picnic table served as a dining surface when the sun was out (and often when it wasn't). Sooz strung some outdoor fairy lights and garlands of fabric flowers for some party and never took them down—ditto for the two floppy camping tents that Peter bought for a festival. This was the kingdom of the Nine—and it was all coming to an end. When this week was over, everything was over, so the party had to rage on as intensely and as long as possible.

There was a knock at the door and Peter appeared, with his sleepy-eyed smile.

"Lost my lighter in the car," he said. "Can I use yours?"

All of the Nine were smokers except for Theo and Yash. Angela planned to give it up after this week.

"It's in my bag, the blue one, on the bed."

Peter went over to the bag and fished out the lighter. He put the cigarette between his lips and joined her at the large window.

"Any chance you want to help us run some scenes this week?" Peter asked, striking a light.

"We're supposed to be relaxing," Angela reminded him. "This is a party, remember?"

"Sure, but there'll be time."

Peter always had his eye on the future. Only he and Yash planned on making an actual career out of comedy, which was not known for being the most stable of livelihoods. She never doubted they would make it, though. They were fantastic writers and they never stopped working. She was a writer as well, but she never felt like she could keep up with the two of them. Well, she was a historian really. A researcher. That was her calling.

Or maybe she had failed. She just didn't have their commitment. If you wanted to be funny, you needed to be deadly serious about it.

She sat on the windowsill and leaned out a bit farther to let the cool air brush her face.

"Careful," Peter said. "I don't think we're supposed to be falling out the windows this early in the week."

"Remember that time," Angela said, "that Yash fell out that second-story window while trying to make a girl laugh?"

"The Spider-Man impression."

"What college was she from? Kings?"

"Pembroke," Peter replied. "His ribs still hurt him. I don't think those breaks healed properly."

"Breaks never do, do they? I broke my wrist when I was a child. It's always been a bit funny."

Peter was looking at her curiously. She had the light, tingling feeling like he was about to kiss her. It made sense that this might happen now. They had never come together romantically in the last three years. It was one of the few couplings that hadn't come up. The Nine tended to date internally and reconfigure themselves regularly. To keep up with their love lives, you needed a chart. Julian and Sooz were tied for most romantically active within the group. Along with her two stints with Julian, Sooz had dated Peter for a full year, Yash for a week, Noel for several scattered weekends, and Angela for two months. All the girls had taken their turns with Julian, including Angela. Sebastian, too, had a dalliance. Angela had a tender, brief kiss with Yash their first year, and then dated Noel for much of the second year.

It was like a logic puzzle, keeping it all straight. They

often couldn't do it themselves and would forget who was with who—or they would at least pretend to. This friction is what made the Nine what they were—webbed together by a meshed network of nerves and veins, reacting to each other's pain and pleasure. They were an organic soap opera with eighteen swinging arms. The tension and the drama was part of what made it all work.

Peter wasn't handsome in the way Julian was (few people were). He wasn't romantic, like Yash, or rubbery and goofy like Noel, with his 70s clothes and spindly energy. Peter was thoughtful, with heavy-lidded eyes that missed nothing. Sooz had only good things to say about his physical attributes (and Sooz was nothing if not forthcoming). He had a broad, athletic build, a soft flop of coppery hair. But the sexiest thing about him was that he was funny—the funniest of them all, really—but that was something you only came to understand over time. Peter wasn't one for the witty exchanges, like Sebastian, or physical gestures, like Noel or Yash. He was quiet. He saved it, wrote it all down, refined it.

She wanted to say something to Peter about her growing fear of the future, of being without the rest of them, of all the changes, of not being flanked by the Nine at all times. She wanted to grab him and press her face into his chest. She wanted to hold on to all her friends and never, ever let them go. And from the look on his face, he felt exactly as she did.

There was a flash of light followed by a tremendous crack in the distance. The sky opened and the rain came all at once. Instead of taking this moment for its romantic value and inviting Peter to meet her right now, on the floor, what she said was:

"Do you think we'll still play?"

And that was that. All the tension dispersed. His whole demeanor changed. She had ruined the moment.

"I'm sure we will," he said, handing the lighter back to her. "See you downstairs."

He left Angela alone with her dreary thoughts, plus a bonus of embarrassment and disappointment. She needed to get herself together. This misery wouldn't do. This week was going to be incredible, the most fun they'd ever had, and they'd had a *lot* of fun. She would make a point of revisiting the moment with Peter. Maybe that would be her project for the week.

She distracted herself by going to the mirror to examine the bald girl who looked back at her. She still wasn't used to it, even after two weeks. Angela hadn't meant to cut off all her hair. She had simply woken up one morning with vague memories of a game of truth or dare and all her hair was in the kitchen sink. She laughed in front of the others and cried in her room, not because she hated it but because she didn't recognize herself. It wasn't so bad. Maybe she loved it. It was tough, decisive. There was a little hair sprouting now, a soft fuzz. She liked the way it felt.

Another knock. This time, the door opened before she could call out. Rosie popped in.

"Ange," she said in a low voice, shutting the door behind her. "I need to talk to you for a moment."

"What's Jules done?"

"Not *everything* is about Julian," Rosie replied, shutting the door. "Jesus."

"Tell that to him. He'll faint from shock."

Usually, Rosie would flop back on the bed to have a chat; tonight, she sat on the edge, her expression grave.

"What's wrong?" Angela asked. "Are you all right?"

"I don't know. I mean . . . I'm fine. It's just . . . I saw something. Something I didn't understand. But I think I might understand it now. It was in the paper. And now that I've seen the photos . . ."

"What are you on about?" Angela said, sitting next to her.

"You won't believe me," Rosie said. "*I* don't believe me . . ."

Before Rosie could say anything else, there was another knock and Sooz joined them. She had a bottle of champagne and three water tumblers tucked under her arm. Rosie shook her head at Angela, indicating that she should say nothing about the conversation they'd been having.

"I'm furious at you," Sooz said to her friends.

"What?" Angela said. "Why?"

"You don't have a drink. Sebastian's family left us six crates of what he's calling third-rate champers, which means it's better than anything we've had in a while. You look sad, and I won't have it. Julian's caused enough trouble."

Rosie put her hands over her face and stifled a scream.

Sooz popped open the champagne, causing it to foam up and spill onto the bedspread. She filled the tumblers and passed them out. The warm champagne went right to

Angela's brain, creating a pleasant warm fizz behind her eyes.

"No long faces," Sooz said. "This week is for us and we're going to have a good time. Now drink up like good girls and come with me. Anyway, it's time to play the game."

Whatever Rosie had been about to say, she had decided to hold for the time being. Much as they all loved Sooz, everyone knew she wasn't great at secrets. She didn't seem to believe in them as a concept. Everything was to be shared— her possessions, her thoughts, her body. It's what made her such a good performer and generous friend, and what made her a bit of a nightmare if you were trying to keep something to yourself.

"You're right," Rosie said. "Let's go and play the game."

"There's a good girl. Come on. Let's go."

As they followed Sooz out of the bedroom into the dark hall, Rosie gave Angela a tug on the arm to hold her back for a moment.

"I'll talk to you after," Rosie said to Angela quietly. "Come up and meet me here after the game."

"But what's it about? What's going on?"

Rosie shook her head.

"Not now," she replied. "It's too important."

Over the years, these words would replay in Angela's head. If only she had pulled Rosie back into that bedroom, waited a few more minutes to go downstairs, sat her back down on the wet bedspread and made her explain. If only she'd listened to her gut for once, maybe things wouldn't have happened the way they did. Her life—all their lives—would have been different.

But Angela did not do that. She followed Sooz and Rosie down the steps of Merryweather, past the family portraits and the landscapes, to where the others were waiting.

Events spun on, toward the inevitable.

2

BACK IN HER ROOM, STEVIE SAT ON HER BED AND GNAWED ON A PIECE of the chocolate cake she had acquired. The first bite revealed a terrible but inevitable fact—it had maple in it. In Vermont, there is maple syrup in it—it doesn't matter what *it* is. Cake. Ice cream. Coffee. Soup. Mustard. Concrete. The water supply. This chocolate-maple cake was way too sweet, but it was in her mouth now. There's no going back with cake. She crinkled her nose from the cloying taste and took another swing at the reading.

Defining Bias: How We Interpret What We Read

When we consider the topic of bias, we must first consider the writer, and to consider the writer we must consider the audience . . .

Stevie sighed and looked at the ceiling, concentrating on the rosette that housed the overhead light. The heat clanged through the radiator. It was so hot. She got up and opened her window a few inches, went over and rearranged some things on her bureau, and picked up the phone she had put there to keep it out of her hands while she was doing homework. No messages. Nothing to distract her.

She set the phone down and looked at herself in the mirror. Her hair was getting weird. She'd meant to get it cut over the summer but forgot, so now she had a blond demi-shag. She'd tried to cut it herself earlier in the semester, but Janelle told her it was great. Stevie relied on Janelle for this kind of advice because Janelle understood clothes and hair. This knowledge gene had skipped Stevie. She didn't get how she was supposed to look. All she knew was the black hoodie that comprised 90 percent of her personal style, and the vintage red vinyl raincoat that made up the other 10 percent. She owned a little makeup—a massive eyeshadow palette Janelle had given her for her birthday, a lip gloss, some kind of highlighter in a tube.

She picked up the latter and began to apply it to the high point of her cheekbones. Her face was round; this highlighter was supposed to do something about that.

It was sticky. And now she had shiny lines under her eyes. She would watch a video. She would learn how to do this.

What if she gave herself bangs? She could give herself bangs. She went over to her desk to look for scissors, then remembered that Janelle had taken her scissors two weeks before because Stevie had said something out loud about maybe giving herself bangs.

Nate was right. She had become the person with the

long-distance boyfriend.

There was a David-sized hole in everything. They texted constantly and spoke at least once every day, but that didn't make up for the fact that he was in England doing his first semester of college in London, and England is far from Vermont. He was five hours ahead, so he tended to talk to Stevie throughout the day and then between six and eight o'clock for their long call of the day. Which meant she had the rest of her night to stare slack-jawed at her friends and not get any work done. She hated being this person, but she didn't know how to make it stop. Her feelings rolled over her thoughts. Being in love had killed her brain. She needed to *focus*. She had to read this goddamned thing. She returned to her bed and picked up her computer to try again.

Defining Bias: How We Interpret What We Read . . .

She seemed to be constitutionally unable to read the first paragraph. It was like there was a force field around it. She knew exactly when she would be able to read it—on her phone, on the way to class, in a panic.

Why was she like this? Other people seemed to be able to do stuff in a reasonable fashion. Some had detailed online calendars. Others, like Janelle, kept fancy planners that they marked up with special pens and stickers. Some people simply knew what they were supposed to be doing and did it, and those people were the worst of all. Stevie's brain had to hit a white-hot pitch of panic before it was willing to do any real work. It would work quickly then. It was a good brain, but it had only two modes—fog and frenzy.

Maybe she could cut her hair with nail clippers. It would be slow, but it could be done.

"Oh my God," she said out loud.

Defining Bias: How We . . .

Stevie gagged on cake when her laptop unexpectedly made a ringing noise. David's name and the video call icon popped up on her screen. She had crumbs on her face and her teeth were probably covered in dark brown cake jackets. She rubbed her face and ran her tongue over her teeth before answering.

"You're calling late," she said.

"It's never too late for my princess."

David was leaning against a fake wood headboard and looked down at the camera, in that angle that was flattering to no one except maybe to adorably jowly dogs and to David.

"Are you drunk?"

"Not *drunk*," he said. "Just hanging out with some people. I had two beers. Maybe three. I had four beers. So, those five beers I had . . ."

God, he was handsome. He was sexy. Whatever *sexy* was, David was that. He was loose curly hair, long-limbed and comfortable in his skin. When Stevie had arrived at Ellingham the year before, David had been the school's most famous reprobate, rumored to be drunk or high most of the time. His reputation was exaggerated, but still, he was the kind of guy who always had weed somewhere nearby and wasn't going to turn down a drink. He attended classes on a need-to-know basis—with the criteria being what he felt he needed to know and when he thought he needed to know it, which was not much and maybe later. His greatest performances on campus included sleeping on the roof, five a.m. screaming meditations, sleeping in class in a Pokémon comforter, and releasing several dozen squirrels in the library. After he left—after he was removed from school—he completely cleaned up his act. He finished school remotely with high grades, graduated, and spent the summer working to register voters. He was a model citizen now, and even in England, where you could legally drink when you were eighteen, he never seemed to do so. Most nights when he was on video calls with Stevie, he was stone-cold sober and working.

She liked slightly drunk David. She had missed him.

"So here's the thing . . . ," he said.

Stevie's stomach contracted itself into a tiny, hard fist. It was reflexive. Every hanging sentence burned along her nervous system. This was when he told her he'd met someone in England. Someone smart and funny with an accent, who raised horses or something.

"What?" she said when he trailed off. "What?"

"You're *pretty*. And you've got a shiny face. . . ."

Her adrenaline levels dropped, but her heart was still pounding and her stomach churning. She rubbed at the highlighter with the back of her fist.

"What?" she said again.

"God! Okay. So, I was thinking. You know how I'm here and you're there?"

Stevie nodded and gestured with her hand that he should get to the point.

"Well, it's not good, right? So I was thinking, do you want to come here?"

"What?"

"Do you want to come here . . ."

"I heard you," she said. "And of course I want to go there. But I can't."

"Why not?"

"Because . . ."

It wasn't that she didn't want to go. Of course she wanted to go. Everyone wanted to go to England, and she especially wanted to go to England, but it wasn't possible. She didn't have a clear answer on why it wasn't possible, but it was something, something, school, life, something.

"Okay, but here's the thing . . ." He slid down the headboard a bit and had to straighten up, putting the laptop on his knees and changing the view. "I was talking to the people who brought me here and I was saying that you should come here too because . . . because you should and they said they would talk to someone at the American embassy who works in educational tourism or something and he just got back to me and . . . you're a pretty little starfish . . ."

"What?"

"Okay! Okay. You wouldn't stay in my building, but they have some rooms in the building connected to this one. They said they could get up to four rooms for a week or ten days or something and you could call it study abroad or something, like, you'd have someone to call at the embassy so if Quinn gets up your ass about it . . ."

"Wait . . . you got . . . four rooms? For . . ."

"For you. And for Nate and Janelle and Vi, because I know that is how this would work. You just . . ." He gestured expansively and knocked the computer off his knees. She was looking at the ceiling for a moment before he righted it. "Study abroad. Thing. This guy can help with that. You tell the school you're looking at museums or some shit and you come here."

Stevie was so distracted that she set her cake on the front of her hoodie, by her collarbone.

"I need a passport. Don't I? I don't have one."

"You can get one. It doesn't take that long. Just come here, stop being a dick about not being here right now and come here. There's, like, a queen. So come here. Just do it. Come on."

Stevie didn't precisely rip Janelle's door off the hinges a few minutes later, but there was a bit of violence inflicted on it. While Janelle called Vi, Stevie ran to the end of the hall and rattled Nate's doorknob. He didn't answer, so she texted him until the door cracked open and he peered out.

Everyone wanted to go to England.

Stevie woke the next morning assuming that everything she remembered about the conversation was a dream, but there were multiple messages from David waiting for her—a name, an email, a phone number, the address of a building in

40

London. It was a genuine offer with a genuine person at the American embassy prepared to back it up.

She spent every moment between classes and lab and yoga looking up flights and passport information. She had some money—the result of work she had done over the summer with a guy named Carson who ran a company called Box Box and wanted to make a true crime podcast. She'd been under-cover at the summer camp he'd bought and helped him solve the cold case of the Box in the Woods. He'd paid her decently for her time at the camp, plus he'd advanced her some money while he put together the podcast about the case. It wasn't a fortune, but it was way more than she'd ever had before, working at the mall or the grocery store. She could buy a fancy coffee every once in a while, and she had invested in some new black hoodies. There was enough for a plane ticket, plus a little pocket cash for each day to pay for food and things.

Over dinner that night at the dining hall (maple-glazed pork with mashed sweet potatoes with a little bit of maple syrup in them), the four set about creating their presentation—their pitch to Ellingham about why they should be permitted to go to London. There aren't many advantages to having a bunch of murders happen at your school. They tend to bring down the mood. However, in the search for silver linings, there was one—the school had fully embraced the concept of remote learning. Before, Ellingham expected its students to be there all the time, "going to class" and "being part of the school community" and that kind of thing. But once the murders started, they decided to get a bit more flexible. It turned out you could do a lot of school stuff outside of school. Ellingham still wanted you to go to class, but if people had to travel home, or go on college visits, or do a project somewhere, there were far more opportunities to do so. You could join your class remotely.

It took about four hours, and many cups of coffee, but by the end of the night, they had collectively hammered out something that looked like a legitimate case—a detailed day-by-day schedule in spreadsheet format, listing cultural and historical locations of interest and what they intended to do there and how this related to their individual academic goals. They reviewed the plan until midnight, at which point they emailed it to Dr. Quinn, the head of school. They weren't expecting anything else to happen until tomorrow, but she replied within ten minutes to everyone with the following words: *My office. Tomorrow. Six p.m.*

Stevie was going to England. Maybe. If Dr. Quinn said it was okay. Which was not a guarantee. Because of things like the murders and Stevie's propensity to get involved in them.

She just needed a yes.

June 23, 1995
11:00 p.m.

"THERE YOU ARE, MY DARLINGS!" SEBASTIAN SAID AS SOOZ SHEP-herded Angela into the sitting room. He popped a bottle of champagne and put the foaming mess to his lips. Some of it made it inside his mouth; the rest went down the slim-fitting deep purple shirt he was wearing. He used his champagne-sticky hand to sweep his dyed black hair back off his face.

"We're seriously going to play when it's pissing down?" Yash said from the sofa.

"Of course!" Sebastian intoned. "We are not *cowards*!"

"Don't speak for me."

Angela sat next to Yash, sinking deep into the cushions. This was a proper old sitting room sofa, the kind that enfolded you in soft flocked fabric and broken-down filling, inviting you to stay for hour after hour, drinking and reading and enjoying the fire.

"We could stay inside," Yash said. "Like normal people. We could drink."

"Sounds like someone's worried," Peter said, coming into the room with a tarnished horn he'd picked up from one of

Merryweather's countless displays of antiquities. He tooted it speculatively, but it only made a spluttering fart noise.

"I don't even know why we have to play this game every time we are here," Yash went on.

"Tradition!" Sebastian said.

"How's it a tradition if we've only been here three times? That's not even a habit. It barely qualifies as a trend."

Noel threw himself over the back of the sofa and slid down between Yash and Angela. Noel rejoiced in weird movements and liked to throw himself around the furniture, down the stairs, up into the rafters.

"Now," Sebastian said as he grabbed a bag and began distributing small packages containing disposable clear rain ponchos. "I'm the starting seeker. I'll count to a hundred to give you all time. As I find you, you'll join the seeker team. I'll give you a yellow poncho to show you've switched sides."

He held up a yellow poncho as an example.

"When you find people, bring them to me for the poncho. Oh, and don't even bother with the outbuildings. . . ."

He reached down into the front of his trousers and fished around for a moment.

"The evening has taken a turn," Yash said. "It's a bit early to get your cock out, Sebastian. Even for you."

Sebastian jerked his arm up and triumphantly displayed a set of keys. "Everything's locked, and these are the only keys."

He held them aloft, stared at them for a moment as if he wanted to question them about the nature of keys and locks and how they fit in to the grand plan of the universe, then shoved them back down the front of his trousers with a roughness that made everyone wince.

"There," Sebastian went on, wobbling a bit. "The keys are now down with the other family treasures."

"Why?" Yash said. "Why *there*?"

"Didn't fit in the pocket. Throws off the line of the trousers. So, no outbuildings. The boundaries are anything within the proper grounds—the house, any of the gardens, any wooded area within the stone boundary wall, and nothing beyond the ha-ha. We have to put some limits on it or we'll be doing this all week."

"So you're going to sit in here, nice and dry?" Noel said.

"No, darling. I'm a good sport. I'll use the folly by the pond as a base. And we'll make it a rule—once anyone leaves the main house, there's no going back in until the game is over."

"We get torches, don't we?" Sooz asked.

"Torches are for seekers!" Peter said. "That's always been the rule."

"Correct," Sebastian replied. "Last person to be found is the winner. Where is Rosie? It's time to start."

"Having a slash," Sooz said. "She's coming."

Sure enough, there was the sound of rapid footfall down the stairs and Rosie appeared at the door, looking a bit distracted.

"Right!" Sebastian said. "Now we can start. The count begins. One, two, three . . ."

The group scattered. Theo and Yash remained inside,

but the others all went for the many doors that led to the outside. There were certainly plenty of places to hide inside Merryweather—the house had many bedrooms and reception rooms, multiple all-purpose rooms for washing and household use, box rooms, crawl spaces, closets, a cluttered and rambling attic, and a genuinely cavernous basement. If one ventured outside, there were acres of gardens with tall borders, an orchard, and dozens of dark pockets and nooks between trees and behind buildings. An ambitious player could hide indefinitely.

At the count of one hundred, Sebastian opened his eyes and surveyed the empty sitting room. He listened carefully for the sound of movement overhead. Nothing. The rain beat against the windows, but he heard no creaking footsteps. He smiled and gulped back the remainder of the closest glass of champagne.

"Here I come!" he shouted.

He began in the house, and he found Theo first, which was not a surprise. She was crouching in one of the understairs cupboards. Sebastian and Theo were best friends, so she likely put herself close by to join him. Yash was next, having somewhat half-heartedly pressed himself under the bed in Noel's room. No one else turned up in this first review of the house.

The team of seekers was now three. They donned their yellow slickers and stepped out into the rain, which had intensified a good bit. The drops drove themselves into the ground. Visibility was poor, and the rain made a deafening noise as it hit the hoods of the ponchos.

"I'll do a sweep of the front garden and then head to the folly," Sebastian said. "Theo, take the gardens around the orangery and head back round the house. Yash, go from the other side. Start with the tennis courts."

It would be over an hour before the next person was found. This was Angela. Theo found her lurking around the stables. Just before one in the morning, Yash found Peter hiding under a bench in the back garden. By this point, the rain had become violent. The ground was saturated, so muddy that it sucked in running feet. The lightning got closer. But the Nine continued, running and yelling in their ponchos, flashes of torchlight cutting through the dark. Sebastian held court in the folly, waving a bottle of champagne and drunkenly yelling encouragement over the onslaught of the storm.

It was almost one thirty when Peter caught Sooz, who had pressed herself in between some tall hedges along the inner edge of the walled garden. Two o'clock approached, and three of the Nine were still unaccounted for. The search took on a frenzied quality. The searchers taunted the hiders with their calls. They flashed their lights into the shadows, poked under benches with sticks, stood sentry in front of doors and ends of pathways. They tried pincer movements to force them out of hiding. There was one tremendous boom, and the lights in Merryweather went out all at once.

Now it was very dark indeed.

Yash ran up to Sebastian at the folly.

"We should pack it in," he said. "That was too close."

"One last pass!"

This final push produced a result. They located Julian, who had ambitiously gotten on top of a pergola and clung to the vines for hours in the rain. He might never have been found, except that he sneezed when Angela was walking underneath.

"Back to the castle!" Sebastian yelled. "Official time-out! Drinkies! Gather the troops!"

The call echoed out around the grounds, through the rain, and one by one the Nine returned to the house, dripping wet and with a tremendous thirst. They knocked their way through the dark house by torchlight, laughing and falling. Sebastian produced some candles and lit them, and Peter stoked the fire and added more logs. The sitting room felt smaller with the cloak of darkness over it.

"Where are Rosie and Noel?" Theo asked. "Didn't they come in?"

The names Rosie and Noel were yelled in the direction of the stairs and out the front door, but there was no reply.

"Seems they are committed to the game," Sebastian said. "Admirable."

"I think they're committed to something," Sooz replied. "Maybe not the game."

"Don't diminish their achievement. Now. I know what we need."

Sebastian dropped to the floor and began crawling toward the dark side of the room. He started this trip holding

48

a candle, but Yash plucked it from his hand as he went past.

"What are you doing?" Angela said.

"The good stuff...is...down here. The whisky. Not just *any* whisky. The 1936. We *must have it.*"

Sebastian continued his creep across the floor until his head made contact with a cabinet against the wall. He rolled onto his back and jammed his hand down the front of his trousers to retrieve the keys, writhing like an inverted insect trying to gain purchase and right itself.

"I think I just witnessed the end of the family line," Yash said, wincing as Sebastian triumphantly yanked the keys from his waistband.

He jangled the keys and began stabbing at the wooden door of the cabinet in an attempt to find the lock.

"We don't need it," Theo said.

"How dare you!" he said. "Where is your resolve? We didn't win the war with that kind of attitude."

Thud, thud, thud. Scrape.

"Let me bring you some light, mate," Yash said.

"I don't need light! I am an artist! Stay back!"

Thud, thud. Jangle. Thud. The battle of the cabinet was now a performance. A struggle for the ages.

"Once more unto the breach!" Sebastian cried, audibly scratching the wood. "Dear friends, once more . . . or close up this cabinet with our English dead."

"And we've reached the misquoting Shakespeare part of the evening," Julian said.

"Silence! In peace there's . . . something, something . . .

but when the blast of empty glasses blows in our ears, then imitate the action of the tiger! Stiffen the sinews, summon up the blood . . . Disguise fair nature with . . . something. What do we disguise fair nature with? A wig?"

"He's really making a meal out of this," Yash commented.

Even for him, this was a touch over the top, a sketch that went on longer than it should.

"And . . . scene," Peter said, dropping to his knees and crawling over to Sebastian. Sebastian held out his hand dramatically to pull his friend in.

"And you, good yeoman!" Sebastian replied. "Whose limbs were made in England! You come to help your king! A horse! My kingdom for a . . ."

"Bottle of whisky," Peter replied, taking the keys from Sebastian's hand before he carved the cabinet to shreds. Sebastian face-planted and pretended to be dead as Peter worked through the keys and found the right one. As soon as the cabinet door opened, Sebastian popped back up.

"You are the light of the nation," he said to Peter. "I'll see you're remembered on the honors list."

He plunged his arms into the cabinet, shoving bottles out of the way, causing them to violently clank together as he sought his prize.

"Ah," he said, sliding one toward himself. "Here we go. The 1936. The most precious."

He kissed the bottle reverently.

"Should we at least wait for Rosie and Noel to open it?" Theo asked.

"No, it will be waiting for them when they decide to come in."

Sebastian poured nine glasses with great ceremony, muttering some kind of incantation as he did so. These were distributed to the seven people in the sitting room.

"A toast!" Sebastian said, raising his glass. "To us. The most brilliant, talented, attractive, and humble group of wastrels in all of Cambridge, perhaps even the world. May we always land the punchline, play the fool, embrace disaster, and love absurdly. I adore you all to the bottom of my black and cold heart, and my life would be nothing without you."

Angela audibly sniffed.

"You wrote that in advance," Yash said.

"Maybe I did. Now drink, you disgusting peasants."

Sebastian had not lied. The whisky tasted of ancient fires in the Highlands of Scotland. It rolled smoothly down the throat, sending a column of warmth up the bridge of the nose and into the third eye. It slipped into the blood like an eel, and in its thrall, all the legends were true. The morning would be bad—even the soon might be sticky—but the now was exceptional.

"Oh God," Yash said. "I can't feel the palms of my hands. I only have fingers now. Loose fingers."

"Tell me more," Sooz cooed.

The group lost themselves for a moment in the warmth of the whisky, and the fire, and the booming storm outside the window. After what could have been five minutes or several hours, Peter rose unsteadily to his feet.

"I," he said formally, "am going to be very sick. I may be some time."

Soon after, Angela also acknowledged defeat and decided to go to bed. Theo followed, first stopping in the kitchen to pour a few glasses of water for herself and her friends. This was Theo's way: after every night of hard drinking, she left a glass of water by her friends' bedsides.

Sebastian, Julian, Yash, and Sooz remained in the sitting room. The night was long now, and the dark crowded them. Sebastian put on Blur. The three of them fell into a pleasant silence for a while, enjoying the fire and the blankets and the whisky. Sebastian's head tipped back awkwardly in what was either sleep or a long consideration of the plasterwork on the ceiling.

"Rosie and Noel have really committed to this," Yash finally said. "What time is it, anyway?"

Julian raised his hand in the direction of the fire to consult his watch.

"Three thirty."

"Anyone else notice they've been getting a bit close in the last week?" Sooz asked. "I hope they're out there shagging away in the mud all night."

She glanced over at Julian, who looked unconcerned as he sipped his whisky. Sooz was not going to be ignored, not after a night in the rain and the better part of two bottles of champagne and one of Scotland's finest whiskys.

"You were all over that Canadian at the pub a week ago, Julian," she went on. "You can't complain."

"I'm not complaining," Julian replied, looking up from under the thick curtain of lashes that shaded his eyes. "I didn't say a word."

"What Canadian?" Yash said, but Sooz did not appear to hear him.

"Now that we're here—you know—now that we're leaving—we need to be honest," Sooz went on. "We need to resolve things. If anyone's got things to say, we need to say them."

"I always have things to say," Sebastian said.

"I mean important things."

"What Canadian at the pub?" Yash asked again woozily.

"Some Canadian at the Horse and Feathers," Sooz said.

At this, Julian did look uncomfortable, and he stared down into his glass.

"The Horse and Feathers?" Yash mumbled. "I met a Canadian girl at the Horse and Feathers . . ."

"It was the same girl," Sooz said. "Julian got in there before you showed up."

"What? Oh, come on, mate . . ."

"You got together with her on Saturday," Julian cut in. "This was Friday. I wouldn't do that to you. You know that."

The room settled into an uncomfortable but familiar silence. To be one of the Nine was to live with the twitching underbelly of feeling, and dramatic pauses were common.

Yash stood, wobbling a bit.

"Right, well . . . I'm . . . I have to . . ."

With that, he left the room, taking a slightly sinuous

path that included a direct hit on a side table and the edge of the door. A minute later, the distant sounds of retching came into the room, echoing from one of the downstairs loos.

"I can't believe you sometimes," Sooz said after a while. "Betraying Rosie and Yash in the same moment. A new achievement for you."

"I didn't . . ."

"You did."

Julian got up and started walking around the edges of the room, running his hand along the books on the shelves. He cut the figure of a romantic poet in the flickering candlelight, with his sparkling eyes and beautifully furrowed brow—he was Lord Byron in a flannel shirt, oversized jeans, and shell necklace.

"I didn't betray Yash," he said. "He hadn't even *spoken* to her yet. You *know* I wouldn't do that."

"And Rosie? Well, that's a given, isn't it? You certainly betrayed her. But that train is never late, is it?"

"Sooz, are we going to do this forever? Can we do anything else? Is it always Berate Julian O'Clock?"

Sebastian broke into a dramatic snooze and a sharp snort.

"What's that?" he said. "I died just a moment there, when you two were doing the thing you do where you yell at Julian for being Julian and you, Julian, do the dramatic thing and try to get out of whatever you've done by being good-looking. You two—either shag each other or shut up. Make a choice. I don't care which you choose, but you have to choose one."

Sooz made a disgruntled noise and went to the window

facing the front of the house to get as far from Julian as the room allowed. From the loo in the hall, there was a final cluster of retching coughs and the flush of a toilet.

"I'm fine," Yash called weakly to no one. This was followed by the sound of him unevenly ascending the stairs, punctuated by one or two full body falls.

More silence after that. Julian kept his position on the far side of the room, and Sooz was riveted to the window. Sebastian sighed.

"*Boring*," he said. "Sooz, come back over. I'll tell you a terrible story I just heard."

Sooz remained at the window, her focus fixed at something out on the lawn.

"There's someone out there," she said. "I just saw a torch flash. Did you give Rosie or Noel a torch?"

"No," Sebastian said. "Torches are for seekers."

"They must have found one, because I just saw a torch flash by. They must still think we're hiding. I'll go get them."

She went out to the main hall and yelled to them from the front door, her theatrical voice pushing back against the storm.

"Nothing," she said as she came back into the room. "There's no way they didn't hear me just now. It seems like they don't want to come in."

"Should we go out and get them?" Julian asked. "I mean, it's absolutely shitting out."

"Let's leave them to whatever it is," Sebastian cut in before any more discussion of Julian and Rosie resumed. "It's a violent night, but they have each other. Now. Who's hungry? Fish fingers? Oven chips?"

And so, Rosie and Noel were briefly forgotten, superseded by some frozen fish dumped onto a baking tray and shoved into an unheated oven. The rain beat on against the windows and walls of Merryweather, as if to mock its name.

Sebastian was right—it was a violent night. Just not in the way that he meant it.

3

"WHAT DID YOU ALL DO THIS TIME?" LARRY SAID AS A GREETING.

Security Larry had been fired over the course of the events of last year, and then subsequently rehired after he trekked up the side of a mountain in a blizzard to help Stevie and some others who were stranded there. He was now at his traditional position by the front door of the Great House, at his desk with his tin mug of coffee. He regarded the four students before him with a resigned sigh, which was Larry's way of showing affection.

"You know I don't answer questions like that without my lawyer," Stevie replied. "And they had pumpkin maple rolls left over from this morning." Janelle slid over the container.

"What's the mood?" Stevie asked.

"She was humming when she came in."

"What does that usually mean?" Vi asked.

"Hard to say. Might be good, but one time she was humming after she saw someone on an electric scooter ride into Lake Champlain. You can go up."

Stevie let her gaze float up the grand staircase, to the

balcony above, where Dr. Quinn was waiting in the lofty quiet.

The Great House was at the heart of the Ellingham Academy campus. When Albert Ellingham constructed his school in the 1920s, he'd built himself a mansion right in the middle of it. It was an elegant monster, made of tons of imported hardwood, cut crystal, stained glass, and marble. It had been the scene of great tragedies, which were immortalized in a family portrait that hung at the landing—a surreal image of Albert, Iris, and their daughter, Alice, as painted by Leonard Holmes Nair.

There were no paintings of the more recent tragedy.

Dr. Quinn had taken over the office formerly occupied by Dr. "Call Me Charles" Scott, the overly enthusiastic head of school who had left the position the year before. When this had been Charles's office, it had signs on the door that said things like I REJECT YOUR REALITY AND SUBSTITUTE MY OWN, QUESTION EVERYTHING, and CHALLENGE ME—the last of which was generally considered the most odious. They had, in fact, challenged him. It was no longer his office. Instead of the posters and the corkboard, the door had been restored to its original smoked-glass panel with delicate Art Nouveau swirls etched into it. There was a simple and elegant brass plate on the door that read: DR. JENNY QUINN, HEAD OF SCHOOL.

They stood in the dark of the hall and Stevie gently rapped on the door.

"Come," said a voice from inside.

Dr. Quinn was seated at her desk, her attention focused

on her laptop. She wore Actual Fashion—expensive, confusing things with lots of folds and extra material, and heels with red undersoles. She was the kind of person you would expect to see at a global summit, probably because she attended global summits sometimes. Her job as the head of Ellingham Academy was a bit simplistic for her, but it was a prestigious school, with a massive endowment and excellent skiing right on the doorstep. She could jet off to New York City or Washington, DC, if she was needed, and she had the summers to go around the world, negotiating treaties or wrestling alligators or whatever it was you did for fun if you were Dr. Jenny Quinn.

"Sit," she said, not looking up.

This room had originally been Iris Ellingham's dressing room; it still had her dove-gray silk paper on the walls. There was a hole in one of those walls that had been patched over to the best of the ability of the maintenance crew, but there were still tears in the paper, clear signs of where the wall had been punctured last December. These four students had been in the room when it happened—had put the hole in the wall, in fact.

When Dr. Scott had been in charge, the room had been full of sofas and Funko Pop figurines. That nonsense was gone. The only things that had been kept were the large, framed map of Ellingham Academy that hung between the windows and the green marble clock on the mantel that was said to have belonged to Marie Antoinette. Dr. Quinn had her own bookcases installed and a wooden desk that could house a family of four.

Janelle, Vi, Nate, and Stevie planted themselves in the chairs arranged in a horseshoe and waited until Dr. Quinn finished typing. She looked up, removed her glasses, and regarded the students in front of her with the disappointed look of a hanging judge who'd been denied a rope.

"So," she said.

Nate cleared his throat nervously, which was a mistake. It was important not to show fear in front of Dr. Quinn. Or was that bears?

Same difference.

Dr. Quinn did what police detectives in interrogations do—she let the silence accumulate past the point of comfort. People can't help but fill it. It's human nature, and it's what sinks a lot of murderers. This was something Stevie knew from her compulsive viewing of interrogations on YouTube.

"I've sent you the spreadsheet. . . ." Janelle began, breaking the silence. "About our proposed week of study abroad."

"I've seen it," Dr. Quinn replied. "I want to hear it from you in person. Tell me what it is you plan to do if you're allowed to go. Explain it to me."

The "explain it to me" didn't sound good.

"The first few days would be dedicated to cultural landmarks," Janelle continued. "The Tower of London, the Houses of Parliament, the Victoria and Albert Museum, the National Gallery. If you look at page three, you'll see I've compiled a list of supplemental reading that I'm . . ."

Dr. Quinn waved her hand, indicating that Janelle should stop talking.

"You," she said, "I'm not worried about. Let me hear from someone else."

Vi stepped up.

"I want to concentrate on the impact of colonialism," they said.

"That's a broad remit," Dr. Quinn said.

"I'm going to narrow it to the British Museum," Vi said, "and the question of ownership of cultural artifacts."

"What about you, Nate?"

"Book stuff," he said. "Writers . . ."

"Can you be more specific?"

"British Library. Um, I'm going to . . . There are manuscripts there. I'm going to look at. Them. The originals. And there are literary tours."

Dr. Quinn leaned back in her chair and rolled her fountain pen between her thumb and forefinger for a moment.

"And what about you, Stevie?" she asked. "This trip seems to be at the invitation of David Eastman, so I assume you have something significant planned and you're not just making up an excuse to take time off school to visit your boyfriend. Or some other ill-advised reason."

"Well," Stevie said, "I was hoping to, just . . . the museums. The . . ."

She'd practiced. She had a whole list of places, justifications, full-bodied lies. But in the scorching rays of Dr. Quinn's stare, her mind had become a dry and barren place.

"The . . . ?"

Use your words, Stevie.

"The . . . specific role that England plays in media portrayals of crime. Mysteries. Why we like English mysteries. How English mysteries got to be a thing, especially during the period between World War One and World War Two. Murder as a comfort activity. Reading about it, I mean."

That was jumbled, but she got all the main concepts in there.

"I see. Well. You can understand why I'm a bit nervous to allow the four of you to travel as a group. Things tend to happen when you move as a unit."

"It's not really our fault," Stevie said.

"A case could be made."

"This is an academic trip," Janelle said. "I mean, it's also exciting. I want to see London. We all want to see London. We got an offer with a place to stay. This is the only way we can afford to do it. And because it's Thanksgiving week, we'd only be missing about four days. It's an opportunity we're not going to get again."

Smart. Well played. Janelle landed that last note with just the right tone of voice.

More pen rolling. Silence, except for the clank of the heating starting up from some dark corner of the Great House.

Tick. Tick. Hisssssssssss.

"All right," Dr. Quinn said. "I understand this pitch you've put together is largely a ruse to get my approval, but it is a good opportunity. London is an amazing city. I'm giving this my tentative okay. But there are conditions. Once these plans are approved by your teachers, you will make a schedule and you will stick to it. You will stay together as a group. You will not deviate from the plan without permission from me. I have many, many contacts in London. My eyes and ears are everywhere. I will also be calling you. The calls will be at random times. And when I call, you pick up and show me where you are and what you are doing. Think of me as always being with you."

Stevie Bell had faced murders, run for her life, fallen from great heights, and in various other ways looked into the abyss. None of those things quite brought the dread of the thought of Dr. Quinn hauling herself to an airport, boarding a plane, and going to another country just to bring Stevie home because she'd screwed up.

But she had her yes.

June 24, 1995
8:30 a.m.

THEODORA BAILEY PEELED HER HEAD AWAY FROM THE PILLOW AND looked at her watch. She rubbed her face hard. On one hand, she knew she should go back to sleep. She'd only crawled into bed three hours before. On the other hand, she knew trying to go back to sleep was useless. She was constitution-ally unable to sleep past six in the morning, no matter what she had been up to the night before, so this eight thirty in the morning thing was decadent enough. When she started training in the hospital in a few months' time, she would fre-quently be sleepless, but she would still have to perform her duties. This was good training. She pushed herself out of the wonderfully comfortable bed, considered throwing up, let the moment pass, and got to her feet.

Out of everyone in the group, she'd had the least to drink the night before, but that still meant four or five glasses of champagne. Or six. Who knew? Sebastian refilled them before they were empty, so it could have been any amount. On top of that, there had been the whisky. It felt like some-one had pulled a woolly jumper over her thoughts.

It appeared she had tried to change her clothes before going to sleep—she was at least wearing an oversized Prodigy T-shirt as a nod to pajamas. She pulled on some tracksuit bottoms she found on the floor next to her. When she had started Cambridge, her hair was natural and long. With each passing year, she'd taken inches off it. Doctors needed something easy to manage, that didn't get things in it, like your friends' sick when you assisted them to the loo after a long night. It was now flat on top and close cropped; as she ran her hand over it, she found that it harbored a leaf and some organic detritus from crawling under a yew border a few hours ago. She plucked these out. The damage could be much worse—they were lucky none of them had been struck by a falling branch during the storm. Or an entire tree, for that matter. She could handle a leaf or two.

After a quick wee and a splash of her face, she made her way down the main staircase, taking care to step on the edges of the steps rather than the center. (The center of the step always creaked more than the edge.) Not that she was likely to disturb anyone in a house this size. Living packed together as they did in Cambridge, she was hardwired to step lightly and try not to wake her friends.

She went to the kitchen, drank a full pint glass of water, and washed it down with a cup of instant coffee and some loose Hobnobs she found on a plate. The kitchen had suffered a grave assault during the middle of the night feast. She soaked the oven trays with the carbonized remains of the burned fish fingers and chips. She threw wrappers in the garbage, swept the floor, and washed plates and mugs. Then she began the circuit to take stock of the wounded.

Sebastian and Sooz were still fast asleep on their sofas, so she padded back upstairs and made her way along the halls, peering inside bedrooms. Yash, Peter, and Angela were all in their bedrooms, in various stages of undress and in a variety of positions. Yash had burrowed under the blankets, with only a bit of his hair sticking out the top. Angela was facedown on the bed, fully clothed. Peter was in his underwear, sleeping sideways across the bed, his head and feet dangling. It took a bit longer to find Julian; he had decided to sleep on a chaise longue in the library. She put a throw blanket over him.

Wherever she looked, she could not find Rosie or Noel— not in the bedrooms they had claimed, or the empty ones, or any of the other rooms inside the sprawling maze that was Merryweather. The more she looked, the more determined she became to find them. She opened cupboards, she looked in closets, she went into the pantry, the cellar, all the bathrooms and anterooms. This was strange, but not even remotely the strangest outcome of one of their parties. One time she'd found Sebastian asleep on the front doormat. He'd walked all the way home from the pub, gotten to the door, and curled up and gone to bed. Another time, she found Sooz in a shopping trolley in the back garden. If Rosie and Noel were tucked away in a folly or outbuilding, there was nothing much in that.

Still, it bothered her. She liked to make certain that everyone was all right. Also, it could get a bit boring being the responsible one who was up hours before anyone else. Normally, she would let them sleep, but that was when they had all the time in the world. Now, time mattered, every precious second of it. After this week, they went back to the house, boxed up their things, and broke away. Sooz, Sebastian, Peter, Yash, and Angela were all going to London. Julian was going up north to work in law. Rosie was going back to Dublin, maybe, or perhaps to Manchester, she still wasn't sure. Noel was uncertain where he was going, but for now he was moving back to his home in East Anglia. Theo had a few years left in her medical studies at Cambridge and at various hospitals. It took years to become a cardiologist, and she would be doing them without the eight other pieces of herself.

She puttered around a bit longer, then she decided it was time to do some gentle poking. They would be sad if she woke them and had no good reason for them to get out of bed. She would make bacon sandwiches for everyone. They would all sit up for a bacon sandwich—everyone except for Rosie, the resident vegetarian. She would get some vegetarian sausages on toast.

The smell of bacon lured Peter first. He came shuffling into the kitchen and sank into a chair. From his gait and expression, Theo could see that while he was awake, he was not sober yet.

"How are you so good?" he asked.

"Just am," Theo replied. "You look awful."

"Thanks."

He accepted the bacon sandwich and consumed it

greedily, then reached for a second.

Yash and Sooz wandered in next, collapsing together on a small sofa by the windows. Theo distributed tea and bacon sandwiches to them, which they ate, but with slightly less gusto.

"I still can't believe it," Yash muttered, his mouth full of sandwich. "I finally meet someone. I meet one person, and Julian had to get in there as well."

"Before you met her," Sooz said reassuringly. "She clearly liked you much more."

"I gave her our number and address. I lent her a Pulp CD. She said she was going to listen to it and bring it back. I really . . . I liked her."

"Julian is an arse." Sooz leaned her head onto Yash's shoulder.

"He is an arse," Yash replied.

"We all know Julian's an arse," Peter said. "But he didn't do anything wrong this time."

"Aside from cheat on Rosie," Sooz said.

"The leopard doesn't change his spots. She had to have been used to that. You got used to it."

"I never got *used* to it, Peter."

"I'm just saying . . ."

"Rosie's smarter than I am, anyway. I stood for it more than I should. Rosie didn't. Or, not as often. And I was just as bad as he was. I'm simply saying that Noel and Rosie are meant for each other and I'm glad they're getting together. And Yash, my darling, don't worry about Julian and this Canadian girl."

"She never did ring. She probably went home. I liked her. And she liked my idea for the sketch where we all had buckets on our heads but never acknowledged it."

Peter closed his eyes.

"That sketch is not going work," he said.

"It just needs some polish."

"My God, you two," Sooz said. "No wonder you never get any. You can only pay attention for ten seconds before you're thinking about writing sketches again. Weren't you heartbroken a moment ago?"

"There's probably a sketch in that," Yash said.

The toaster popped up, and Theo put the finishing touches on a few more sandwiches, which were loaded onto a plate. She put these on a tray, along with more cups of tea, and went to the sitting room with it. Sooz, Peter, and Yash followed her, like ducklings—well, ducklings who wanted more tea and bacon sandwiches. As she set the tray down on a table, Sebastian was seized by a jolt of energy and propelled himself out of the armchair.

"Right," he said. "Right. What's happening now? What are we doing?"

He drank the contents of the nearest glass, which had two fingers' worth of brown liquid in it, and possibly a little cigarette ash.

"I'll go and get Julian," Theo said. "He's asleep in the library."

Angela drifted down the steps, shuffling along and rubbing her eyes. She swiped a bacon sandwich and sat on the rug to eat it. Theo returned with a bleary Julian, who was rubbing his blond hair. Julian managed to look more beautiful when tousled and sleep deprived.

"Have you seen Noel and Rosie?" Sooz asked them.

"I looked," Theo replied. "I couldn't find them."

Sebastian rested his head on the marble of the mantel and groaned.

"They're still at it?" he said. "Chester is coming in the afternoon. He has a delicate disposition. Catching two people in flagrante delicto might do him in."

"You should go and find them," Sooz said.

"Why me?"

"It's your house. You're lord of the manor. It'll be your dead gardener. And we all need some of your special something to get through this morning."

"You're going to make me go out there, into the *blinding sunlight* . . ."

He poked his finger toward the window and the gray morning it framed.

". . . because our friends are raging nymphomaniacs?"

"Come on," Theo said, handing him a cup of tea. "Drink this. We'll go have a look together."

Sebastian sipped it and made a face.

"My God, there's no alcohol in this. Are you trying to kill me?"

"Yes," Theo said. "Drink your tea. And some water."

"I am," he said, stifling a burp, "the Honorable Sebastian Holt-Carey, the future sixth Viscount Holt-Carey. Honor me."

Sooz threw a discarded crisp bag at him. It landed on his shoulder.

"I'll ignore that, peasant," he said, "because there are still some crisps in here. Fine. Send me out to my death. Theo, you're with me. Let's make this terrible journey into the burning desert sun."

"How many bottles do you think we got through last night?" Theo asked as they made their way over the spongey grass. The steely tint of the sky suggested that the torrential rain of the night before might soon be repeated.

"Who can say? Probably twenty or so of the champagne. It would be embarrassing if we drank less than that. Plus, whatever else."

"And your parents won't mind?"

"Who cares if they do? That's what the stuff is for, anyway. We don't leave Cambridge every day."

"What do you think of Rosie and Noel?" Theo asked.

"Long time coming, like some other pairings I could mention."

He looked at Theo pointedly.

"Don't," she said.

"Yash has always liked you, and you've always liked him. Why are you waiting? This is the time to act."

"We've talked about this, Sebastian."

They passed through an archway in the garden wall and stepped into the driveway. The gravel crunched under their boots.

"No. I ask and you don't answer."

"Because I still have training to finish, and . . ."

They came upon an overturned wheelbarrow and a bucket.

"Chester usually keeps that locked away somewhere," Sebastian said. "That's his favorite wheelbarrow. He's precious about it. I think he . . ."

His words trailed off. They had reached the woodshed. The door hung open. The padlock was still locked, but someone had gotten around that by ripping the latch away from the wood.

"Bugger," he said, hurrying over. "Bugger . . ."

"Burgled?" Theo said.

"It sodding hell looks like it. I don't think our lot actually tears the buildings open."

Sebastian stepped into the shed and reached for the light switch, but nothing came on.

There was little in the woodshed to steal, unless you were in the market for wood, spiderwebs, or old, broken tools. It contained only one thing of real value, and Sebastian was checking on that now. He grabbed for something by the side of the door, which turned out to be a long-handled axe. He went deeper into the shed and held the axe up over his head, reaching around with the blade end delicately until it found purchase on a small loop of rope. He pulled down on this, lowering a set of folding wooden stairs.

"Everything's fine up here," Sebastian said from his position halfway up the steps. Theo could see only his lower half—the rest of him was up in the crawl space above the shed floor. "They didn't get what they were after, if that's what they came for. Floor's soaked. The door must have been open most of the night. Seems like they went to a lot of effort for nothing. . . . What?"

Theo was staring at Sebastian with a strange intensity as he came down the stairs.

"Your face," she said.

"What about it?"

"You've cut yourself. You're bleeding. Right side."

"I don't think so," he said, touching his cheek. "How would I have done that?"

He examined his fingers. They were streaked with blood. He touched his cheek again, feeling for a cut, but there was none there. The blood was coming from nowhere.

"I'm not cut," he said. "Where's this come from?"

Then he noticed it. The thing on the floor, near the woodpile. At first, he thought it was a log. But then he saw that this particular log seemed to be wearing a Wellington boot. It was a bare leg sticking out from a pile of wood.

Theo had also seen the leg and was down on the floor, pulling wood off Rosie.

At the very least, she was pulling the wood off what remained of Rosie.

4

THE DEPARTURE WAS NOW SCHEDULED FOR THE SATURDAY BEFORE Thanksgiving. Her parents were at first saddened by the thought of Stevie not being home to argue with them over a medium-sized turkey and boxed stuffing, but when they heard that David was involved, everything changed. Stevie's parents loved David. They loved him in a way that was irritating and unnerving. They loved him because:

a) they were the kind of people who felt that Stevie's having a boyfriend was a primary mission in life and

b) David was the son of their hero, who happened to be an incredibly toxic politician, now disgraced and temporarily off the radar doing whatever it was that toxic politicians do while waiting for the public to forget about their mistakes. Public memory is surprisingly short when it comes to these things.

Whatever the case, this worked in Stevie's favor. That hurdle was easily cleared.

The others had their respective conversations with their families, and everyone was granted permission for this educational opportunity. They had an email from some dude at the American embassy, and sometimes, that is enough to make your weeklong plan of tours and photo opportunities seem more legitimate than it is.

She went to class. She did the readings (usually). She went to study parties in the yurt. She saw the leaves change to gold and red and finally to brown and fall off the trees. She ate maple syrup and pretended to be a functioning member of the student body. She was physically present. Her body showed up. Mentally, not so much. For weeks, she was flooded with the kind of excitement that borders on panic. Everything was new and fresh and alive. The air smelled sweeter. Her classes were more interesting. Math seemed relevant. The new students were sparkling citizens of humanity, and her established classmates close as family. The sheep loved her and she loved them.

Her thoughts circled one subject, like water in a drain. A few days before their departure, Stevie decided she couldn't handle her questions alone, so it was time to go to the expert. Stevie knocked on Janelle's door. Janelle looked up from some physics homework, a TV show, and crocheting—all of which she was watching or doing at the same time, because she was Janelle.

Stevie sat on the floor and picked at the wood for a moment, trying to find the words.

"When we go to England," she said. "I don't . . . get to see David that often. And I've been . . . because he's been gone, and I . . . I think I . . . I want to . . ."

She knew the words but was having trouble uttering them.

"I think we . . . I . . ."

"You want to have sex with David," Janelle said plainly.

Stevie pointed at her, indicating that she had guessed correctly.

"How did you know?"

Janelle smiled in a way that suggested that Stevie was a beautiful tropical fish, so simple and so precious.

"What's the question?" Janelle asked. "I'm kind of not an expert on the whole male anatomy thing, but I know the basics."

"No! No. No . . . What do I . . . do? Not . . . what do I *do*. But, what do I do? For it? I mean, to make it happen? To get ready? I just want to be ready, in case . . ."

"You mean, contraception? Is that what you're asking?"

"No. I mean . . . like, I've got to . . . wear something?"

"Actually, you don't. That's kind of part of it."

"I mean, something for before. Like, an outfit."

"Ohhhhh." Janelle nodded. Clothing choices. This was her wheelhouse. "Well, first thing, I'd say you have to feel comfortable. It's about what makes you feel sexy. What makes you feel sexy?"

"Are you seriously asking me that? Nothing."

"I mean, what do you feel like you look good in?"

Stevie cast her gaze around the room helplessly.

"A . . . hoodie?"

Janelle leaned back against the bed. This was a challenge,

and Janelle liked a challenge.

"There is no such thing as a sex hoodie," she said. "At least, there is probably not such a thing as a sex hoodie."

"Please stop saying sex hoodie."

"What about . . . underwear?"

"I own underwear," Stevie confirmed.

"Maybe you can get nice underwear?"

Stevie had considered this, but nice underwear was not for her. She got three-packs of cotton briefs, usually in black. They were all stretched out, except for one pair that held on to its elastic for dear life. It was the magic pair, and Stevie saved it for special occasions, like when she might be bending over more than usual or the day her favorite podcast released a new episode. As for bras . . . half the time she forgot to wear one, and the other half of the time, she wore the same sports bra she'd gotten on a clearance rack. So really, it was bra. Singular. Very stretched out. Had deodorant marks on it that were never coming off.

"Let's do a little online shopping," Janelle said, pulling up a browser window. "See what we can find."

Janelle motioned for Stevie to sit next to her and breezily started searching for lingerie. Like that was a thing anyone could just do. Like looking at store websites was free or something.

"Let's start high end," Janelle said, going to a gauzy, soft-focus site full of people lounging on sofas in coordinated underwear in the dappled sunlight, looking smugly content. "Let's just get a sense of your bra style. What do you like?"

Stevie didn't know what there was to like or dislike. Bras were a standard construction: two bumpy bits, two strappy things, and something to hold it all together.

"Push-up?" Janelle asked. "Half cup? Lace?"

Stevie tapped her nails nervously on the floor.

"Let's start with something basic," Janelle said, clicking on one of the offerings. It was some kind of lace situation, black, with a silver trim. There was a suggestion of a French maid costume about it, and it was $90. While Stevie had some money now, she didn't have endless money, and not $90 for a bra kind of money.

"That's basic?" Stevie said.

"Black lace is pretty standard."

"It's ninety bucks!"

"What's your price point?" Janelle said.

"I . . . I don't know. I didn't think about it."

Everything was wrong with everything Janelle suggested. Pink was wrong. Too bright. Janelle offered a plain black bra, which was too severe. Red was out of the question. There was a blue bra that she was almost okay with until Stevie saw that it had different-colored lace, which disqualified it at once. Janelle was delighted by a bright yellow set, but more for her than for Stevie, as yellow was her favorite color. White made Stevie feel like a sacrifice. A green one just confused her. She would turn into a plant.

"I don't think it's the color," Janelle finally said. "You don't want a bra. Okay. We'll move on."

"We don't have to," Stevie said. "I think maybe I'll just . . . I'll think about it?"

She had thought about it over those weeks. She had purchased something. It was in her suitcase. And now it was on the plane with her.

Stevie had ambitions for the flight—things she was going to read, homework she was going to do so she would be ahead for the week and would have less to worry about. She was going to be productive.

What she actually did, when the plane took off into the night and the cabin lights dimmed, was go into a fugue state and stare blankly at the tiny screen in front of her. She poked her finger at the entertainment selection because it was there, in her face, and her brain was so overloaded from the experience that she could almost hear it sizzling. She found *Murder on the Orient Express* on offer. She had seen this movie at least ten times, which was why she put it on again. It would be overstating the case to say she watched it. It was in front of her. She was aware of its presence.

Dinner came around and Stevie accepted the item described only as "chicken." She became obsessed with a pack of salad dressing that refused to open, so she tried to tear it with her teeth. This worked too well, and as she ripped it open, the contents exploded down the front of her black hoodie (the one she had planned to wear for most days of the trip and now forever tainted by the "sex hoodie" conversation), and a little into Nate's hair. Nate did not notice, because he was reading something, and she didn't want to tell him.

Eventually, the line of peachy sunrise brightened, and they passed over a channel of water. The land looked like a green patchwork quilt—great squares of it, rimmed with lines of hedges and trees and meandering motorways. Then they dipped down over what Stevie could clearly see was London. There was the Thames, snaking along. The plane bumped twice as it touched the ground.

She had already decided to swallow the cost of turning on her data—it went against her every budgetary instinct, but there was no way she was going to be without it. There was a series of texts from David waiting for her.

Did you take off?

Are you flying the plane?

I'm watching your plane. You're near Iceland. Wave at Iceland.

Are you here yet?

She tried to respond, but her phone was slow in recognizing its new location, and there was a sudden rush to get bags and flee the aircraft like it was about to be filled with poisonous gas. Stevie was caught in the hubbub, pulling her backpack out from under the seat in front of her, shaking crumbs from her lap, and shuffling her way out. She looked at the remains of the flight, the carnage that the passengers had wreaked on the plane—wrappers, crumpled blankets, empty Pringles cans, overturned plastic cups, discarded eye masks.

It looked less like an international flight and more like a dull rager had taken place.

The first impression Stevie had of England was a series of hallways and lines. The corridors of Heathrow Airport were endless, with people striding along or hustling down the moving walkways, past advertisements of people with their arms open wide, welcoming them. There were winding pathways to get to immigration, where they waited with hundreds of other people. She approached the end of the line with her squeaky new passport. She was sure for a moment a customs agent would open it, take one look at Stevie, and say, "No way, weirdo. Not letting you in." Or maybe, "Are you the girl who solved those murders? Because I think I found a body in a suitcase."

It turned out they didn't even need to speak to anyone. They were each shuffled into a little glass compartment, where they put their passport facedown, then a creepy little computerized eye slid down and took their pictures. The compartment opened, and Stevie was unleashed into the United Kingdom.

While they waited for their bags, she sent David a text saying they had landed. Stevie glared at her phone, waiting for a response. Nothing came, not even when they went through the strange barrier that wanted to know if you had anything to declare. (If you didn't, you went through a green section, where she kept thinking someone was going to stop and check or at least ask something, but no one did. They seemed to take you at your word.) She held her breath a little, hoping that David might be one of the people lined up just outside the arrival doors, the ones holding flowers and signs and balloons.

She was the balloon now, deflating softly. There was no David waiting at the barrier. Or over by the transportation desk. Or the coffee place. Or the ATM. As much as she didn't want to be seen with her salad dressing and her glowing red eyes, she wanted that moment to be real—the one where he was leaning over, waiting for her.

There was, however, a man in a brown sweater with a clipboard that read:

JANETTE FRANKLIN, NATE FISHER,
VI HARPERTOMO, STEVE BELL

"I win," Nate said, dragging his suitcase. "Steve. Janette and Vi and Steveeeeee."

The man, who had a thick Cockney accent, told them to follow. They did so, through the arrivals area, up the elevator, out to a car park. They followed him for so long that Stevie started to wonder if they were the victims of a very lazy kidnapping. She had hoped for one of those big black cabs that looked like bowler hats, but it was a black minivan with the words *Addison Lee* written across the back window. Within minutes, they sped along down a highway, and as much as she had prepared herself for being on the other side of the road, it still messed with her senses for a few minutes. She watched the trucks, which were vaguely different in a way she couldn't place. There were also some sheep in the pastures along the road, so it was like they had taken a little bit of Ellingham with them.

There was no sign that said WELCOME TO LONDON, POPULATION LOTS, PLUS WE HAVE GHOSTS or anything like that. There were suddenly just more things. More houses along the road. More shops. More trucks and cars and overpasses. Then she saw the first double-decker red bus, and it all came into focus in her head. Red pillar postboxes. Ornate street signs in white, red, and black. Grander houses in brick with arched windows and wrought-iron balconies. Endless buildings with a low, severe grandeur—long rows of white-fronted buildings. Union Jack flags flapping in front of hotels. The distinctive Tube signs with the red circle crossed through with a blue bar. Then she saw the first landmark she clearly recognized—the statue of Eros in Piccadilly Circus. They wound through streets of theaters and restaurants, down to a much faster road that followed the river. Then a series of turns past a massive gray stone building that looked like a palace. A few more turns around a confusing block, then the car came to a stop in front of a building made of red-gold brick (they really liked bricks in London), with long windows. It was five stories high, with multiple peaks and arched windows. Next to it was an identical building, and the two were connected by a lower structure.

"Here we go," said the driver.

Early in the drive, Stevie had been texting updates to David. She had been too entranced to do so for the last half hour, and only now looked down at her phone to see a message.

Sorry, something has come up. I'll try to see you tonight.

Her eyes almost filled with tears.

"What?" Vi said.

Stevie held out the message for them to read.

"It's fine," Vi said. "We'll unpack and then you'll see him."

I'll try to see you tonight. What the actual hell?

Nate leaned over and read the message as well.

"Oh good," he said. "I was hoping for some weird tension."

"Come on," Janelle said, opening the door. "We're here!"

Stevie took a gulping breath and opened the door on her side, almost knocking into someone on a bike. She heard a shouted swear word as the bike moved on.

"Look to your right," said a voice.

A head appeared in the open doorway. It came in from the side, almost upside down. There was a shock of near-black hair, a shag of half-curls and wisps, a twisted smile. "How's it going, jerks?"

5

DAVID EXTENDED A HAND TO HELP HER OUT OF THE CAR.

"You . . ."

"A joke. You love jokes!"

"I hate jokes," she replied, breaking into a smile. His hand was warm, and the gesture so genteel. This was the first touch, the first contact. He was real.

"Oh, that's right," he said. And then he swept down and kissed her. It was fleeting—truly, it was just a brush of the lips.

Now that he was standing upright and she was in front of him, everything shifted into position. She had looked at him in hundreds of photos since he'd been in England, and over equally as many video calls, but in person, she could see how his slightly longer hair moved in the breeze, the tips of the curls snapping back and forth. He was wearing his fine, long black dress coat. The coat. It had apparently caused a two-thousand-dollar dent in his father's credit card. He'd bought it to impress her, to dress up for her, and probably to piss off his dad as well. In both these things, it had succeeded.

It was hard to explain the effect it had. It swept the backs of his calves. The lapels seemed to draw out the angles of his face. It was a magical piece of clothing.

Under it, he wore the worn-out Yale sweatpants that had belonged to his father—the white letters crusted and crumbling along his leg. She took a step closer and noticed an unfamiliar smell. New detergent. A strong scent. This was his English scent. She wanted to grab him, to push him flat against the side of the minivan, to kiss him until her lungs turned inside out from lack of air, until night fell and the sun rose again. She wanted to disgust the world and not care. She wanted vengeance on months of lonely nights. She wanted to taste his skin.

What she said was: "You suck."

He threw his arms around her waist and picked her up, spinning her once, almost hitting the driver with her legs. The driver dodged around, making a low grumble, and went to haul their suitcases out of the back of the car. David greeted them all. Vi and David had always gotten along well, so a warm hug was exchanged. Janelle had never been as fond, but she accepted a hug. Nate was simply not a hugger, so they nodded to each other.

Stevie had been gripping a ten-pound note in a sweaty hand for the last half hour of the trip, and she presented it to the driver before he left. She was unsure from his look whether this was a lot or a shameful pittance. She decided she would worry about this for days. It would wake her up at night.

"Welcome to London," David said. "This is Craven House, where you will be staying. That building"—he pointed to an identical building to the one that they stood in front of—"is where I live. It's connected to this one through this lobby and the common room. You live this way."

He grabbed the closest suitcase and started pulling it along. It happened to be Nate's. Nate was perfectly content with having David do his lifting. There is no elegant way to drag your suitcase up some steps and into a lobby with too many fluorescent lights, which Stevie was certain turned her skin a fetching shade of grayish green, like a sad cabbage. It was still late November, but a small Christmas tree was up in an empty corner of the lobby, looking like it was at a party at a stranger's house and hating every minute of it.

At the front desk, their photos were taken and printed onto ID cards. Stevie tried not to look at hers, with her bloodshot eyes and salad dressing hoodie. Each of them was handed a key on a plain ring.

"Room 5-19," the person behind the counter said to Stevie. "Fifth floor."

There were elevators, but they were hilariously small, clearly designed to aid people who needed it and not to carry stupid American suitcases up five flights. They pressed into the elevator in two loads of people and bags, and it made the begrudgingly slow ascent to their floor.

"This way," David said, grabbing the handle of Stevie's suitcase and pulling it along.

To get to their rooms, they had to pass through three

separate heavy doors that segmented the hallway for no clear reason.

"Someone's in the pocket of Big Door," Nate said.

"They love fire doors here," David said. "Something to do with the whole city burning down."

Most of the doors along the hall were closed, and there was only a faint sound of voices behind some of them.

"Seems empty," she said.

"Well, it's the pub hour. A lot of people go down for drinks or food or to hang out in the lounge around now. There's kind of a routine. I'll show you. This one's yours, Vi. Nate, here you are. Janelle, I think you're down a few doors. And here . . . nineteen."

Stevie opened the door of a compact, utilitarian room with front-facing windows that looked out over the street. Unlike Ellingham, which had big, quirky rooms, this room was a modern blank canvas—plain white walls, empty corkboards, built-in lights overhead and next to the bed.

David half closed the door and embraced Stevie, looking down into her face.

"You actually came," he said.

"Wait. Were you joking about the invitation?"

"Yeah," he said. "Can you go back?"

All the time and distance that they'd been apart fell away, and Stevie was full. Full of love and feeling, not just for David, but for everything—the built-in wardrobe, the slightly crooked window blind, the reusable plastic water bottle with the school logo; taking in the general vibe.

"I was only sort of joking about being busy," David said. "I have a lecture I have to go to. I'll be back in about two hours. You guys can get settled and then I'll meet you back here at four? I'll take you guys over to the local, and then I have a surprise."

"What?"

"A *surprise* surprise. The kind where you don't know what it is."

"The *local*," Stevie clarified. "What's the local?"

"That's what they call the pub. Your pub is your local, and we have a local. And you have to go. It's the law."

Then he took her face in his hands and kissed her. It wasn't designed to be a long kiss, since he had to go—but it was also the kind of kiss meant to make up for time already lost. A strong kiss, one that made solid contact and held it and seemed to ask, "Are you really here?" She grabbed him around the back of the neck, pressing him harder into her. She forgot how you could hear the other person breathe, feel the warm exhale, know that they were alive, that they wanted to be with you so much that they pressed their mouth against yours and then the room spun away.

David broke the embrace first, taking a step back and smiling.

"There will be plenty of time for that," he said. "I wish I could skip. See you in an hour."

When he was gone, Stevie unzipped her suitcase and looked down at what she smilingly had called her "packing." Unlike Janelle, who had planned outfits for every day and layered them in day-to-day order in compressed packing cubes, Stevie packed like someone who just heard that reports of the monster were true, and it was headed toward the city. And what was weird was that she had *really tried*. She had pulled things out of her drawers and closet at Ellingham and put them on the bed and tried to make sartorial sense of it all. She was the kind of person who had both kinds of shirts: the T-shirts with writing on them and those without. There were the jeans she liked, the ones that fit okay, and the ones that fit badly but she'd bought them and was therefore stuck with them for the rest of her life, or whatever it was that happened to jeans. She'd brought the one dress she owned, which was black and still had the tags on it. All these things had been shoved into the bag in a teeth-grinding frenzy the day before she left because she was up late the night before writing a paper that was already two days late. She had, she discovered, only brought three pairs of socks.

One thing, however, was securely packaged and packed. She removed this and took it down the hall, where Janelle was delicately removing her journaling supplies from her carry-on bag and lining up her pens and notebooks on the desk.

"I need to show you something," Stevie said, coming in and shutting the door behind her. "Do you want to see what I bought? For the thing."

Janelle's eyes opened a bit wider.

"Let me see!"

Stevie ripped into the packaging.

"I got it yesterday right before we left," she said. "I had to shove it in my bag before I could even open it."

She ripped through the inner plastic bag, knocking loose two silica gel packs. She shook out the garment and held it up for inspection.

Janelle stared for a long moment.

"Is that a union suit?" she said.

"It's a fleece-lined onesie."

"I can't believe it. You found a sex hoodie."

"Hear me out," Stevie said. "It doesn't seem like it's for sexy times, but it's got all these buttons . . ."

She indicated the buttons as proof.

"And you can undo the buttons and . . ."

Stevie looked at the onesie that hung from her hands. All the details stood out to her—the brightness of the black-and-red check, the body-obscuring thickness of the fleece, the sturdy closures. It had made so much sense when she'd picked it out.

"I think whatever works for you is the right thing," Janelle finally said. "And that is the most you thing I have ever seen."

June 24, 1995
8:00 p.m.

IN THE AFTERNOON, THE RAIN STARTED UP AGAIN. NOT LIKE LAST night this time—it didn't pound the roof and windows. It pattered. It misted the glass. It rinsed the flowers and turned the earth soft, releasing the smell of ozone. The house fell into soft shade, and the Nine sat inside it, quiet and broken, as the day slipped away. Outside, there were three police cars and a van, officers in uniform walking across the muddy lawn. Sooz watched them from the sitting room window. An hour before, she had been sobbing so hard that she had been physically ill.

They had been asked to remain in the house, and specifically in the sitting room, while the police examined the rest of the house. One by one, they had been taken out to give statements. Sebastian had been asked to come out for a second round, as it was his house and the police had some additional questions. They were waiting for him to return. Angela sat between Peter and Yash. Theo curled in on herself in a reading chair and stared at the cold embers in the fireplace. Julian paced around the room, looking at the shelves, the walls, the backs of the furniture. It was cold inside Merryweather, but no one had the initiative to start a fire, nor would it have been clear if they would be allowed to do so. Could you burn logs after a murder?

"What the hell is happening?" Sooz said, mostly to herself. "Are we having a nightmare? All of us?"

There was a creaking sound. Sebastian was returning down the stairs from his questioning. They all turned to look at him as he entered the room. The normally bouncy and smiling Sebastian was now hunched. The color had not returned to his face, and he kept rubbing his skin as if there still might be blood somewhere on it. He had washed his face at least six times, rubbing the skin until it was raw. He walked straight to the bar cart and reached for the nearest bottle.

"They said we're allowed to go to our rooms if we want," he said. "They're finished up there. We still can't go outside. We'll have to stay here at least for tonight. After that . . ."

He let the sentence trail off. After that . . . who knew? The future had changed.

"They also said there have been a string of burglaries recently," he went on. "Four times in this area in the last few weeks. They've been nicking tack and things."

"Burglars," Yash said after a moment. "Fucking *burglars*?"

It was so horrifically absurd. It sucked the meaning out of the world.

Sooz began to tap her foot on the floor, then got to her feet and circled the sofa.

"I don't understand," she said. "Wasn't that shed locked?

You said everything was locked. How did Rosie and Noel get in there if it was locked?"

"I don't know." Sebastian swirled his drink to steady himself. "I suppose Rosie and Noel went in after the door was ripped open. They must have heard them or seen them, tried to stop them. Or they went in there and the burglars came back and found them."

Angela stood up suddenly.

"You all right, Ange?" Peter asked.

"I need to change my clothes," Angela said. "I need to take these off. I need a bath." She rubbed her arms violently and hurried from the room, back up the steps.

Angela felt like a ghost, moving out of time. Yesterday, they had rushed down this hallway, screaming with laughter as they grabbed their favorite rooms. Now the doors were all cocked open from when the police had trampled through. There had been strangers in the house, strangers in the suitcases, strangers in the drawers and closets. The view outside was just as lovely and lush as ever. Just outside the window, there were wild dog roses with their delicate pink petals and sunny bellies. Their beauty offended her. Confused her. She wasn't sure if she was real. Real was Noel—long and lean Noel, with his slow smile and moony face and his nerdy-cool 70s style. Noel who said the most surprising things sometimes. The freckles under his eyes you could only see in the bright sun. She remembered a night that she and Noel stole a shopping trolley and pushed each other down the street and looked up at the sky and talked about how much they loved

Bagpuss. Noel who asked so little of everyone else, who always did the washing-up, who could not drink tequila or he would turn into a strange creature who liked to run naked down the road. Noel, the nice guy who played villains shockingly well, who let anyone use his car.

Real was Rosie's green eyes that always held laughter, the jeans she had been wearing that had nail varnish on the knee, the rope bracelets on her wrist. Rosie sitting with her before Christmas, the two of them wrapping gifts, Rosie telling Angela how she thought the Blur album *Modern Life Is Rubbish* was her album because it had a song on it called "Villa Rosie" and one called "Pressure on Julian." ("It's fate, Ange, me and Jules. Damon Albarn is sending us messages.")

Rosie, coming to her room the night before with a secret.

I saw something. Something I didn't understand.

Dramatic Rosie.

But I think I might understand it now.

No.

Frightened Rosie.

Dead Rosie.

And now Angela had seen something too. Something she didn't understand.

If she didn't get into the tub of hot water, she would die. The water would make the world make sense, stop the ringing in her ears. She turned on the taps, ripped off her shirt and jeans and let them fall to the bathroom floor, and sat on the rim of the tub. She tested the water with her hand, found it was far too hot, and got in anyway, letting her skin prickle against the burn. It made her itch all over, and she rubbed her legs and let her face flush. The pain of the heat distracted her. The water was loud. Let it wash everything away. Scald it off her.

When the water was higher than it should have been, she leaned forward and closed the taps, then sat, hunched over her knees, watching the rain.

I saw something. Something I didn't understand.

Her mouth was so dry. Her head hurt. They'd had so much to drink the night before.

There was a rapping on the bathroom door.

"It's me," Theo said. "Can I come in?"

The Nine lived and worked on top of one another. Between changing backstage, the house, and the romances, they had seen each other in every stage of undress. There was nothing strange about having visitors when you were in the bath. Theo slipped in and set the mug down on a chair next to the tub.

"I brought you this," she said. "I know you don't like sugar in your tea, but you need it right now."

"How are you so calm?" Angela asked.

"I'm not calm," Theo said plainly. "I'm in shock, like we all are. It will wear off in time, for each of us, in a different way. The shock is why you're so cold. I'm cold as well. We need to stay warm. To eat. Stay hydrated."

Theo went to leave, but Angela stopped her.

"Wait a minute," Angela said. "I need to talk to you. Shut the door."

Theo closed the door.

"Something's not right, Theo. When we got here yesterday . . ." Angela lowered her voice, which echoed around the bathroom and the water and the tiles. "Rosie pulled me aside and said she had something to tell me."

"About Julian?"

"Not Julian. Something else. It was something . . . I don't know. Something serious. And I know Rosie is . . ."

She was not prepared to say "Rosie was."

". . . kind of dramatic sometimes, but this was different. She said she *saw* something. She said it was something she didn't understand. She needed to tell me about it but she didn't have a chance. She was going to tell me after we played the game."

"Saw something?"

"That's what she said. It was so odd. And . . . intense."

"And she didn't give you any idea what?"

"There's something else." Angela hugged her knees tighter into her chest and rubbed some sweat that was running into her eyes. "I saw something last night. I've been thinking about it all morning, but I didn't want to say it in front of everyone, because I don't know what it means either. Last night, when we were seeking, I went past the woodshed. *The lock was off the door.* Not unlocked—missing."

"Angela," Theo said slowly. "I saw that lock on the door this morning. The woodshed was locked. That's why they ripped off the latch."

"It was off in the middle of the night," Angela replied. "I

passed the woodshed last night. I saw the lock was off and tried to get in, but the door was stuck on the inside. I saw a light under the door. I called, but no one replied. I rattled the door a bit, and then I gave up. But I'm telling you, the lock was off the door."

Theo sat on the floor next to the tub.

"Ange," she said. "Our heads are going to play games with us. We need to keep clear heads and get each other through this. I don't know how we move on from here, or how we live like this without them, but I know we must take care of each other. I love you all so much and I . . ."

She could not finish.

Angela retreated into herself. She could see it so clearly. She had gone up to the door. The lock was gone and the light was squirreling around inside. The flashes had attracted her over to the door. That's right. She'd seen something. And she could tell there was someone on the other side of that door. Waiting. Listening. She'd felt it.

Hadn't she?

6

EVEN THOUGH DAVID KEPT REFERRING TO THE PLACE THEY WERE
going as "the local," it was a few streets away, past two other
pubs. And as he pointed out, though it was only four thirty
when they headed out the door, it was already night, for all
intents and purposes. The sky was dark and tinged with purple, and orange-tinted streetlights were on.

"It gets dark stupid early here in the fall," David said.
"Especially when it's overcast. Which is a lot of the time."

London's street layout was like the web of a drunk spider. Some streets curved and ended abruptly; some were
honeycombed with passages and mews. Alleys wove the baf-
fling structure together. Words on the street reminded idiot
Americans like herself which way the traffic was coming
from, and every time they went to cross one, she turned the
wrong way.

"You have to choose your pub wisely," David went on.
"This one has the best drink specials, the best music, and
they look the other way when we bring in food from other

places. The others like these weird-ass nachos from the place on the corner . . ."

He indicated a place called Señor Sam's.

". . . but English nachos are very bad. Do not eat English nachos. I swear to God I've seen them put baked beans on them. Fish and chips, however, are very good. That's not a stereotype. That's fact. And that's what we are getting."

They entered an inauspicious place called Mr. Chips: a pocket-sized place, painted stark white, with just three small tables that no one sat at. There was a menu on the wall that was perplexing. Stevie understood the component words, but they were in combinations that seemed to have a magical significance that she wasn't getting.

"I can order for us," David said. "I'll get a mix of stuff. My treat! Two regular cod and chips, two regular haddock and chips, a scampi and chips . . ."

"A battered burger?" Nate said, a certain amount of awe in his voice.

"Go for it," David said. "Arteries are for losers."

Several items were dumped into deep fat fryers, a rich, unhealthy smell filled the air, and they soon were back out into the evening holding a stack of Styrofoam boxes.

The pub was called the Seven Bishops, and it looked more like what Stevie was expecting—something cheerfully Dickensian, painted shiny black with gold lettering and a sign with a picture of a miter on it. The dark facade was broken by a chessboard of windows, and a cheering warm light glowed from within. Inside, there was a wooden bar, studded with tap handles. There were wooden booths with high walls, making cozy chambers for people to gather in. A few of these were still empty.

"We got here just in time," David said, staking one of these with the pile of food. "Drinks! What does everyone want?"

"Like, *drinks*, drinks?" Vi replied.

"Whatever you want."

Janelle had turned eighteen in October, and Nate followed in early November. Stevie, however, would not turn until December, and Vi until February. They had all discussed what they were going to do once they got here. They had planned on this—but being in the pub still felt, well, foreign.

"Stop worrying," David said. "See this?" He pointed to the pile of food in front of them. "This is a meal. You're allowed to have drinks with a meal when you're sixteen."

"Seriously?" Janelle said. "What a weird law."

"Welcome to the home of the weird law. Here's another one I learned in my introduction to UK and international law lecture—the Salmon Act 1986. It's illegal to handle salmon in a *suspicious manner*. I'll be watching. Now, drinks. Come on. What do you want?"

"What's good?" Vi said. "I want something that's right for here. A pint of something? You pick it out."

David nodded and looked to Janelle, who was eyeing the bar curiously.

"I don't like beer," Janelle said. "Is there something else?"

"There's cider," David offered. "It's a little sweeter."

Janelle accepted this. Nate stuck with Coke.

David turned to Stevie.

"I don't know," she said. "I guess . . ."

She felt stupid saying pint. She wanted to do the things—all the things. She just didn't know how.

"I guess . . ."

Someone walked by with a wineglass. She'd had wine before—champagne, actually—warm, in a mug, sitting on the bathroom floor with Element Walker on her first day at Ellingham. That felt right—a toast to Ellie.

"Do you want one of those?" he asked, following her gaze. "A white wine?"

"Sure?"

They settled into the padded green booth and looked out the many panes of the leaded window.

"Well," Nate said, flipping open one of the containers and taking out a fry. "We made it, and nothing weird has happened yet."

"Why would you even say that?" Janelle replied, examining the large pieces of fried fish and delicately removing one.

"I'm saying shit follows us around. I give it three days."

The fries were thick and hot as the tears of the sun, and the fish was every bit as good as David had promised. Overhead, Harry Styles sang out over the noise of the crowd, suggesting treating people with kindness. David returned with the drinks and slid in beside Stevie and slipped his arm over her shoulders, naturally. Stevie sipped at the white wine. It had a friendly taste and filled her head with a happy warmth.

They were all together again. All her friends. David. David so close that she could push her face into the curve of his neck. She had to restrain herself. She wanted to do much more.

"We've got to eat kind of quickly. We've got to leave in"— he consulted his phone—"fifteen minutes."

David was not the kind of person they typically wanted to follow to a second location, but here, he was the guide. It made Janelle visibly nervous. Vi was clearly fine with it, and Nate just wanted something to eat and was prepared to go against his better judgment. They polished off the fish and chips, drained the glasses, and pushed out of the booth, back into the night.

He took them out a back passage, through a short tunnel and over a bridge, finally emerging on the riverbank on the far side. There was no visible rain, but microscopic needles of moisture blew through the air, directly into their faces. David put his arm around Stevie, drawing her to his side. It was awkward walking this way, but nothing in the world had ever been better. The wine was on her lips and there was a happy fuzziness in her head that smeared the lights of London into a painter's palette of shine and color. The dark waters of the Thames plugged along beside them, smelling faintly of the sea. Or was that something else? Her senses were jumbled. She was tired and heavy and extremely awake, all at once.

David had a jaunty, springy walk. He hadn't shaved in maybe a day or two, and there was a bit of shadow over his chin and above his lip. He must have known how good this looked, or else he would have gotten rid of it. It was the perfect amount of stubble, an artistic amount of stubble. The sweater was new—black, formfitting. Was all of this for her? Was the world really this good? The wine warmed her brain, and her hormones warmed the rest.

She needed this night to go on and on and never stop.

They walked briskly back along the river, past the tourist information and the London Dungeon and a merrily painted old-fashioned carousel. Ahead of them was a massive, illuminated wheel. It dominated the riverfront like a spinning crown, glowing a purple blue. This was the London Eye, a Ferris wheel of epic proportions. It didn't have seats—it had pods—sealed glass rooms that could hold maybe twenty people as they made their way up and around. Only a few people were in line. It seemed that not many people wanted to come out on a wet November night like this.

There was a girl, standing off by herself. She was tall and angular, with a sweeping point of a chin. Even through her thick duck-egg-blue coat, you could tell her elbows were pointy. She had a mass of brown hair whipped up into a messy bun, and an oversized pair of glasses guarding a pair of brown eyes with carefully winged liner. She was waving her arms in their direction like she was guiding in a plane.

"Who is that?" Stevie asked.

"That," he said as they approached her, "is Izzy. She's one of my tutorial partners. And Iz, this is everyone."

"You're Stevie," she said. "And . . . Janelle? And Vi. And Nate. Did I get it right?"

She had, in fact, identified them all correctly.

"David talks about you *all the time*," she said. "Constantly. I've been so excited to meet you."

Normally, if someone said this to Stevie, she would have thought they were being sarcastic, or at least overdoing things a bit. Izzy seemed to mean it. She had a bright, enthusiastic fizz about her, along with a vague air of apology. She was one of those people who, like Janelle, knew how to accessorize. She wore multiple stacked rings on her fingers—at least six—earrings that looked like little baskets of flowers, a purple-and-yellow silk scarf knotted around her neck. Janelle was clocking all of this with an approving look.

"We're all set," she said to David. "We've got the last one."

She turned to the group and indicated they should step toward the boarding platform.

"A friend of the family works for the company that runs this," Izzy explained. "The one perk I have is that I can get rides on the Eye for free whenever I want. I've even been on some rides after it's closed for the day if they have a special occasion or are running maintenance. It's great when there are people in town. It's my party trick."

If you watch enough British mystery shows—and Stevie had—London will seem familiar, even to those who have never been near it in person. She had seen the London Eye in this way many times, spinning in the background of *Sherlock*. She understood it was a massive Ferris wheel, illuminated in violet, right on the water's edge. She let herself forget that she was not a fan of Ferris wheels, right up until the time that they were ushered quickly down a platform and into a pod that never stopped moving. Before she knew it, the compartment was sealed and Stevie and her friends were gliding up, up, up, the Thames chugging below them, the Houses of Parliament and London in general shrinking below them.

It was too dark to see details; night brought out the contours, the lines made by artificial light. You could see the circulatory system of London—the roads, the bridges, the moving cars—everything pulsing with energy. The smaller buildings became a dark mass of shadow, and the larger ones presented their outlines. This was a city of jagged spires, ancient towers, and modern glass skyscrapers that jutted into the distant skyline like knives. One was literally called the Shard.

The rain started falling in earnest, striking the pod, misting the glass, turning the view into streaks of light. As they rose, Izzy peppered them with questions about their trip. Had the flight been all right? How did they like their rooms? Were they tired? Were they having a good time—oh, of course they had just gotten here, they wouldn't know if they were having a good time yet. She had long arms and graceful hands, which she swung about in wide, expressive gestures. She insisted on helping them take pictures—group shots, David and Stevie, at least a dozen of Vi and Janelle making out against the London Skyline. ("You may not be able to see the view much but the two of you look adorable.") She seemed to have a deep desire to be around the group, to help them in any way, which was weird. There was nothing off about the way Izzy and

David chatted—it was all casual, references to school and the student house. But Stevie couldn't help but feel uneasy around this pleasant-smelling (she was wearing some kind of perfume that she identified as Jo Malone Orange Blossom when Janelle asked), friendly, accommodating stranger.

"Who the hell is she?" Nate asked Stevie quietly. "Why does she like us?"

Stevie shrugged. "We're likable?"

"Not really," he said. "We're okay at best. Are all English people this friendly?"

"I don't know," Stevie said as Izzy encouraged Vi and Janelle into one more set of pictures.

The wheel was dipping them back toward the water of the Thames and the ride was coming to an end, when Izzy came up alongside Stevie privately.

"I'm so pleased you're here," she said. "I've wanted to tell someone about this for so long, but I had no one to tell, then David told me all about you, and I knew I had to tell you when you got here. I thought I'd wait until the ride was over. You see . . ."

She gripped the rail that ran along the inside of the pod. ". . . I have to tell you about a *murder*."

"There it is," Nate said, mostly under his breath.

7

BACK ON THE GROUND, THE RAIN DROVE THEM TO SEEK SHELTER IN the nearby South Bank complex—a gargantuan bunker of smooth gray concrete that Janelle assured them was in the brutalist style. Signage directed them to what seemed like dozens of spaces: theaters, conference rooms, exhibitions, cafés. They took up residence at a table in one of the latter and huddled over some cups of tea and the last muffins of the day.

"I know people must tell you that all the time, that they know about a murder. But it's true. My aunt saw a murder. She was there. It was her friends who were killed. . . ."

Izzy was talking fast, the words spilling from her mouth.

"When my aunt, Angela, was at Cambridge, she was in a theater group. This was a very close group. They all lived together in student housing. After exams their final year, they went off for a week's celebration. One of them—his name is Sebastian, he's lovely—his family owns a massive house in the country called Merryweather. They all went out there for a long party. On the first night, they were playing a game of hide-and-seek on the grounds. It started to rain, so they all came inside, except for two of them. A few of the group went looking for them the next morning. They found them in the woodshed. Dead, I mean. With an axe. They had disturbed some burglars during the night. That's what I always heard about it, but . . ."

Izzy almost knocked over the remnants of her cup of tea as she leaned into the table.

"Growing up, I heard the story. Never in depth. Just that Angela had been at a house party where some burglars came in during the night and killed two of her friends. She's very sensitive about it, obviously. I know there are places she avoids because of it. She prefers to be in the city. The countryside makes her quite nervous. I never thought any more of it until earlier this year—over the summer, I was staying with Angela after she had an operation on her knee. She tore something at the gym and had to have it fixed and she was immobilized for a week or two. She needed someone with her because she was taking painkillers and she couldn't get up for a few days, so I was there to make tea and bring her soup and things like that. . . ."

An adorable flap of the hand, indicating the many invalid-friendly foodstuffs Izzy had brought to her aunt's bedside.

"She had the telly on, and there was a show on about a murder, and out of nowhere she said, 'I think one of my friends murdered someone. I was there.' So I said to her, 'What do you mean?' And she said, 'My friends. The ones who were killed. The lock was off the door. I saw the lock off the door.' Then she kept saying something about things being planted. I could tell she wasn't hallucinating. She was saying something she really believed but wouldn't have said out loud unless she was off her tits on pain medication."

"Your aunt said, 'I think one of my friends murdered someone,'" Stevie repeated.

"And also that she was there. And the lock and planted evidence, or planting, or something. Then I think she realized what she was saying and stopped. I had no idea what to do. I asked her about it later, and she tried to fob me off."

"Some pain medications are very strong," Janelle said. "Isn't it possible that she was just high? That she was saying things that had no bearing on reality?"

"If you had been there," Izzy said, "you would know. It was real. Her guard was down, but she was speaking with absolute clarity. She had a look in her eye like she was remembering something, like she just forgot who she was talking to about it. I've been thinking about this since it happened and I can't let it go. I've read all I can about the murders, but there's not a lot. The point is—they never found out who did it. No one was ever accused or charged. It was written off as a robbery. But she knows something, and that something is eating her up inside. I didn't know what to do about any of this, and then I met David a few weeks ago and he told me about you, and it seems like fate. I'm a great believer in fate. I've been waiting to meet you and tell you about it."

Now that Izzy had, in fact, told her about it, Stevie had no idea what to say next. Usually, these things came in the form of messages, not people leaning over a café table with wide eyes, smelling faintly of orange blossom, tapping chipped green nails on the table surface and picking at the remnants of a muffin.

"So, I had a *thought*." Izzy's thought floated on the air for a moment, swept up and around the table. "David mentioned you're doing a lot of tours? And that you're going to the Tower of London this week? Angela makes history shows for the BBC. She's an expert in all *sorts* of things about London history. She's making a new program now. I thought . . . if you wanted, we could get some takeaway and have dinner with her! She doesn't live far, just a few stops on the Tube. I know she'd love to meet you and she can tell you *loads* about Henry the Eighth and his wives. She knows everything about the Tower. She's done something about it—an article, or maybe part of a book? Because that's where they were beheaded. The wives. And maybe we could get her to talk about it? What do you say? There's an amazing restaurant down the road from her flat that does the best takeaway curry. Only if you want to, because I know you have plans, but I thought I'd offer since you're here and you're doing this sort of thing and I suppose you have to eat dinner anyway and . . ."

There was something almost elegant about the way Izzy rambled. Her conversation was a ball rolling on a marble floor, effortless in its unbroken motion, unstoppable without an outside force. Everything she said was polite and friendly, offered as a suggestion only—but the longer she spoke, the more Stevie realized that this was going to be the plan. It was too reasonable to fend off. You don't argue with a gentle breeze. Why wouldn't they go to meet with a historian, eat something delicious, and hear about an axe murder?

". . . obviously, I don't want to change your plans . . ."

Everyone looked at Janelle.

"Our dinners are generally open," she said. "And meeting with a historian who knows a lot about the Tower of London seems like a good thing to do?"

"Oh, then *paaarrfect*! We'll meet after you're done with your tours tomorrow. What time would work for you?"

Everyone looked a bit helpless in the face of this polite onslaught. Plus, the group was starting to fade a little, from the lack of sleep and the time change and the cold rain. Stevie had the strong desire to go back to the student housing, get under a warm blanket, and take David with her. The matter was settled.

They walked back to Craven House. Izzy's and David's lodgings were in one direction and Stevie's and the others' were in the opposite. Nate, Vi, and Janelle took the elevator first, leaving Izzy, Stevie, and David.

"Have a good night!" Izzy said. She paused, looking to David to walk in her direction, then shook her head and corrected herself. "Oh, of course. You're going that way. See you tomorrow!"

This was a very public way of acknowledging that David was going with Stevie. Though Stevie had gone off to private places with David many times, it still felt strange to her when someone else threw a spotlight on the fact. Like the world at large was conscious of her business. Which, of course, it was.

As a detective, she observed other people—that other people observed her was the uncomfortable corollary.

Once back in Stevie's room, David put his hands in his coat pockets and made a circuit of the small space. He knew this gesture pulled down on the coat, elongated it. He had a sly smile, a fox grin, as he looked around at the empty corkboard, her bags, the slightly crooked window blind. He stopped at the built-in desk on the wall and took a seat on the edge, then lifted the cheap plastic kettle there from its base.

"Even comes with a kettle," he said. "It's essential. They all love a kettle. Just fill it up and click."

He set it back on the base.

"Did you know about all that?" Stevie said. "The murder stuff?"

He nodded. "She told me. She wanted to tell you. Everyone's got a story, huh?"

"I guess so."

"Well, now you get to meet a TV lady and hear about a murder. See the nice things I get for you?"

There was a pause.

"Come here," he said.

Stevie was right by the light switch. She hesitated. Should she switch it off? That was a direct way of signaling what you expected to happen. It didn't seem smooth. But was it fun? She felt like she should err on the side of fun.

She casually bumped it with her shoulder as she passed, as if she didn't mean to do it. He laughed.

She walked across the half-lit room, trying not to stumble

over the bags she had set on the floor. The street below provided much ambient glare, as the streetlight was just outside. It was enough light to see the contours of his face—his long nose, the little quirked peaks of his eyebrows.

"I'm really," he said, leaning in, "really, *really* glad you came."

She pressed herself up to kiss him, hard. She felt a tremor through her whole body, a warmth, a sense that the entire world was here, running between them. This position—leaning halfway against the desk—was impossible to maintain. They both sank to the floor, ignoring the bed. The cold linoleum was the best surface in the world. His hands slipped under her T-shirt. She tried to shrug it off, but the hoodie got in the way. She sat up to remove the hoodie, remove the T-shirt.

This would have been the moment to deploy the fancy bra that Janelle had shown her, but then, what did it matter? The stretched-out sports bra was just as good, and David was reaching for . . .

The phone.

It was ringing, that is. A video call, from Dr. Quinn.

"Shit," Stevie said, reaching for her shirt. "Shit, shit, shit. I was supposed to call. Shit . . ."

She pulled her shirt on and stood up, her head still spinning and her legs a little weak. She ran a quick hand through her hair, which did nothing. David crab-crawled away a few paces as Stevie answered.

"Oh," Stevie said. "Hi. I'm sorry. I got confused about the

time. I was . . . unpacking."

"In the dark?" Dr. Quinn said. She was leaning back in her chair in her office at Ellingham, making the call from her computer. Stevie got the full effect of looking across the desk.

"I just . . . came in. I was in Janelle's room. Sorry."

She reached over and turned on the little reading light next to the bed. The effect was like pointing a flashlight at her face, like she was trying to tell a scary story. She sat down on the bed and tried to seem casual.

"How's the accommodation?"

"Fine," Stevie said. "Nice. Good. Fine."

"Fine and nice and good. Let's see it."

On hearing this, David began to move around the room, away from the focus of the camera.

"Switch on the main light so I can see," Dr. Quinn said.

"Yeah . . ." Stevie kept David out of frame as she crossed over to the light switch by the door. She illuminated the room and continued panning around. The room was so small that David had to squeeze behind her and step up on the bed to keep out of sight. It let out a small, plasticky creak.

"Oh, hello, David," Dr. Quinn said. "Come over and wave to me."

Stevie opened her mouth in a pathetic attempt at denial, but before she could embarrass herself, Dr. Quinn shook her head. David pulled on his shirt and adjusted it, then stepped in front of the camera.

"Hi," he said. "It's been a while. I was just showing Stevie how the kettle works."

He pressed down the lever on the kettle and it lit up and gurgled happily, as if it were delighted by the prospect of a nice cup of tea.

"It's a complicated machine," Dr. Quinn said.

"Took me a while to master it."

"Leave Stevie's room now. I'll be on the phone with her for a while, so there's no point in waiting outside."

"Yep," David said. "Yep. Anyway, Stevie, that's how the kettle works so, see you tomorrow . . ."

She knew. Of *course* she knew. It could have been an educated guess, or maybe she had someone on the inside, or maybe she had tapped into the CCTV mainframe. She was Dr. Jenny Quinn, so anything was possible.

"I think it would be best," she said, "if David kept out of your room. It's late there, and you must be exhausted from your trip. Jet lag hits fast, though I find it's often worse on the second day. Get some rest. Enjoy your kettle."

DCI PHILLIP STARLING, GLOUCESTER CONSTABULARY

24 June 1995

Background:

Incident took place at Merryweather, a large house on over fifty acres, with numerous outbuildings and extensive grounds. The owners are currently in Greece, and it was known locally that the house might be unoccupied. Son of owner, who attends Cambridge, returned to the house with eight friends for a visit, arriving approximately 10.00 p.m. last night. No staff was present on this evening and all have been accounted for.

Interviews of seven witnesses/housemates paint a consistent story of a house party with a game of team hide-and-seek being played on the grounds between 11.00 p.m. and 2.30 a.m. During this time, all members of the house party were freely running the grounds and were both hiding and seeking. (Witness statements contain details.) There was a powerful electrical storm going on while the game took place.

At approximately 2.30 a.m., the storm took down power lines at the opening of St. Swithun's Lane, which is the only road that leads in or out of Merryweather. Merryweather and the village of

117

Ramscoate-on-Whyle lost electricity, and emergency services dispatched a van to deal with the downed wire and prevent fire or accidental electrocutions. This van arrived at 3.00 a.m. and remained in place until 7.30 a.m. To prevent vehicles or people from going near the wire, they stationed the van across the opening of St. Swithun's Lane, blocking entry or exit. During this time, no vehicles could have come in or out of Merryweather without encountering the van. The workers reported that no vehicles or persons came down the road, which was not surprising, given the hour and the severity of the storm. (Note: Merryweather has an electric gate which is accessed by a numerical keypad. The code is known to many locals who work at or make deliveries to the property. With the power down, the gate would have to be forced open, and there were no signs of forced entry at the gate.)

The seven witnesses returned to the house when the power went out. Two members of the party, Rosalyn Mortimer and Noel Butler, did not respond to calls that announced the end of the game. The witnesses said that there was a romance budding between the two, and it was assumed they had gone somewhere in private and did not wish to be disturbed. The remaining seven stayed in the house the rest of the night, drinking and talking. None reported hearing anything out of the ordinary, but the storm would have easily drowned out any cries for help or noises of intruders. Witness Suzanna Rillington states that she "clearly saw" the beam of a torch at the front of the house. She could not provide an exact time, but given the fact that the sun had not yet risen, she estimated this would have been around 3–3.30 a.m.

Around noon today, witnesses Theodora Bailey and Sebastian Holt-Carey went looking for the lost members of the group. In their search, they found an upturned wheelbarrow in front of a woodshed located near the garage. The woodshed is used for wood and garden implement storage and contains nothing of value. The door of the woodshed had been forced open, tearing the latch from the wood. The shed is locked with a padlock, which was found intact. Assuming that someone had attempted to burgle the shed, the witnesses entered to inspect the damage. Inside, they found the bodies of Mortimer and Butler.

Impressions of victims and scene:
Both victims were found partially covered in firewood, and both had been attacked with a sharp, heavy weapon that left wedge-shaped injuries, consistent with an axe. The axe normally kept in the woodshed was missing. A long-handled axe was found by PC Whitsgale in small stream running through the

property. Both victims had multiple injuries and massive blood loss. The location of the wheelbarrow and the use of the axe indicates disturbance of a crime in progress.

The door of the shed was open and rainwater had pooled on the floor, eliminating any potential footprints and washing away blood and other debris. Light for the shed was provided by a single lightbulb fixed to the ceiling. This had been smashed, and faint traces of blood were found on the edges, suggesting that it was broken by the axe during the attack. Bits of broken bulb were found on top of the wood that covered Mortimer, but *under* Butler's body. This seems to indicate that Mortimer died first. Butler likely entered the scene after Mortimer was already dead and under the logs.

Medical examiner arrived on the scene at 2.00 p.m. Initial impression is that both Mortimer and Butler died around the same time. This time could not be determined with any exactitude; however, the pair had been dead somewhere between ten and twelve hours. As they were last seen at 11.00 p.m., this places the window at between 11.00 p.m. and 4.00 a.m., covering all the hours of darkness.

Several of the witnesses state that they passed the

woodshed during the course of the game and found it intact, with no wheelbarrow in front. There were two keys to this shed: one with the gardener, who was at home, and one on the key ring of Holt-Carey, who had it in his possession at all times. (It was established for the game that outbuildings were locked and off-limits.)

Unless the intruder(s) came on foot, which is unlikely considering the location of Merryweather and the size and weight of potential stolen goods, this suggests the intruder(s) arrived and left the scene prior to the loss of power at 2.30 a.m. Vehicle was likely parked out of view of the house. Note time discrepancy of statement of witness Rillington re: torchlight. If intruders left at 2.30, there would be no torchlight at 3 or later. Likely explanation in that witness had been consuming alcohol all evening and there was a good deal of lightning in the night. Timeline of power services much more reliable.

Addendum 12 July: blood found on remains of lightbulb still in ceiling has been matched to Mortimer.

8

"A PANOPTICON," VI SAID.

They were sitting around a tall, slightly wobbly table at the corner Pret a Manger, having breakfast. Stevie had opted for a large coffee and a brownie, which was maybe not the best choice, but it felt right. She was a little confused about what time it was, and therefore she would need to be powered by all the sugar and caffeine she could pump into her system.

"It's a concept of a prison," Vi went on, picking out the chunks of mango in their fruit cup to eat them first. "It's circular. The people in the prison are arranged around a central guard station that you can't see into. The idea is that you only need one guard, because the imprisoned persons never know *when* they are being watched, so they have the feeling of *always* being watched."

Vi was a student of prison reform, and this was the kind of thing they knew off the top of their head.

"Quinn doesn't have to be everywhere," Vi went on. "She just has to be *somewhere*."

"Do you think she's really got someone in the building

122

who's watching us, or did she get lucky?" Stevie asked.

"Doesn't matter," Vi said. "That's the point."

"Why does she even care?" Stevie said.

"When you're a guardian, you have to make sure sex isn't happening, even when you know it is and there's nothing wrong with it. It's patriarchal hangover. Not even a hangover. Just patriarchal."

Their face took on a disappointed cast, as they had eaten all the mango, the single strawberry, and the three grapes, and now reached the milky-pale melon pieces that lurk at the base of every cup of fruit. Vi was not a waster of food, so they grimly set about consuming the tasteless melon.

Throughout this discussion, Janelle had been consulting the schedule on her phone and nodding at various points to show her agreement. She was looking spectacular for their big day out in London. Janelle had recently gotten into online consignment shopping and had picked up some clothes she referred to as "pieces." She was wearing one now, a form-fitting sweater dress with zigzagging rows of multicolored autumnal shades. ("This is vintage *Missoni*. I got it for fifty-five bucks because it had a little hole in the hem. I can fix that no problem. *Missoni*.") Her hair was up in two bunches, which she had accented with multiple bronze and orange barrettes. Janelle was not playing around on a trip like this.

"We should walk back the way we went last night," she said, "along the river, and catch the hop-on-hop-off bus at Temple Pier, which is really close. So we should finish and go. Nate, are you going to get anything to eat?"

"Not hungry," he said. "We should get going."

The plan, which had seemed so sensible and short and compact when Stevie had first seen it, was now in motion. They bought passes for the hop-on-and-off tour bus and rode around London, Janelle tracking on her phone. They got off to see the changing of the guard at Buckingham Palace, which involved standing at a gate while people in huge black fur hats moved around. Back on the bus to the far corner of Hyde Park. Hyde Park was exactly what the name suggested—a park, and a lot of it. It connected to more park. Travel has so much between time—walking around and trying to figure out where you were. There was Kensington Palace, the Peter Pan statue, the Serpentine, where they considered getting a boat but there was no time, Speakers' Corner . . . then through an arch to more park, a different park. This one was Green Park, which was basically Buckingham Palace's back garden. This led to St. James's Park and St. James's Palace (there were way more palaces than Stevie thought), down to Westminster, to 10 Downing Street and the Imperial War Rooms. Back on the bus. Back in some other direction. Where were they? Covent Garden? Soho? Russell Square. Just names now. Names and massive buildings.

Her head was spinning and her attention flagging.

Izzy. She appeared in Stevie's mind. The point of her chin, her long hands, her fuzzy coat, her masses of hair that looked adorably perfect piled on her head like a glamorous owl sanctuary. Izzy and David spent so much time together here. He hadn't mentioned her on their calls. Or had he?

Maybe once he mentioned an Iz. Stevie probably thought he said "is" or something. Why not mention her? He planned things with her. Like that ride last night. Of course, it was a good surprise. He got her a trip on the London Eye and a murder story.

And yet.

So much time together. So many London nights like the one last night. So many long evenings and drizzling rain, and talking at the pub, and walking these streets . . . the streets she didn't know.

My aunt saw a murder. She was there.

She looked down at her phone and did some searching. She had only a few points of reference for her search. Two murders. 1995. A country house. A burglar.

Google didn't turn up much. She only found one or two articles, and they all repeated the basic facts that Izzy had told her. Nine students, recently graduated from Cambridge, went to a house called Merryweather on June 23, 1995. That night, during a storm, they played an outdoor game of hide-and-seek. Two members of the party never came back inside and were discovered in the morning in the woodshed, murdered with an axe. The matter was thought to be connected to several local burglaries. And that was it. Nothing more.

The two cases she had worked on before—the Ellingham case and the Box in the Woods murders—both had substantial coverage. The lack of information out in the world was both disappointing and intriguing. This was fresh ground, undisturbed.

"We're here," Nate said, tapping her on the arm.

They had returned to their starting point. Stevie hadn't even noticed. She hurriedly grabbed her bag and followed Nate down the steps to the lower level and off the bus. Janelle and Vi had already disembarked.

The dark was gathering over Craven House as they stepped into the greenish light of the lobby. The tree looked slightly sadder today. It was leaning to the left and someone had put googly eyes on a few of the ornaments. Two balls had fallen off the tree and were lolling underneath.

"Harsh," Nate said, noting it as he passed. "You know, the best fanfic I ever read was an erotic story about Thor and Tony Stark living together on a Christmas tree sex farm."

"What?" Vi said. "Was it a sex farm or a Christmas tree farm?"

"Both," Nate replied as they pushed open the doors into the common room. "Mostly sex, some tree. I don't think they were taking the business seriously, because that was no way to handle a wreath."

The common room was a large space with a shocking purple carpet, several wood-framed sofas and large work-tables, with a small bar in the corner that didn't appear to be open. David and Izzy were already there, sitting together on a sofa working on their individual laptops. Izzy was wearing an oversized white blouse with large sleeves. On Stevie, it would have been a confused mess, and it sort of was on Izzy as well, but it was also charming.

Something funny hit Stevie. A little sizzle of something unpleasant.

"Oh!" Izzy cried, getting up. "You're back! Ready to go?"

Izzy's aunt lived in a place called Islington, which was several Tube stops to the north, on something called the Northern Line—a black line on the orderly squiggles of the Tube map. This meant they had to walk to the Embankment stop, which was down along the path they had taken before, by the river.

The Tube. The famous Tube. It was nothing to David now. He'd been here for months and tapped his card lightly on the reader while Stevie and the others fumbled with their tickets. He and Izzy chatted and joked as they rode down the incredibly long escalator into the depths below London. The walls were paneled in screens that repeated the same rotation of advertisements as they went down, trying desperately to get her to buy a new thriller called *Blood at Dawn*, attend a production of *Richard III*, and buy dessert for Christmas at a place called M&S. There was a light, minerally smell, somewhere between fuel and the sweet, unused smell that basements sometimes had.

Another little sizzle as Izzy showed David something on her phone.

There was nothing to be jealous about, was what she told herself as they stood on the platform, looking across at the massive advertisements that were plastered along the curved walls of the Tube. If anything, Izzy seemed more excited about Stevie.

But what if that was what you did when you were trying to hide something?

"Hey."

David was whispering against her ear. The feeling of his warm breath made her tingle, and the entire right side of her body seemed to go into a liquid state.

"Guess what?" he whispered.

"What?"

"Chicken. Butt."

He flicked her ear with his tongue.

There was a rush of wind and the train appeared. There was a polite bong sound, and then the recorded voice said MIND THE GAP in a staid English accent.

"It really does that?" Nate said.

The train was utterly rammed with people. There were no seats to be had, and very little standing room. They all crushed together in a forest of arms, wobbling as the train sped along. Janelle and Vi squished together by a pole. David had looped an arm around Stevie. It was warm on the train and the gentle rocking motion made Stevie start to drift off. She wasn't asleep, but she wasn't as awake as she wanted to be. There was no time to sleep on this trip—this was all she had. Every day was valuable. Every night.

There was a lot of squeezing and standing and wobbling and pressing before the train expelled them at a place called Angel. They emerged on a wide street of shops and restaurants.

"It's not far," Izzy said brightly. "About a fifteen-minute walk."

This was not quite the around-the-corner-sounding place that Izzy had indicated. Finally, after walking down at least a dozen streets, they stopped at a restaurant on the corner called the Rose of Bengal that played old Bollywood movies on a large screen.

"I'll get a selection of dishes to share, if that's all right," Izzy said. "My treat. Are there vegetarians?"

Vi had been transitioning to a vegan diet, so this was noted. Izzy ordered an array of things that Stevie didn't know. All the dishes going to the tables in little copper pots looked and smelled incredible, but she didn't know what they were. It sounded like they were having all of it—lamb bhuna, rogan josh, tandoori prawns, saag paneer, aloo gobi, bindi masala, chana masala, chapati, paratha, Peshwari naan . . . a few of these words sounded vaguely familiar, but she was lost. For the first time since arriving here, she felt the depth of distance. She couldn't even figure out what David's new friend was getting them for dinner.

After a short wait, they were presented with three brimming bags and headed back out, following Izzy down a street filled with rows of identical two-story brown brick terraced houses. Each had six concrete or stone steps leading up to a shiny black door, and a low fence of black wrought iron along the sidewalk, separating off a recessed area where there was a lower level. Stevie didn't really know what things were like in Dickens's time, but she imagined the building much like this, with chimney sweeps and cooks and maids talking to one another on the stoops. Now, instead of horses, there were impossibly small cars and scooters lining the road, and plastic trash bins stationed aside the stoop.

"Hello, Doorknob," Izzy said.

"Did you just say hello to the doorknob?" David asked.

Izzy pointed to the top of a recycling bin next to them, in the tiny forecourt of the house. Sitting on top, like the Cheshire Cat from *Alice in Wonderland*, was a large orange cat, slapping at his own tail.

"This is Doorknob," she said, passing David the food bags and scooping the cat into her arms. "Because, dumb as a. His favorite toy is the wall. He has a cat flap but he can't work out how it works. You're not bright at all, are you? But you're a good boy. She's going to be so excited."

Stevie wasn't sure if she meant the cat, but the cat seemed to be male.

"She?" Stevie asked. "Your aunt? She knows we're coming, right?"

"I texted her," Izzy replied.

Izzy knocked twice, then produced a set of keys and opened the door a crack to lead them into a darkened vestibule, which was tidily full of coats on a row of pegs, a bike, and a stone statue of a Buddha on the floor. She set Doorknob down, and he circled three times before strolling through an open doorway into what looked like the living room. There was a light on somewhere above them, but no sound.

"Hello!" Izzy called up the stairs. "Just me! I brought food!"

Which seemed like an odd thing to say, since it was not

just Izzy, and suggested that food had not been previously discussed. Stevie heard a chair roll back and footsteps. A woman came down the steps. She bore enough of a resemblance to Izzy to confirm that this was, in fact, her aunt. Her hair was cropped to her chin and full of bouncy curls. She had well-manicured eyebrows, professionally full, but wore no makeup. She was dressed in pajama bottoms and an oversized T-shirt.

"Oh," she said. "Hello . . ."

"I brought some friends," Izzy said. "This is David, from uni. And these are some of his friends from America—this is Janelle, and Vi, and Nate . . . and this is Stevie. Stevie Bell."

She said it in a way that suggested that Angela should know the name, and maybe clap.

She did not.

"Oh," Angela said. "Right. Nice to meet you."

She looked at Izzy with an expression that said, *Why have you brought me five Americans? I did not order five Americans.*

"They're doing a tour of historical sites," Izzy went on. "They're going to the Tower tomorrow. And I thought, since I know you never eat when you're working, I'd bring food and maybe we could chat?"

So, Izzy hadn't told her aunt that this was happening. They were crashing. They were crashing with a lot of food, but they were crashing. Stevie looked to David in concern, but he just shrugged and gave a half smile.

"Oh. Right. Of course, yes. And you're well timed. I haven't eaten today and I'm *starving.* Izzy knows me. Yes, let's go through to the kitchen."

Angela recovered from her initial surprise, or at least made a good effort at covering. The kitchen was at the back of the house—a small, cheerful space with pale yellow walls. Izzy dumped the bags on the table and Angela started pulling down plates from the cabinet while the five Americans shifted around and tried not to get in the way, which was difficult.

"Are you over on holiday?" Angela asked politely.

"We're on a weeklong study-abroad trip," Janelle offered.

"Oh, right. That's quite fun."

Izzy kept pulling containers from the bag. It seemed endless. There were little tin dishes of steaming rice with yellow and orange flecks in it, multiple curries, dishes of chickpeas and greens, flatbreads, and then about a dozen tiny plastic cups of condiments, none of which Stevie could recognize. This was one of those moments where she felt like she had failed at some primary task of life, to know the basics of an Indian takeout meal.

Angela sneezed loudly several times.

"I'm getting over a cold," she said by way of an apology for dabbing at her nose with a napkin. "I can just about taste. How much was the food?" Angela examined the receipt. "Seventy-eight pounds. Here."

She went into a drawer and produced four twenty-pound notes and handed them to Izzy.

"Oh no," Izzy said, "really . . ."

Angela gave her an "I'm your aunt and you are taking this

money" wave, and Izzy accepted the notes.

They all filled their plates with the food, which looked as beautiful as it smelled delicious—the rich red and soft yellow of the curries, the charred bubbles on the fresh bread, the bright pops of cilantro. Nate eagerly filled his plate until it almost ran over the edge. There wasn't enough room in the kitchen for seven people, so they decamped to the living room, where Angela tried to make her unexpected guests comfortable.

"So, Stevie and Janelle and Nate and Vi all go to a school called Ellingham Academy, in *Vermont*," Izzy said, sitting on the floor alongside the coffee table and tucking into her meal. "And David went there as well."

She said the word *Vermont* like it was a magical, fictional place of ill repute. To be fair, it was a bit. At least in Stevie's corner of Vermont.

"I've heard of Ellingham," Angela said, tearing a piece of the bread with gusto. "The kidnapping, in the nineteen thirties? They never solved that, did they? Or something happened recently, maybe?"

"That was Stevie!" Izzy said, passing around the condiments on a tray.

She didn't clarify, and Angela didn't ask. It was better that way. Stevie was already in a stranger's house, holding a massive plate of food, slightly stupefied with exhaustion. She was not prepared to give a talk on her *detecting*. She wanted to eat, avoid burping, make out with her boyfriend, and possibly fall asleep on the floor.

To Stevie's surprise, Izzy began to recount the story of Stevie's work on the Ellingham kidnapping and murders—even the stuff that hadn't been in the press. She told the story of the Truly Devious letters and the recent deaths. These were things she could have learned only from David. She knew these things in detail, and she got the details right. This told Stevie a few things. One: David talked about Stevie a lot. Two: Izzy paid attention. Three: Izzy made it sound like Stevie was Wikipedia Holmes, a walking, talking, deducing database that ate true crime and spat out justice.

"Oh," Angela said in reply when Izzy had concluded. "I see. That's really quite something."

It was sort of flattering, but some other, darker emotion was slipping into Stevie's brainpan. Why did Izzy care so much about her? Was it just to bring her here, to talk to her aunt? Or was it to build trust with David? "Oh, your girlfriend! Tell me all about her . . ." Stevie suddenly conjured images of long nights at the pub, their feet touching under the table, Izzy's intent and interested expression. She had warm brown eyes, that soft halo of hair, a dimple on her left cheek. And she was smart. She had been talking with Vi on the Tube about international politics. Vi's and Izzy's interests overlapped a bit—environmental justice, food insecurity, the political implications of prisons. Izzy had started learning Japanese online and Vi, who had studied it a bit longer, was giving her some tips. Izzy was the full package, warm and vibrant and smart and engaged; she was with David all the time. . . .

And then there was Stevie, far away in America, no future plan, and no idea how to fix the planet. She couldn't even figure out how to cut her hair.

There was a loud burst of pops outside, like a scatter of gunfire, and Stevie saw a glint of yellow light. Having participated in school shooter drills since she was in kindergarten, she almost reflexively scooted herself under the window and out of view.

"Nothing to be alarmed about," Angela said, reaching for some more chutney. "Those are just leftover fireworks from Bonfire Night. Someone keeps setting them off in their garden."

"Do you know Bonfire Night?" Izzy asked. "Remember, remember the fifth of November, gunpowder treason and plot?"

"Vaguely?" Janelle said.

Stevie had heard of it in the many English mystery books she read. She knew there was something about a mannequin, but never really understood what it was about.

"Henry the Eighth," Angela said, "you probably know that he had six wives. When he wanted to leave his first wife, Catherine of Aragon, to marry Anne Boleyn the Church wouldn't let him do it. After fighting with them for years, he broke with the Catholic Church and declared himself head of the church in England. He destroyed a thousand years of the Roman Catholic Church's rule in England. He dissolved the monasteries. He took all the wealth the church had, which was a lot. This change in religion caused turmoil for decades, Catholics and Protestants fighting for control of the crown. And in 1605, a group of Catholic zealots launched a conspiracy to blow up Parliament and the king. Guy Fawkes was found hiding under Parliament with thirty-six barrels of gunpowder. Things didn't go well for him. They tortured him until he gave up his confederates. Knobby! No!"

Doorknob had settled his happy orange bulk on Stevie's coat and was sucking on one of the buttons. As soon as Angela moved to get up, he jumped off and skittered up the steps.

"He does that," Angela said. "Likes to chew buttons off things. Buttons, zips, laces. Sorry."

"Tea?" Izzy suddenly popped up off the floor and grabbed some dirty plates. "Anyone? I'll make tea."

She hurried out of the room.

"You're going to the Tower tomorrow?" Angela asked. "That's where they tortured him. I'm going to be doing some filming there in a few weeks. I'm one of those people who host historical documentaries, or I appear in them. Izzy may have mentioned that. This one is *another* program about the wives of Henry the Eighth. There is an insatiable appetite for things about the wives of Henry the Eighth. Everyone loves them. Sex and murder."

"Murder?" Stevie said.

"How else would you describe killing two of your wives?"

It was a good point, and Stevie felt stupid for having said the word like it was a question. Her brain was slow.

"It's the thing people always want to know about," Angela said. "Here's a king so smitten by a woman that he smashes everything to marry her, and he does so, in November 1532. She doesn't give him a son. Within about two years, he's discussing how to get rid of her. He takes a mistress—he's already got her successor picked out. In order to have this new wife, the old wife has to go. And she's not going to go with all the fuss of the first one. I mean, he's just blown the world apart, ripped religion and world order to shreds, so he can't just admit that she didn't work out for him. He's got to *erase* Anne. . . ."

She said it with genuine distaste.

"So she was arrested on mostly, if not entirely, trumped-up charges of infidelity, including the charge that she was in a relationship with her *brother*."

"Yikes," Vi said.

"Yikes, indeed. The king wanted her gone, so she was going to be gone, no matter what it took. The more disgraceful, the better. There could be no questions. Anne was taken to the Tower after her arrest. They'll probably tell you in the tour she came in by the Traitors' Gate, but that's not right. In any case, she's imprisoned there. Henry's already off having a good time with his new love. It all ended quickly, within about two weeks, in May 1536. She was arrested on the second. All the men she was accused of having affairs with were taken off for questioning—that means they were tortured. Anne was tried and found guilty on the fifteenth. The men were executed on the seventeenth, and she was set to die on the nineteenth. Seventeen days. That's all it took from being a queen to being accused, imprisoned, tried, and executed.

The king gave her a going-away present, so to speak. The punishment for the crime that she'd been convicted of was burning at the stake—for women. Because she was a queen, he decided that wasn't appropriate for her. She would be beheaded. But a simple beheading also wasn't enough. He sent for a special executioner from France who used a sword. He did this, mind you, *before* she was found guilty—almost as if he knew how it was all going to end."

Another, smaller, flash and pop outside.

"Here's a little grim fact," Angela went on. "The Tower is big on those. With beheadings by axe, you had to put your head down on a block, like this . . ."

She demonstrated by leaning forward and tilting her head to the side, like she was setting it down on something.

". . . but beheadings by sword were different. You knelt, but you kept your head up. When Anne climbed the scaffold after she spoke—and she gave a moving speech—she had to remove her cloak, her headdress, all her jewels. She even had to pay her own executioner with a bag of money she had been provided and formally forgave him. That was all procedure, but it always affects me when I think about it. They put a cap on her head, knelt her down, put a blindfold over her eyes. Now she can't see. The executioner, to his credit, is good at what he does. He has a method he uses to get his victim's head in the right position. He calls to his boy to bring him his sword, except, there is no boy. He's already got the sword. He does this because the victims will naturally turn their head in the direction he's calling, waiting to hear the sword being brought to the scaffold. It seems so simple, this little misdirection, but it works. A little bit of fakery did so much. One swing of the sword was all it took. What's odd is after all that—the trials and torture and bringing a swordsman from France—no one planned for the body. The body they knew would be there. No one had arranged for a coffin. One of the yeoman had to go to the armory and find a box."

Izzy came in with a tray full of steaming mismatched mugs, along with a wrapped roll of chocolate Hobnob cookies. She distributed the mugs, handing Stevie a pink polka-dotted one.

"As a coda to all of that," Angela said, accepting a mug of tea, "Henry didn't bother with the swordsman for the murder of his fifth wife, Catherine Howard, six years later. He let them use the axe."

The word *axe* seemed to be the perfect jumping-in point. Stevie saw Izzy reaching for the conversational baton.

"You know," she said, passing teas to the others, "I was telling Stevie—because she's done work in this area, real work, like I said—here's milk, Vi, do you take sugar? I'll leave it here—about what happened to you. With your friends. You know. The murders."

9

ANGELA STIFFENED HER GRIP ON HER MUG. IT WAS NOT A GRACEFUL transition of topic.

One did not simply mention *the murders*.

"I know," Izzy said quickly. "It's very hard for you, but . . . since Stevie is . . . well, an expert in these things, and it was never solved . . ."

Again, she waited for Angela to take the lead, but she did not. Despite what Izzy had told them, Angela clearly had no idea this was going to happen. Angela didn't know they were coming, didn't know she would be giving a history lesson, didn't know about dinner, and hadn't expected to talk about what must have been one of the most terrible days of her life.

"Izzy . . ."

"It really is all right," Izzy said, even though it was not for her to say what was or wasn't right for Angela. Janelle shifted in deep discomfort. Vi stared into the remains of the chickpea curry on their plate. Nate was so utterly expressionless that he was no longer with them in spirit. He had moved on to some other plane of existence. Even David gave Stevie a bit of concerned side-eye.

"When I was leaving uni," Angela explained, "two friends of mine were killed. It was horrible. It was a burglary. They never found out who did it. For obvious reasons I don't like talking about it."

Which was fair. But there was something in her manner that suggested otherwise. She had moved to the edge of her seat on the sofa. She wanted desperately to talk, but she was stopping herself. Was Stevie the only one seeing this?

The surefire way to get someone to tell you something you want to know isn't to ask them about it. What you do is start telling the story yourself, say what you think happened, and say it *wrong*. People may not want to discuss things, but they will correct you, every time.

"I think I read about this," Stevie said.

"You did?" Angela said. "It didn't turn up much in the news. I doubt you've heard about it."

"Something about a game? At a manor? Hide-and-seek? And someone drowned?"

Izzy opened her mouth to correct Stevie, then seemed to realize what was going on and shut it.

"No," Angela said. "Well, there was a game. It happened at a manor. But . . ."

"In a pool?" Stevie went on.

This was intolerable to Angela, both as the friend of the victims and as a professional historian. She couldn't sit there and let this wrongness go on. She got up and went up the steps.

"Uh-oh," Vi said.

Angela returned half a minute later with a small framed item, which she passed to Stevie. It was a poster, hand-lettered, photocopied on mustard-colored paper:

THE NINE PRESENTS
BINGO HALL SEX PARTY
45 MINUTES OF SKETCH COMEDY THAT YOUR
AUNTIE WOULDN'T LIKE

There was a photo on the page—obviously a print photo that had been photocopied, so it was in black and white and not very sharp. Still, Stevie could make out clearly enough that these were nine people who wanted you to know this was comedy. They each wore a costume, but none that related to any of the others. There was a tall woman in a dirty formal dress. One was wearing a top hat. One of the guys was wearing nothing at all and had a bingo ball turner strategically placed over his groin.

"What happened was this," Angela said. "When I was at Cambridge, I was in a theatrical group. There were nine of us. We met during freshers' week and at some auditions in our first year, and we all became friends. We wrote and performed shows together."

"The Nine?" Stevie asked.

"That was what we were called," Angela said. "Despite

how this looks, we weren't bad. We weren't the Footlights or anything like that, but we had a good following. We went to the Edinburgh Fringe Festival twice and did well. Sooz . . ."

She pointed to the tall woman dressed in the tattered evening gown.

". . . is an actress. She does quite a lot of Shakespeare, occasional television. She's always working. She's an amazing impressionist. And Yash and Peter . . ."

She pointed at the guy wearing nothing and holding up the bingo balls, along with the guy in the cowboy outfit.

"That's Peter, the naked one. And that's Yash in the hat. They're a writing team, and they work on loads of shows—comedy panel shows, sitcoms, all kinds of things. In fact, Peter and Yash just won an award for their latest show the other week. They're always doing that. So at least three of us ended up performing. And I do some television work, so that's four, I suppose. Anyway, we got a house together in our third year, all nine of us. We were each other's entire lives, really. Sebastian's family had a big house in the country called Merryweather. We would go there sometimes, after term. Our final year, after exams, Sebastian invited us there for a graduation party week. His family had gone away to their other house in Greece so the house was all ours. On the night we arrived, we were playing a game—a group hide-and-seek. We played it all the time. One person would start as the seeker, and as each person was found, they'd join the seeker team until only one person was left. We played until the early morning hours, but we went inside after the storm became

143

too intense. Two of my friends—Rosie and Noel . . . we didn't realize they were missing at first. We assumed they were . . . that they wanted time to themselves. In the morning, we found them in the woodshed. They'd disturbed burglars in the night, or the burglars disturbed them. Either way, they were killed, with a wood axe from the shed. They never found who did it. That is the story."

"But what about the lock?" Izzy said.

Angela didn't exactly scream or throw a plate across the room, but the word *lock* had a chilling effect on her. She cocked her head to the side. For a moment, she made no reply, before coughing out a "What?"

"The lock," Izzy repeated. "Your friends were found in a woodshed that was supposed to be locked. You told me, you said the lock was off the door in the night."

The color was draining from Angela's face.

"When did I ever say that?"

"When I was staying with you after you had that surgery on your knee, earlier this year."

The mood in the room changed completely.

"There's nothing about a lock," Angela replied in a way that made it clear that there was something going on with the lock.

"You said something about planted evidence, and that . . ."

Angela was no longer trying to disguise her discomfort.

"It was strong medication, Izzy."

"You said you thought one of your friends was a *murderer*. I know this is terrible for you, but it was *real*. I could see it was real. Stevie can help. She's done this before."

Doorknob worked the ankles of the assembled as the awkward silence fell over the group. That had effectively cut the conversation off. There would be no more talk of murder.

"I hate to be rude," Angela said, "but I have an early call in the morning and more work to finish up tonight."

"What did you think?" Izzy said when they were back on the street and walking toward the Tube entrance.

"It was . . ."

What had it been? Evasive, for sure, but evasion was a reasonable response to a group of foreign teenagers showing up at your door unannounced and then being asked to talk about the greatest trauma in your life. But there *was* something there—a look in Angela's eye when that lock was mentioned. The lock had not been conjured out of prescription opiates. The lock was real, or it was a genuine memory. The memory might be faulty, it might be irrelevant, but it was one she'd had long before she took her pain medication, and it was one she had right now. It had conjured something in Angela that Stevie couldn't place.

"It was odd, wasn't it?" Izzy went on. "She didn't want to talk about that lock. There's something there, isn't there? I wish you saw what I did when she was on those painkillers."

The ride back was less crowded, but Stevie found that the food had settled happily in her belly and now her body was sedate. The train rocked. London whipped past in a series of Tube stop names and flashes of tile and tunnel and people.

She sat on one of the upholstered train seats (fabric seats on a subway? That seemed risky. What lived on these seats?). She put her head on David's shoulder and began to drift.

"Hey."

The shoulder bumped, and Stevie snapped up her head with an audible snort.

"We're here."

Stevie had heard of jet lag, but she didn't really jet that much, so was not sure what the lag was supposed to feel like. Apparently, this was it. You just fell asleep. She was in a stupor, dragging herself along, back to Craven House.

"You're toast," David said, running a finger along the edge of her chin when they got back. "You're going to crash. Jet lag is worse the second day. I have some work to do tonight. You should sleep."

She didn't want to be tired. She wanted to go somewhere with him now. But it wasn't happening. Her body was turning out the lights for the night.

"Tomorrow," he said. "After you're done. Want to go on a date?"

"A what?"

"I know, right? A real date."

"Gross," she said.

He smiled, kissed her, and she dragged herself into the elevator with the others. Once in her room, she pulled off her clothes as she walked and flopped onto the bed. She listened to the squeak of the plastic against the frame, looked at the corona of light coming from the streetlamp outside. Someone kicked a glass bottle on the street, and people were laughing. Her stomach was full of curry. Her hormones were dancing and her vision was blurring from exhaustion.

There's nothing about a lock. It was strong medication, Izzy.

Angela was lying to them. Why? Why bother lying when she could have been dismissive? Why say there's nothing about a lock when everything about your voice and body says there was *definitely something* about a lock, and that the lock was important?

As she winked out of consciousness, Stevie caught the tail end of a realization. She knew the emotion she'd seen playing over Angela's features as she'd been telling her story. It wasn't sadness about what had happened, or annoyance that she was being prodded to tell a traumatic story to a bunch of strange teenagers in her house.

It was fear.

24 June 1995

Q: Can you describe the nature of the group here at the manor right now?

A: We're housemates, at Cambridge. And we have a theater group. We're celebrating graduation. We . . . we were celebrating . . .

Q: And you arrived at what time last evening?

A: Almost ten.

Q: And this game you were playing started . . .

A: Around eleven. We were picking rooms and chatting and then we started when it got dark.

Q: Where did you go at the start of the game?

A: I went out the main door in the front. Rosie went out that way as well.

Q: Did anyone else go out that way?

A: No. It was just the two of us.

Q: And then where did you go?

A: Rosie went to the left, toward the drive and the woods. I went straight ahead. I almost fell over the ha-ha. I realized I'd made a bad choice running that way, so I looped around, behind the stables, to the back of the house and hid in the garden. After an hour or so, I got tired of being in the mud, so I crawled out to find another place to hide, somewhere warmer. That's when I went past the woodshed.

Q: Did you try to get inside?

A: No.

Q: Why not?

A: Sebastian said it was locked.

Q: But did you see if it was locked?

[silence on tape]

Q: Miss Gill?

[silence on tape]

Q: Miss Gill, was there something about the lock on the woodshed?

A: No. I'm sorry. I feel quite . . . The lock . . . was . . . secure. Quite secure. During the game. Yes. I saw it. It was locked.

10

THE TOWER OF LONDON, STEVIE WAS EMBARRASSED TO FIND, WAS not a tower. The name was misleading. So many things she was told to expect in life did not pan out as she anticipated. What this thing was, was a massive stone boundary wall, with turrets along it and a grassy ditch where a mast used to be, and inside a dozen or more peaks and towers and structures of all kinds. And this whole thing sat in the middle of a congested business district within sight of the glass towers (actual towers) of modern London.

"We're supposed to budget about two to three hours for this," Janelle said, consulting her phone as they waited in line for the opening for the day. "But we have the Old City of London tour at one, and it's almost ten now so I guess we should try to do this in two so that we can eat and send our first video report. Everyone has the tour app downloaded, right?"

Stevie gulped at her coffee and stared over at the iconic Tower Bridge—the one that was on all the posters and pictures. There were carts selling magnets and tea towels and phone cases with the Union Jack flag on them, the sure sign that this was the place for them. They were capital-*T* Tourists, and eventually they would be worn down and get a shirt or a hoodie that said LONDON on the front.

There's nothing about a lock. It was strong medication, Izzy.

On one hand, Angela was a witness to a crime, a crime she wanted to leave in the past. That's what she said. She wanted no part of this tale she supposedly told when on pain medication. But that was the thing. The discordant note. The *problem*. In this case, the problem of the lock. She could see it in her mind—a hunk of metal with a loop on the top, opened with a key on the bottom. Your average padlock, holding closed a piece of metal on a wooden door.

And the idea of it terrified Angela. Why?

The line began to move forward. Stevie tripped over a crack in the sidewalk and milk foam flew out of the coffee hole, some going up her nose, a bit more onto the sleeve of her coat, and a disappointing amount down her front. She found herself about to lick the sleeve when she caught herself.

Travel was making her disgusting.

"Happening already, huh?" Nate said, falling into step next to her.

"What?"

"The murder story. From last night. You're gone already."

"I'm not gone. Besides, who kills their friends with an axe?"

"That seems like a strange thing to say considering what we've seen."

"Yeah, but we didn't see *axe* murders. That's messed up.

I mean, all murder is messed up, but that's really messed up. Angela was high on pain medication. It's probably nothing."

"I know you think it's a thing because you haven't said a word all morning and you were just about to lick your sleeve. Yeah, I saw that. This is how you get."

"Doesn't matter if I am or I'm not. There's not a lot I can do about it."

"That's never stopped you before."

Stevie paid her admission (which was breathtakingly expensive—now that she had a little to spend, she noticed how quickly it went). Nate was behind her, and as he tapped his card, the machine made a noise of disapproval. He tried again.

"That card isn't working," the person in the booth said. "Do you have another?"

"I, uh . . ." He scrambled for his wallet, which contained a single twenty-pound note, which was not enough.

"Here," Stevie said, tapping her card for him, "pay me later."

"Thanks," Nate said. "I think I messed up the chip or something."

He smiled weakly, but there was a crinkling in the corners of his eyes that struck Stevie as odd, like he was worried about the card. Nate had money. Nate probably had more money than any of them. He had a book out. She didn't know how much he made from it, but it was probably substantial. And they had all gotten paid for their work at the camp over the summer—not a fortune, but it had been decent.

She was reading too much into it.

Once through the main tower gate, they found themselves in the walled complex, almost an entire town: the Salt Tower, the Broad Arrow Tower, the Martin Tower, the Brick Tower, the Flint Tower, the Beauchamp Tower . . . all these strung together by battlements and interwoven with lanes and greens and paths. The voice on the app breathlessly said that the tower was still technically a royal residence. It had been a palace, a defensive structure, a torture chamber, a munitions site. The tower had served as a jail for everyone imaginable, from unrepentant religious leaders to World War I spies to deposed royalty to actual sorcerers who scratched cosmic guides on the walls. It was protected by Beefeaters, or yeoman guards, who got to live there in one of the many charming residences that lined the walls. They even had their own private pub, full of historical relics. This place had seen over a thousand years of reigns and wars and bloodshed and millions of tourists.

It had even, the voice on the tour app continued, been host to an entire zoo for hundreds of years, because what else do you give to royalty who have everything? You give them baboons, leopards, tigers, an elephant or two. At one point, someone gave one of the kings a polar bear, which he put on a leash and took down to the Thames to fish. Because when you're king, you have weird pastimes. But for most of those hundreds of years, no one knew how to take care of the animals, so the monkeys kept biting everyone, the lion ate someone, and the keepers thought ostriches could eat anything so they fed them metal. Eventually, the death zoo was closed and relocated to an actual zoo.

The audio started to devolve into dates and kings, various Henrys and Charleses or Richards or Edwards or whoever who lived or died there, who each built a tower or a chapel, until the place turned into such a maze that if you tried to attack it, you'd get lost inside, chasing whatever Henry or Charles or Edward owned the place at the time. Stevie tried, but she couldn't get herself interested in who had a bed here in 1300-something, or why the fireplace mattered. Angela had tried to explain the significance of a lot of this last night, but once they got on the subject of murder, Stevie overwrote all those mental files. That information was gone.

The doors, however, attracted her. These were heavy doors, several inches thick, with great big locks.

There's nothing about a lock. . . .

They left whichever tower they had just come through and were back out on the paths that wound around the Tower.

"I need to pee," Vi said. "And more coffee."

The Tower had multiple cafés and stalls within its walls. Nothing completed an eleventh-century fortress like a cappuccino, after all.

One of the yeoman guards stepped out in his distinctive hat and uniform with a plastic container. This, a tour guide pointed out to a nearby group, was the Ravenmaster, in charge of the ravens that were always in residence at the tower.

"Ravenmaster," Nate repeated. "*Ravenmaster.*"

The Ravenmaster proceeded to offer his ravens their favorite snacks, which included biscuits soaked in blood.

"Gross job," Nate added. "Still, best name."

"Blood?" Stevie asked. "Just . . . blood? Loose blood? They should really say where they're getting the blood."

"Never explain where you get the blood," Nate replied, looking at Stevie enigmatically.

"And now," the tour guide said, "the spot everyone wants to see. This is Tower Green, the site of the execution of some of the Tower's most famous prisoners. These include Lady Jane Grey, the nine-day queen, and Anne Boleyn, the second wife of Henry the Eighth."

This was a true privilege, as most of the poor bastards imprisoned in the Tower (not the exact words of the tour guide) were taken out to Tower Hill to be killed in public; only fancy people got to die on Tower Green. There was art-work there now—a glass cushion—representing where they put their head for the executioner.

Everything in Stevie's mind meshed itself into a single fabric—the Tower of London to Izzy's aunt to Henry the Eighth and these poor students who were cut to pieces with an axe in the 90s. It wasn't hard to follow this mental path, especially as the guide went into gleeful detail about how the severed heads used to be displayed outside and on the bridge, just so prisoners knew what was in store for them.

"Here for a bad time," Nate said, "not for a long time."

Janelle and Vi appeared from around a corner without coffee.

"Line was too long," Vi said, a strange smile on their face. This may or may not have been true. Clearly, they had slipped off for a minute to be romantic and adorable, maybe to make out or take pics of themselves.

"It's the jewels next," Janelle said, consulting the app, "then the White Tower—that's this big one—and then we're done."

They went into a large building that was dark and heavily guarded by real soldiers with real guns. They saw the Crown Jewels. ("Magic hats," Nate said. "Magic wands. Magic orbs. Magic spoons. This is all wizard stuff." "Literally all of this was stolen," Vi added.) Then it was into the White Tower, the dominating structure at the center of the complex. This was an old palace, a fortress. Janelle couldn't help but admire all the armor. ("It's clothes *and* it's metalwork.") There was even a little murder mystery corner for Stevie—the place where the bones of two children were found, assumed to be the lost princes of the Tower, the ones supposedly murdered by Richard the Third. As they wound out, there were the rooms of weapons, weapons, cannonballs, and weapons. The tour cheerfully ended in the torture chamber, where they saw the rack, the manacles, and something called the Scavenger's Daughter, that compressed people until they juiced. Like lemons.

After two hours of this, Stevie's brain was raw from towers and cannonballs and ravens and kings. They found a place with Wi-Fi to get in touch with Ellingham and give Dr. Branfield from the history department their observations about what they'd seen. Vi had clearly been paying the most attention and gave a detailed report of many of their observations of pillage, detailing the jewels and where they had all come from.

There was time enough for a quick sandwich, then it was another walking tour, this one of the Old City of London, covering the square mile at its heart. She was not paying attention to the fragments of Roman wall, the magical stone called the London Stone that was hidden behind a bit of grating, or the re-creation of the Roman temple that was now located under an office building. London refused to stop. The main lesson of all the tours and the buildings and the dates and the spires and statues and stones was that everything took a long time to build. And then it would burn. Or someone wanted a new, different thing, and would continue building the thing in some other style. Everyone died in a plague? No problem. Build on a plague pit. The dead were stacked under them in some kind of archaeological seven-layer dip. Every once in a while, someone would try to repair a road and up came a skeleton, waving a bony hello. It happened so often they had teams of archaeologists to deal with it.

Death. Plague. Destruction. Torture. Beheadings. Merry old England!

She couldn't help but admire the mastery of Izzy's play. Izzy had set her up to hear Angela's story, and to hear Angela talk about this place of beheading and violence and torment. Once you start thinking about murder by axe, you tend to keep thinking about murder by axe.

Axe murder is serious business. In the Tower, it was a brutal message and vengeful justice. It was rare in most murder mysteries—axes were scary movie territory. Someone might sneak around with a knife or a gun or a bottle of poison, but someone will notice your axe. In this case, it sounded like a weapon of convenience. It was in the shed, most likely, since it was a woodshed. If someone in that group of nine had murdered two of the others, it must have been on the spur of the moment.

Also, there was the practicality of it. How did one person with an axe murder two people in a shed? Was it a crazed bloodbath? Why didn't the two take on the one?

What was it Angela had said? *A little bit of fakery.* That's what the swordsman had used to get Anne to turn her head, to make it easier to kill her.

Maybe that's all it took to murder someone and get away with it. A little bit of fakery.

11

When they arrived at Craven House, having walked many miles and thousands of years through London, David was waiting for them in the lounge. He was wearing a dress shirt and a tie and already had the coat on. He had been curating a mist of shade around his jawline. Somehow, it never got to stubble. Between that and the way he leaned back on the steps, stretching out his legs . . . he knew exactly what he was doing.

"Hey, sicko," he said, getting up to kiss Stevie on the lips.

That feeling never got old. That moment of contact. Feeling that warm puff of air from his nose, the softness of his mouth, the way he reached around to cradle the back of her head, his fingers in her short hair.

"Ready to go?"

"Now? Could I . . ."

"Five minutes, Bell. Then we ride."

"Where are we going?"

"Another surprise," he said with a wolfish grin.

Again, they were going to walk, taking the same path

they had the other night—snaking down the streets. There was a special pleasure in knowing the path a bit now. It was already a little familiar.

"You keep looking at me weird," he said.

"You just . . . you look good. You're all dressed up. And, you know, the coat . . ."

"You only like me for my coat," he said.

"Yup," she replied. "It's a long game I'm playing to get that coat."

"Starts at five," he said.

"What does?"

He shook his head.

They went to Embankment Station and took the Circle Line, which was a yellow spaghetti on the map, one that was twinned with the green District Line. They took the eastbound train, getting off in a few stops at a place called Aldgate. He walked her down a wide commercial street, mixed with large, modern office buildings made of glass, countless construction sites, some older, ornate places of gold brick, several betting shops, and a Burger King.

"Seriously," she said.

"Almost there."

As soon as she saw the first sign that said WHITE-CHAPEL, she knew. They turned a corner and found many people milling around—all tourists, like her.

"This way for the original tour," a man in a top hat said. "Tickets are available. You should have a code if you bought online, so please have your mobile out so I can scan it and we can be on our way."

"Is this . . . a Jack the Ripper tour?"

"Nothing's too murdery for my princess," he said. "I even coordinated with Janelle."

David held out his phone and allowed the jowly man with the shock of long white hair to check them in.

Like any person who followed true crime, Stevie knew the basics of the Jack the Ripper case. London, 1888. A man haunted the streets and killed sex workers, women who were poor and trying to survive. He was famous for his rapid mutilations, some in places where he could easily have been discovered. But what he really was, was some dirtbag. The press had given him the nickname Jack the Ripper, and the case had been pumped up in the press. There was debate about how many victims he had, but most people had settled on five. Now he was a spooky folk hero.

She had by now been on a lot of tours. Unlike the other places she had been visiting, there were no fine buildings on this walk—no towers or turrets, no marble busts or spires. Henry the Third had never come this way. Instead, this walk led them down some pretty mundane streets in East London, mostly deserted for the night. They walked past fried chicken places, banks, pubs, vape shops, fabric stores . . . most of them were closed. There were streets of old warehouses of brown brick, now converted into luxury flats. The guide gave a low-key summary of the socioeconomic conditions of Victorian-era London, and the fact that the canonical victims of Jack the Ripper had been forced into sex work because they needed to eat. Many were addicted to the cheap gin that was sold absolutely everywhere, and was the only thing that made the rough life on the streets of the East End at all bearable.

Except he didn't say it quite that way, and he didn't call the victims sex workers.

People had come for the murders. People always come for the murders. Stevie had to admit that she was one of the people who had come for the murders—but it was not as simple as that.

"For weeks, all was quiet," the guide said dramatically. "Then, on the thirtieth of September 1888, Jack the Ripper struck twice in one night—twice in *just forty-five minutes*—in what is now known as the double event. It was a vicious, miserable night, raining and hailing, gale winds . . ."

There was a buzzing noise coming from David's coat pocket.

". . . how does he do it? How does he kill two people, in two different parts of town, in that short a time? How does he do his evil surgery in the dark of Mitre Square? Is he a phantom?"

"No," Stevie said to herself.

Murder stories were always about the same thing at their heart—some twerp thought it was acceptable to take the life of another person. Murderers were small inside. People had died here, and they died because they were poor and vulnerable.

More buzzing.

"Who is that?" she asked.

"Izzy," he said, looking down at his texts.

"Murderers are shadows," the man said. "That's their defining quality."

"Murderers are assholes," Stevie said, just loud enough to be heard. "*That's* their defining quality."

Someone turned. The guide gave a wry smile that suggested that he had met her ilk before, these young people with their ideas about society, and he found it amusing. As he moved the group along, Stevie put her hand on David's arm and held him back.

"I really appreciate this," she said, "but . . ."

"No. I've been wincing for the last half hour. There were some other Jack the Ripper tours. But I went with this one because the guy had a hat. I think maybe I picked a bad one. This was a hat-based mistake."

"What does that even mean, murderers are shadows?" Stevie said to David.

"Who the fuck knows? Well. Seems like we have some time, then. How about dinner and some light entertainment? I can think of a few fun things to do. . . ."

And there it was. The spark. The electric moment.

This was the night. She could sense it now. She could feel the energy coming off the golden-brown bricks of the Victorian warehouses that were now apartments, the orange glow of the lights, the people slipping down the dark streets on electric scooters. It would happen.

Except his phone kept buzzing. He pulled it out of his pocket, thumbed a reply, and dropped it back in.

"Sorry," he said. "Izzy's freaked out."

"About what?"

"Her aunt hasn't replied to her texts. She's worried that she's mad about last night."

"Yeah," Stevie said. "I think she might be. I think Izzy kind of sprang all of that on her."

There's nothing about a lock. It was strong medication, Izzy.

"Come on," he said. He wrapped his arm around her shoulders and took comically long steps, walking toward the Tube stop they'd passed a few minutes back. "I know where we should go. I'm taking you to the best restaurant in all of London."

It was called Ali's of London. It was, again, a plain white storefront with bright fluorescent lights, with a TV mounted on the wall playing a soccer match. In the window, there was a rotating vertical spit of roasted meat, off which one of the men behind the counter was expertly slicing thin pieces. David leaned against the counter with both hands, watching him work.

"Ali is an artist," he said. "Look."

Ali smiled and held up a slice of the meat. It was so thin you could almost see through it. As someone who had worked a deli counter for two weeks over the summer, she knew good meat slicing when she saw it.

"This," David said, "is the food that keeps England running. This is the doner kebab. It is magnificent. Look."

Another man was slapping flatbreads on the grill. The smell of the warm bread and the meat was intoxicating.

"People say fish and chips," David went on. "No. People say sausages and mash. No. It's the doner kebab."

"He's right," Ali said as the man at the grill dropped the flatbread into a Styrofoam clamshell. "You want everything?"

"She wants everything," David said. "This is my girlfriend. From America. She's a famous detective."

"Oh yeah?" Ali nodded absently as the kebab was loaded down with shredded lettuce and red cabbage, sliced tomatoes, cucumbers, pickled peppers, and squirted with a white sauce.

The two containers were ready, and Ali rang them up. David reached for his wallet, but Stevie swatted his arm.

"I've got it," she said.

"Famous detective," David said again.

"Good," Ali said approvingly. "You should marry her."

"Maybe I will," David said with a smile as he scooped up the containers.

What?

What?

It was a joke, of course. Something shouted by a man with a sandwich. But David had answered. He'd said *yes*. Could you joke about that? What did it mean?

They went to sit on a bench at the riverside, despite the slight spittle of rain that had started.

"It's seasoning," he explained. "Everything here tastes better with it. You start to get used to it. You start to think it's warm out when it's only kind of cold, and that a little rain isn't rain."

"Is this how you normally eat? Sandwiches in the rain?"

"I am eating fancy this week because you are here. Most nights I eat spaghetti from a can. Go on. Try it. Eat the art."

Stevie tried to pick up the massive gyro neatly, but this was impossible. She leaned in to take a bite. It was as good as promised, fatty and garlicky and messy.

"You see?" he said. "The best meal in town."

They ate for a moment or two. Stevie found that she was starving from all the walking in the cold.

"He made me an offer," David said before he took another massive bite of the sandwich.

"Your dad?"

A heavy nod.

"Yup." He wiped some gyro from the side of his mouth. "He cut off all money months ago. No school money, nothing. But he called me two weeks ago. He offered to pay my tuition if I stay here and finish school. He said it was because I was doing well here, but he wants me out of the country. I'm a liability. If he can keep me out of the US for three years, that's one less thing to worry about."

Stevie's heart was fluttering nervously. They had danced around the topic of David's school. This was only supposed to be a semester abroad. It was almost over. And now . . .

"I do like it here," he said. "But I don't want his money. I told him I would see him at Christmas and hung up."

"So you're not . . ."

"There are good things about being here. I like it. I really do. And I like being away from him. But you live kind of far, which I don't like. What about you? I mean, I know you're not sure yet—I mean, you've never mentioned anywhere you wanted to go. You could study here. They have good criminology programs here."

"Yeah, but how?" she said.

"How what?"

"I don't know how to . . . get the money for that. Or how to set it up. My grades are fine. They're okay. Mostly. But I don't know if I'd get in."

"I got in."

"It's easier for you. Your dad may suck, but it does make things easier for you."

It came out badly.

"I mean . . ."

"I know what you mean," he said. He didn't seem mad about it. "You've solved *murders*," he said. "I don't solve murders. I just hang around with someone who does."

"Yeah, but that's not something colleges ask. There's no question about how many murders you've solved."

David regarded her curiously for a long moment.

"You don't get it, do you?" he said. "You really don't."

"What? You think I'm being modest or something?"

"Something."

"I'm not," she said. "I like myself fine. But I'm confusing

for colleges. I've done stuff, but I also missed a lot of classes on the way. I'm not Janelle. . . ."

"No one's Janelle. Maybe not even Janelle."

"I don't speak multiple languages. I don't know about art. I don't play an instrument. Unless there's some kind of true crime quiz on the application, I may be screwed. I only applied to Ellingham because I knew that case."

Suddenly, she could no longer finish her massive sandwich. It had been delicious, and garlicky, and full of tasty, oozing things—but the concept of the future had stripped her of her appetite. She got up and threw the remainder of the sandwich in the trash, feeling bad about the waste. She went over to the wall that ran along the riverside and leaned her elbows on it. The famous Thames. Her mental image of the Thames had come from TV and books, and she had compressed it, making it quaint and pleasant. The real Thames was wide, with a powerful current, full of large vessels. It smelled faintly of the sea—or at least some primal element. It splashed against the supporting walls. It was a tough river.

David came over and opened his coat, invited her inside. She hugged him by the waist and pressed her head into his chest.

"Fuck," she said quietly. "I hate it."

"Hate what?"

"Not having everyone around me. Forever. I want to be with you. And Janelle and Nate and Vi, and that's not going to happen."

"Yeah, but . . . you're here. We'll figure it out. Come on. Look! You're in London! We're supposed to be having fun. Do you want to have fun?"

"What kind of fun?" she said, lifting her head to look at him.

"I can think of lots of fun things to do."

Stevie could feel his heart rate increase, and hers sped up to match it. This was it. It was time to have the conversation. David was fully here with her, right now, and they could . . . do anything.

"I need to ask you something," she said. "Have you . . ."

She had worked this out in her mind—how to ask this. It was a straightforward question. Well, it had straightforward aspects. *Have you had sex before?* But now that the moment was here and she was supposed to say this in actual words that came out of her actual mouth, they had been reduced to particles, blown apart in the winds of meaning. What counted as sex? What precisely did she mean? And then, if the answer was yes (she had always been pretty sure the answer would be yes), what then? Did she continue the line of questioning like she was in court? What kind of sex and what exactly and with who and how many times and can you draw the locations on this map . . .

He was still waiting for the rest of the question. He had a twitching half smile. Did he know what she wanted to ask and did he find it funny? Or was he really waiting to see what the hell she wanted because "have you . . ." could lead to anything and what she was, was a maniac who didn't know how

169

to talk to anyone about anything. Also, would he ask her the same? She was sure he already knew the answer. No. No, she had not. Her experience in this department was limited. To be honest, she had shocked herself in her encounters thus far by having any idea what she was supposed to do at all. It was amazing that she hadn't flopped and flailed or fallen out a window by accident or something during any physical encounter.

David was still waiting. It had gone beyond anticipation to that point where the question was starting to break apart like smoke on the wind.

There was a ding and a buzz as a text message came in. David didn't reach for the phone in his pocket, but Stevie could feel it against her hip. It buzzed again, like a persistent bee.

"Do you want to get that?" she said.

Another buzz.

The moment had passed.

"Is that Izzy?" Stevie asked.

"I don't know. I didn't look."

"You hang out a lot," she said, stepping away from his chest and back.

"Well, yeah. What about it?"

"I didn't say anything about it," Stevie replied.

"You kind of did, because you mentioned it."

Stevie could see clearly that this was going badly, and it was happening fast. Time to turn it around. Laugh it off. Convert this conversation into something else. A joke. A moment. But David was looking down at her with that slight tilt of the eyebrow that meant he was engaged, and that slight tilt of the eyebrow made him more attractive to her and annoyed her in the same moment. Which meant that there was something in this, and no, she would not be able to let it go. It was a loose tooth that demanded wiggling. A hole in the fabric that required picking and expanding.

No. Make the conversation stop.

"That's all it was. I was just saying."

Her tone was too flat. She invited combat.

"She's in my tutorial," he said. "It's just me and Izzy and this guy Graham who keeps loose cheese in his pocket and we think is an online predator, so Izzy and I kind of stick together. I live here right now. There are people here . . ."

"*Obviously* there are people here. They are people everywhere. I didn't mean . . ."

"You did mean. You need to trust me. Do you think that I can't control myself or something? Like I'm not serious about you? What have I done to make you feel like that? Because I've kind of worked hard to stop being fuckup David and be this new one? Also, fuckup David felt the same way about you too and never cheated. I just failed more classes and hung out on the roof more."

"Forget it. Okay?"

"I'm actually trying."

"So . . ."

David took a beat and nodded. This happened to them sometimes. They went to a hundred. In fact, her pulse was quickening, beyond the point of happy excitement and into the territory of fear. It made her neck throb and electric shocks run down her arms.

"Oh shit," she said.

"What?"

Not now. Not here. Not this.

But that's the thing about an anxiety attack. It shows up when it likes. It barges into the situation and takes over. The world warps.

"Stevie?"

She didn't know what to ask him to do. She fumbled for her bag, yanking the zipper open and feeling around for the key chain that held her emergency anxiety medication.

"Are you sick?"

She shook her head.

"Anxiety attack," she said as her fingers found the small container. She unscrewed it, removed the pill, and swallowed it dry.

"Okay," he said, scooping his arm around her, giving her support. "No problem. Walk with me a little. Breathe that stanky air. Smell it? That's cold, nasty river water."

She was a useless piece of human furniture, confused, tucked under his arm. Were other people looking at them? What did they make of her? They were in the other world, the one that made sense.

"Just take it easy," David was saying, close to her ear. "Breathe nice and slow."

As if it was that easy. But she tried. She knew it worked. She knew it would end, and all the things that had fallen over would be put back in place, and the world would reassemble itself. She had been through this many times—not usually in public, though. This tended to happen more before bed or when she was asleep, when she could break apart in private, climb under the sheets, rest on the floor, pace from familiar wall to familiar wall. This was London, dark and bright and loud and strange, and there was only David to cling to in this moment.

He was her only guidepost as they walked back to the Tube and made their way through the clamor and bright lights of the station. On the train, she had to turn and put her face into his shoulder because the view out the window was too much—the whoosh through the tunnel, the bright subway ads flashing by, taunting her with offers for travel insurance, human-sized pictures of chocolate bars, better phone rates . . . all the flotsam and jetsam of life. Numbers and houses and futures and food. Why did all this stuff have to fly into her face? Who needed it all? Why go this fast?

"Breathe," David was saying.

"I'm breathing," she mumbled.

She was breathing. In and out. That was one for the win column. She was breathing. Her therapist had told her this was the thing to grab on to. You are breathing. You are okay. Grab hold of your breath. Make the exhales longer than the inhales. That was all she had to do. In for four. Hold for five.

Out for six. Her own warm breath cocooned her against his coat. It was a blanket, something she could grab with her hand and understand. She had her own breath and a handful of coat and she was going to take those two things and put the planet back together with them.

This was how they got back to Craven House.

By the time they arrived, the medicine was starting to take effect. Things were still racing, but they were slowing down. She pressed close to David, but her knees were more stable, her gait more regular. The lights didn't strobe at her quite so much. She was almost able to enjoy the moment, her body against David's, the way he held her.

He said nothing as he helped her into the elevator, then down the hall. Nate's door was open, and he looked up as David came in with a stunned-looking Stevie.

"What's going on?" Nate asked.

"No big deal," David said, taking the key that Stevie was fumbling with and helping her open the door.

"Are you drunk?"

Stevie shook her head heavily and stepped into the half-lit room. The medicine she'd taken would knock her out soon enough. She shrugged off her coat and let it fall to the floor, then climbed into the bed, the plasticky mattress squeaking as she huddled under the duvet. Her thoughts kaleidoscoped in her mind's eye—the streets of London, the view of the bridge, the socioeconomic realities of 1880s London and the taste of garlic on David's lips, Izzy and her aunt and the lock on the door, her stubbornness. David's face. His long, angular face. The softness of his coat and the warmth of his breath. It all blended together and rode along the tracks made by the ambient light coming through the blinds and slicing up the wall. And then, the full effect of the medication kicked in, and everything faded out.

Q: If you could take us through the night, please, starting with this game you were all playing. Where did you go when the game started?

A: I went outside through the back, out the mudroom door. The gardens here are vast. I thought the back garden was a good place to start. There's a yew maze back there.

Q: Did anyone go that way with you?

A: Julian did, but we went separate ways once we got out.

Q: Where did you go?

A: I ran around the back garden for a few minutes, but I couldn't find anywhere that seemed suitable to hide. I ended up in the walled garden on the north side of the house. It has an edge of shrubbery lining the inside. I wedged my way in there.

Q: Do you know when you were found?

A: It felt like ages standing there in the rain, but I don't know when it was.

Q: And who found you?

A: Peter. I had just come out to move again when he came through the garden. That's the trick—don't move.

Q: And you were taken to the folly to get a new poncho?

A: Yes. And then I started seeking.

Q: Were you ever by the woodshed at any point when you were hiding or seeking?

A: I went past it a few times but I didn't check it. It was locked.

Q: How do you know that?

A: Sebastian told us. All the outbuildings were locked. I walked past that area but I didn't really look at it. I think I would have noticed if the door was open and the wheelbarrow was out. I feel I can say that for certain.

Q: At any point when you were outside did you see Rosie or Noel?

A: I think I may have seen Noel running through the back gardens when the game started, but I'm not sure. Noel's quite a good climber. He may have been going for the trees. I don't know, though.

Q: When would this have been?

A: I don't know. Early. Early on.

Q: Did you see which door he used to leave the house?

A: No.

Q: And the game itself ended when . . .

A: There was this tremendous lightning and a thunderclap and all the lights in the house went out. Right after that, we all decided to go back inside. We didn't want to be hit by lightning, and we needed a fire and a drink anyway.

Q: Do you know what time this was?

A: I think around two thirty. There's a grandfather clock in the entryway hall. It chimes on the half hour and hour. I remember it making a noise soon after we came in, because the hall was dark and it was quite an eerie sound.

Q: And Rosie and Noel never came in?

A: No. We thought they were off together somewhere. Romantically, I mean. They had been getting closer over the last week and we thought they were out having a night together, so best to leave them to it.

Q: Romantically.

A: Yes.

Q: And that was recent?

A: Yes. Rosie had been . . . well, she'd been dating Julian up until recently.

Q: There had been a breakup?

A: Yes. Julian is a bit of a lothario. Rosie had had enough.

Q: She split from Julian?

A: Yes, but . . . he wouldn't, I mean . . . if you're suggesting that—

Q: I'm not suggesting anything. We're merely trying to ascertain the facts.

A: Julian is a tomcat. Everyone is used to his ways. This sort of thing happens a lot with us. We may get mad at each other, but the most violent thing that's ever happened was Rosie pouring a bottle of Coke over Julian's head. We care for each other. We love each other. We . . .

Q: Do you need a moment?

A: No. I can do this. Please. Carry on. I need to do this for them.

Q: And what happened once you were back inside?

A: We went to the sitting room to get warm. Sebastian was desperate to get at a certain bottle of whisky, something quite special that was locked in a cabinet. He was crawling over the floor to get at it and he almost knocked the wall in trying to open the cabinet. Peter had to get down on the floor to help him. It was a very special bottle, and we drank some and toasted and talked. I think it may have been too much because Peter felt ill, and then Angela drifted off to bed. Theo went to give everyone glasses of water before going to bed herself—she always does that. Future doctor. Always taking care of everyone. Yash was ill as well. Sebastian, Julian, and I stayed there to finish the bottle. We were talking, and then I saw the light.

Q: The light?

A: Something flashed outside! Not lightning, I mean a torch or something. It was on the ground, a beam of light. I thought maybe it was Rosie or Noel.

Q: Where was this exactly?

A: Somewhere just outside. Close to the house. I think it was coming in the general direction of the drive, from the left. Across the front patio. Like someone was coming around the side of the house. That's what it looked like. I got up to see if it was them, and I was thinking it was strange because you could only have a torch if you were a seeker, and neither of them had been found. Sebastian and Julian didn't see it, but Sebastian was facing away from the window and Julian was doing something, not looking that way. But I was facing the window. I saw that flash clear as anything.

Q: When was this?

A: I honestly don't know. I was a bit beyond telling the time. It was a torchlight in the darkness, though. The sun comes up quite early this time of year, around four or four thirty. So before that, but I don't think much before. I thought that must be Rosie or Noel, so I went to the door—the main door out the front—and I called to them and told them to come in, the game was over. I kept shouting for them. I shouted. I called to them . . .

Q: Are you all right? Do you need a moment?

A: May I have a cup of tea? I'll be all right. I . . . Please may I have a cup of tea?

24 June 1995

Q: This is your family house, correct?

A: That's correct.

Q: And your family is away?

A: In Greece. We have a house there. They go several times a year.

Q: And you've come up from Cambridge with your friends to celebrate graduation?

A: That's correct. Do you mind if I have a cigarette? I'm . . .

Q: That's fine. So these are your friends. Housemates, is that right?

A: Yes.

Q: Your family knew you would be here?

A: They are aware.

Q: And what staff is there at this house?

A: There's no live-in staff. There are cleaners who come in a few times a week. There are gardeners, at least four, usually. The head gardener is Chester Jones. He lives in Ramscoate.

Q: There were no staff on the grounds last night?

A: No. It was just us.

Q: Do you think it would be known locally that your family was away?

A: I would imagine so. You know what it's like in a village. Everyone knows everyone else's business.

Q: Is the gate at the end of the drive always locked?

A: Always.

Q: Who has the code to get in?

A: I don't know. Everyone who works here or makes deliveries, I'd imagine. I don't think the code would be much of a secret around the village.

Q: How does one access the gate if the power is out?

A: It can be unlocked with a key.

Q: And who has a key?

A: I do, my family. Chester.

Q: You told the others the outbuildings were locked, is that correct?

A: Yes.

Q: And that includes the woodshed.

A: Yes. We recently put a lock on that because of the burglaries in the area. People break in to steal tack. We've lost a number of saddles over the years.

Q: How did you know everything was locked? Did you check?

A: I didn't have to. My family is in Greece. They lock everything before they go.

Q: During this game, you were the "seeker"?

A: Yes.

Q: What did that entail?

A: Standing down at the folly, mostly. Shouting. When

the team found people, they'd bring them to me. I'd give the new seekers yellow rain slickers and a torch. It's a silly game.

Q: So you were standing in the folly most of the night?

A: Yes. I had some shelter from the rain.

Q: And the game ended when the power went out?

A: Yes. The lightning got far too close. It felt a bit like tempting fate to run around outside when trees might fall on you or lightning catch you in the open. We made one final push, found Julian clinging to the top of the pergola, and suspended play.

Q: Who found him?

A: Angela.

Q: Who decided you should all go back inside?

A: It was a collective decision.

Q: What time was this?

A: I believe it was around two thirty.

Q: What happened when you came inside?

A: Well, we went back into the sitting room to get warm, wrapped ourselves in some throw blankets, stoked the fire. There was a very good bottle of whisky in the cabinet that I thought we needed to drink to mark the occasion. I got it out.

Q: Using your keys?

A: Yes. But it was awfully dark. I fumbled with them for a bit. Got the bottle out. We drank it. People began to peel off to retire.

Q: Do you recall who went first?

A: Angela or Peter, maybe? Theo went at some point. She usually does a Florence Nightingale run after a long night, delivers water to everyone's bedside. I know I was in the sitting room with Sooz, Yash, and Julian. Yash became ill and left. Julian and Sooz were having a silly spat about something, and Julian decided to go off. Sooz and I finished the bottle and passed out where we were.

Q: Did you see or hear anything out of the ordinary?

A: Well, it would be hard to hear anything. The rain was hammering at the windows and whistling in the chimney—it was that kind of night. At some point Sooz said she saw a torchlight go past the window.

Q: Did you see it?

A: No. But I was not . . . incredibly focused.

Q: What time was this?

A: I don't know. Julian was there, I think. I just remember her saying she saw a light, and she called for Rosie and Noel, but no one answered. Other than that, nothing. The next thing I remember is that it was morning and Theo was standing over me with a mug of tea, saying we should go and look for Rosie and Noel.

Q: Are you currently under the influence of alcohol?

A: I am, yes. I prefer not to be sober today.

Q: It might be best to have some tea or coffee instead. Perhaps something to eat.

A: No, thank you.

Q: All right. You can return to the others. Thank you.

12

Rain. The promised rain of England—that endless dribble and steel clouds. That was the morning outside the window.

The morning after an anxiety attack was always odd in its ordinariness. Hours before, the universe had been collapsing like a flat-pack box, and now day had come and everything had slid back into place. Aside from feeling tired, she was okay. Anxiety was just a weird creep sometimes.

Of course, she had also lost a night in London with David. Winked it right out of existence in a haze of terror and medication. That was what he was saying not to worry about, of course. Last night had not gone precisely to plan, but it had not been a failure either. Tonight would go better.

Today's schedule was another dense program of tours. She was late waking up, so she took a quick, cold shower and pulled on her hoodie and jeans. Someday she would make more of an effort than that, but today was not that day. There was a raging blister on the back of her left heel. She shoved a folded tissue down the back of her shoe. It wasn't a great solution, but it would have to do.

"You okay?" Nate asked her as she stepped out. He was leaning in his doorway, dressed in an oversized and pilled brown sweater and slouchy jeans. The gray English light suited him. It was light for indoor people, for ghosts, for royalty and urchins. For writers.

"Fine," she said.

"Are you sick?" Janelle asked as she and Vi came down the hall. They had put in the usual effort. Vi was wearing a pair of purple overalls with a silver-gray turtleneck underneath. Janelle wore a fuzzy, open-weave red sweater that she had knitted herself, along with a matching hat.

"Just an anxiety attack," Stevie said. "It's fine."

Vi reached over and gave her arm a reassuring squeeze. Then it was out into the cold, busy streets of the London morning.

"We should take the bus," Janelle said. "I've worked out the map. We're going to Westminster, and it's not far. Most of the stuff we're going to see today is close together."

They joined a group of morning commuters at the bus stop and clambered inside the bus, taking the steps up to the second level. They scored seats at the front and brushed away some candy wrappers and soda bottles to take in the view. From here, they got a strange, floating perspective of London and the street, and there was the illusion that cars and bikes were being sucked under the bus as it went along, like a land whale gliding down the street, consuming all in its path.

They were starting at Westminster Abbey, which was a place that Stevie had often heard mentioned but had never taken the time to think about at all. Abbey made it sound like monks or nuns would be living there, but it turned out to be a cathedral on a massive scale. Another day, another tour guide enthused about dates and walls and people named Edward and Henry. Westminster Abbey turned out to be the work of Henry the Third again, who was so obsessed with a guy named Edward the Confessor that he had to go and build a cathedral about it. When he was done, he moved Edward's body into it, putting it on a massive plinth that had been picked bare of ornament by people coming to worship at it.

"This is what happens when fanboys get out of hand," Nate said, looking at the monument and then up at the expanse of ceiling. The abbey was designed to make you feel small. Look at this ceiling—look at it barreling up toward heaven. Listen to the spooky echo of the organ, the ethereal sound of human voices in harmony spinning around the room. You got lost in it. The building wanted you to know your place. No matter what you did, no matter how hard you tried, someone was doing more.

It was also, the guide informed them, the place where England kept a lot of its famous dead—over three thousand of them were buried there, and many more memorialized in marble and stone and glass. There were many kings and queens there, buried under mounts of marble with statues of their bodies in repose. You could do a selfie with Elizabeth the First, and people were.

From there, it was across the street to the Houses of Parliament and the Palace of Westminster, the seat of the government of the United Kingdom. It wasn't where the beheadings happened, but it was often why.

Another break. Another sandwich. Obligatory pictures with the giant lions by Nelson's Column. A relentless trip through the National Gallery in clammy clothes. The tissue stuffed into her shoe kept sliding out of place and sticking out the back, so she kept hopping and shoving it back in. Eventually, she took it out and allowed the pain to come through.

Art, art, art, art, art. At a certain point, nothing made sense. It was bulk information, stimulus overload. Things to check off a list.

"I've got twenty-one schools still on my list," Janelle said out of nowhere.

"What?" Vi had been considering a dark painting of an arrangement of fruit with what appeared to be genuine interest. It was hard to tell. Vi was great at putting on a neutral face of interest—they wanted to go into some kind of international work to fix the world, and that was going to require going to a lot of meetings about boring things and talking to terrible people. They had mastered the blank stare. It was a gift.

"I was just thinking. Twenty-one schools. Seven are in Boston—well, not just Boston. In Massachusetts. I need to get that list down."

"Okay." Vi didn't seem that interested in the topic of colleges at the moment, so Janelle turned to Nate.

"That's too many, right?" she said. "I can't apply to twenty-one schools. That's crazy."

"It seems fine," Nate said. Nate had not been looking at the paintings of fruit with any interest. Nate would tolerate most things for about an hour if he knew there was the promise of a snack and the chance to be left alone in the near future.

"When the answers come back, that's going to be more to decide. I want to make the cuts now. I mean, I'm not saying I'd get into all twenty-one . . ."

"You will," Vi said.

". . . but if I did, then I have to figure that out. Plus, that's about two grand in application fees. And all the stuff to write and get. I feel like, I don't know, seven is a good number? Or ten? How many are you applying to?"

"I don't know yet," he said.

"Probably not twenty-one, though, right?"

"No," he said.

Janelle had not included Stevie in this conversation, perhaps because Stevie had riveted herself to a picture of a cluster of men dressed in black, standing around a table in their big hats. Why ask Stevie about college? You might as well ask one of the billions of Trafalgar Square pigeons their thoughts on inflation.

Stevie was delighted when her phone buzzed and she saw a message from David.

Where are you guys now?

National Gallery, she wrote.

Are you almost done? Because we're outside.

"We?" Stevie said.

Sure enough, they were on the steps. With David, shivering in an oversized pink coat, was Izzy.

"I need your help," she said. "My aunt is missing."

"Missing?" Janelle said.

"She's gone," Izzy said, nodding. "She hasn't answered any of my texts or calls since the other night. She doesn't *do* that. She *always* answers me. So I went up this afternoon to see what was going on, and I went in and . . . she's gone. All the things from the other night are still out. Food. Dishes. She would never leave those. Something is wrong. And! I looked on her tablet, which gets her texts. Look at this."

She pulled a tablet out of her bag and showed Stevie part of a long text chain. The messages were marked from the night they had been there to visit.

9:23 p.m. ANGELA: I'd like to propose a get-together. Maybe this weekend? I think we should have a talk. Seb, is Merryweather free?

9:23 p.m. ANGELA: I wouldn't ask if it wasn't important.

9:27 p.m. SEBASTIAN: The house is free and I think I could make the weekend work. What's going on?

9:28 p.m. THEO: I could possibly get coverage. Is something wrong? Are you all right?

9:29 p.m. SOOZ: Currently backstage. I have a performance Saturday evening, but we're dark Sunday. What's going on?

9:31 p.m. PETER: I'm scheduled to take the kids to Peppa Pig World this weekend, but I'm happy to bow out of that.

9:31 p.m. PETER: But same question.

9:32 p.m. THEO: Ange?

9:33 p.m. SOOZ: Ange are you all right?

9:41 p.m. YASH: You make it sound serious, Ange. What's happening?

9:45 p.m. ANGELA: it's about what happened

9:45 p.m. ANGELA: we need to talk

9:46 p.m. ANGELA: and I don't think it can wait

9:46 p.m. ANGELA: She had the button

9:47 p.m. THEO: ?

9:48 p.m. SOOZ: What Theo said.

9:48 p.m. YASH: Button?

9:49 p.m. PETER: what?

9:50 p.m. SOOZ: I have to go back onstage. Please someone explain to me what is happening.

9:51 p.m. SEBASTIAN: Can you ring me?

9:55 p.m. THEO: Ange?

9:57 p.m. THEO: Ange can you pick up?

9:58 p.m. PETER: I just rang as well and it went to voice mail.

10:16 p.m. SOOZ: I'm back. Can someone tell me what's going on?

10:18 p.m. YASH: Genuinely confused about what's happening rn

10:21 p.m. JULIAN: I'm at a dinner. Is something wrong? What's going on? My phone keeps pinging.

10:22 p.m. THEO: Ange please ring me whenever you get off the phone.

10:24 p.m. SOOZ: Which one of you is talking to her?

10:25 p.m. YASH: Not me. Does anyone know what's happening?

10:26 p.m. PETER: Not me

10:27 p.m. JULIAN: Is there something wrong with Ange? I need to rejoin the dinner.

10:29 p.m. THEO: Ange please ring

"It goes on," Izzy said, "just lots of texts from everyone asking where she is. Including me."

"What's this about a button?" Stevie asked, scrolling down.

"I have no idea," Izzy said.

"That's not a phrase? An English thing?"

"No."

Izzy was right. This didn't seem good.

"So I thought," David said, "that we could help? Maybe by going to her house and having a look to see if anything seemed off? That's kind of your thing."

He laid on a particularly charming smile. He was right. Going into other people's spaces was Stevie's thing. She had done it at Ellingham several times when one of their classmates was killed and another went missing. She had even done it to David himself, something he didn't let her forget. Her proclivity for investigating spaces was both a serious thing and a joke between them. He wasn't supposed to just talk about it like that.

Still. Probably a good idea to have a look through Angela's house.

"Can we talk for a second?" Stevie asked Izzy. "We just have to figure out what we're doing."

"Of course. Of course!"

Stevie stepped off to the side with Nate, Janelle, and Vi.

"Do you think this is a thing?" Vi asked.

"I don't know," Stevie said. "Angela had a serious trauma. And then she said weird things on painkillers. Every story I've ever heard about a crime . . . every person that's been through something that traumatic, they have theories. They try to work it out. She was high. I don't know."

"But now she's gone," Vi said.

"People freak out," Stevie replied.

"And need help when they do," Janelle said. "You should go and do it. We can put together the report for today."

It was time to go through a house.

13

Outside the snug little house in Islington, Doorknob was waiting for them, meowing loudly and throwing himself against their ankles and rubbing for all he was worth. Izzy scooped him up.

"You poor thing! Look at him. Look. He's hungry. He's scared."

Doorknob seemed to be neither of these. He thrust his head into Izzy's chin and purred, then rammed his face down the front of her sweater.

Izzy produced the keys and admitted them into the house. As they stepped into the dark hallway, Stevie slipped on something and grabbed the wall. She looked down and saw that she had almost been taken down by a pile of mail, including some glossily finished flyers for Domino's pizza.

"See?" Izzy said, extracting a local council statement from under Stevie's shoe. "Today's mail. And look. Her coat and bag are normally here." Izzy indicated some empty pegs on the entryway wall.

There was a stillness—an odd quality houses get when

they are left to their own devices, even for a short while. Everything appeared just as they had left it the other night. The living room was in order, with a few mug rings and left-over crumbs on the coffee table from where their tea and cookies had been.

In the kitchen, the remnants of the takeaway were still in evidence. There was the bag, the containers. There could be no question that this was the same meal: the receipt was stapled to the bag with Izzy's name on the order. The dirty plates were in the sink, still stained with curry and with rice sticking to them. The tea mugs were sitting by the sink, and the pack of Hobnobs was on the counter, half-open.

"She left these plates," Izzy said. "That's not her. She wouldn't go away and leave plates like this. She wouldn't leave food out."

The rest of the kitchen seemed to indicate this was true. The small table was clear, save for an ornamental striped bowl, filled with apples and oranges. Stevie opened the cabi-nets and looked inside at the jumble of mugs—many patterns and types, but all where they were supposed to be. It didn't seem like the kind of place where leftover curry would be allowed to sit out for days, the plates allowed to crust over and collect flies. This was a house out of its own rhythm.

Doorknob yowled by his bowl, so Izzy got a pouch of food out of the cabinet and filled it. He began to eat at once, in noisy chomps. Maybe Izzy had been right about Door-knob. He ate with urgency. This was a cat not used to missing meals. Stevie went back through the living room, took a long look at the elaborate cat tree in the corner and cat toys that were scattered around the room. The litter box in the downstairs bathroom was overflowing and ripe.

She walked the downstairs again, testing the windows. All were closed and locked. There was a cat flap out of the kitchen window leading onto the roof of the level below, but no human was going to get through something that was only a few inches high.

"What's under this apartment?" Stevie asked. "Another apartment?"

"No," Izzy said. "Someone rents it for storage. They run a catering business and leave extra tables and chairs and things down there."

"Did you check upstairs?" Stevie asked Izzy.

"Of course! I checked the whole house. I'll show you."

Angela's home office was just off the landing. It was a small space, with file cabinets, stacks of books, pinboards filled with references and business cards and pictures. Her laptop was open on the desk. Stevie tapped it awake. It asked for a password.

"I know what it is," Izzy said, sitting down. "I had to use her laptop once when I couldn't find my phone. It's Cleves. As in Anne of."

"Anne of?"

"Anne of Cleves. Henry the Eighth's fourth wife. The lucky one. But I went through this already. I opened every folder and file. There's nothing on here but script notes and parts of the book she's working on. I looked through all her email. There's nothing of note. Her schedule says she has a meeting at the BBC in two days."

"What about her search history?" Stevie asked.

They checked. Angela had a mundane online life. She updated her social media. She searched furniture sites for rugs and cat supplies. She looked up simple recipes and ordered takeout. She paid some bills. Most of the time she was using libraries and online archives to do Tudor research. It wasn't promising, but Stevie copied it anyway and sent it to herself.

Stevie took a moment to open the file cabinet drawers. They contained bills and household records—utilities, insurance, a passport.

"She didn't leave the country," Stevie said, holding it up.

They then examined Angela's bedroom, which was slightly less tidy than the rest of the house, but within the bounds of reason. She had some clothes on a chair, but the bed was made and decorated with a small silver throw pillow.

"If we're going to look," Stevie said, "we need to look. That means the drawers, everything."

The three of them set about opening all the drawers, the cupboards, the closets. They found nothing out of the ordinary. Stevie examined the bathroom. Every single sign pointed to the fact that Angela had left the house sometime after their visit and had not returned.

"You see?" Izzy said. "She left after we were here. I'm worried we said something—I said something—something that upset her. This isn't her. She wouldn't just *go* and not tell me."

Izzy and David looked at Stevie expectantly. Everyone was waiting for her to do something—to pull a rabbit out of her hat. But all Stevie could see was a house with a missing owner. She went into the bathroom in an attempt to look busy while her wheels were turning. She felt the towels (they were dry), opened the medicine cabinet (just normal stuff, nothing marked POISON), checked for a toothbrush (an extremely fancy electric one that looked like it connected to an app).

It was hard to look like a brilliant detective.

"There's still the box room," Izzy said.

"The box room?"

Izzy motioned them back out into the hall. She reached up and pulled down a hatch that Stevie had not noticed. This revealed a folding set of steps. Izzy pulled them down and Stevie climbed up.

The box room was just barely a room—it was more of a glorified crawl space with shelving taking up three of the walls, and a sloping roof that made it impossible to stand up. These were full of standing magazine boxes full of papers and binders. There were slim document boxes with labels like, "Star Chamber, primary document copies," "Thomas Cromwell 1517–18," "Naval history, lecture notes." A whole room of documents, as you might expect from someone who researched for a living.

Stevie sat down, and Izzy and David came up and crushed into the little space with her. There were boxes of materials from her time at Cambridge—course catalogs, syllabi, printouts of research papers. In with these was a box of scripts from the Nine, rustic early computer printouts with gray lettering. The three of them opened every box, but it became evident that these were Angela's old academic records and archived research materials.

Stevie's phone began to ring. Quinn. Of course. The evening call.

"Hi," Stevie said, trying to look casual.

"Where are you?"

"At the historian's house," Stevie said. "The one from the other night?"

Always tell the truth when you can. Lie only when necessary. This was true.

"You look like you're in her closet."

"In her attic—or, her archive. She's letting me go through her research."

She slapped her hand around until she found something printed out on an ancient printer, titled "Burning Faith: England During the Dissolution of the Monasteries."

"Are you developing an interest in the Tudors?" Dr. Quinn asked.

"Yeah," Stevie said. "The Tower got me really interested. In . . . Henry the Eighth. It's sort of about crime, right? He was a murderer, really. What else do you call a man who kills two of his wives?"

This was a direct swipe from Angela, but Stevie didn't think she would mind.

"An interesting point," Dr. Quinn said. "Are you doing this on your own?"

"No," Stevie said. David was there, but so was Izzy. Stevie swept the camera around so Dr. Quinn could see.

"We're working together," Stevie said. "That's Izzy. Angela is her aunt. She studies with David."

A long pause.

"I look forward to hearing your thoughts on this topic over the next few days," Dr. Quinn finally said. "And maybe we'll incorporate some Tudor history into your program."

"Definitely," Stevie said with a nod. Her lips were dry, and her smile was flat.

"Do you think she actually believed that?" David asked when the call ended.

"I think she's not sure. Probably not. But I'm not doing anything wrong by sitting around with some history papers, so she can't say anything."

Dr. Quinn was gone, and the moment passed. Stevie was just a weirdo sitting in a pile of someone else's old homework.

"Does this tell you anything?"

Izzy had a hopeful look, like she had expected Stevie to have found her aunt inside one of the boxes.

It didn't. None of it did. What the hell else was there? Just piles of history, dirty dishes, a hungry cat. What did detectives do now?

The partner. Of course.

"Who else is in her life?" Stevie asked. "Was she seeing anyone?"

"She has an ex-husband. His name is *Marvin*. He's fine. He's a journalist. He lives in Hong Kong. They haven't seen each other in years—not one of those angry things. They just broke up because he was always traveling the world for the BBC and she was here."

"Anyone else?"

Izzy shook her head.

"What about your family? Angela is your mom's sister?"

"Oh." Izzy compressed her lips together a bit. "Yes, but my mum died when I was a baby. I've gotten closer to Angela since I moved to London. My dad wouldn't know where she was. I'm the only one who would know. I don't know anyone she works with. It's just me and her friends."

Stevie pinched her nose and ran her hand down her face. She smelled of dust and old paper and she was out of ideas.

"I think we can put this stuff back," she said.

They attempted to restore the box room to the way they'd found it and descended the ladder, then went back downstairs. Stevie wandered in circles for a moment, looking around the living room. What could she learn? What did she see? The bricked-up fireplace with the beautiful art deco tiles. The books. The rich patterns of the wallpaper. The smell of the old food and cat litter.

She had forgotten the most important thing.

"The trash," Stevie said.

"I suppose we should take it out."

"No," Stevie said. "We *need* the trash."

They returned to the kitchen and turned on all the lights. There was a silver step can in the corner, as well as two recycling bins. There was a pair of rubber washing gloves resting on the sink. Stevie grabbed these, then looked in the cabinet under the sink. Trash bags. She pulled out the roll and ripped a few off.

"Here," she said to Izzy and David, "spread these out."

The kitchen floor was soon covered in slippery plastic trash bags.

She picked up the silver step can. The trash had been festering for several days, so it had developed a pungent hum—a sour stink that made Stevie scrunch her nose involuntarily. She pulled out the bag and dumped the contents onto the floor. She did the same with the recycling, making a separate mound a few feet away.

"Well," David said, "if she comes home right now, this will be nice for her."

Stevie put on the kitchen gloves, then got on her knees and started picking through it. Trash was archaeology. Trash always told the truth. The recycling for a start. It was all clean. Everything had been sorted correctly. Angela took lids off and broke down boxes. There were two empty wine bottles. Seven empty sparkling-water bottles. At least a dozen containers from ready-made meals from the grocery store: premade soup, lasagnas and salads in plastic containers. A single person's diet. Someone busy.

The trash must have been emptied recently because there was very little in the bag. Some plastic shrink-wrap from a package. A chewed-up shoelace. Two receipts from Boots, which was the major drugstore chain. Angela had had a cold recently. She'd purchased a decongestant and throat drops, as well as body wash and a toothbrush. Nothing strange.

Stevie lifted the lid of the compost bin and dumped the food scraps and piles of used tea bags onto an empty corner of plastic.

"She drinks a *lot* of tea," Stevie said, nudging around the disgusting pile. "She doesn't finish most of her meals."

Doorknob had been interested in these proceedings and chose this moment to make a move. He saw a piece of old chicken, snagged it, and ran off.

"No!" Izzy said. "Doorknob, no. You'll be sick. . . ."

She hurried off after the cat. David squatted down and looked at Stevie from across the pile of garbage.

"Hey," David said. "We go on the best dates, huh?"

He said it mirthlessly. Stevie nodded.

"What do you think?" he said in a low voice, craning his head to make sure Izzy was out of earshot. But there was no worry—Izzy could clearly be heard running around the living room calling for Doorknob.

"It looks like . . . she's gone," Stevie said, pointing out the obvious. "No sign of forced entry. No sign of a struggle. It seems like we ate dinner with her, and then, she left. You asked me to look and . . . I looked."

She indicated the pile of trash she was lording over as proof.

"I know," he said.

What was that tone in his voice? It was dispirited, but what did it mean? She had failed. The great Stevie, the one who busted into places and turned up things—she had

204

nothing. She had not performed the trick. All she'd done was spill a lot of garbage. She wanted to say something, explain herself, but before she could, Izzy called them.

"You should come in here," she said.

They found Izzy on her hands and knees on the floor. She had pushed back an armchair that was tucked into the corner where the stairway met the wall. The bottom half of her body was sticking out. She crawled backward and looked up at them.

"Doorknob dragged the chicken bone back here. There's a little opening. Look."

She pushed back the chair. The paneling under the stairs had been papered in a lush tropical print, and at the corner, the panel had been pushed back a few inches, just enough for an enterprising cat to squeeze through. Izzy felt the panel and found that it was hinged. It was the opening to a very small cabinet.

"I didn't know this was here," she said. "So, this is where the Hoover is. And this is where Doorknob has been keeping things."

Stevie leaned in to look. Sure enough, this was the spot Doorknob collected his little treasures. His toy mouse. Part of what looked like a real mouse. A used tea bag. Two buttons. A crumpled tissue. A dirty cotton swab. A grape stem.

Izzy pulled out the canister vacuum cleaner and stuck her head into the opening. She dragged out a heavy, blocky briefcase.

"Look at this," she said, pushing it farther into the center of the room so they could see it.

"It's a fire safe," Stevie said. "Document storage."

This model had no key lock. It had a keypad instead.

"No chance you know the code, is there?" Stevie asked.

Izzy shook her head.

"I had no idea she had that. What's it for?"

"Important documents, usually," Stevie said. "Records. Wills. Insurance. Passports. Important stuff. It's a safe, basically, that keeps your papers safe in fires and floods."

"I think she keeps all that kind of thing in her office. So what's in this?"

"Unless we have the code, we won't know."

"People tend to use bad passwords and codes," David said. "The password really is 'password' a disappointing number of times. What's her birthday?"

"The ninth of February."

"So, 0209," Stevie said, putting in the digits.

"No. 0902. Other way around."

Right. England. Many things were flipped here. She tried both versions. Neither worked.

"Birth year?"

Izzy counted back.

"1974."

That didn't work either.

"Okay," Stevie said, standing up and making a circuit of the room, peering at the bookshelves. "She's a historian. Loads of dates in history."

"It's pretty much all dates," David pointed out.

"But she does Henry the Eighth a lot, right?"

"Her specialty is the Tudor period," Izzy replied. "Which is . . ." Izzy consulted her phone for this information. "1485 until 1603."

Those two dates were tried and did not work. Nor did the year Henry the Eighth became king, the beheading of Anne Boleyn, Elizabeth the First becoming queen. Eventually they tried every number between 1485 and 1603.

"What about 1066?" Izzy said. "That's the big year in English history. *1066 and All That.*"

It was not 1066.

"This group," Stevie said. "They're called the Nine. Is it something to do with that?"

The only thing they could think of that would work was 9999, which did nothing. Nor did 1995, the year of their graduation and the event at Merryweather. For good measure, Stevie also tried the default 1234, just to make sure Angela hadn't kept the factory setting. She had not. The box refused to divulge its secrets.

"Could we force it open?" David said.

Stevie shrugged to indicate this was worth a try. They looked around the flat for something to use to pry it open, finding a large flathead screwdriver in the utility closet. They all attempted it, but the box resisted.

"It's pretty solid," Stevie said. "It's designed to take a beating."

"What now?" Izzy said. Her frustration at not being able to open the box, at the sight of the house and the growing evidence that something was wrong—all of it was making her tearful.

"I think we take this with us," Stevie said. "If she turns up, we just bring it back to her. But we keep trying to get it open. Is that okay?"

Izzy nodded emphatically.

"But there has to be more we can do," she said. "I'm going to talk to the police tomorrow. I've walked around the area; I've even talked to some neighbors to see if they saw or heard anything, but no one did. What do I do now?"

She looked at Stevie with such an open, pleading expression. She needed help. She needed Stevie. Stevie had failed in the house, but Izzy had not given up on her. David was looking at her as well.

Think, Stevie. What do you do?

"She thinks one of her friends committed a murder," Stevie said. "She texts those friends to say she wants to meet. She says something about a button, something about going to Merryweather. This is about the Nine. Do you know any of them?"

"A little," Izzy said. "I've met Theo before. She came over several times after the surgery to check in. She's a doctor. And the others have all been around. I don't know them well, but I know them."

"If Angela was talking to them that night, then we need to talk to them. They were the last people she was in touch with, and it sounds like she wants to see them. Are they around here?"

"Um . . ." Izzy considered. "Theo, yes. Sooz, yes. And Peter and Yash, I think they are too. Julian—I think he's an MP in York or somewhere up north. Sebastian lives at Merryweather, which is up near Cheltenham. So, four of them are in London."

"Okay . . ." Stevie scratched at her forehead in thought. "We need to talk to them. But . . . we need to do it now. Soon. Can you text them? Ask if we can meet with them. As soon as possible."

"I can do that," Izzy said, pulling out the tablet. She typed furiously for a moment. "Theo's working twelve hours tomorrow," she said. "Sooz . . . has a show in the evening. She can do the afternoon. And . . . Yash . . . Yash and Peter. They say they'll go to Sooz's house. We can meet them there. At two?"

She looked up hopefully.

Two was the middle of their carefully scheduled day. She would have to make it work.

"Two," Stevie said. "Where do we go?"

24 June 1995

Q: Can you walk us through the events of this morning, starting from the time you woke up?

A: Yes. I . . . I woke around eight thirty. I'd gone to sleep around three, so I was still quite tired, but . . . I can't lie in. I went downstairs. I cleaned up the kitchen a bit. Then I started walking around the house to see if everyone was all right. Not sick, I mean.

Q: Where was everyone?

A: Angela, Yash, and Peter were in their rooms. Sebastian and Sooz were asleep in the sitting room. Julian was in the library.

Q: The aftermath of a party?

A: Exactly. And I kept looking, knocking on doors, checking all throughout the house for Rosie and Noel, but they were nowhere. And as everyone woke up and got hungry, I decided it was time someone went looking for them. They'd been out all night. I assumed they were passed out somewhere. I wanted to make sure they were . . . oh God . . . may I have some water, please?

Q: Are you all right to continue?

A: I'm all right now. I can continue. I went with Sebastian. It's his house, and he looked like he could use some fresh air. We started by going down the front garden, up toward the folly, then we wound our way around the formal gardens on the orangery side, around the back, checked in the pavilion at the tennis court, then came around through the trees where the woodshed is.

Q: I'm sorry, but I must ask you to describe the scene as you came upon it.

A: I understand. I know. The woodshed is just beyond the drive, in the trees. There was a wheelbarrow. On the ground. In front of the woodshed. Tipped over in the mud. There was a bucket. And the door to the woodshed was open, about halfway open, so we could see a bit inside. And we could see the latch had been forced, the door was ripped open. It was clear someone had broken in. It was very wet inside, puddles of water on the floor. The woodpiles were knocked about into these odd stacks on the floor, these mounds . . . and at first it just seemed like someone had broken in and made a mess of the place . . . but then Sebastian had this odd look on his face, and then I saw what he saw. There was a boot under one of the mounds, and part of a leg, and . . . I thought . . . that's odd. Someone is hiding under a pile of wood. But the leg was so still. I didn't . . . I couldn't make sense of it. It didn't make sense. I went over and started moving some of the logs away and . . .

Q: Take your time.

A: Yes. I'm all right. Yes. What I saw was . . . not

consistent with life. I did not have to check her vital signs. Sebastian had backed up, and in doing so he found Noel. Noel's condition was the same as Rosie's. Sebastian and I left the woodshed. Sebastian was starting to go into shock, so I moved him away from the area and got him back to the house. We called you.

Q: You said the others went out shopping while you were looking for your friends?

A: Yes.

Q: It was just the two of you who came upon the scene?

A: Yes.

Q: Did you move anything, aside from the logs?

A: We got out as quickly as possible. We didn't want to touch—once we saw. I've tried to be clinical. I've tried to report to the best of my capability. I find I'm quite cold and my head . . . I'm sorry.

Q: You've done very well. You can go back to your friends, have a cup of tea.

Q: Can you tell me where you went as the game began?

A: I went out the mudroom door, at the back of the house.

Q: Did you see anyone else go out that way?

A: Sooz . . . Suzanna.

Q: Where did you go?

A: I made a loop of the back gardens, which are extensive. There's a maze, but that seemed too obvious a spot to hide. And there are so many little topiary spaces back there, rooms, but there's nowhere to hide in them. I left to find a better place. I circled the house at least twice, running all around, looking.

Q: Did you ever go past the woodshed?

A: Yes.

Q: Did you try to get inside?

A: No. The outbuildings were locked. There was no point in that.

Q: And you knew that because Sebastian had said so or because you saw it locked?

A: We were told it was locked. It certainly appeared to be locked. Eventually I had an idea that I would climb up the pergola, hide on top. That's what I did. I thought I'd get rumbled, but I was there for ages.

People walked right under me. At first I was pleased, but I was soaked to the bone. I was there for hours. Literally, hours.

Q: Did you see Rosie or Noel at any point during the game?

A: I saw Noel.

Q: Where did you see him?

A: In the back garden.

Q: Where precisely?

A: In one of the topiary areas. That place is a maze. It's hard to say, but it was in there somewhere.

Q: And he was alone?

A: Yes.

Q: When was this?

A: Early on. Very early on.

Q: Could you be more precise than that?

A: I only know it was early. I'd say within the first fifteen minutes of the game? It was during my first pass of the back garden.

Q: Did you speak to him?

A: No. I don't think he saw me. He was moving quickly. He went out one of the exits and I didn't see him again after that.

Q: And what about Rosie?

A: I didn't see her.

Q: You and Rosie, you two were recently in a romantic relationship?

A: Yes.

Q: How long had that been going on?

A: A year. Or a little less than a year.

Q: A year? So, quite a long time, then.

A: Yes. I suppose. Yes.

Q: But it had recently ended?

A: Yes.

Q: Why was that?

A: Does it matter?

Q: We need to ask these sorts of questions. Can you please tell me about the end of the relationship? Was this recent?

A: Within the last few weeks.

Q: And what was the cause?

A: I . . . I did something that upset her.

Q: What was that?

A: This really matters?

Q: Please answer the question.

A: About a week ago, we were all at the pub. We were having a laugh. I'd finished my exams and I'd had maybe one too many, and I think I knew Rosie and I wouldn't be continuing the way we were, and I . . . I kissed another girl. Just some girl I met there that night. It wasn't serious, but Rosie found out, of course. Everyone saw. But that's what our . . . these things, we . . . it happens. I'm not . . . I'm sorry. I'm sorry, Rose. I'm sorry.

[Unintelligible.]

Q: We'll end this for now.

14

THE NEXT DAY, THEY FOLLOWED THE SCHEDULE. THEY BEGAN AT THE Natural History Museum, which was an ornate palace of rocks and bones. From there, they went to the Victoria and Albert Museum, the design museum, which contained, among other things, a massive collection of clothing and fashion-related items from the ages. Janelle was beside herself looking at Victorian ribbon corsets, ancient Egyptian shoes, Balenciaga ball gowns, and Frida Kahlo's used cosmetics. From there, they were supposed to go to the Science Museum. They took this opportunity to call Dr. Quinn.

"Calling a little early," Janelle said. "We're going to the Science Museum after this and there's an interactive program about climate change that starts at two."

It helped that this was the truth.

The plan was that Stevie would leave them at this point and take the Tube to meet Izzy. David couldn't come—he had a class. Going into the Tube by herself turned out to be an exhilarating and nerve-racking experience. Something about being on her own in this place for the first time, without anyone to notice if she was going west instead of east or getting on the wrong train entirely. London was hers in this moment.

She stuck to the plan. Stevie watched the stops carefully, fearful of missing hers. Knightsbridge, Hyde Park Corner, Green Park . . .

Piccadilly Circus. She stepped off the train into a kind of free-for-all of people and coats and bags, a massive crush of humanity that drifted back to the upper world on long escalators, with more of the flashing, synchronized advertisements. It was madness. There were way too many doors leading out and she got turned around and caught up in the crowd and had to make her way back around to meet with Izzy, who was waiting by the statue of Eros. Izzy looked sleepless. Her winged eyeliner was not quite on point, and her cheeks were flushed pink with cold and effort.

"I went up to her flat again first thing this morning," she said. "To see if she was back and to feed Doorknob. Still nothing. What do we say when we get there?"

"Your aunt thinks that one of her friends might be a murderer," Stevie said. "She talks when she's under the influence of painkillers, but that's the only time. She's probably kept her suspicions to herself. We don't tell them about what your aunt said about the lock. We just get them to talk. We ask if anyone has heard from your aunt, and then see if we can get them to talk to me about the case. Let them say anything that comes into their minds. Just let them talk."

In London, there were no street signs on poles at corners. The elegant street plaques were on the corners of buildings themselves, often at second-story height, so Stevie was always looking up. She looked up at buildings stately and twee, buildings that looked like old soot and others that were pastel mint and butter yellow, or finished in fine decorative work from a different age. The streets got narrower, barely the width of a car. They passed down the proud Old Compton Street, which was clearly the center of the gay district. They wound around corners and through alleys. This was deep in an old part of London, something lively and varied, probably a bit questionable at times.

Sooz lived behind a stark black door on a street of cafés and shops that were so perfectly adorable and expensive-looking that Stevie felt poorer just being near them. Sooz's particular door was between a vegetarian café painted sky blue and a purple-gray bao shop. Izzy hit the button for flat 2, and the door popped open with a gentle buzz. They ascended a set of creaky internal steps carpeted in red, several of which slanted toward the left, like the house may have been knocked over at some point and hastily propped back up again. Flat 2 was at the top of the stairs and was fronted by a modern door that didn't match the rest of the interior.

It opened, revealing a tall, redheaded woman with

enormous almond-shaped eyes. She was dressed all in black—slim black trousers, a formfitting black turtleneck sweater. Stevie didn't really know how cashmere was different from other materials, but somehow, she knew that everything Sooz was wearing was made of it.

"Isabelle!" She wrapped her arms around Izzy. It was a wide, all-encompassing embrace.

"This is Stevie," Izzy said. "She's a friend. I brought her along because—"

"No need to explain. When I was at university, I went everywhere with my friends as well. You know that. Come in, come in. Peter and Yash are on their way. They were just finishing up a rehearsal."

They were admitted into a small but perfectly outfitted apartment. The main space had a white shag rug and two cobalt-blue sofas. There was a lot of black and silver and mirrors in curious places. By the door there was a rattan organizer that held shoes, magazines, books, purses, a hairbrush, a makeup case. The kinds of things a working actress might drop on the way in late at night or need on her way out the door again. Every inch of wall space was in use, encrusted in pictures and framed posters from shows. Dozens of them. Pictures in frames on the shelves. Pictures magnetized to the fridge and the hood of the stove. Pictures rotating through multiple digital frames. Sooz had selfied long before the world knew what a selfie was. There was Sooz with some vaguely familiar faces. Stevie had to look twice before she recognized an actress from one of her favorite English detective shows. There was Sooz in black and white, dressed as a ringmaster. Right by the galley kitchen was a long photograph of an entire class from Cambridge, all in white skirts, draped in black academic gowns, arranged in a formal photograph taken outside. In calligraphy at the top, around a double crest of two shields, were the words *Cambridge University, Magdalene College, Matriculation, 1995.*

Sooz noticed Stevie pause in front of it.

"Several of us in that one," she said. "Angela, Peter, Noel, and I all went to Magdalene."

She pronounced it "Maudlin."

"Cup of char?" she asked.

"Oh, yes, please," Izzy said.

At Stevie's puzzled look, she clarified.

"Tea. Sorry. Would you like some?"

Stevie nodded.

"I've been racking my brain," Sooz said as she filled the kettle. "I've been texting. I've been talking to the others. It makes no sense. It makes no *sense*, Izzy. She's not like this. Not Ange. I don't understand it."

"That's why Stevie and the others are here. Stevie is—"

"Sebastian told me. And I read about you when he explained. Can you help us?"

It was always a bit weird when strangers put their faith in her. Just this morning, Stevie had almost eaten the stopper they put in her coffee. She wanted to say something wonderful and brave and inspiring, but what came out was

"Uh . . . I can . . . try . . . to . . . do . . ."

Sooz fidgeted around the kitchen, letting Stevie run out that sentence. She peered out the window to a roof beyond it, where three cats sat in a triangular formation, staring at each other.

"They do this," Sooz said absently. "For hours. Stare at each other like this. I'm afraid one of these days they're going to tear each other apart."

"Which one is yours?" Stevie asked.

"Mine? Oh, none of them. I'm allergic to cats. Hives all over."

Everyone considered the impending battle as the kettle began to rumble to a boil. Sooz was on it as soon as it clicked, dumping hot water into mugs. It seemed to focus her. She fussed around, grabbing tea bags and mugs and tiny spoons and a tray. She moved with the lilting motion of someone who ran through life on the tips of her toes.

They sat in the living room. Sooz draped herself elegantly in the corner of one of the sofas, tucking her bare feet under her, and stared out over the steam of her tea. No sooner had she done so than the buzzer rang.

"That'll be Yash and Peter," she said, bouncing up.

Yash Varma was a tall man, with dark brown skin and a thick, well-sculpted beard that rounded his jaw. He had sparkling brown eyes—there was genuine merriment there. He seemed like the kind of person who laughed easily and often. He came in, peeling off a green peacoat and revealing a scrappy Nirvana T-shirt and jeans.

"Sorry we're late," he said. "Terrible read-through for the show. We're going to be absolutely bricking it by the time we film tomorrow unless we suddenly get much funnier."

"I don't hold out a lot of hope for that," his companion said. Peter Elmore had a tousle of reddish-blond hair, which appeared even redder against the rust-colored pullover he wore. Everything about Peter had an air of intentional slouch, a comic casualness. Yash was the high energy, and Peter was the slower, lower note.

Izzy commenced with the introductions, explaining Stevie's presence.

"We want to find out what she's been doing recently," Izzy said. "We're just trying to get information in general."

"Of course," Sooz said. "Anything."

"When did you last see my aunt?" Izzy asked.

"Last week," Peter replied. "She was at a party I had at my house. We were all there."

"Pete and I got an award for our show, so we were having a celebration," Yash said.

"It wasn't a tough competition," Peter added. "We were only up against one other show, which wasn't very good."

"I wrote that other show," Yash shot back. "That's why he's saying that. He's been smug about it."

"I gave you the idea for that show."

"You wish."

"You two," Sooz said. "Shut it."

"And how was she?" Izzy asked. "Did she do or say anything out of the ordinary?"

The three looked at each other.

"No," Sooz said. "She was in good spirits. She's working on that new program about Henry the Eighth. She was telling us about that. She's always happiest when she's working on a project. She was in a wonderful mood. We all had a bit to drink."

"Maybe too much," Yash said. "It was a proper, old-school party. I think she ended up sleeping on your sofa, didn't she, Pete?"

"I gave her the bedroom," Peter said. "I slept on the sofa."

"She brought me a lip balm," Sooz said. "I'd given her one a week or so before when we were out and her lips were chapped. It was a nice one—Penhaligon's Orange Blossom. Nothing beyond the pale, but they cost maybe eleven quid. It's my favorite. When she got to the party she had a replacement, the same exact one. That's Ange. If she borrows something, she *always* replaces it. *Always* pays you back. She never wants anyone to worry or be put out. She wouldn't go off and leave everyone worrying."

"Would you mind talking a bit about what happened in 1995?" Izzy said. "Stevie really is an absolute genius. She has a way of working things out. I know it's not an easy subject, but my aunt was talking about it with us that night, and maybe it was on her mind. Maybe if we knew more about it we could figure out if it played a role in where she went. . . ."

The soft wind of Izzy's conversation blew across the room, lulling them into a state of compliance. The excessive praise and discussion of her methods made Stevie start to sweat under her vinyl coat. She stripped it off, revealing the hoodie underneath, the traces of salad dressing still down the front.

"All right," Sooz said. "If you think it would help. We all met as freshers at Cambridge. We came from different colleges. We met at auditions, and drinks after auditions, things like that."

The three of them engaged in a little back and forth for a moment about who met who at which pub or party or school event and who introduced who to whom and where, and then, sensing that they had strayed from the discussion at hand, Sooz waved her hand in a graceful gesture that suggested the words "or something like that, it doesn't matter."

"We sort of just—well, came together right away. We were best friends. And we decided to make our own theatrical group, write and perform our own comedy sketches. That's a common thing students do."

"We all did a bit of everything," Peter went on, "but we had some loose roles within the group. Yash and I wrote together, like we do now. That's where we started. We were the main writers."

"Angela wrote a lot as well," Yash said. "And Rosie did some writing."

"Theo directed," Sooz said, and the others nodded. "She also did a lot of producing—getting us spaces to perform."

"Sooz, Julian, Sebastian, and Noel were our primary performers," Peter went on.

"Noel was our special character," Sooz said. "He was good at playing authority figures. He had a hilarious way of *being* onstage. He just made you laugh without doing much of anything at all."

Peter and Yash nodded at this.

"We weren't bad. And we lived together. It was the end of university. It was time to pack up our house. It was like the world was ending and starting again. That's how it felt, before . . . we had no idea. None."

Sooz rubbed her mouth with the back of her fist to prepare herself.

"We went to Merryweather," she said. "That's the name of the house . . . you've probably heard that. It belonged to Sebastian's family. It's his now, along with the title of viscount. We'd go there every once in a while, on breaks, when the family was away. Incredible place. I grew up in a little house outside of Southampton. I'd never seen anything like it. It was magical. We drove down in two cars. It was hot that day—there was a heat wave that summer. We were blasting *Parklife* the whole way—that's an album by Blur. Blur is a band. You've probably never heard of them, but they were the biggest thing. Remember?"

"It was a huge story that summer," Peter said. "Blur and the other major band of the moment, Oasis, had had a public dispute and were challenging one another. Everyone took a side and had an opinion on which band was better . . ."

"Oasis," Sooz said. "Most of the others thought otherwise.

225

I was the only one standing up for the Gallagher brothers."

". . . they released a single on the same day, and there was a huge furor about which band would come up on top," Peter went on. "They called it the Battle of Britpop. So funny to think of that—it was such a bright summer and the big controversy was whose band was best."

"We arrived well into the evening," Sooz said. "Remember? We left late because most of us had hangovers and we'd been packing up the house. We got there right as it was getting dark and the rain started. We ran around and picked our rooms—that was always fun."

Her brow furrowed. She'd hit a memory.

"Something was odd," she said. "Rosie was in a strange mood the whole way there, I remember. Something to do with Julian. Rosie had been dating Julian, and things with Julian were always . . ."

She shook her head.

"Drama," Peter said. "There was always some drama about Julian."

"Not just Julian!" Sooz said. "We were all big, passionate, messy. But yes, that day was about Julian. I knew what that could be like. I dated him twice, and for most of our second year. Julian and Rosie were together for most of our last year, and they split up right near the end. At least Rosie was in the process of leaving him for Noel. That last week we were at Cambridge, I saw them going off together. We had this tatty tent—someone bought it for a festival and put it up in the back garden afterward, and we never took it down. We'd go in there sometimes. It was disgusting, muddy, moldy, but private. I saw Rosie and Noel slipping in there during finals week."

"Did Rosie and Julian fight?" Stevie asked.

"No idea. Probably. Not a serious fight—not anything . . . not violent! Stupid things. Julian was, and still is, very, very attractive. *Everyone* flirted with him, and he flirted right back. When you were with Julian, things got messy. He wasn't always faithful—and by that, I mean he was never faithful. Who is, at that age? I had my moments as well. But Julian was the worst of us when it came to that."

"But he could have been angry with Rosie and Noel, right?" Stevie said.

Sooz wrapped her hands around her teacup and tucked her knees together as she considered her reply.

"No," she said.

"No?"

"That's not how it was with us."

"And Julian had no right to complain about anyone," Peter added.

"Oh God," Yash said. "We're always talking about Julian."

"What I mean," Sooz said, "is that we were . . . sort of a commune, almost? We always shared things with each other. Anything you brought into the house, you knew it belonged to everyone. By the end, I don't think any of us knew which clothes were ours. If you found it on the drying rack, it was fair game. Clothes. Bicycles. Hairbrushes. Books. Food. There were no possessions in our house, and in a way, no possessiveness? I think we all dated each other at some point. There were so many showmances. Even though we all dated and broke up, we were friends. I mean, Yash, you and I got together in our first year, and Peter, you and I had a good year in there. Right?"

The two shrugged and indicated this was so.

"We might be heartbroken or furious, but the others would get you through it. We were constantly annoyed with each other—constantly, always—but we were always loyal as well. If Rosie stopped dating Julian and started dating Noel, that was within the bounds of how we did things. There was always a frisson of tension—it was quite exciting, actually."

"More than a *frisson*," Yash said. "The atmosphere could be *thick*."

"But that was the fun of it," Sooz said. "The undercurrent. Anything could happen."

"And usually did," Peter replied. "Loudly. At all hours. Frequently against the wall we shared with Julian's bedroom."

"That's why I can sleep anywhere now." Yash stretched and cracked his neck. "I once fell asleep during a performance of Stomp, during the part where they're banging the dustbin lids. Lulled me right off."

"Anyway." Sooz waved her hand, moving the topic along. "Rosie was up in her room with Angela having a chat, and I dragged them downstairs for champagne. We had quite a lot of champagne that night, and some other things as well. It started to pour down with rain, and then we were going to play our game. It was team hide-and-seek. Sebastian was the seeker. The rest of us hid. There weren't many rules, just you couldn't go back inside once you went out, and the outbuildings were out of bounds."

"Sebastian shoved his keys down the front of his trousers," Peter said. "Remember that?"

"Oh yes," Yash said.

"The last any of us saw of Rosie and Noel was as we ran out into the rain in the dark. They never came back in. What we *figured* is that they were off shagging somewhere. The next morning, they still hadn't come back in. Sebastian and Theo went out to look for them . . ."

She trailed off.

"Theo and Sebastian found them," Peter said quietly.

That was clearly the end of what they were prepared to say on the matter.

"You have a lot of pictures," Stevie said to Sooz.

"Oh yes. I was the photographer of the group. You used to have to buy film and get it developed, and it was expensive, but I knew someone who worked at Boots who developed my pictures for free—so I took loads and loads of them."

"Did you take any . . ." Stevie proceeded carefully. ". . . that weekend?"

"I did," she said.

"Would you mind?" Izzy said. "I know it's a bit of a strange ask, but . . . could we see them?"

Sooz nodded.

"Of course. I'll go and get them."

She was gone only a moment and returned with three

black paper sleeves full of printed photographs.

"These are the last photographs I took of all nine of us," she said, crossing her arms over her chest and looking down at the sleeves. "I've never been able to digitize them. I don't even like looking at them. I keep them separate. I don't know how they could help, but . . . if anything helps find Angela . . . Go ahead. Feel free."

She waved her hand toward Stevie, indicating she was welcome to examine the photos. She tucked herself back on the sofa.

"Some are from the week or so leading up to our going away," she said. "I'd just gotten the first two developed before we left for Merryweather. I remember showing them to the others in the car. I took the last roll while we were there. For a long time, I couldn't pick up my camera again. There's about six months between the photos in that last pack."

There was a lot of red-eye, flashes caught in windows and mirrors. No filters. Just people glancing up from their lives and being caught in a moment, bent over to pick up a beer or a book. Making faces behind each other's backs. The same nine people, over and over. Occasionally there would be someone else on the side of the image, but the stars of the show were always the same.

"Look at this!" Peter said, holding up a picture of a bald Angela. "Remember Ange shaved her head right before we went away."

"Oh yes, that's right," Sooz said. "That was . . . a game of truth or dare. We were all a bit stoned. Sebastian had some powerful joints. He grew his own special blend. I think I set that dare. Didn't think she'd do it. I thought she looked great. Very Sinead O'Connor."

"This one," Yash said, pulling one out of the stack. "This is probably the last one of all of us together. It was taken when we arrived at Merryweather."

He handed Izzy and Stevie a group photo. Nine people—goofy smiles, suitcases, looking a little worse for wear and very happy. And there, behind them all, was a structure. Gray wood, plain, with a little closed window above the door.

"That's it," Sooz said quietly. "That's the shed. That's where . . . that's the place. We took the photo there because we'd just arrived and I put the camera on the car and set the timer. When I saw it later, saw what I had in the photo . . ."

She was unable to continue.

"What were they like?" Stevie asked. It was a good question to ask to get people to open up and talk.

"Rosie?" Sooz let out a short laugh. "Rosie was . . . fierce. She was from Dublin."

"Stubborn," Peter said, nodding. "She could drink with the best."

"And how," Yash confirmed. "I once saw her drink twelve pints in an afternoon. *Twelve.* Barely had an effect on her."

"She was incredibly loyal," Sooz went on. "If you had a problem, day or night, Rosie was there for you. If you were sick, Rosie was by your side. If she was mad at you, you knew it. She was wonderful. And so funny. I don't think I've ever met anyone as funny as Rosie. She would have been famous. I believe that."

"I could see Rosie hosting *Bake-Off* now," Peter said. "Or doing panel shows."

"She'd have been great on our show," Yash added.

"Noel . . ." Sooz let her gaze drift to the ceiling. "When I first got to Cambridge and met everyone, Noel was someone I couldn't figure out. He seemed very straitlaced, serious. Really into poetry. He played the straight man in comedy brilliantly. He played baddies as well. You could play off Noel in any scene. He had that gift. He kept his feelings close to his chest, but . . . I believe that all along, Noel was in love with Rosie. I felt it. I could see it. But he didn't work up the courage until the very end. I'm glad that, at the end, they had a moment."

Peter cleared his throat and Yash looked toward the window.

"Right," Sooz said, collecting herself. "We're going to figure this out. Despite being absolute rubbish, Julian's done well for himself and does good work. He's an MP. I know he's making inquiries. He'll call everyone in the world if he has to. I trust him on that, and he's maybe the only one of us who can do something directly. But we're going to do all we can. I've been posting online. We've all been. Whatever you need from us, you ask."

"Day or night," Peter said.

"And wherever she is," Yash said, "off looking for Henry the Eighth's old pants or whatever she's doing, we're going to give her an earful when she's home. It'll be all right, Izzy. You have all of us. And we never leave each other alone."

15

"So," Stevie said, "all of these people slept with each other all the time. That's a lot of what we learned."

The group was seated around a large, circular booth in a restaurant in Chinatown in Soho. Over plates of Singapore noodles, ho fun, and shredded duck pancakes, they told Janelle, Nate, and Vi about the information they had gleaned from Sooz, Peter, and Yash.

"Also . . ." Izzy reached for a spring roll. "Everyone seems mad at Julian a lot. Julian Reynolds. He's an MP from up north. He has a good track record on issues but he's been in the papers for having a lot of partners. All of it is interesting, but it doesn't tell us anything about where my aunt is, does it?"

"Anything new from the police?" Vi asked.

"They say they're going to go through the CCTV tomorrow. It would be more helpful *now*. Anything could be happening. What the hell do I do?"

"Get the word out," Vi said. "Post it everywhere."

This kind of thing was very much Vi's wheelhouse, and

soon the table was in a discussion about graphics, messages, and influencers. After they finished their meal, they knocked together a flyer, got a thousand copies made, and went up to Islington together to shove them into letter flaps and post them everywhere they could.

By the time this was all over, it was almost midnight. They returned to Craven House with a heaving bag of junk food from Tesco Express and a sense of having done something in this general effort. When they reached the lobby, David and Stevie looked at each other.

"Want to hang out?" David asked.

She did, in fact, want to hang out.

They decided to go to his room. It was much like Stevie's in layout, with a few more personal touches. But not, Stevie noted, as many as she expected. He hadn't been able to bring that much with him to England, so most of his things were new to her, and the room was sterile and blank.

Which mattered not at all. The door was no sooner closed than he was kissing her, backing her carefully toward the bed. She was reaching for it, trying to find it so she knew where to sit and when to lean back. He was on top of her, kissing along her chin, down to her chest. He was reaching up under her shirt, running his still-cold hands over her stomach, up higher.

"All night," he said. "We've been out there all night and . . ."

She silenced him by putting her mouth on his, tugging her shirt up. They were working with frantic speed. And then came the fervent rapping on the door. David broke off the kiss. He closed his eyes and shook his head, then pulled down his shirt and leaned back as if nothing was going on. Stevie did the same.

"Come in," he yelled.

"There have been developments," Izzy said, rushing in, paying no attention to the close atmosphere in the room. "Two things. One, Julian got information. On the night she disappeared, my aunt got a call from an unknown mobile number at 9:53. That's right in the middle of the chain of texts. Here."

She pulled up Angela's texts and pointed to the spot.

9:46 p.m. ANGELA: She had the button
9:47 p.m. THEO: ?
9:48 p.m. SOOZ: What Theo said.
9:48 p.m. YASH: Button?
9:49 p.m. PETER: what?
9:50 p.m. SOOZ: I have to go back onstage. Please someone explain to me what is happening.
9:51 p.m. SEBASTIAN: Can you ring me?
9:55 p.m. THEO: Ange?
9:57 p.m. THEO: Ange can you pick up?
9:58 p.m. PETER: I just rang as well and it went to voice mail.

"So she mentions the button. That's the last time she speaks on this chain. The call comes right after Sebastian asks her to ring. And Peter says down here that her line is engaged and goes to voice mail. An unknown mobile number."

"That's not hard to do," David said. "Set up an online burner account."

"But someone went to the trouble," Stevie said.

"That seems bad." Izzy wrapped her arms around herself. "Very strange. She gets this unknown call and then she's gone. But there's more. Tonight, they all kept talking on the chain. They've all decided to meet at Merryweather. Tomorrow. They're going to spend the night. I had an idea. I texted Sooz separately, pretending I didn't know about their going. I was saying how scary this situation is and talked my way into being invited. And then I asked to bring you. All of you. To Merryweather."

"Us?" Stevie said. "Where is it?"

"Gloucester. Outside of Cheltenham. Only two hours or so on the train. I'm going mad here and there's nothing more I can do. The answer is there, isn't it? With them? We need to go where they are, and it will be all of them!"

Stevie felt stupid having to explain that tomorrow they had a boat tour of the Thames to learn about the work of someone named Isambard Kingdom Brunel who was apparently a very important Victorian-era engineer who made tunnels and bridges but who looked like the kind of guy who had a basement full of urchins. Stevie didn't particularly care about this, but Janelle was eager and had been planning to do an essay about it.

"There's a train at noon that would get us there by

midafternoon," Izzy said. "Please. This may be the chance to find out what's going on."

Stevie ran through the math in her mind.

On one hand: missing person.

On the other: limited time in England, every second of which was dripping away. And they had a schedule to follow or else.

On the third hand: missing person who was present at a murder at a country house and thought something was up with that murder.

On the fourth hand (officially too many hands now): it wasn't that she came here to be with David, but . . . manor house. With David.

Minutes later, Stevie walked back over to the other side of Craven House. She found everyone still awake, sitting in Vi's room and eating their feast of chips and cookies.

"So," she said. "Something's come up. Hear me out."

She started with the positive approach. Didn't they all want to go to a manor house? They'd been invited by a viscount, for whatever that was worth. She expected more enthusiasm than the tepid silence she was getting. Vi picked at the dust at the bottom of a bag of pickled-onion-flavored chips and Nate wrinkled his nose as if holding back a sneeze. Janelle met Stevie's eye.

"Stevie," she said, "I don't know if we can, or should, for a bunch of reasons. We only have two more days here. We still have all of Vi's and Nate's stuff to do. I mean, a manor house sounds cool, but it's just a house, and we have things here in

London. Vi has an interview with a curator from the British Museum tomorrow. It's a big deal for them. They need it for their applications."

"The answer is there," Stevie said with increasing desperation. "Angela was on to something, or at least she was working on something. We show up, Izzy brings up the fact that Angela was talking about the lock when she was high, Angela sends a text to the others saying she needs to talk to them and they should go to Merryweather, and now she's gone. Wherever she is, it has something to do with what happened at Merryweather, and the way to find her is to find out what happened."

"We all get it. It's important that Izzy finds her aunt. We really do understand that. But her aunt vanished *here*, right? That's why we just helped with the posts."

"Well, she was last *seen* here . . ."

"But what are the chances she's at Merryweather?"

Nate and Vi had gone silent and watched this back-and-forth warily.

"Quinn isn't going to let us go," Janelle said. "She's already on edge with us here. We're supposed to follow the plan. If we say we're going to some manor house, she *will* look up that manor house. She *will* find out there was a murder there once. She *will* realize what is going on."

This had already occurred to Stevie. She'd taken a few minutes back in David's room to look up Merryweather. The first link was to the official site, which was designed to entice couples looking for wedding venues and production crews looking for locations. It had a Wikipedia page, and various mentions of Christmas parties and weddings and gatherings held there. The gardens were apparently famous, and people came to visit them to see the flowers changing over the seasons. Sebastian had done a lot to make sure the murder stuff stayed out of the searches as long as possible. But if you kept looking, it was there, buried in the lines of a few old news articles. If you put in "Merryweather" and "murder," it came up right away. It wouldn't be natural to do that, unless you were Dr. Quinn and you knew Stevie and her ways.

The best answer she had come up with was:

"What if we just . . . went? For a little? One night. If we don't ask . . ."

"Without telling her?" Janelle said. "Oh, she'd kill us. She will get on a plane to come and *kill* us with her *hair*."

She had a point, of course. If Dr. Quinn found out that they had taken off across England to bust into a murder mansion, she would, in fact, kill them all with her hair.

"Stevie . . ." Janelle brushed imaginary lint off her yellow sweater. It was the color of lemons—Janelle's favorite. "We're in another country. And . . . we need to graduate."

"I need to graduate too," Stevie said.

"I know that. I didn't say you didn't."

"So I can go," Stevie said. "On my own."

"So Quinn can expel you? For real, Stevie, have you even *started* your applications? I haven't seen you do anything. All that stuff is due soon. You have to make plans. You're always running after whatever shows up in front of you, but you can't do that forever."

This was unexpected. Stevie felt it in her solar plexus. The thing that was never said, the thing she felt over her shoulder but kept telling herself wasn't there, it was real. Her friends saw her for what she was. Janelle and Vi and Nate—they were doing the work, and Stevie was a free-floating object, pinging around, looking for focus. Looking at garbage.

Janelle was almost shaking with upset. She got up and left the room. Vi followed her. Stevie heard them go to Janelle's room and shut the door.

"That didn't go well," Nate said.

"No."

"If one of us was missing," Nate said, "and you were worried, would you invite a bunch of strangers to come to your house when you were freaking out?"

"If one of those strangers solved things like that, I would."

"I think it's weird. And Janelle may have a point. Do you really think you can find her by going to Merryweather?"

Five minutes ago, Stevie had been sure, but her confidence had been shot out. Her best friend had just leveled a heavy blow.

A few minutes later, Vi came back with Janelle in tow. Janelle was quiet. There was still tension in her posture.

"I'm sorry," she said. When most people apologized, they looked down. Janelle looked right in Stevie's eye. "I'm just . . .

I worry. And we're on thin ice as it is. I have a proposal. If you call Quinn and she says we can go, I'll go. And Vi said they would go. Nate?"

Nate shrugged a general acceptance of this plan.

"But if she says no, you'll stay," Janelle added. "We stick together. Deal?"

It was one in the morning there, which meant it was eight o'clock at night in Vermont.

"She might be gone for the day," Stevie said.

Janelle shrugged as if to say, *Not much I can do about that*.

"Fine," Stevie said. "It's a deal. I'll go call her."

Stevie returned to her room, her face flush with anxiety. Having Quinn call you was bad enough—calling Quinn after hours was not a pleasant prospect. She had to be gone by now, off to some dinner or cocktail thing or a tryst with a lover or a meeting with a spy or whatever the hell it was Quinn did when not running Ellingham. Stevie called the number, clenching and unclenching her fist involuntarily, when . . .

"It's late there, isn't it?" Dr. Quinn said.

She was there, still at her desk, looking tired and puzzled.

"Yeah. Um. I wanted to ask something? Sorry it's late."

"What is it?" she asked, indicating that Stevie should get on with it.

"We've been offered a chance to go to this place called Merryweather? It's a manor house. The owner invited us. He's a . . ."

How did you pronounce *viscount*? She knew it wasn't the

way it was written, but she couldn't remember the right way to do it.

"He has a title. And he's a friend of someone here. And it's really nice. It has a site. You can see it."

"And he invited you to do what?"

"Just visit for the night. It's sort of like a hotel, like a venue, so there are a lot of rooms."

A tapping sound on the other end. She was looking it up.

"I see."

"It has . . . really famous gardens."

She could almost hear Dr. Quinn's synapses firing. This was the problem with having a smart head of school—she knew something was up. But her game always recognized game. Stevie had presented a highly suspicious but ultimately reasonable plan. The flaw was not obvious. She was intrigued.

Tap. Tap. Click. Click. She was looking it over.

"It's a beautiful place," Dr. Quinn finally said. "But I think you should stick to your schedule."

"Okay, but we . . ."

"Stick to your schedule. You have enough to do in London. No side trips. I believe you have a tour tomorrow that focuses on Brunel? I think that's more important. Good night."

She was gone.

Stevie sat on her bed, thinking.

Angela Gill was missing. She needed help. Stevie was sure—*sure*—that she could get at the answer at Merryweather.

She was pretty sure, at least.

It was a possibility. A strong one. But Quinn had said no.

Stevie got up, took half an anxiety pill, gulped back the contents of a can of some drink she'd bought the day before and forgotten about, then returned to her friends.

"She said yes." Stevie arranged her expression into a mask of pleased disbelief. "It turns out she really loves gardens."

It was so easy to lie. So frighteningly easy.

24 June 1995

Q: Can you tell me where you went when the game began?

A: I went outside. Inside would have been nicer, but if you're playing the game, you have to play it. There are more hiding places outside. More ground to move around.

Q: How did you exit the house?

A: Through the library—well, through the orangery that's connected to the library. I started off trying to hide in the gardens out that end, but there wasn't anywhere to go. I ended up going to the back gardens. Plenty more places there. It was bucketing down. I pressed myself under a bench.

Q: And did you see Rosie or Noel at any point when you were outside?

A: No. I didn't see much aside from the ground.

Q: And who found you?

A: Yash. And quite pleased he was about it too. I was fine with it. I'd been there for ages and I was freezing and had a cramp.

Q: You became a seeker.

A: Yes, I was taken to the folly for my slicker and a torch. I managed to find Sooz almost straightaway.

Q: At any point did you approach or attempt to enter the woodshed?

A: I probably ran past it at some point, but I never went over to it. All the outbuildings were locked. Sebastian made sure we knew that.

Q: What happened after the game was suspended?

A: We went back inside. We lit some candles. The fire was going in the sitting room. It had gone down a good bit since we'd been out, so we put more logs on it, got it going again. Sebastian was talking about some whisky and was determined that we were going to drink it. He was making a tremendous fuss about it. That proved to be my undoing. I'd taken a bottle of champagne outside with me and I had the entire thing, plus the drinks from before, plus whatever else . . . the whisky was the last straw. I had to go upstairs and be sick. Then I got into bed. Theo came through with glasses of water. Then I woke up sometime around . . . eleven, I think, or noon. I felt all right, because you usually do after you're ill, don't you? Get it out of your system.

Q: I've had that experience, yes. And you came downstairs?

A: Some of the others were awake. Rosie and Noel still hadn't come in. We were all feeling moribund. Someone, Julian maybe, said they wanted a fry-up. Eggs, sausages . . . someone wanted Monster Munch. So we decided we were going to go to the shops. Theo and Sebastian went out to find Rosie and Noel and bring them in.

Q: I understand there were two cars, one belonging to Sebastian and one to Noel. Which car did you take?

A: Sebastian's. Noel's keys were . . . with Noel, I suppose. We drove to the shops and when we came back, you were here. Not you, I don't think, but a police car, I mean.

Q: I understand. I think that's all we need for the moment.

24 June 1995

Q: Please tell me what you did when the game began at eleven o'clock?

A: I'm not a huge fan of the game, but I play it because . . . because that's what we do. There's a rule that once you leave the house, you can't go back in or you forfeit, so I decided to start inside and stay there as long as possible. I went and hid under a bed in one of the bedrooms. I wanted to be indoors.

Q: And you were found?

A: Almost straightaway. I thought it would take longer. I was a bit drunk. Thought I was being clever. Hiding under a bed isn't very clever.

Q: So you, Sebastian, and Theodora were seekers.

A: Yes. Together we searched the house top to bottom, which probably took us an hour. We may have stopped to have a drink before going outside.

Q: What time do you think you went outside?

A: Somewhere around midnight. We were all a bit reluctant to go, but we had to. It was absolutely bucketing down. Sebastian went down to claim a base position at the folly, and as we found people, we brought them to him.

Q: Did you go past the woodshed in your searches?

A: Oh yes. Several times.

Q: And you noticed nothing out of the ordinary?

248

A: Nothing at all.

Q: Did you check the door to see if anyone had gotten inside?

A: Well, the outbuildings were all locked, so there was no need to go through them.

Q: You didn't check?

A: No need. Sebastian had the keys. He stuffed them down the front of his trousers right in front of us.

Q: Down the front of his trousers?

A: Yes. It looked quite painful.

Q: Did you notice anything at all out of the ordinary?

A: Nothing.

Q: Any cars on the drive, aside from the ones you came in?

A: Truly, there was nothing. And I was making loops of the house and grounds. I never saw a thing that I'd consider odd.

Q: You found some people?

A: Yes, I found Peter. He was crouched under a bench in the back garden. His hiding spot was almost as bad as mine.

Q: When was this?

A: Not sure. Within my first hour of searching, probably. This place is enormous.

Q: Yes, it is substantial, isn't it? What happened with the rest of the time you were outside?

A: I know Peter found Sooz hiding in some bushes. Ange had been found. There was a godawful clap of thunder, and all of the lights in the house went out. We stayed outside for a few more minutes, found Julian hanging on top of the pergola, and then it was clear that we should get inside.

Q: What happened when you returned to the house?

A: Sebastian was banging on about this special bottle of whisky we had to try. It was very dark and he was crawling across the floor, fumbling with his keys. It looked like he was doing battle with the cabinet, so Peter had to get down on the floor and help him unlock it before he pulled the wall down trying to get in there. We opened it and we all had some. I had one glass, but by that point I was feeling it. We'd all had a lot. Angela had come to the end and went up to bed. Peter went upstairs to be sick for a bit. I didn't make it that far—I remember being ill in the downstairs loo, then I crawled up the stairs and got into bed. I remember Theo putting a pint glass of water next to me and that was it until morning.

Q: Do you know what time this was?

A: I knew nothing by that point.

Q: So you were in bed the rest of the night?

A: Yes.

Q: Did you hear or see anything?

A: No, I was absolutely shattered. A plane could have landed next to me and I wouldn't have known. The next thing I remember was Theo again, back with some tea. It was morning.

16

IN THE MORNING, THEY WERE AT PADDINGTON STATION, WHICH STEVIE was embarrassed to realize she hadn't known was real. She thought it was made up, for the bear. Paddington Station really wanted to sell her a Paddington Bear. There had been no time to eat, but Paddington was rammed with restaurants. Stevie bought herself Brie and apple on a baguette, a water, and the biggest coffee available. Then they headed off to the massive overhang where the trains came into the station.

The box had to come with them—whatever was in it, whatever it was, it would not be left behind. But it was clearly a fire safe, and they couldn't just turn up to Merryweather with a fire safe like that was normal. It would have to be hidden in something else. Stevie had pulled her suitcase from the corner of the room, tipped out the dirty clothes she had been storing in it, and managed to fit in inside. She had just enough room to wedge the onesie in with it. It was good packing material. So she dragged a massive, heavy suitcase full of fire safe behind her and carried her supplies for the night in her backpack.

There were some tables available, with four seats around them. She sat at one of these with David by her side, and Izzy and Nate across from them. Vi and Janelle sat behind, in a set of two seats. Stevie could hear them speaking gently to each other behind her head.

Once they were on the train and the doors slid closed, they all settled in with their food. Izzy stared at her phone, preoccupied, hoping for updates that didn't seem to be coming. Nate was reading something on his. David also pulled out his phone to watch something, slouching over and tilting his head in Stevie's direction. The last views of London were the backs of houses—gray and brick—with neat rectangles of back gardens.

She had done this. She had led her friends on this trip. With a lie.

Lies, she noted, took energy. They *weighed* a lot. She had to think about everything she said and did now to support the lie. It sat there in her head, giving off *vibes*.

Lies were radioactive.

She had to try to do something. Figure something out. But she had so little to work with. She had Sooz's photos. That would have to do. She pulled out her tablet to look at them and enlarge them, to take them in and make them part of her own memory.

Noel was a beanpole in massive glasses and 70s clothes. Sebastian's character came through loud and clear. He almost always had a glass of something in his hand, and his posture was theatrical. Theo was often with him. Her hair was short, and she wore a multicolored sweater vest over a white T-shirt. Angela was often to the side in the pictures, smoking and watching. Peter and Yash tended to appear together. Yash looked like he was twelve, swamped in a massive T-shirt. He had no beard. He always appeared to be in the middle of explaining something or telling a joke, a smile cracking his face. Peter almost looked the same as he did now. His ginger-blond hair was floppier, but he looked much like the man Stevie had met. Rosie was small, with long blond hair she often wore in pigtails. She too was often laughing in the pictures. The camera loved Julian—his blue eyes with their long lashes. He was the 90s incarnate, from his shell necklace to his flannel shirts to his boy-band sweep of blond hair. Sooz took most of the pictures, so she wasn't in many, but when she was, she was the star—in front, arms or legs spread, hugging, jumping, her massive brown eyes taking the focus.

These were the players.

The conversation from Sooz's house began to play on a loose recording in her head, skipping and looping. One phrase was on repeat:

When you were with Julian, things always got messy. He wasn't always faithful—and by that, I mean he was never faithful. Who is, at that age?

That last sentence had changed her day, made her feel twitchy and cold. Was that a 90s thing? Or was it true now? They were halfway through this trip to England. The journey had been a destination for so long, she had forgotten about the other side of it—the cliff edge, where she left, plummeted back to earth. Every evening was closer to the last evening. Just like the Nine and their doomed trip to Merryweather, counting down to the last moments of togetherness.

Behind her, Janelle and Vi were going through the schedule for the last full day of the trip. Tomorrow. Tea. Theater. After this, just one more full day.

"What is *Richard III* about?" Janelle asked Vi. "I've never read it, which I guess is embarrassing, but I don't really like Shakespeare."

Who is, at that age? College age is what Sooz meant. Which was around the age Stevie and her friends were now. David would remain here, in the warm air of pubs and the student house and the London Tube. This was his life now. Who knew what would happen next? And they were spending so much time with Izzy, or doing something for Izzy or related to Izzy. Izzy had done nothing wrong. She'd been complimentary, excessively so. She seemed to believe in Stevie more than anyone. But maybe that was something you did if you were covering for something. Because apparently no one was faithful. . . .

"Paranoia," Vi said.

Stevie dribbled coffee down her chin and onto her tablet.

"It's about paranoia," Vi went on. "And wanting a horse really, really bad. I think. I just read the Wikipedia entry."

"I've been thinking," Janelle said. Anyone was invited to listen, but it was mostly directed at Vi. "Maybe I should do an engineering degree, and then a medical degree. To make medical devices. You can do that without being a doctor, but

254

a doctor would really know how they'd be used. Right?"

"That's so much school," Vi said. "You'd be in school forever."

"Well, the engineering degrees, those are four or five years, depending. I could get it done in four. And then probably one year to do the premed requirements. Then four years of medical school. Then the intern period, which is somewhere around three or five years . . ."

"That's so much school," Vi said again. "You'd be in your thirties before you were done."

"Yes, but I could still make things all during that time. I could . . . I don't know. It's just a thought. But if we were going to school in Boston, we'd have so many options. Or New York . . ."

The conversation fizzled quietly. Nate squeezed the air in the bag of potato chips he was holding and it came open with a surprise pop.

Pop.

Something moved inside the dark corridors of Stevie's brain. Something was alive in there. An idea. A pop. A noise. An unexpected noise. Like a firework. A leftover firework from Bonfire Night. The big celebration every year to mark the time Parliament didn't explode.

"Get up," she said to David, who was still watching something on his phone. She nudged him out of his seat and went to the luggage area at the head of the car. She hauled her bag out. She knelt in the aisle, taking it up completely, as she attempted to find the space to get it open. Someone was

255

trying to get back from the bathroom and found Stevie on the floor in the way.

"Sorry," she said, tugging at the fire safe. "One second."

It was more than a second. It was an awkward struggle that took several minutes. She lugged the fire safe back to the table, forcing everyone to clear cups and wrappers. She took the aisle seat, which David had vacated for the window one.

"When you need to remember something . . . ," she said to the group. "You're a historian and you need to remember. What do you remember? Remember, remember . . . What's the date again? The date to remember? The one with the fireworks?"

"The fifth of November," Izzy said.

She tried 1105. Nothing.

But that was the wrong way around, of course. Here, it would be 0511.

The case clicked open.

17

"WELL," DAVID SAID. "WILL YOU HOLY SHIT THAT."

The six of them were pressed around the little train table. Janelle and Vi leaned over David's and Stevie's seats. Before them, spread out in a neat array, was a selection of documents.

Official documents. Police documents, mostly. Full-sized prints of thirty-five photographs. Seven witness statements. A copy of notes from the detective in charge of the case. Autopsy reports. A photocopy of a newspaper article. And on top, a note on lined notebook paper in what Izzy identified as Angela's handwriting. It read:

> Order of events, times approximate:
>
> Right before game Rosie said
> "I saw something I didn't understand,
> but I do now"
> "It was in the paper"
> "You won't believe me, I don't believe

me" does not believe self

Sooz came

Talk later because game starting

11 p.m. game begins, last sighting of Rosie going out front door with me, no one else sees her

11.15 Theo found (inside house, found by Sebastian)

11.30 Yash found (inside house, found by Sebastian and Theo together)

Time unclear, but probably before midnight: Julian and Sooz see Noel in back garden

12.30 I am found (stables, found by Theo)

1.00 Peter found (back garden, found by Yash)

1.30 Sooz (walled formal garden, found by Peter)

2.30 lights go out, Julian found, return to house

3–3.30 Sooz sees torchlight at the side of house, coming from the general direction of the woodshed and drive

"She was investigating the case," Stevie said. This was obvious, of course, but this treasury of documents was so monumental, she couldn't help but state it out loud. "How did she get all of this?"

"She's a researcher," Izzy said. "That's her job. She knows people and knows how to get things. But this means the thing about the lock was *real*. What she said about thinking one of her friends was a murderer was *real*."

"Well," Stevie said, "it means that she was looking into the case, which she could still do even if she was looking for burglars who murdered her friends."

Izzy tapped on the timeline notes.

"She's making notes about where everyone was," she said. "Because she thought one of them did it."

Stevie ran her eye over the pile. One of these things didn't belong. The newspaper article. It had nothing to do with the events at Merryweather.

BODY OF MISSING AMERICAN STUDENT FOUND

The body of missing American student Samantha Gravis has been found in the River Cam near Grantchester Meadows. Local resident Donald Worth was walking his dog along the riverside early yesterday morning when his dog became attracted to something in an area of natural debris and overgrowth. As he tried to move his dog from the spot, he noticed what appeared to be a human form trapped in the collected sticks and plants. Police positively identified the victim as Samantha Gravis.

Gravis, 18, was from Portland, in the state of Maine. She had recently graduated from secondary school and was visiting England for the first time. She had been staying with a friend studying at Magdalene College. Gravis spent the week sightseeing and socializing. She was last seen by her friends at 2.00 a.m. on the morning of 15 June. The friends had been having a small party for Samantha's last night in Cambridge. She was planning to move on to London to continue her trip. Her friends said that Samantha was moderately inebriated and in very good spirits that night. She told them she had something she needed to do and refused the offer of company on her errand. When she failed to return by the next morning, her friends went looking for her and then alerted the police.

Gravis had expressed to her friends the desire to go punt running—the local Cambridge tradition of running along punts as they are tied up at dock. They had dissuaded her from doing so on previous occasions.

"From our conversations with her companions, we believe the deceased may have been inebriated and punt running," said Detective Chief Constable Nigel Rose. "She had a small wound on the side of her face, consistent with a fall. We believe she was temporarily knocked unconscious, and she drowned. Her body drifted and her foot became stuck on a shopping trolley that was on the bottom of the river. We must emphasize that punt running is extremely dangerous and results in many injuries. This tragic event is evidence of that."

"I assume this was what she means by the thing in the paper," Stevie said. "Does this mean anything to you?"

Izzy read through the article and shook her head.

"No," she replied. "No idea. I mean, aside from the fact that it's dated the same day as the murders."

Stevie took the page back. She had missed that. Sloppy. She couldn't be sloppy.

It didn't seem likely that Angela just collected newspaper articles from the day of the Merryweather murders. This person, Samantha Gravis, had something to do with the case. A quick Google search turned up very little—nothing more than the article had provided. She was American. She was visiting Cambridge. She hit her head and fell into the river and died.

"An American girl falls into a river in Cambridge and dies," Stevie said. "A week later, there's a story about it in the paper. That same day, the Nine leave for Merryweather and two of them are murdered that night. Whoever Samantha Gravis is, she has something to do with this case." Stevie tapped her nails on the table. It was so much to take in. "Okay . . ." She looked at the pile of information. "We need to read through all of this."

They passed the documents around. Stevie began with the crime scene photos. The woodshed was a plain wooden structure with a peaked roof. The wood was variegated, brown in some places and an ashy black in others. It had a solid wooden door with peeling gray paint, partially open. Directly above it was a small ventilation window, much too small for a person, which was propped open a few inches. There were close-up photos of the door and the handle. The door had a rough wooden handle, and the lock system was a metal latch with a padlock. This had been ripped away with a crowbar or some other tool, splinting the wood. The lock was still intact. Just outside the woodshed, about four feet away, there was an overturned wheelbarrow and a bucket in the mud. The interior of the shed was dark in some photos. These revealed a plain, rough space, the back of which was covered in stacks of wood, which also spilled onto the floor. There were scattered tools on the ground—a rake, a shovel. Stevie had to squint to see the form of a human leg coming out of one of the piles.

She did not have to squint in the next few photographs. These were illuminated by police lights, and they showed the true horror of what had taken place. She set the photos down and Izzy reached for them.

"Just so you know," Stevie said, "they're rough."

Izzy picked them up anyway and winced as she sifted through them.

With the picture of the scene in her head, Stevie glanced through the autopsy report, not that there was much of a mystery as to what had killed Rosie and Noel. She exhaled slowly and looked out the window. The backs of houses were gone. Suddenly, they were somewhere entirely different, an open place, with great spreads of land, cut through and quilted into patches by lines of trees or high hedges. Some of these patches of land had horses or sheep or cows grazing. They were in the country now. London was gone, and a different England presented itself. The spaces were wide and wild. And for the first time since this started, she felt a real sense of the danger here.

Angela had not gone off to be by herself. Someone had taken her. Because of this case, because of something she knew or might have been on the verge of knowing. And they were all going right into the heart of the beast. To Merryweather. To the Nine.

18

THEY DISEMBARKED AT CHELTENHAM.

There were several cabs waiting by the station, none of which were the fancy black cabs. They were just normal cars with decals on the side. David, Izzy, and Stevie got into the one, with Janelle, Nate, and Vi following right behind.

"We're going to Merryweather," Izzy said to the driver. "It's . . ."

"I know where it is, love," the driver replied. "I drive people there all the time for weddings."

They were off, down tight roads lined with cottages. Then they were out of the town, driving past fields neatly checkerboarded by hedgerows and rustic fences. The turns were many, and tight, and came without warning. Stevie let out an involuntary low scream as a van came barreling right at them. Izzy smiled and patted her arm. The taxi driver, completely unfazed, pulled as far off to the side as humanly possible, the hedges scraping the car. The van squeezed by, inches from the cab.

"He just went the wrong way?" Stevie said, turning around to watch it drive off.

"This is a two-way road," the driver said. "You're American? You have quite wide roads in America, don't you?"

This was not a two-lane road. This was a tiny, tiny, tiny path surrounded by a high wall of greenery that blocked the view. It was a deathtrap, a meandering thread of madness. It suggested that there was something about English people that she may never understand.

She looked to David, who had the decency to look a little startled himself, though he had not actually screamed.

They turned down an even more narrow road, which ran along a low stone wall and ended in a gate. The driver, seemingly used to this, accessed a button that was concealed on a panel in the overgrowth. After a polite pause, the gate swung inward. They drove down a track between a higher brick wall and trees, and then the vista on the left opened onto something that was right out of any one of the many period dramas or mysteries that Stevie had seen. There was a vast house of sand-gold stone that seemed to be alive with climbing vines of a shocking autumnal red.

"Can't pull up the front," the driver said, guiding the car into a gravel parking area off to the side. Moments later, the second car stopped next to them.

"I'm never doing that again," Nate said, stepping woozily out of the back of the car. "Whatever that Six Flags reject ride was."

"It was a small road," Janelle said, looking equally uncomfortable. Only Vi seemed to have enjoyed the experience.

"Hello!" called a plummy English voice from the other

side of a high brick wall. "Hell*o*!"

A black gate in the wall opened, and Sebastian appeared. There was no mistaking him. He was more ample in his build now, his face a bit more jowly and his hair silvered. He was dressed in gray pants and a simple but likely expensive black sweater, with white detailing down the sleeves. He made his way quickly across the gravel, talking as he went.

"Oh, you're here! I hope the train ride was all right. Izzy. Izzy!"

He wrapped her in a massive embrace.

"Has there been news?" he said, pulling back enough to look down at her.

She shook her head.

"How are you?"

"I'm not sure," she said.

"Well, quite, but we're going to sort it all out, don't you worry. Now, is this everyone? Please introduce me."

Izzy made the round of introductions. Sebastian took note of all the names as she went and then repeated them back correctly.

"Right," he said, clasping his hands together. "Come through the front, won't you? I'll take you in the proper way."

He indicated a different gate through another high brick wall, which led into a private garden, lined with topiary, with benches and planted beds, with a winding gravel path.

"Welcome to Merryweather," he said, turning as he led them along past a small fountain.

He put his arm over Izzy's shoulders and leaned in to

266

speak to her. David fell in beside Stevie as they made their way through the twisting garden path.

"There's something going on in your head," he said quietly. "I saw it on the train. What is it?"

"Can't," Stevie said in a low voice. "Not now."

David frowned.

There was a break in the topiary wall that Stevie didn't even see. Sebastian stepped up to it and led them to a long front stone porch. Did you call this a porch? Her house in Pittsburgh had a porch, with a crooked mailbox, a God Bless America banner, and two wicker chairs that housed generations of spiders. This was not a porch—this was a stone stage, balustraded, punctuated on the corners with lichen-marbled urns. Below it rolled lawns and gardens that seemed to stretch on for miles and miles, taking in the hills around, which were patchworked in dark green hedge lines and trees. Far down, sheep grazed freely, baaing and milling around. It seemed like they were utterly alone in the world here, in a peaceful idyll.

A stage waiting for an audience. That's what it was.

Sebastian ushered them under a columned portico, in through an outer then an inner door, into a grand, high-ceilinged hall. Even though there was a fair number of them coming into what should have been an echoing space, Stevie was immediately aware of how Merryweather seemed to eat sound. There was the grandfather clock by the stairs that made a loud, ticking heartbeat.

"They're here!" Sebastian bellowed. His voice was big—a

professional voice—which took up that void. "You can set your things here, and leave your coats just there, on that table."

He indicated a long side table with a marble top and no visible function. Above it hung a painting of a man with a shotgun and a dog, which felt like more of a warning than a greeting.

"Come through, come through," Sebastian said. "We're here in the sitting room. Just made some tea."

Of course there was tea. Stevie had started looking forward to it. This one had already been laid out on a large tray on an ottoman. Sitting by the fire was a Black woman dressed in a gray cowl neck sweater dress, black tights, and tall, flat-soled boots. Her hair was cropped close to her head.

"You remember Theo?" he said to Izzy.

"Of course!" Izzy accepted a hug from Theo.

The introductions were made again. Theo, they were told, was "an A&E physician" at St. Thomas's Hospital in London.

"I've got everything organized," Sebastian said. "All the rooms are ready. Sooz will be here any moment. Peter and Yash are on the way. Julian will be coming later this evening, probably after dinner."

Tea and a few biscuits were quickly consumed, then Sebastian guided them back out into the hall. Their American voices seemed to echo baldly through the space. The man in the painting was unimpressed. Even his dog wasn't happy about their sudden appearance. They went up the stairs, which were lined with portraits of people who looked like they hated being in portraits. There were so many paintings—paintings of large, sweaty horses, fainting women, thin sunrises breaking over cottages and pastures, several ships in perilous seas, drooling Labradors, a man in medieval clothing being stabbed through a curtain. It was sadness, seasickness, and dread in frame after gilded frame. And there were *things* everywhere. At the top of the stairs, a porcelain bowl sat on a small table for anyone to knock over. Against the wall—a cabinet full of . . . fancy rocks? An oar above a door. A desk with a lute on it. Glass-fronted bookshelves. Ancient, framed photographs. A dish of old-fashioned keys. The jaw of a monstrous sea creature (possibly obtained in one of the sea battles pictured before?). Vases. More vases. A shepherdess made of china. Rugs on top of rugs.

It reminded Stevie of her grandparents, who had a serious addiction to buying things at yard sales and the Harbor Freight store, except they had six air fryers, a whole bunch of old computer monitors, a dartboard from a bar, and a Skee-Ball machine salvaged from a Chuck E. Cheese that had gone up in flames in an insurance fraud arson.

This stuff was different. It was at least more expensive.

"I think I'll put you here, Izzy, in the Bishop's Room," Sebastian said, switching on the light in a sprawling bedroom with pale blue wallpaper and a four-poster bed. "Janelle, how about right here. The Rose Room. The ghost of my great-aunt lives in here, but all she ever does is move people's eyeglasses, so don't worry. She's otherwise charming. Vi? This way, darling. The DeVere Room. Nate, was it? Smashing room over here—the Regent Room. Stevie and David, right this way, around the corner. I've got two lovely rooms back here that face the garden."

David got a room called the Mountjoy Room. His was in bracing shades of deep blue and green. Stevie was guided down two more doors.

"And here you go, Stevie," Sebastian said. "The Lilac Room. You might not be used to English heating. These houses get drafty. There are extra blankets in the chest at the foot of the bed."

"Thanks," Stevie said.

"Not at all, not at all. Let me just pop back downstairs and have a butcher's to see how dinner is coming along. Come and join us when you're ready."

Stevie had absolutely no idea what he meant by "have a butcher's" and was not going to ask.

Once he was gone, she shut the door, took the fire safe from her suitcase, and stashed it under the bed. She went to the window and pushed it open. There were no screens on the windows, so she could lean out a bit and touch the climbing vines that surrounded the window and snaked up the walls. The garden seemed to be functional, with sections of green vegetables and herbs all set out in neat rows, supported with wires and many covered by arches of netting. Some pear trees grew flat along the wall and were heavy with fruit. Beyond the garden was more garden, and beyond that green land rolling along, going right to the hills and the trees. England. Endless, green England.

It would be easy to fall out a window like this, she also noted. Lean out a bit too far to look at a rose or a cloud or a sheep and you'd be sprawled on the terrace stones in no time, Agatha Christie–style.

She shut the window.

The bathroom was nice. There was a massive claw-foot tub and a small sofa. Just to sit on. In the bathroom. She sat on it for a few minutes, staring at the tub, pushing down an anxiety attack that threatened to rise. She breathed slowly, making her exhalations longer than her inhalations.

Angela. That's why she was here. Sure, she had brought everyone here under a bit of a lie, but it was a lie for a good reason, and if you lied for a good reason, was it even a lie?

She needed to tell someone. Nate. Nate would understand. She had to let Nate know, and then she would tell Janelle and Vi and everything would be fine and then she could get on with the business of finding Angela.

She stepped back into the dark paneled hallway and the warren of doors. Stevie crept along, though she couldn't quite tell why she was creeping. There was something about the ornate carpets and runners and all the eyes on the walls and the grandfather clock that suggested that creeping was the only acceptable way to move around a house like this. Clomping was vulgar. Walking was for *poors*. David stepped out of his room.

"Hey," he said. "Going back down?"

"Just need to talk to Nate for a second," she said. Then, lowering her voice, she added, "Do you think they're really fine with us being here?"

"They're English," David said. "They complain when your back is turned. They'll never say it to your face. And they sort of expect Americans to be rude so it kind of doesn't matter."

"Not rude," Sooz said.

Stevie let out a startled sound. A weird one. Kind of like *beep*. Sooz had apparently arrived and had dropped her things in a nearby room. Today she was wearing a deep blue jumpsuit with silver piping. Her curly red hair bounced as she walked.

"Good to see you again. Most Americans I meet are lovely. And I *would* tell you if everyone was annoyed, but the others probably wouldn't. They're more polite. It really is fine that you're here. We might as well be together. Better than sitting alone at home sick with worry. Come down. Sebastian was just saying that he wanted to give you a tour of the grounds."

"I'll be there in a minute," Stevie said.

"I'll come with you," David offered.

"Good. Sebastian!"

Her voiced boomed through the space.

"Yes, darling?" came the reply.

"Do you have anything for a little afternoon bring-me-down?"

"There's a nice little cabernet left over from a wedding a few weeks ago. In the kitchen."

David glanced back at Stevie, then descended the steps.

Stevie continued, backtracking until she found the door of the room that she was pretty sure had been assigned to Nate. She knocked and found him in a room with maroon walls, deep and saturated like drying blood. He had stationed himself on the bed and was looking at his phone.

"Are you enjoying your stay in the *Rocky Horror* house so far?" he asked. "When do we Time Warp?"

"I need to talk to you," she said, shutting the door.

"Why does that fill me with dread? You never need to talk to me about finding a baby dragon or a bottomless pit of KFC. It's always something terrible."

"Quinn didn't say we could come."

Nate lowered his phone to his lap.

"What does that *mean*, exactly? I thought you asked her?"

"I did ask her, but . . ."

"But?"

Stevie looked at her friend.

"But?" he prompted.

"She said no."

Nate put his hand over his eyes.

"That's a joke, right?"

"We'll be back so soon," Stevie cut in. "And I'll take all the blame. All of it. I'll tell her I told you guys she said it was okay. I will take it. All of it."

She allowed him a moment of silence, the heel of his hand pressing into his forehead. He finally lowered it and looked at her seriously.

"You have to tell Janelle and Vi."

"Are you mad?"

"You do this shit, Stevie. This is how you are. I guess I probably knew on some level that Quinn said no and we were going anyway. That's just what happens with you. Lying kind of sucks? And, I don't know, Vi and I can probably take it, but you shouldn't lie to Janelle."

For some reason, this was more painful and difficult than Nate just being mad. He was right. Nate and Vi might roll with this nonsense, but Janelle didn't play around with the truth.

"How bad will it be, do you think?" she asked.

"Bad," he said. "Do it now. And then we have to figure out what to do when Quinn calls."

"I already thought of that. She can't tell where we're calling from, so we can . . ."

He just stared at her.

"Yeah, I . . ."

"Everyone!" Sebastian called. "Would you like the tour?"

"Tell her soon, Stevie. Shit. *I'm* not telling her, and I'm also not going to lie to her."

Lie. It was such a gross word, with spikes on it. She was a *liar*. A fiendish thing. Her throat felt dry.

"I'll tell her tonight," Stevie said. "I promise."

19

Sebastian guided David and Stevie out the front door, and they stood a moment on the grand flagstone porch, overlooking the rolling greens and the sheep and the sunset. Nate had opted out of the tour, and Janelle and Vi had vanished somewhere in the depths of Merryweather. Izzy was deep in conversation with Theo, so only David and Stevie were making the rounds outside.

"Good of you to come with Izzy," Sebastian said, leading them down the steps to the lawn. "How is she doing?"

"She's nervous," David said as they descended the low stone steps onto the lawn.

"So are we all. Julian should be bringing news. Until then, keep calm and carry on, I suppose. And you get to see a bit more of England. See a place like this. My family has lived here since 1675. Somebody in the family did something or other for the king and got the land and an old house as a gift. This is the kind of thing I'm supposed to care about and remember, but I don't. They tore that house down and built a new one, and then a hundred years later, some other ancestor of mine decided that house wasn't quite right and ripped it down and built this one. Madness. But here it is."

He waved a hand in the direction of the house that reared up behind them.

"I'd never be able to keep this place if it didn't pay for itself," he said. "It's absurd for one person or family to own something like this, but here we are. Now it earns its keep by hosting weddings and events, film shoots, things like that. Spring and summer, Christmas and New Year's . . . those are the busiest times. But there's going to be a film crew here in two weeks' time to shoot some scenes for a new period drama. It's quite fun when that happens. I've worked as an extra in a few things. I played a butler once. Even got a line."

He smiled.

"All the grand rooms, I leave those open for guests and filming. The top floor is where I live. Those are the poky servants' rooms, but there's loads of space and I knocked a few of them through to make myself a bigger bedroom and lounge. My husband is an antiques expert for Sotheby's. He's in Vienna at the moment, appraising items for an auction. He's absolutely mad for boot sales—or yard sales, you call them? He can spot a treasure in a pile of dreck and picks it up for a tenner or something. And so, we live in a pile of tea sets and Georgian tripod tables that people found in their attics and basements."

"When did your husband leave?" Stevie said, trying to sound casual. "For his trip?"

"Last week. These large estate sales are complicated affairs."

They walked down and around a small pond at the base of the lawn. At its far edge, facing the house, was what looked like a tiny Greek temple.

"The folly," he said. "Very good spot for wedding photos from here. Careful!"

He grabbed Stevie by the arm.

"Ha-ha," he said.

Stevie stared. He indicated that she should look at the place she was about to step. The lawn cut away suddenly and there was a sheer drop of about four feet. There was nothing there to mark it—no wall or ornament of any kind. It was not clearly visible at all.

"This is a ha-ha," he explained. "It's a kind of garden architecture designed to keep animals out—in this case, the sheep and deer—without affecting the line of the vista. The point is that you can't see them. I suppose that's why they're called ha-has? Sorry, I should have warned you. This way."

He guided them toward the drive, to where the lawn gave way to a line of trees where the ground was littered with a rich, soft layer of golden brown.

"Back in the day," Sebastian said, taking a high step over a fallen branch, "we had a head gardener named Chester. He was about a hundred and sixty when I was born. His father was one of the original gardeners. He grew up here and knew every corner, every plant. He tried to teach me about them when I was a child. I had little interest in most of them, but I always had a thing about mushrooms. They're the odd little children of the forest. I suppose I related. There . . ."

He squatted down and pointed to a toadstool with a bright red cap and white spots.

"That," he said, "is called fly agaric. Very common. Pretty. Your basic *Alice in Wonderland* mushroom, or if you like Mario games, that's the kind of mushroom they're indicating. Mildly psychoactive."

David regarded the mushroom with interest.

"Believe me, I tried all the ones that I thought were magic," Sebastian said, noting this. "Threw up quite a lot but never poisoned myself, which is lucky. Once he realized I was eating the mushrooms, Chester made sure I knew what was what. Over here—they're often over here—yes, there's one . . ."

He tromped over to a nondescript bit of fallen leaves and vegetation, knocking some aside with a stick. He indicated a plain brown mushroom with a thick stem.

"*Amanita phalloides.* Death cap. Doesn't look like much, but it's *very* dangerous. Absolutely will kill you. They think this is what killed the roman emperor Claudius. It's always the quiet ones, you know? This boring-looking mushroom is the deadliest thing around. You're a detective. I thought you'd like to know the deadly things of the woods."

Stevie did, in fact, want to know that kind of thing, and she appreciated that Sebastian understood that.

Sebastian took them up the gravel drive, and then along an ivy-covered high brick wall, and through a gate into an elaborate garden, full of sections of flowers, a fountain, a pathway, and a burbling tiny stream that trickled through it.

"We're more famous for the gardens than the house. They were designed in 1910 by my great-grandfather, Sylvester Holt-Carey, who was mad as a bag of gravy about gardens. Had squadrons of gardeners make the place, got cuttings and plants from all over the world."

They could see through the sitting room window. Theo was standing and speaking to someone. She saw them go by and raised a hand. Sebastian raised a hand in greeting back. They passed through the formal garden, through a kitchen garden, and then to the back of the house. Unlike the front, which had a clear, rolling path, this garden immediately put up several walls of greenery, some low, some high. This was another mansion, just outdoors and made of organic materials, rooms and rooms of plants, fountains, trees, and paths. Now she knew what they all meant about the back gardens—the whole thing was a confusing maze of plants and path and wall and border. If Sebastian left them alone in here, it would take them a half hour to find their way out.

They entered a perfect circle, walled with tall topiary yew trees, with a small pavilion and a burbling lion's head fountain.

"I've partnered with an organization that works with people who are struggling with addiction. We host at least four retreats a year here to help people get away for concentrated therapy. My goal is to turn it into a residence where people can be treated—a proper home for people who need it. I just have to make the house work for itself a bit longer to get all the repairs done so the floors don't cave in. It's not very restorative to have an entire bedroom land on you. This space is particularly good for meditation. Many of our guests have said so."

"Can I ask you something?" Stevie said.

Even though she had only just met Sebastian, and he her, there was no time to waste.

"Please do," he replied.

"Is Angela the type of person who goes away and doesn't tell anyone?"

"No," he said. "Ange has her moments of spontaneity, but she wouldn't go away and leave everyone worrying. She was texting us that very night, said she wanted to meet us all. Here, in fact."

He pulled out his phone, navigated to the text chain he wanted, and passed it to Stevie. Stevie did not mention she had seen this exact chain before, and having it handed to her made questioning that much easier.

"What did she mean about the button?" Stevie asked.

"I have absolutely no idea. I assumed that was an autocorrect."

"When did you last see Angela?"

"At a party," he said. "A few weeks ago. At Peter's house. Yash and Peter won an award for their show, *Fish in a Barrel*. It's a comedy panel show about current events. Don't know if you've ever seen it. It's very good."

"How did she seem?"

"Utterly normal," he said. "Much fun had by all. I only drink tonic water and I'm early to bed, so I left first, with

Theo. But Ange was there and in fine form."

"So why do you think she wanted to come here and talk about . . . what happened?"

"Well . . ." Sebastian sat on a bench alongside the yew border. David and Stevie perched on the edge of the fountain. "I'll tell you something. The events of that night—they changed us. Obviously. I mean that it fundamentally altered who we all are. It's funny, living here, with that memory. That's the thing about places like this—they've been witness to so many events. Wars. It's like they're built to absorb those kinds of blows. They become part of the place. By seeing it every day, maybe I've been able to process it more. But at times we all need to. It can't be avoided. It must be faced. It must have been on her mind."

"But there was nothing going on? No suspect or anything?"

"They'll never catch them now," Sebastian said, shaking his head. "I don't think this is the kind of case DNA will solve. The rain had gotten in, and I don't know if they kept everything."

"Do you mind talking about it?" she asked.

"No," he said. "Like I said, I keep it present in my thoughts."

He crossed his long legs and sat back in the position of a person who is about to tell a tale.

"My father, the late and unlamented fifth viscount, was a bit of a bastard. He had one child, me, and he did not want a gay son. He made that *very* clear. So I took that as a challenge to become the most flamboyant, most lively person I could be. I drank. It was university. Everyone drank. That's how it is. But I *really* drank. I took all the prizes. I also smoked a remarkable amount of cannabis. I read chemistry, believe it or not. Always been good at it. That may be why Theo and I have always been so close—we're the science-y ones. Of course, she worked bloody hard and I worked as little as possible.

"There are four grades when you take your exams and leave Cambridge. You can get a first—that's for the brilliant people who kept their pencils sharp and put in the hours. That's what Theo got. Then there's a two-one and a two-two. Those are the middle grades. The two-one means you did quite well indeed. The two-two is acceptable and maybe you enjoyed a little too much sport and time at the pub, but good enough. A third means you made it through somehow. And because the exam results are ranked, I worked out in advance how to do the absolute bare minimum and still pass. I wanted the bottom grade. I got the exam paper, did precisely what I needed to do, then was the first one to walk out of the exam room and make it down to the pub. I took great pride in that. It didn't matter anyway because I wanted to act. But then, *it* happened. The events of June 1995."

He looked up at a massive black bird that had landed on the head of the figure on the fountain and was cawing at them relentlessly.

"I do not handle complaints in person," he said to the bird. "Please contact us via our website."

This seemed to satisfy the bird. It flew away.

"So," he said, "I went to London. I had some money—a little something that came to me from a relative. Not a lot, but enough to get a grubby flat, which I shared with Sooz. She put her all into auditioning and performing. I put everything I had into being the very best lout I could be. Things got very, very bad indeed. I started taking any drug I could get my hands on. I never wanted to think or remember. Sooz tried to help me, but I think I could get away with some of it making it seem like I was just a bon vivant. A year and a half after the incident, it all came to an end. I found myself on the floor in the toilets of some club, the paramedics over me. Who even knows what I'd taken. I wound up in the hospital getting my stomach pumped. Apparently, it was quite a close call. My family wasn't speaking to me at the time, because of the drugs. It was this lot . . ."

He pointed in the direction of the house, but Stevie knew he meant his friends.

". . . who came to my side. It was Theo who was there when I opened my eyes. They talked to me. They got me into a program. They supported me every step of the way. I got clean and sober and I remain clean and sober. But I think it's because I went down very low and got quite a lot of therapy that I overcame the horror of it. Or I learned to live with it. I came out the best of all, but I had to go all the way down before I came back up. And I was gifted with this place. I'm the lucky one, and I never, ever forget it. The others are . . . lonely. Theo is an emergency doctor, so she barely has time for herself, let alone anyone else. Sooz has partners who come and go. Angela was married to Marvin, but . . . I never saw that lasting, and it didn't. Peter's been married twice, and both times it ended badly. Yash never seemed to have any luck in the romance department, though I think there's someone he's been pining for, for many years. Julian, well . . ."

He shrugged apologetically.

"Julian is the textbook politician. The one who gets caught cheating and has to give a speech about the mistakes he's made. But he is very good at what he does, so his constituents vote him back in. Which is the right thing to do if you ask me. He works very hard. But I think it . . . if I say it cursed us, that sounds diabolical and supernatural. I mean that it broke us all in some way. We're still the Nine. We're still in many ways the most important people in each other's lives. As long as we have each other, that's all that matters."

Those words struck her. His friends—they were all that mattered.

She had lied to her friends. She was *in the state of lying* at this very second.

"Come on," Sebastian said, standing up and breaking the mood. He led them back the way they'd come, out of the back gardens and off to the side of the house, where there was a garage and two parked cars.

"Over here," he said, leading them through a few trees.

And there it was. The woodshed. It was bigger than it looked in the photos.

"I should tear the damn thing down, but it feels wrong," he said. "I can't do it."

The door of the woodshed was new, and it locked with a normal door key, not a padlock. Sebastian opened this, revealing a plain box of a space, containing a rider mower and dozens of hay bales. The windows were coated with old cobwebs that had stuck together and formed gray strips, and the windowsills were lined with cans of WD-40 and other cans and bottles of oils and garden sprays. It smelled of sweet hay and gasoline. This was not the first time Stevie had stood at the site of a murder. What struck her here, as it had in the past, was how ordinary it was. No neon sign. No arrow. No statue or marker. It was a shed—a big shed, but a shed. She walked its perimeter to get the size of it. It looked to be about ten feet by fifteen feet or thereabouts, something about the size of two cars. It appeared to be in the same condition as it was in the photographs, not freshly painted, but in a similar state of faded gray and brown. She examined the door. The latch had been replaced, of course, but upon close inspection she could see minute scars in the wood where the old latch had been ripped away.

There was something else in what Sebastian had just said—the thing about the death cap mushroom. It looked so innocent. So dull. So ordinary.

"Just a nasty old outbuilding," he said, looking around. "I don't use it for firewood anymore. Built a new shed for that. Now it's mowers and these hay bales, which we use for event seating outside. Sit around the fire on an autumn evening,

285

have a hot chocolate or a nice glass of port."

Stevie looked up and around. Something was confusing her. Something she'd just seen, or hadn't seen, in those crime scene photos. The shed had a window, high up, near the peak of the roof. When she looked up now, there was no high window, no peak. The ceiling was flat, and now that she thought about it, it was lower than the overall height of the building. Which meant there was something *above* them. A quick scan of the ceiling revealed a rope pull and the faint outline of a pull-down opening.

"What's up there?" she asked.

"Just a crawl space," he said.

When you want someone to tell you something—don't ask, tell it wrong.

"Oh," Stevie said. "That's where the robbers hid, right?"

"Oh no," he said. "No. No, that wasn't used. The floor was rotted away."

"So no one could have hidden up there?"

"No." Sebastian shook his head. "My parents sealed it up. It was a deathtrap."

Perhaps sensing that this was the wrong choice of words, he rubbed his eyes.

"It's since been replaced for safety reasons," he added. "Considering what had happened in there, we didn't want anyone else hurt."

Maybe it was all the time she'd spent around tour guides in the last week, but Stevie could now feel in her bones when the tour was coming to an end.

"Would you mind," she said as Sebastian went to the door. "I have this school thing I have to do. I need to take some pictures, and it would be great if I could pose on the hay bales? Would it be okay to use one or two? I'll put them back."

Sebastian accepted this and left them, perhaps thinking that American schools gave out vague, hay-adjacent assignments and hoped for the best. It wasn't entirely wrong.

"Hay?" David said as soon as Sebastian was gone. "What are you doing?"

Stevie closed the woodshed door, leaving them in darkness. She pulled her phone out and turned on the flashlight, pointing it toward the ceiling. She reached for the rope pull, but it was just an inch or two out of her grasp.

"Grab that," she said to David. "Pull it."

"Buy me dinner first."

She elbowed him in the ribs, maybe a touch too hard, because he started coughing. He reached up and pulled on the rope, opening the hatch. There was a folding ladder, which Stevie indicated he should pull down.

"It's a nice change," he said. "Usually, we go into creepy holes in the ground. I've enjoyed going up into creepy holes instead."

Once the ladder was down, Stevie wasted no time climbing up. She expected that she might be about to stick her head into the home of a million billion spiders, that would immediately swarm her. Instead, she got a strong smell of old leaves and dirt. There was nothing up there, really. Just a bit of dead space, about four feet high, containing nothing but dirt and a few broken-down cardboard boxes. She banged on the floorboards a few times with her fist, both to test their sturdiness and to shake out any mice or other creatures that might be around. No visible movement.

Stevie got as high on the ladder as she could, while resting her body on the crawl space floor and sliding along. She elbow-crawled forward. She pushed herself up to a crouch and went over to the window. It was even smaller than it looked from below. She tried to raise it up, but the wood had warped, and she was barely able to move it more than a few inches.

David hoisted himself up and into the crawl space to join her.

"This is nice," he said. "What are we doing?"

Stevie scanned through the photos on her phone.

"Look," she said. "Here's the photo Sooz took when they arrived on the night of the murder. This window . . ."

She pointed at the window behind them.

". . . was closed. But then look at this police photo from the next day."

Stevie had, of course, taken pictures of all the documents on the train. She pulled up the police photo that most clearly showed the outside of the shed.

"It's open," she says, pointing at the window. "Sometime between the night they arrived and the time the police were here the next day, this window was opened. Sebastian just said the floor up here was rotted away and there was no access. And look . . ."

She pulled up another crime scene photo, one that showed the blood splatter on the ceiling. It also clearly showed the hole where the rope pull should have been.

"No rope," she said. "So how does someone come up to this supposedly inaccessible place to open a window a few inches after a murder?"

"Does it matter?" David asked. "Nobody could get through that."

"Well, not nobody. There are people who can disjoint their collarbones and squeeze through dog doors. Or people who can do certain contortions."

"So, creepy people. Or circus folk."

"Also, why? They busted the lock off the door. Why dislocate your collarbones and crawl through an impossible opening when you can go through the door? Which is what happened."

"Maybe the police opened it?"

Stevie frowned.

"Policing was different then," she said. "Crime scenes weren't handled as well. But I feel like they wouldn't *open the crime scene window* and then photograph it that way. There's nothing in these reports about coming up here. I mean, I read them pretty quickly on the train, but I would have seen something about a crawl space above the murder site. That's kind of critical. No. The police had no idea this space was here. They never looked."

"What does that mean?" David asked. "Someone came to a place that seems to be inaccessible, to do something that has no point?"

"It means," she said, "that this matters. This crawl space. That window. This whole woodshed. It's locked, it's unlocked. The floor is rotted and there was no way to get up here, yet someone was up here."

"You make it sound like Sebastian was lying about the rotted floor."

Stevie was silent for a moment, as the last of the daylight ebbed away.

"Maybe he was," she said.

"But Sebastian was the one person everyone could see the whole time, right? Up at the folly? So why lie about this? I don't get it."

"I don't either," she said. "We better get back inside. I think we may have left our friends with a murderer."

20

Dinner, as they say, was served.

Merryweather's dining room was the kind of place that could accommodate eleven people for dinner and have plenty of room to spare. Because it was used for weddings and events, there were multiple tables and chairs folded along one of the sides of the room. There was a massive silver mirror over a marble-tiled fireplace. The walls were papered in a buttery yellow silk with a painted pattern of crawling vines, birds, and flowers.

"Forgive the simplicity," Sebastian said as everyone was seated. "I just had time to put together a basic menu."

A woman appeared from a hidden door that blended right in with the rest of the wall. She was short, with close-cropped black hair and an intricate tattoo sleeve of twisted ivy, flowers, and barbed wire.

"This is Debbie," he said. "She's the events manager. I asked her to pop round and give me a hand."

A general round of hellos for Debbie.

The basic menu started with a cauliflower and chive soup, served up in plain white catering china, along with baskets of warm bread. Debbie served these to each person as Sebastian wound around the table with bottles, pouring drinks.

"White or red?" he asked as he got to Stevie. "I have sparkling elderflower as well."

Stevie had had wine before, but no one with an English accent in a long dining room in a country house had ever approached her before to offer her wine like she was an actual goddamned fancy adult. Because she was not one. An adult. Or fancy. She didn't come from the kind of family that had wine with dinner. They had Diet Coke, like decent Americans. If her parents had been offered red or white wine with dinner, they'd probably have pulled a gun in surprise.

"Uhhhhhh," she explained.

Sebastian gracefully turned to Izzy to give Stevie time to compose further remarks.

"I'll just have the elderflower," Izzy said. "Not really feeling up to wine tonight."

The group nodded sympathetically.

Stevie had recovered enough to figure out her drink. She would do what Izzy did—she would have whatever sparkling elderflower was. (It turned out to be sort of like Sprite. Fancy Sprite, for fancy people.)

"This dairy-based, Seb?" Sooz asked as the soup was set in front of her.

"No, darling. It's vegan. I checked."

"I'm vegan," Sooz explained to the newcomers, though

that much could have been gathered from the previous exchange.

"You've been known to eat meat," Sebastian said.

Sooz's mouth twisted into a grin.

"Not for years," she said. "No. I'm entirely plant-based now."

Theo frowned at this and turned pointedly to Stevie and the others.

"Is your school food quite dismal?" she asked politely. "Or is it all right?"

"It's a lot of syrup," Stevie said.

"And moose," David added. "Moose steak with syrup. Delicious."

This remark was allowed to die a peaceful, polite death.

"Pete," Sooz said, "Yash—what were you two talking about before?"

"Just a new show idea we've been bandying about," Yash said. "Early doors."

"Oh!" Sooz said. "What's it about?"

"It needs work," Peter replied.

"They're always like this," Theo said. "Always have been. Yash pitches the ideas. Peter shoots them down. Yash refines. Peter figures out the problems. And together they eventually come up with something brilliant."

"I come up with ideas all the time," Peter said. "Just because I'm not indiscriminate . . ."

"That's what your mum told me last night," Yash replied.

"You see what I'm working with?"

They continued like this, bantering without pause as the dark night settled down around them. Debbie brought out dishes of sausages and mashed potatoes and salad. ("The mash is plant-based, right, Seb? And which is the veggie sausage?") The group spoke breathlessly, endlessly, grabbing the tails of each other's sentences, understanding every nuance. What they were talking about, Stevie largely had no idea. This was the conversation of people who had known each other for a long time, who were so intimately aware of each other that they had their own language. They all seemed to have a deep, penetrating knowledge of everything going on in the world—politics, art, books, music. They all sounded so self-assured. That wasn't surprising, considering that they were older and successful.

Izzy slid right into this conversation, speaking confidently on the subject of wind farms, some scandal in Parliament, and *Bake-Off*. Her royal-blue sweater, which, now that Stevie was looking more closely, was both small and large on her in precisely the right way. It was a shape and size of sweater that had evolved from all the lesser sweaters of the past, achieving this effortless final form. Had Stevie worn the sweater, it would have ended up wrong somehow. The neckline would suddenly be weird, and the shoulders would sag. She would disappoint the sweater. Stevie only truly understood hoodies, which felt very American and unsophisticated and maybe a little Unibombery. She pulled down on her sleeves to cover her hands, then realized what she was doing and pushed the sleeves partially up to her elbows. This too was wrong, so she let the sleeves fall back to her wrists.

That salad dressing from the plane was still visible on her hoodie.

Stevie wasn't an unaware person. She read a lot. She knew the basics. But she found herself struck dumb, confused, and freaked out. Janelle could easily keep pace with almost everything being discussed, especially if it involved science or crafting. Vi was shockingly up to speed on UK politics, even more so than David, who was here studying international affairs. Only Nate and Stevie kept to themselves. Nate focused on the food, and Stevie watched the people. Everyone around this table was pointedly avoiding the reason they were all here. There was no mention of Angela. Everything was light, flowing, and desperately avoiding the terrible matter at hand. Stevie got the sense they were waiting for something—a boom to go with the tick tick of the clock.

As she ate her sausages, she looked at the intricate design of the walls. It took a few moments to work out that the pattern was not repeating. This wasn't just some nice wallpaper that had been carefully lined up to make the pattern match—it was a continuous, varied piece of art, not repeated designs.

"It's silk," Sebastian said. "Hand painted."

He had obviously seen her intently examining the walls.

"It's one continuous picture. I think it was done sometime around 1920. It's a little worn in places, but with the lights low you can't tell. It's quite a piece of work. I'm not sure you could get something like it now that could wrap the whole room in a big piece of art."

One long, continuous picture. Not pieces. One picture.

"So," Yash said as the plates were cleared and Debbie came in with sticky toffee puddings. "Tell us about detecting. You've solved two cases?"

Stevie wrung her hands in her lap.

"Well, four. Kind of. Or . . . it depends on how you count them."

"How do you do it?" Sooz said, leaning over the table. "You don't have a DNA lab in your room at school, I assume. How do you solve murders? What's your *process?*"

"I . . . I just kind of . . . look at everything."

"Old-school," Peter said.

Perhaps realizing that discussing Stevie's career might take the conversation down some dark paths, they moved on to Nate.

"You wrote a book?" Theo said. "*The Moonbright Cycles?*"

"I read that," Peter said, perking up. "My daughter loved it, wanted me to read it. So I did."

He did not, Stevie noticed, say he loved it. That didn't mean he hadn't liked it. But Stevie had spent enough time around Nate to know now that if someone read his book and didn't specifically say they liked it, then he assumed they hated it. It would be worse if they said they liked it. If that had happened, Nate would have crawled into the fireplace and set himself on fire. Writers were weird. Talking to them was like talking to spiders—the mere breath of speech sent them running.

Nate began shoveling sticky toffee pudding into his mouth. They moved on to Janelle, discussing her engineering skills, the machines she made, her Rube Goldberg entries. Vi talked about becoming a translator.

"And what do you do, David?" Yash asked.

David nodded. "As little as possible," he said, taking a sip of red wine. It was a glib reply, but everyone gave it a polite laugh and Sebastian toasted him with a glass of water. "I have learned a lot since I've been here, though. Like about the Salmon Act 1986. It's illegal to handle salmon . . ."

". . . in a *suspicious manner*," Yash and Peter said, almost in unison.

"We write jokes for a news show called *Fish in a Barrel*," Peter explained. "It's our job to know stupid laws about fish."

"There are more than you would think," Yash added.

Stevie didn't like how that conversation had gone down. David was smart. David could program. David studied international relations here and had volunteered for a voting rights organization at home, but he didn't quite have a *thing* like the rest of them did. And he joked about it, but she saw him shift a little in the chair. The smile was thin. She was about to say something about all the volunteer work he had done over the summer, but there was a sound in the hallway. Someone was coming into the house.

Everyone at the table straightened up.

"Jules," Sooz said, pushing back her chair.

A minute later, a man entered the dining room. Well, other people *entered* rooms—Julian Reynolds changed their spatial orientation. All chairs, eyes, and energies magnetically pointed toward him.

His hair was the color of beach sand, with an elegant soft gray on the sides. He was immaculately dressed in gray pants and a royal-blue shirt that he must have known brought out the color of his eyes. Stevie had read the phrase "piercing blue eyes" many times and never knew why eyes would be described that way. Eyes are notoriously round and squishy and would burst like a water balloon if deployed as a weapon. Julian's were blue like pool water, and just as clear. They invited you to dive in and examine their depths. You were in the wordless, intimate conversation that comes with making such strong eye contact with a stranger. You were hooked.

"Sorry I'm late," he said, gracefully removing his camel-colored coat. "I had surgery this evening."

Debbie hustled over to disappear the coat, and all the Nine got up to greet their friend.

"You know Isabelle, Ange's niece," Sebastian said. "And these are her American friends."

He said all of this like they'd been friends for life—as if he'd been waiting for the moment where he could introduce them.

"Can I bring you a plate of food?" Debbie asked. "It's still warm. Sausage and mash, and some soup?"

"I had a sandwich on the train, thank you," he said. "But a pudding would be lovely, and some coffee. I have some things I'd like to discuss."

"Why don't we go through to the sitting room?" Sebastian said. "We'll have coffee in there by the fire."

Everyone made their way out of the dining room and into the main hall.

"I think they want to talk," Janelle said in a quiet voice. "We're going to go upstairs."

"I think that's the move," David added.

Everyone in Stevie's contingent made their way toward the staircase, though Stevie wanted to go in and find out what was going on. Luckily, Izzy wanted the same.

"Stevie," Izzy said, "could you come? I think it would be helpful."

Nate gave Stevie a pointed look before turning and heading upstairs.

"Did he just say he had surgery?" Stevie asked before they stepped into the sitting room.

"Oh. He's an MP. When they have public hours that constituents can come in and talk—that's called surgery."

Nothing made any sense here.

It was dark now. The fire had been replenished with wood. Sebastian drew the heavy curtains against the night as Debbie came in with a tray of coffee and tea and a pudding for Julian. She set it down on an ottoman.

"That's all for tonight, Debs," Sebastian said. "Thanks so much for pitching in."

"Is one of these soya or oat milk?" Sooz asked, looking at the tiny jugs on the coffee tray.

"That one with the roses on it is plant-based," Sebastian said, reaching forward to pass it to Sooz. There were only so many times that someone could say the words *plant-based* before they lost all meaning.

"I've been in touch with the police," Julian said, pouring himself a coffee. "I spoke to them on the way here. I've got some information. CCTV shows Ange leaving her house right around ten that evening. She used her Oyster card and took the Tube to Waterloo. She tapped out of the station at ten fifty-five. There's footage of her leaving the station, but it was raining and she put up an umbrella, so it becomes hard to follow her."

"What about her phone?" Stevie asked. "They can check where it pinged."

Julian made a noise that suggested this had not been fruitful.

"The last ping they had was about an hour after that, and fairly close by."

"So she left her house and went to Waterloo," Theo said. "She left the station. On her own?"

"Yes, on her own."

"And nobody saw her hurt," Peter said.

"Exactly," Sooz said. "No news is good news in many

ways? Ange has gone off on an errand or mission, or maybe she just needed some time to herself. People do."

She reached over and patted Izzy's arm.

"I'll keep working on it," Julian said. "I'm scheduled to speak to someone again later this evening."

He drained the rest of his coffee.

Stevie watched Julian for a moment. Despite the liquid ease with which he moved, there was a twitchiness to his movements. Under the shadows of his long eyelashes, the blue-sky eyes clouded with storms.

Unlike everyone else, he was not pretending all was well.

21

A FEW MINUTES LATER, AFTER MAKING HER FAREWELL, STEVIE ascended the creaking steps of Merryweather's grand staircase on her own, the ticking grandfather clock beneath her, and the eyes of the Holt-Careys of the past boring down on her. The ceilings in here were tall enough that pictures were not at eye height—everything was *up*.

She had a choice now. Which room to go to? She could knock on Janelle's door, get this over with. It was nine o'clock, and Quinn still hadn't called. She had to do this soon. She started walking in that direction, but everything began to swim in her head. Angela and the lock. The text about the button. Samantha Gravis. The power outage and the tree down on the road. The rules of the game and the statements about where everyone was that night.

Too many things. She needed to think. She would talk to Janelle in a minute. She returned to her room and paced around, staring at the silver-lilac walls, the painting of a horse, the detailing on the side of the wardrobe. A moment later, there was a soft knock and David stuck his head in.

"Hey," he said, coming in and shutting the door quietly behind him.

"Did they seem really . . . calm to you?" Stevie asked. "No one was talking about Angela."

"They're English," David said, sitting on the bed. "That keep calm and carry on thing is real. You know. Don't talk about stuff that's bad. Talk about tennis! That's how they are."

"It's more than that," she said. "There was something weird about the whole conversation, about all of this. They let us come here with Izzy . . . something is off with all of it, and I can't figure out what it is. It feels . . . claustrophobic."

"I think it's just a weird situation," David said. "And being foreign. Things feel different. You feel out of place a lot."

"But Angela is gone," Stevie said.

"What if she doesn't want to be found? If she thinks one of her friends is a killer, then . . ."

"I thought of that. She sends the texts, realizes she's made a mistake, then takes off. But . . ." Stevie shook her head. "Did you see how many cat toys were in that house? The pictures? She loves that cat. She's not going to leave her cat, not without telling anyone. She's not going to leave that mess. She's not going to go without mentioning something to Izzy—anything, just to keep her from worrying."

David leaned back against the headboard.

"So what does it mean that her phone last pinged by the river on the night she vanished?"

"What do you mean?" Stevie said. "I thought it was near Waterloo Station?"

"Which is directly on the river. It's near where we were the other night, close to the Eye."

See, this was the kind of thing Stevie needed to know to figure out what the hell was going on here.

"Well, that's not good," Stevie said. "I think we can say that Angela is not safe right now. If we want to find Angela, we have to figure out what happened here."

Stevie felt like the answer was dangling nearby, in her peripheral vision. If she turned her head too quickly, it would move. Maybe if she stayed very still, it would float into view. She went over to the window, opened it, and got a face full of cold, autumnal air, loamy and refreshing. It was so dark here. She could see so many stars flecking the sky, and there was a fat moon, glowing white.

Another knock on the door. Even softer. David called for them to come in.

"Sorry," Izzy said. "Am I disturbing you?"

"No," David said. "We were just talking."

Izzy came inside like an embarrassed ghost and shut the door. She took a seat in one of the lavender-colored armchairs in the middle of the room.

"They're in the sitting room talking about shows they used to do," Izzy said. "Julian seems to be the only one *doing* anything. And the thing with her phone . . . should we go back to London right now, to where her phone last was? Why isn't her phone on?"

"So many things could be going on," David was saying to Izzy, trying to reassure her. "She could have just dropped her phone. Or gotten rid of it."

"Why would she get rid of her phone?"

"If she's investigating," David said. "She doesn't want to be found. She's working the case. Right? She could be working the case."

This was to Stevie, who was too distracted by leaning out the window to answer.

"Do you think we should go back to London?" Izzy said. "It's late for a train, but maybe we could borrow a car."

Such an easy fall out this window. Why had she come to the window? Something made her want to come to the window. The window. The garden.

"Stop," she said, holding up her hand.

This was a weird and dramatic way to break into a conversation, but it had to be done.

She slid the fire safe out from under the bed. Even though she had scanned the documents, she wanted to see the original photo for a moment. Feel it in her hand. She dumped all the pictures on the bed, all those scenes printed up in a large, glossy format. She shuffled through them, pulling out the one of the exterior of the woodshed and the one of the missing rope pull. She had snapped a picture of it from the inside before they left the crawl space. She pulled it up and stared at it.

"What did your aunt say to you again?" Stevie asked Izzy. "What *exactly* did she say?"

"What I told you. She said the lock was off the door. She said she thought someone—"

"About the planted evidence. What *exactly* did she say? This is where you need to think carefully, remember what you can. Did she say evidence? Or did she just say planted? Or . . ."

Izzy sat neatly on the edge of the bed and concentrated.

"I can't remember precisely. Let me see. The day she told me, I'd been down to Sainsbury's. I'd gotten her a bunch of soups, and I made her a leek and potato. She was on the sofa in the lounge, watching telly. I think she was watching the Channel 4 news. And . . . that's right. There was something about a murder. That must have been what made her say it."

Izzy did what Stevie did—link events, make a story in her mind.

One continuous picture . . .

"And she said, something along the lines of, 'My friends were murdered, did you know that?' And I said I did. And she said something about how it was all wrong. It was wrong because the lock was off the door. That she thought someone she knew committed murder. And then . . . she mumbled about the planted things."

"Did she say planted? Or did she say *plants*?"

Stevie had locked in on Izzy now, watching her expression. Izzy's eyes were drifting in a way that all the body language books she'd read suggested that she was remembering or trying to recall.

"Planted. Plants. Planting? I don't know. I thought she said planted, because that made sense, but . . . now that I'm saying it . . . maybe she was saying plants?"

Plant-based. Planted. Planting. Plants in the garden below the window . . .

"Plants," Stevie said.

She had no immediate follow-up to that.

"Plants," David repeated.

Stevie remained silent.

"What's happening right now?" Izzy asked.

David motioned for her to wait.

Stevie felt the thing that had evaded her creep into the corner of her vision.

"The window doesn't need to fit *people*," she said out loud. "It's the Orient Express. God, they said it. They practically told us."

"What's happening?" Izzy asked again.

"Something," David replied. "We never know until it happens."

Oh yes. Something was finally happening.

The six of the Nine were still exactly as Stevie had left them, though some had moved on to glasses of whisky. Sebastian was pouring himself a cup of tea. Stevie, Izzy, and David joined them and they were all welcomed graciously and offered tea or whisky. David helped himself to the whisky, while Izzy sat down next to Theo and tucked herself in tightly. Stevie went straight across the room to the fire.

"Everything all right?" Sebastian asked.

"We need to ask you about something," Stevie said.

From this position in front of the fire, she could be seen

by everyone. This made her butt very hot. She tried not to think about this. She reached into her hoodie and produced one of the crime scene photos.

"What is that?" Yash said, leaning forward. "Is that one of Sooz's pictures?"

"It's a police photo."

"How did you get a *police* photo?" Julian said.

"This," Stevie went on, "is a photo of the exterior of the woodshed on the afternoon after the murder. This photo shows the scene as it was found. Notice the window is open . . ."

She passed the photo to the nearest person, who happened to be Sebastian. He took the photo in silence and stared at it before passing it on.

"But something doesn't make sense about that," Stevie said, "because in the photo you all took when you arrived, the window is closed. Why was the window closed before the murder but open the day after?"

"The burglars must have done it," Theo said, barely glancing at the picture as it went past her.

"Except that Sebastian just told me outside that that space was rotted, that no one could go up there. The police didn't. There are no photos of the crawl space. I guess that's because there was no pull cord. . . ."

She held up the photo of the ceiling, focusing on the little hole where a pull cord had been.

"There's blood splashed across the ceiling," Stevie said. "That hatch to the crawl space was closed when Rosie and

Noel were killed. So how and why did burglars go up into a space they couldn't access, with a rotted floor, to open a window? Makes no sense, right? Unless . . ."

This time, Stevie nodded. They had discussed this upstairs. It was time to tip their hand. Izzy shifted to the edge of her seat.

"After my aunt had surgery earlier this year," she said, "she was on painkillers. I was at her flat helping her, and she started talking about the murders. She kept saying something about the padlock being unlocked, and that something had been planted."

"Except," Stevie said, "she probably didn't say *planted*. Angela was talking about *plants*. It's not that one of you is lying . . ."

Stevie spoke slowly, as the thought assembled itself before her.

". . . it's that you all are."

June 24, 1995

1:00 p.m.

IT WAS THE SMELL THAT THEO REMEMBERED MOST VIVIDLY. SHE would become familiar with it in her career. The metallic smell of blood, the odor of a body. Effluvia. It rolled over her, flooding her nostrils.

Rosie and Noel were partially obscured by the woodpile, some of which had been pushed on top of them. For the rest of their lives, both Theo and Sebastian would be thankful for this small mercy, that they could not see the full extent of the horror. They saw enough, though. A leg. A hand. Some clothing. The dark, wet marks on the floor, and the blood that was all over the handle of the axe that Sebastian had used to pull down the rope hook of the hatch in the ceiling.

They stumbled out of the woodshed and into the strange light of day. The dots and streaks of blood across Sebastian's face made Theo's stomach churn. It was the only color on his face at all—he had turned gray and seemed to be unable to move.

The birds chirped and swooped overhead, unaware that anything was wrong at Merryweather.

"We need to call . . . an ambulance . . ."

Theo didn't have to explain to him that an ambulance was unnecessary at this point. Sebastian was just saying things. Ambulance. Police. Help. Someone. Whoever you called when your friends had been murdered in a shed.

The police . . .

They would come, and they would find the ladder down and a room of cannabis plants and growing materials and two dead students.

They would come to the wrong conclusion.

Theodora had been a medical student for three years now—she had learned to deal with serious things. To save anyone she could. Triage. Rosie and Noel could not be saved, and someone else was in danger.

"The plants," she said.

"The plants? Who cares about the plants?"

"*They're* going to care about the plants, Seb," she said urgently. "When they find that room full of cannabis plants, they'll arrest you. They may think you did something to Rosie and Noel, something because of the plants."

Sebastian seemed to be past understanding or caring. His knees decided it was time to tap out, and he wobbled before sitting heavily in the mud.

"What then?" he asked. "What are we supposed to do?"

A good question. Theo was a director. She was a planner. She took care of people. She was a doctor in training. She could do this. She *would* do this.

The plan began to assemble itself in her mind. The

adrenaline fueled her, made her brain go faster. Fight or flight.

"*Here* is what we are going to do," she said, taking long, even breaths. "We need to go back inside. We need to tell everyone what happened. We need to work together. We have to keep calm."

Sebastian started to laugh, which was fair.

Theo reached out her hand to help him off the ground. She guided him to a remote bit of one of the walled gardens.

"Take off your clothes," she said. "I'll be right back."

Sebastian complied, pulling off the boots and his fitted shirt and trousers. He stood in the garden, barefoot and mostly naked aside from his underwear, waiting for Theo to return. She did so promptly, with dry clothes, a towel, a glass of water, a bottle of whisky, and a roll of loo paper. She set to work cleaning him up. She rolled up wads of the paper, moistened them with the water in the glass, and cleaned the blood from his hands and face.

"We can flush it, you see," she said, mostly to herself. "We don't want it on the towels or in the bin."

When the blood was wiped away, she handed him the whisky.

"Drink," she said. "For the shock."

He complied, taking a long draw. He let this glide down his esophagus, and when it hit his stomach, he felt a flush come over his face. This provided enough clarity to dry himself off and change into the jeans and T-shirt that Theo had grabbed from his room. She had him lift his feet, which she cleaned before he reinserted them into the boots. She gathered up the bloodied tissues. Sebastian carried the clothes and the towel. As they made their way back to the house, she made them both dunk their booted feet into the stream in the garden, getting rid of blood on the soles.

Relatively clean, they returned to the house, where Theo shoved the clothes and towel into the washing machine along with some used kitchen drying-up towels and set it going. This wasn't ideal, but they could certainly explain that they needed to clean some clothes and towels after a night spent playing in the rain and mud.

Now, the hard part. This was where she stalled. Sebastian saw it happen and put his hand on her shoulder.

"I'll do it," he said. "You've been doing all the lifting."

He took an exceptionally long draw on the bottle.

The two of them proceeded on to the sitting room, where everyone was laughing and talking and eating bacon sandwiches. It was like Theo and Sebastian came from another world—they were ghosts in the world of the living, the world of the before.

Julian noticed them first, his face falling into a confused grimace.

"You all right there, Seb?" he asked. "Theo?"

The laughter and conversation faded as everyone became aware of the silent pair in the doorway.

"Something's happened," Sebastian began.

Later, people would tell Sebastian that he was the one who gave the news, but he would have no recollection of it. He had a distant memory of the reaction. A strange laugh from Yash. Silence from the others. Disbelief. Someone started screaming. Possibly Angela? Sooz said something about the police, which was when Theo blocked her way out the door.

"There's something we have to do first, and we need to do it right now," she said. "We need to clear out all the plants. They'll arrest Sebastian otherwise."

She didn't need to say any more. The point was communicated around the room wordlessly. They could sense each other's thoughts.

"How?" Julian asked.

"We touch as little as possible," she said. "One of us goes up into the loft space to get them. We clean out that space, we get rid of all the plants and equipment, and then we call the police. We have to be quick about it. The gardener will be here this afternoon."

Once she started on the plan, Theo found her mind clearing. It wasn't that this was easy—it was not. But at least there was something she could *do*. Keep busy. Keep moving. Later, she would process. She would find a way to deal with the trauma.

"We need bin bags," she said. "Lots of them. And gloves. Washing-up gloves will do. Bins, gloves, a broom, cleaning supplies, some gardening sheers or scissors, rope."

The group, now seven, made their way through the gardens, propping each other up and carrying supplies. The scene was as Sebastian and Theo left it—the overturned wheelbarrow, the door hanging open. It had not been a dream.

"I'll go inside," Theo said. "I've already seen . . ."

She almost said it. *It* was *them*. Rosie and Noel. Noel and Rosie.

"I have to see," Sooz said, stepping forward.

"Sooz . . ."

Sooz made it as far as the doorway, froze, and backed away.

"I . . . I can't. You're sure? Theo, you're sure? You're *sure?*"

She began to shake uncontrollably. Peter got to her first and moved her back, holding her tight.

Theo put on the gloves.

First, she put a trail of unrolled plastic bin bags on the ground between the door and the ladder. The floor was soaked from the lashes of rain that had come in during the night. Theo took off the boots to climb the ladder. No footprints. Once upstairs, she opened the little window. It was tiny, but they would be able to get the plants through it. The other things—the grow lights, the tarps—those might be harder. Those could go down the steps, if necessary.

They formed a brigade. Theo lowered the plants from the window in the bucket. Someone on the ground dumped them directly into a bin bag. Bit by bit, the room was emptied. When it was cleaned out, she swept it for any remaining cannabis on the floor. She tipped the dustpan's contents into a bag. She considered closing the window, but there was still a smell of cannabis plants in the space. The window had to be open. There was a breeze today— anything they could do to air out the space would be good.

On the way down, she wiped the ladder rungs clean.

When she was done upstairs, she cut the rope that opened the hatch and removed it, leaving only a small hole where it had been, and pushed the hatch closed with the handle of a shovel. She backed up out of the shed, taking the tarps with her as she went.

One last thing. The axe. It was on the floor where Sebastian had dropped it. She forced herself to look as she wiped it, picked it up in a bin bag, covering it so the others couldn't see. She stepped out of the woodshed and walked several yards back, to the stream that wound through the woods into the garden. She shook it out of the bag, dropping it into the water, kicking at it until it was entirely submerged.

She stared at the axe for a moment, peacefully resting there among the rocks. Reality fragmented for a moment. She was cleaning up a murder scene. Rosie. Noel. She had a mental flash of Rosie's body under the wood . . .

"Keep it together, Theo," she said to herself. "You're going to be a doctor. You do whatever needs to be done to help others. You have to do this."

She shook her head forcefully, as if trying to knock the picture out of her mind. It worked, at least enough for her to pick up her chin and march back to where the others were loading the cars.

"Where do we go with these?" Yash said, regarding the bags. "The woods?"

"They might search," Peter said. "They might find them."

"There's a lot of woods."

"There's probably going to be a lot of police."

Peter and Yash, refining each other's ideas even now.

"A few miles up the road," Angela said. "There was a skip by some construction. I saw it as we drove in. Some building site, close to the pub. We could take them there, drop them in with the other rubbish."

Everyone agreed that this was the correct thing to do.

"Who feels like they can drive?" Theo asked.

"I think I could," Julian said. "I have no idea why or how, but I think I could."

"You five go. Get rid of the bags and drive to the shops and get bread or milk or sauce rolls or something, so if anyone says they saw a car leave here in the morning there'll be a good reason. While you're gone, we'll call the police. Once we start this, we need to stay together on it. Not just today. Always. Do we agree?"

One by one, each of the group nodded their assent. Julian, Sooz, Angela, Peter, and Yash backed out of the driveway with their terrible cargo, leaving Theo and Sebastian.

And Rosie and Noel.

Theo reached for Sebastian's hand. The stage was set. Ready or not, showtime always came. You had to go on even if you felt underprepared.

22

The fire crackled and licked the dark air. The clock on the mantel did its part and made a gentle, slow heartbeat sound. The Nine circulated a look. They spoke wordlessly to each other. It was weird how they could have an entire conversation this way. Stevie could feel it, even if she couldn't hear it.

Her butt was way too hot. She stepped forward a bit.

"I didn't start putting it all together until dinner," Stevie said. "I didn't know what I was looking at, at first. But a few things got me thinking. If you hadn't said *plant-based* so many times, I don't think it would have occurred to me what Angela was really saying. Plants. Then I started thinking about all the things Sebastian told me when we were outside. That he used to smoke a lot of weed. He learned about plants from the gardener. When you add it all up: plants, weed, the window closed one day and open after the murder, the rope missing from the pull—it all equals . . ."

"Grow house," David said, breaking into a smile.

Nothing from the assembled. Too much nothing. She had stepped out into the void and . . .

Then someone sighed.

"This is my fault," Theo said.

"Don't you *dare*, Theo," Sebastian said. "If it's anyone's fault it's mine."

"It sounds like it was mine," Sooz added. "Maybe it was my subconscious talking."

"It's not anyone's *fault*," Peter said. "No one's fault. It was . . ."

"What we had to do," Julian concluded.

. . . and she had landed on solid ground. Across the room, David had a strange look on his face. Not a smile, exactly—a kind of grimace of amazement.

"Do you know where my aunt is?" Izzy said to them.

Everyone shook their head. A chorus of nos.

"We don't!" Theo said. "If we knew, trust us . . ."

"We would be there," Sooz said. "We want to know as much as you do. This . . . the cannabis . . ."

"It has nothing to do with it," Peter said. "Nothing."

"There's no harm in explaining now," Sebastian said. "You seem to have a handle on the situation. And it's all down to me anyway. You're right. I had cannabis plants up there. Not many. I put in some lights and fans and grew a few plants—barely anything. I'd pick some up when I visited home. When we came upon the scene that morning, saw the door ripped open, the first thing that occurred to me was that someone must have found out and had come to steal the plants."

"And had they?" Stevie said.

"No," Sebastian replied. "Nothing had been taken. We

just found . . . Rosie and Noel. So we got rid of the plants before the police arrived."

"Carefully," Theo added. "We tried to disrupt as little as possible. When we got there, the floor was soaked—there were puddles of water everywhere, so there were no foot-prints. We still used other objects to avoid stepping on the ground. We removed everything from upstairs, very care-fully, and got rid of it. The only things we altered downstairs were the axe and the rope handle."

"Where was the axe when you arrived?" Stevie asked.

"Exactly where it always was," Sebastian said. "Standing upright by the door. It had a long handle, so I'd use it to hook the rope pull. That's what I did that morning. I grabbed it and pulled the hatch down. I didn't see Rosie and Noel until I had come back down the ladder."

"We had to cut the rope handle because it had blood on it," Theo continued, "and the police might go up there and find residue of the plants. We had to clean the axe because Sebastian's fingerprints were on it. We cleaned the handle and threw it in the stream. I've never regretted what we did that day. We couldn't help Rosie or Noel, but we could help Sebastian. If those plants had been found he would have gone to jail, and maybe he would have been accused of murder."

"No regrets," Sooz said.

This was generally echoed around the room.

"And my aunt knew?" Izzy said.

"Of course," Theo replied. "It was all of us. She helped."

"All of us," Sooz said.

"Every one of us," Peter added. "We used a brigade system to take the plants down. We loaded them into a car and got rid of them."

"And then I phoned the police," Theo said. "As quickly as I could."

"And what about the lock on the shed?" Stevie asked.

"What we said about that was true," Sebastian said. "We found the lock intact and the door ripped open. Must have been easier for the burglars to crowbar it open rather than mess about with the lock."

Stevie had to move away from the fire. It was too much heat. She moved to the darker side of the room, nearer to where David was perched.

"Question," Yash said, raising his hand slightly. "You still haven't explained why you have crime scene photos and police reports."

"My aunt had them," Izzy said. "We found them in her house. She's been researching this case."

"You mean, she's looking for the burglars?" Yash replied. "For some DNA evidence or something? She never mentioned this to me. Did she say anything to any of you?"

A chorus of shaking heads.

"If Angela is researching the case," Sooz said, "is *that* where she is? I mean, she'd have to be here, right? Where else could she look? And why not just tell us she was doing it?"

Because she thinks one of you did it, Stevie thought.

"What does she have?" Julian asked. "What did she learn?"

"Only what the police knew at the time," Stevie said. "She has the photos, the statements, the notes, the coroner's report."

"The entire police file?" Julian said.

"And one other thing. Who is Samantha Gravis?"

Six blank looks.

"Who?" Sooz asked.

"This was in with the police file."

Stevie pulled out the newspaper article and passed it around.

"I don't know who this is," Julian said.

"Nor do I," Theo said, passing it to Sebastian, who shrugged. Peter and Yash held the clipping between them and studied it.

"You know," Peter said, "there's something. Vaguely something I can't place."

Yash frowned in thought. The others crowded around the sofa. Sooz leaned low over the back of the sofa, her elbows on her friends' shoulders.

"Well, the article is dated the day we arrived at Merryweather—June twenty-third, 1995," she said. "That was also the day that Rosie and Noel were killed."

They all conferred, trying to make sense of it. Their confused buzz seemed genuine. They really did not seem to know who Samantha Gravis was, and they wanted to figure it out.

Stevie was on the verge of asking something when Janelle appeared in the doorway.

"Dr. Quinn was just on the phone," she said. "Can I talk to you for a second?"

Stevie ushered Janelle to the far side of the entrance hall, under the disapproving portrait of the man and his dog. This made Stevie too nervous and was still within hearing distance of the sitting room, so she motioned them into the library and shut the door. She slapped at the wall, looking for the light switch, but was unable to find it. This talk would have to happen in the dark, which suited Stevie just fine.

"Figured some stuff out," Stevie said. "In there. About what happened."

"I heard," Janelle replied quietly.

There was no "great job, Stevie!" or "you're brilliant!" or "this makes everything fine!"

"So I'm getting closer," Stevie said quickly. "Not there yet, but if we figure out who Samantha Gravis is—"

"You did hear me say that Dr. Quinn was on the phone, right?"

Stevie sucked in her lips and bit down hard.

"Mm-hmm."

"I didn't pick up in time," Janelle went on. "So she called Nate. I heard Nate saying that we were in the student lounge watching a movie. And since we're not in a student lounge watching a movie . . ."

The wind was picking up outside, and the trees were running the tips of their bare branches on the house, skinny fingertips tapping and scraping. There was a hollow whistle from the fireplace.

"Okay." Stevie breathed out the word in a violent exhale. "I can explain . . ."

"Nate already did."

"I was trying to find a time to tell you . . ."

"That you lied and said we had permission to come to this house when Dr. Quinn actually thinks we're in London?"

"Yeah," Stevie said, curling in on herself a little. "But you know why I did it."

Nothing from Janelle for a moment. The dark library may have been a bad choice for this discussion. The windows were tall and cast long rectangles of moonlight on the floor. The books stood as silent sentinels, witnesses to Stevie's shame. There was some kind of threatening piece of art nearby, something with beady eyes. The air smelled faintly of furniture polish, book dust, and judgment.

"I know why you *think* you did it," Janelle said. "You think you did it because you had to help Angela and you had to get us all here any way you could."

"You said you wouldn't come if Quinn said no . . ." Stevie shot back.

"But don't lie," Janelle countered, an edge of emotion in her voice. "You should have told me what she said. Vi didn't know. When did you tell Nate?"

"When we got here," Stevie said quietly.

"I guess David knew, not that it matters for him. He

doesn't have to answer to Quinn."

"I didn't tell him either," Stevie said. "But you know . . . you know why I had to lie."

"No," Janelle said. "I know that you did it, but you didn't have to. If I can't trust my friends—if I can't trust *you*—who can I trust?"

Stevie's eyes burned with tears. She coughed and thumbed them away.

"I'm stupid for lying to you," she said, "but I'm honestly scared for Angela, and here, this is the only place to find out what happened to her. So I did a shitty thing. I'm a shitty friend, but for a good reason."

"Did lying to us get you closer to finding Angela?" Janelle said.

"I'm closer. She's out there somewhere, and she's in trouble. And there . . . there isn't a me without us. Angela needs *us*."

She landed on the *us* as hard as she could. It was true. There was no Stevie without Janelle and Nate and Vi and David. They were one, like those people in the other room. They were an organism. A system. Even in the dark room, Stevie could see Janelle's cheerful yellow sweater, her neat wrap of braids in an orange-and-brown scarf—bright yet autumnal, always in the moment. The friend who backed her at every turn, who fixed the broken things, who did the hard math. The person you could go to in the middle of the night.

Janelle's stance softened a little; she was always sensitive to people who needed help.

"You know," she said, "if you'd told me what Quinn actually said, we'd have figured it out. It's not like I don't care that Angela could be hurt. I was mad at you for screwing around. If you'd told me . . . we could have come up with a solution together. But you didn't trust me."

"I trust you," Stevie said. "With anything. I just didn't know what to do. What do I do to make it up to you?"

Janelle sighed.

"You tell me the truth," Janelle said. "Lies are poison. But Stevie . . . we only have a little over a day left here in England. So you have, what, thirty-six hours? I believe in you, but this one . . . there may be no time. You may have to leave it to someone else to find her. That's just reality. Is there anything specific you think you can do in that time to work it out?"

The answer to that question was no. No, Stevie did not know what came next. She never did. The moves always came to her as she worked out the puzzle. There was no advance plan, no method, no organized way of dealing with this.

"Tomorrow," Janelle said softly. "We go back to London. We do what's on our schedule. We have our tea. We go to the theater. We finish our trip. We can't screw up our lives on hunches, Stevie. We need to plan, and we need to trust each other."

The words landed hard, each one in her gut.

"I won't do it again," Stevie said. "I promise."

"You better," Janelle replied. Then, after a long moment,

she added, "But you did good in there. You're lucky you're so smart."

"I'm lucky I have you."

"You're right, but don't push it," Janelle replied. It came out stern, but Stevie could hear the smile on her face.

23

Stevie had exhausted her mental resources for the evening. Between her revelations and the talk with Janelle, she had nothing left. She wanted to burrow into the massive bed upstairs and sleep—sleep for a week. She stepped out into the shadowy main hall, where David was waiting on the steps.

"I've missed these kinds of nights," he said. "You solve everything, all hell breaks loose. Usually we end up in a hole or something too. We're making out well tonight."

Stevie had no energy for the banter. She sat next to him on the step. By craning her neck forward, she could see that the conversation in the sitting room was still engaged, photos were still being passed around.

"Quinn didn't say yes to you coming here, huh?" he said in a low voice.

"Not exactly," Stevie said.

"You never change," he said.

"You mean I'm a shithead."

"Take that however you want. It's not the word I'd choose."

"Seems to fit," she said. "But what else was I supposed to do?"

Instead of replying, he took her hand. Using his thumb, he made slow, soft circles in her palm. It was reassurance. It was love. This tiny gesture also made every nerve in her body stand at attention. There was a quiver, a gentle, repeated note, like an orchestra warming up. A rising energy. The anxiety and exhaustion converted into something more liquid. Emotional catharsis. Also, horniness, plain and gloriously simple.

"Can we go upstairs now?" she asked quietly.

David stood, and the look in his eye told her everything.

They did not turn on the lights. They didn't even make it that far into Stevie's room. As soon as the door was shut, David turned. She moved first, with a hungry, nervous energy, kissing him hard and accidentally bumping his head against the wall. To her delight, he scooped her up and took her over to the bed, dropping her the last foot. She bounced gently. He hopped up, tenting himself over her. She thought he was about to lean in and kiss her. She was ready to go the full *Bridgerton* here at Merryweather. But he was just hovering there, looking at her with a faint smile.

"The other night," he said. "I think you were going to ask me if I'd ever had sex. Weren't you?"

To her surprise, her awkwardness with the question had gone.

"Yes," she replied.

"But you didn't ask. What answer did you want?"

"The real one. Because I'm guessing yes."

"That's the right answer," he said.

There was a little twinge inside her—part upset, and part satisfaction. It was okay. It was a little strange. It was good. It was all those things at once.

"A lot?" she asked.

David laughed, but not unpleasantly.

"What's a lot?"

"Did you win any awards for Most Sex?"

A real laugh this time. He got off his hands and knees and rolled next to her, so they were face-to-face on the pillow.

"My last girlfriend before I went to Ellingham," he said. "And once at Ellingham. Well, not at Ellingham. I went to Burlington with Ellie for a party. I met someone there. It was just the once."

Ellie. Their friend from Ellingham. It was odd to talk about her this way, out of context of all the terrible things that had happened there.

"Is there anything specific you want to know?"

"I don't think so," she said. "Not right now."

"What about you?" he said, propping himself up on his elbow.

"Do you really need to ask?"

"I mean, I think the answer is no, but I'm asking."

"You think right."

"Are you asking for . . . a reason?"

"I think so."

He considered this for a moment.

"Okay," he said. "Do you want to . . . talk about that? Because . . . we should talk about that. Before . . ."

"Yeah," she said. "But I've thought about it. And . . . would you . . . want to?"

A short laugh.

"Yeah," he said. "Of course. But . . . we don't have to. We can do whatever. I'm saying yes. I'm also saying that whatever you decide is good with me. You know what I'm saying . . ."

There was a little nervousness there now that was unlike him. She looked at his face, which was framed in the squares of pale moonlight coming through the glass.

If not now, when? This was about as ideal a time as she'd ever hoped for. This was what she had thought about and considered and researched.

"I'm saying yes," she said.

"Tonight, or in general, in the future?"

"Tonight," she said. "Now."

"I brought condoms," he said. "I didn't say anything."

"Where are they?"

He reached into his back pocket and produced a small package.

"If you say stop, we stop. Talk to me. And we don't have to. Just so we're super clear on this."

"Same."

Now that they'd had the discussion, they were left for a moment looking into each other's faces on the pillow. For a moment, she thought the spell was broken. But then they both burst out laughing at the same time. People made out

331

like this stuff was so serious—it wasn't. It was stupid and fun. It was taking turns rolling on top of each other, biting ears and kissing necks and getting stuck in your own clothes trying to get them off. It was feeling muscles moving under skin, feeling the warmth under the covers. She didn't know precisely how it was all supposed to go, but she was getting an inkling that was growing all the time. She was vaguely aware of noises in the hallway, but they didn't matter. She was gone—out of the mansion, in some kind of skyscape made of David's hair and the inside of the covers. Nothing mattered, not the future or college or anything but . . .

There was a knocking on the door—a strong, steady knock that increased in urgency.

"Who is it?" Stevie finally called, breathless.

The person responded by throwing open the door. Sooz stood there in a long red dressing gown, over royal-blue pajamas with a pattern of leaping tigers.

"I know who . . . *oh*." She looked at the two of them together, blinked in confusion, then shielded her eyes as a nod toward privacy. "I thought you said come in. So sorry."

She stepped back out of view, but kept the door open a crack.

"It is important, though. You've got to come downstairs. I know who Samantha Gravis is."

Sooz gathered the residents of Merryweather in the kitchen rather than the sitting room. She had roused the entirety of the house, including Janelle, Vi, and Nate. Everyone else was wearing, if not formal sleepwear, then something generally presentable. David had pulled on his Yale sweatpants and his T-shirt. Stevie had grabbed the closest thing at hand—her sex hoodie.

"Oh," Janelle said, noting the onesie that Stevie was wearing (now well zipped). While modest enough, it had never been intended for a wide audience. She wondered if she was still flushed, still sweating. She could feel moisture at the base of her neck. Her hair was probably standing on end. Luckily, no one cared what Stevie looked like—they had all been roused and brought around to the table, where Sooz's laptop was open.

"I couldn't get to sleep," Sooz said. "I was thinking about everything that happened tonight and the face of the girl in the newspaper. I was sure I had seen her before. So I looked through my photos. It took a while, since I have so many, but . . . I found her."

She indicated a scan of a photo that she had pulled up.

There were members of the Nine—young and shiny faced, with their 90s hair and communal clothes—lined up against the bar at a pub. Behind them were the decorative handles of the beer taps, and a bartender caught unawares by the camera, his eyes glowing red as he looked up from filling a glass. On the far end was Sebastian, his eyes closed in a squint and preening for the camera. Theo was tucked under his arm, smiling at something or someone out of view. Noel, tall and slouched, in oversized glasses and a flop of dark hair. Angela was next to him, thrusting a flower in the direction of the camera like a sword. Peter wore a green-and-blue-striped rugby shirt and had his head thrown back in laughter, while Yash had his mouth open and his hand out in a wide gesture, still in the middle of telling a joke. Only Julian tried to work the camera at all, a half smile on his lips. He wore a loose T-shirt and had a flannel shirt tied around his waist.

There was one more person, far to the edge of the frame. An afterthought who almost didn't make the cut. She looked away slightly, but her face was clear enough. She wore an oversized Oxford sweatshirt.

Sooz pointed to her.

"There she is," Sooz said. "The *Canadian*."

"What?" Yash almost dropped his mug of tea. He hurried over and leaned in to look at the screen.

"Canadian?" Stevie repeated. She went in for a look, but the members of the Nine had crowded around Sooz and her computer. Yash scraped back one of the wooden chairs and sat down.

"The Canadian," he repeated, rubbing his forehead. "My God."

"Why do you keep saying she's Canadian?" Stevie asked.

"Because she told us she was Canadian," Sooz replied.

"It used to be a thing," Theo explained. "Some people weren't overly fond of Americans? So some Americans would say they were Canadian instead. Can't really tell the difference. American and Canadian accents sound the same to us, generally."

"Okay," Stevie said. "*Who* is the Canadian? I mean,

Samantha. She's Samantha. But how did you know her?"

"We didn't," Peter said.

"Well, we did in a way," Theo added. "But not really, like Peter says."

"We did," Yash said. "I did."

"Julian certainly did," Sooz cut in.

It was like they were talking in riddles.

"In our last week or so at Cambridge," Sooz said, "during exams or right after, sometime around that period, we were all at the pub one night, and we met the Canadian. The American . . . Samantha. I don't think we knew her name, did we? We called her something else."

"Monty," Yash said. "Because she was Canadian, and I said something about Mounties, and she thought I said Monty or something. It was just one of those things that happen in a pub. She probably told us her name but we called her Monty. She seemed to like it. It made her laugh."

"I took the picture," Sooz said. "And you can see we're all in it except for Rosie. Which means this happened on the night Julian cheated on her."

Julian lifted his head.

"Sooz, do you have to . . ."

"I'm trying to explain. Rosie was out studying for an exam or doing a lab or something, and we were all at the pub without her. And Julian met the Canadian and he snogged her. The Canadian was the reason Rosie and Julian broke up . . ."

Julian again lifted his head in protest.

". . . which sounds worse than it should. Everyone broke

up with Julian when he cheated, which was always and with everyone. We broke up, what, four times because of that?"

"It wasn't always me that did the cheating in that case, Sooz . . ."

"The point is that's how Rosie and Noel ended up together," Peter summarized.

"But you didn't recognize her?" Izzy said.

"I remember the Canadian," Julian said, "but I didn't recognize her photo."

"Julian had a lot of encounters," Sooz said.

"Sooz, can you . . ."

"She hung out with me the next night," Yash said. "She was fun. She was funny. She was really into music. She said she liked being in England because so many of the bands she liked were here. Unlike Julian, I didn't shag everything that moved, so this stood out for me. I really liked her. She was going to be in England for another day or two, so I lent her some CDs in my bag. I gave her our address so she could visit and bring them back, but she never came. I just thought she took my CDs and went back to Canada."

"But she didn't," Sooz said. "She died. I don't know how Angela put that together or why, but we knew her."

"She died punt running?" Stevie said. "That's a thing?"

"Oh yes," Sebastian said. "Cambridge is on a river—the Cam. The punts are the boats used on the river, mostly by tourists. At night, they're tied up in rows, and people run across them while they're drunk."

"How easy is it to fall in?"

"Very," Theo said. "It's generally harmless, except the rumor was that you'd get Weil's disease from the water—leptospirosis. It's not as common as people thought, or else everyone would have had it. You'd be in more danger of snagging yourself on a shopping trolley someone had dumped in the water. But it sounds like she hit her head on the way down, which is also easily done."

"It looks like she was found near Grantchester Meadows," Peter said. "That's between town and where our house was. Yash, she could have been on the way to our place. Maybe with your CDs."

Yash leaned back in his chair and rubbed his forehead.

"That's so sad," he said. "Oh God."

"So a girl you all met," Stevie said, "caused a breakup, disappeared, and drowned a few days before Rosie and Noel died, and could have been on the way to your house when it happened. And on the day you left for Merryweather, an article appears in the paper saying her body has been found. That night, Rosie and Noel were killed. Angela put this part together, and now Angela is gone."

"*Where is my aunt?*" Izzy said.

But there was no answer.

24

There had been, to put it mildly, a vibe shift.

The whole house was awake. Not just the people—Stevie felt like Merryweather itself had been roused from slumber. She was acutely aware of the faces from the portraits on the wall, the groan and creak of the wood, the autumn wind striking the windows. Her head was thrumming with information as she made her way back upstairs.

They'd made a mess of the grand bed. The duvet was piled and almost knotted around a sheet. There were creases where they had sweat and twisted. Stevie smoothed them out and climbed in. David got in beside her and leaned in to kiss her, then sat back.

"It's been a weird night," he said.

"Yeah," she said. "Maybe we can just lay here?"

He raised his arm, making space for her to tuck herself next to him. He played with her hair as her thoughts drifted over this new information. She wasn't sure how much time passed before she noticed his hand was not moving and he was fast asleep. She propped herself up on her elbow to look at the outline of his face in the darkness for a moment, then slipped out of the bed as silently as she could, grabbing her tablet in the dark, and went into the bathroom. She sat on the sofa under the window. (How could she not? Who has a bathroom sofa?) The moon was full and white, gleaming the gardens.

When Stevie had tried to get into the spirit of a cold case, sometimes she had to immerse herself in sound, something to help her brain slide along. Nineties. Britpop. They kept mentioning the band Blur, so she looked it up. She didn't know any of the songs, but there was one called "Country House." It started with a bold series of descending chords that sounded like the lead to a party. A very English voice said, "So the story begins . . ."

Stevie set it on repeat and let Blur sing into her ears as she looked at every document again. She tried to walk through it in her mind. Samantha Gravis was an American visiting England, just like her. Samantha's time there was limited, like Stevie's. She met the Nine, like Stevie had. She kisses two of them. She borrows CDs from one and gets their home address. It seems like Samantha Gravis, a bit drunk, starts to walk to their house to return the CDs and visit them. It's 1995, so she has no phone to guide her. Maybe she has a map, or just some idea of which way to go. It's late. It's dark.

Who would have a motive to hurt Samantha?

Samantha had kissed Julian and Yash. Julian and Rosie had been dating, and Samantha was the reason they broke up.

Did Rosie kill Samantha Gravis? Was that what this was

all about? Was that what Angela was referring to? When she said she thought one of her friends was a murderer, did she mean Rosie? And then what? Someone kills Rosie and Noel in retribution? Yash?

As they told it, all these people were involved with each other. There was a lot of hooking up and jealousy and breaking up and making up. *Anyone* could have been mad about what happened.

Stevie must have dozed off for a little while. She came to with a start when her tablet fell from her lap and hit the bathroom floor. She snorted away, looked around in confusion at the bathroom and the big tub, and checked the time. It was five in the morning.

She turned off the music and rubbed her face with both hands. She had no answers. Coffee. She needed coffee.

David was fast asleep in the bed as she passed, the massive fluffs of white duvet pulled up to his nose, one arm hanging off the edge of the bed. It was the arm he wore his watch on—the old watch his father had given him. It was a large watch, but David had heavy, strong wrists. Something about seeing his arm outstretched like that—she considered getting back into the bed, waking him with kisses, finishing what they had started. She stood there for a moment, pulled in two directions, then resignedly moved toward the door.

There was just so little time and so many questions.

Stevie moved along the upstairs hall of Merryweather, past the porcelain bowl and the vases and the grim portraiture. She made her way down the grand staircase, where the ticking grandfather clock stood sentry below. She crossed the wooden floor, smelling the leftover smoke from last night's fire. She made her way back to the massive kitchen and found the lights. The chairs were still pushed out from the table from the conference of a few hours before. She went over to the kettle. She filled it at the sink and put it back on its base, then switched it on to boil. It wasn't a complicated move, but it made her feel like she belonged there.

She could fit in there. She could live there. She could go to school there, with David. Maybe this could be her life, going to places like this. . . .

The kitchen window faced a brick wall. She leaned over the sink a bit to look up at the dark early morning sky. There was a figure reflected in the window behind her. She gasped, even as she realized it was just Nate, shuffling in, wearing a large brown hoodie and blue plaid pajama pants, and holding his laptop.

She nodded. He took a seat, stretching out his legs and spreading them wide.

"Did you figure it all out yet?" he asked, indicating the kitchen, Merryweather, the mystery, and life in general. Stevie shook her head no.

"What's that for?" she asked, nodding toward the computer. "Are you writing?"

"Yep," he said a little too quickly.

"This is a whole new you," Stevie said. "You used to avoid writing, and now that's all you seem to be doing."

"I just couldn't sleep," he said, setting his computer down.

"We're living in a Clue board right now. I heard someone moving around and saw it was you. Probably a good move to be in here. Lots of knives."

She narrowed her eyes at him. It was definitely something. He had his hands resting on his closed laptop, like it might spring open and reveal all his secrets. But Stevie had bigger fish to fry at the moment. Nate's squirrely writing activity would have to be examined another time.

"I've been reading over all the stuff Angela got," Stevie said. "It just . . . it doesn't point at anything. Nothing I can see." She bit her lip and shook her head. "Maybe it was a robbery, now that we know what was in the shed."

"Someone came to steal the weed?"

Now that she said it out loud, the idea had a bit of shape to it. Had she been too quick to dismiss it? Was it worth at least looking around outside with that in mind?

"Do you want to go for a walk?" she asked.

"Are you being serious right now?"

"I just asked if you wanted to go for a walk."

"Nighttime walk at axe murder manor? For sure. Especially if you heard a noise and want to investigate."

"It's almost dawn," she said.

"It's *dark*."

"Murders don't keep happening at the same place," she said. "They're like lightning. Never strikes twice."

"We literally come from a school where murders kept happening."

"Well, we can't keep going to places where more than one

342

murder happens," Stevie said. "So now we're definitely safe."

"Seriously, no. Just wait until the sun comes up."

"We don't have a lot of time," she said. "Anything I'm going to find out, I'm going to find out today. Soon people will be awake, and that's when I'll be able to talk to them. Now's the best time to finish looking at the grounds. Besides, they don't have guns here."

"They have axes."

"Much slower. Harder to use."

She turned off the kettle that she had set on to boil and was now rumbling on its base. She went through to the boot room and looked for the pair of Wellington boots she had worn earlier. She took a coat as well. There were flashlights on a shelf by the door. She grabbed one for herself, and one for Nate, who came into the mudroom a moment later.

"You know one of these times I'm not going to follow you," he said.

"Really?"

"I don't know. Maybe."

He sighed and grabbed the nearest Barbour coat, pulling it on over his hoodie, and accepted the flashlight she held out to him.

"Do you think we should bring something?" he said. "Seriously. For safety."

Stevie glanced around and saw a hammer sitting on top of a pile of garden implements and tools under one of the benches. She took it and shoved it into the deep pocket of the coat, as far as it would go.

"There," she said.

"Hammer," Nate said, nodding. "Great. Let's take our hammer to the woods."

The door was locked from the inside, so she turned the key and stepped out into the cold.

The air was thick was moisture and the smell of leaves and vegetation. The moon was heavy and bright, spilling milky light over the land. They almost didn't need their flashlights. Also, they had experience with being in the woods at night. Ellingham Academy was in the woods on a Vermont mountaintop, much more remote than Merryweather. And they'd spent the summer in the woods looking into a murder. This wasn't all woods anyway—this was countryside. The tree line broke at points, revealing sprawling fields and lawns and bits of wall.

These were all points Stevie ran through her mind as she gripped the handle of the hammer. It was fine, though. She was pretty sure of it.

They walked down the gravel-and-dirt drive, which was maybe a quarter of a mile long, until they reached the very sturdy wooden entrance gate, which was at least six feet high. She consulted the photos on her tablet. It looked to be the same one, or very similar.

"This gate closes automatically," she said. "It's electric. When the power went out at two thirty that morning, the gate would stop working. It would have to have been pried open, which it wasn't. The road just beyond this gate was blocked off from three thirty to seven thirty in the morning to fix the power. There's basically no way anyone came here with a car or van. So what do these burglars do? Walk all night in a torrential rainstorm to get here?"

"Maybe?" Nate said.

"And *no one* sees them? Not any of the many people running around the grounds? Just Rosie and Noel, and only at the woodshed? But there's a problem with that as well. Let's just say you're Rosie and I'm a burglar. You discover me or I discover you. I could just run away, but okay, I freak out. I grab an axe. I kill you."

Stevie mimed this with the hammer, perhaps a little too closely for Nate's liking.

"I've killed you. Oh shit. My bad. What do I do? I should run now. I don't run. I *bury* you in wood. I break the glass lightbulb sometime around here, so I guess I'm still waving the axe around? Why? Whatever. I take so long that someone else shows up. Again. I don't run. I kill them."

She mimed with the hammer from farther away this time, making token gestures.

"I bury the second person. Why am I waiting around?"

"Rain?" Nate offered. "I mean, it's not a great reason . . ."

Stevie shook her head.

"And these geniuses who walked in the rain to steal a few weed plants and end up committing double murder manage to avoid being seen by anyone else. Except, Sooz says she saw a flashlight go past the window of the sitting room, but the police just disregard her because she was drunk and because it doesn't fit what they clearly wanted it to fit. And all of it ignores the hard facts that Rosie knew something was wrong and must have seen this article about Samantha Gravis, which appeared in the paper that very morning. No."

She shook her head. Now she was more certain than ever.

"This has an order to it. Samantha Gravis. Rosie. Noel. One leads to the other. Problem leads to problem."

"I know an old woman who swallowed a fly," Nate said.

"What?"

"You know that song? We sang it in kindergarten. It's about the old woman who swallowed a fly. And then she swallows a spider to catch the fly and keeps swallowing progressively bigger crap to deal with the last thing she swallowed."

Stevie turned and started walking back. On their right was woods, and on the left, trees and low wall and the opening of the great lawn. As they got nearer to the house, Stevie turned in that direction, climbing over the short bit of stone wall and walking on the grass toward the small pond and the folly. To get there, they had to cross the slender stream that went through the property, but it was only about two feet wide and a few inches deep where they were and could be managed with a single stride.

Follies came up a lot in murder mysteries. People liked to put bodies under or around them. That made sense, because they were pointless bits of architectural extravagance—what you built if you were a rich, grown-ass adult and wanted a playhouse. Why *not* build a tiny Greek temple out on the lawn? You'd be weird if you didn't.

This folly was made to look like the front of a temple—four columns and a peaked roof. It had no inside room; it was just a little overhang, a place to stand out of the sun or rain, maybe have tea or a picnic.

"I've been reading these witness statements all night," she said. "I looked at Angela's notes. She tried to figure out who was where and when. And that's great, but the point is that from about eleven until two thirty in the morning, pretty much everyone was just somewhere on the grounds, not seen by the others. They pop up here or there, but everyone was out of view except for Sebastian, who was here. He had the keys to the woodshed down his pants. It's pretty on display, huh. Nowhere to hide."

Behind them was the pond, which looked to be maybe three feet deep at best and was home to some koi. Stevie watched them glide under the surface.

"The medical examiner looks at the bodies at about two in the afternoon," she went on. "They estimated that Rosie and Noel died around the same time, between eleven p.m. until four in the morning. So, the murders could have happened at any time during the night and pretty much anyone could have done it."

She leaned her forehead against a column.

"I'm never going to figure this out," she said, mostly to herself. Her breath puffed in front of her, a delicate feather of white mist. "It's impossible. I've got a murder mansion, a house full of suspects, a pile of evidence, and *nothing*."

She pushed herself away from the column and walked off to look at the sheep in the fields below. They were already complaining to each other, in long, lowing baas. A few deer poked through the trees and sampled the early morning grass. Nate came up beside her. He was about to take another step when she remembered.

"Ha-ha," she said, clutching his arm.

She pointed down.

"The fuck?" he said, looking down at the sheer, unmarked drop.

"It's supposed to keep the animals away while preserving the view. They call it a ha-ha."

"Like that laugh the kid from *The Simpsons* makes? What is *wrong* with people?"

"A lot of things," she replied. She sat down on the ground, letting her legs dangle over the edge. She felt the wet grass soak into the butt of her onesie. It was not designed for this sort of use. Possibly any use. David was asleep upstairs right now. She had so little time left here, but it all seemed so hopeless. Why bother?

Because Angela was out there somewhere.

"Can we talk about something else for one second?" he said, sitting down next to her.

She turned in surprise.

"Well, since we seem to be in the middle of goddamned nowhere with no one around, and I was planning on . . . I figured this trip was a good time, and since we're out here at dawn for no particular reason . . ."

Nate was struggling with words, squinting at the pale moon above them.

"What?" she prompted.

"Okay," he said. "You know, like, you and David?"

Stevie cocked her head in confusion.

"You and David," he said again. "Vi and Janelle. I don't know if you've noticed, but that's not . . . me."

"What's not you?"

"Romance," he said. "Being with someone."

"I've noticed," she said.

"No," he said. "I mean . . . ever."

Stevie turned this over in her mind for a second.

"I'm saying I'm ace," he said. "Asexual. I always knew, but I only kind of put the words to it in the last few months," he went on. "You're the first person I've told."

That Nate was ace wasn't a surprise, really—but him taking her aside to share something this important was. Stevie found herself unexpectedly choking up. She pretended to shift a hair out of her eye to clear a little tear.

Nate eyed this sign of emotion warily.

"Are you going to tell the others?" she asked.

"Probably soon," he said. "Janelle will probably crochet me an ace pride scarf or something."

"Ask her to make you an ace pride drone."

"She would actually do that, wouldn't she?"

"And she'd knit a little hat for it," Stevie said, nodding.

"I'm going to wait until we get back. I can only handle

so much of this kind of stuff at once." He rubbed his eyes sleepily. "We already have a lot going on. But I wanted to tell *you* while we were here, and this seemed like the right time. I mean, I was up and you got up and we're out doing something stupid."

"Wait." Stevie pivoted toward him sharply. "Does this have anything to do with all this writing you're suddenly doing? Did coming out help you start writing again?"

"Oh my God," he said, rubbing his forehead. "Shut up. I'm just writing. I write. I always write."

"You don't," Stevie said, half under her breath. "But whatever."

Nate inhaled sharply through his nose and Stevie moved quickly to redirect the conversation.

"You know how I feel about you, right?" she said. "Like, if you needed a kidney or something, you should definitely come to me after you've asked everyone else you can think of."

"This is why I decided to tell you first," he replied. "You're sort of as close as I get to that stuff. That's why I keep following you to second locations."

They exchanged a long look of understanding. Nate, shaggy and lanky and surprisingly strong, the sleeves of his hoodie pulled down over his palms. She couldn't even remember being a Stevie without a Nate. A silver dawn started to bloom. It was misty—droplets of moisture on everything with a gentle light shining through it. Everything had a magical air, softened, as if reality had been put through a soft-focus filter. It wasn't daylight yet, but it was coming.

"Okay," he said, getting up. "We're done with feelings, right? Let's go back inside. My ass is freezing."

As soon as Stevie got up and turned back toward the house, she saw a figure striding across the wide expanse of the front lawn in their direction carrying something in their hands. She felt a jolt of fear, and the sudden desire to push Nate off the edge of the ha-ha to safety. This was it. She had taken him out to this remote place and they were going to die.

Except it was Theo, carrying two steaming mugs. Unlike Stevie and Nate, she was fully dressed for the day—jeans, a sweater, a wool coat, and a matching hat.

"I saw you through my bedroom window," she said. "I always wake up early. Never have been able to sleep in. I thought you might be cold, so I brought you something to warm you up. Americans generally prefer coffee in the morning, I think? I hope instant is all right."

This behavior of Theo's had been recorded in the statements. Theo bringing people tea and water and coffee. Always the doctor, taking care of everyone.

"Bit early to be out walking," she said. "But it looks like you never went back to bed."

"Just thinking everything over," Stevie answered honestly.

"I was doing the same," Theo said.

Theo sat down on the stone step of the folly, and Stevie did as well. Nate lurked a bit, leaning against a pillar.

"It's a very strange feeling," Theo said, "a secret I've been holding all these years being out in the open at last. What you did last night was impressive. It's . . . so strange. I feel like something's missing. Of course, something—someone—is missing."

"Do you have any idea where she might be?" Stevie asked.

"If I had the *slightest* clue where Angela was, I'd be there right now, not here."

"Because you think she's in trouble," Stevie said.

Theo looked at the ground.

"I work in emergency medicine," she finally said. "I see so many things, every day, from the most mundane to the utterly bizarre. Many things can happen. I don't speculate. I treat the situation as it comes to me. In this case, all I know is that Angela left her house the other night, took the Tube to Waterloo, and hasn't been seen since. None of that bodes well."

"Do you work nights at the hospital? I mean, if someone had been brought in?"

"I work during the day. Benefit of seniority. But I checked, believe me. I checked every A and E in London, and I know the police have checked all over the country. Coming here—at least we could be together, support Izzy, not worry by ourselves."

Theo rubbed her hands together against the morning chill.

"Whatever happened," Stevie said, "it probably has something to do with what happened here, what she believes happened here. Was there anything she ever said about it to you? About investigating?"

"Not about investigating," Theo replied. "The only thing she ever said . . . it was the day we found them. That afternoon. The police interviewed us all, one by one. Angela was cold—shock can do that—so she went upstairs to take a bath. I went up to bring her tea. She was very upset. We all were, obviously. She was having a strong physical reaction to the news, shaking all over. She told me Rosie had pulled her aside when we arrived and wanted to talk to her about something important, but she didn't have the chance. Then Angela started talking about seeing the lock off the door of the woodshed during the game and something about a light inside."

"You knew about that?" Stevie asked.

"You must understand, Stevie. We were all drunk during the night and in shock the next day. I'm not sure how reliable any of our memories or accounts are. I also don't know what Angela's story about the lock means, even if it's true."

"She mentioned a button in her texts to you all that night," Stevie said. "Do you know what she meant?"

"No idea at all. I'm sure it was a typo. Anyway, there'll be breakfast in an hour or so. Sebastian has enough food in there to feed an army."

With that, she stood and made her way back to the house, with the focused stride of someone who walks the halls of a hospital all day and always has somewhere to be.

"Did you get the feeling she didn't just come out here to bring us instant coffee?" Nate asked, holding his face over the hot steam coming off his mug. "I felt like she was trying to tell us something. I mean, there was the stuff about Angela coming to her, but it seemed like something more."

Theo had made it to the low stone steps that rose to the terrace, then passed under the portico and out of sight.

"I think . . ." Stevie said slowly, running her gaze over Merryweather's grand facade, ". . . that Theo can't sleep because she just realized things in 1995 didn't go down the way she thought they did."

"I guess that would be a bad surprise."

"I think she's more than surprised," Stevie replied. "She's a really smart woman. I think she's terrified."

25

WHEN STEVIE GOT BACK TO HER ROOM, SHE FOUND DAVID WAS gone. She put her hand on the side of the bed he'd been sleeping in and found that the sheets held a trace of warmth. In the hall, she heard voices and creaking footsteps—Merryweather was waking up.

She showered quickly under the luxurious rainfall shower, taking advantage of the fancy products that were stocked in the bathroom. She emerged smelling of gardenias and orange blossom, with her blond hair wet. She shook it out, pulled on her jeans and hoodie, and made her way back downstairs.

Julian was pacing the main hall, talking on the phone and running his hand through his hair.

". . . yes, I know, Fiona, but the vote is on Tuesday. Yes. Yes, I *know* . . ."

"Morning," said a voice behind her. Sooz was coming down the stairs, her curly red hair a halo against the sober dark paneling of the staircase. She wore a petal-pink jumpsuit, rolled at the ankles, and white combat boots.

"I hope you got some more sleep last night after I woke you," she said.

It may have been Stevie's imagination, but she seemed to linger on the word *sleep*.

"There's coffee and tea in the kitchen," she said, continuing past Stevie and going in that direction. Yash and Peter were in the sitting room opposite each other, each with his laptop open and an intent look on his face. Peter had a slouchy way of sitting. He was dressed in jeans and an orange-and-red-striped sweater that made his own golden-red hair stand out. He had such a heavy-lidded expression that he looked like he might be falling asleep, but Stevie could see his eyes were intently focused on Yash. Yash was dressed in a hoodie and sweatpants and was making a gesture that was either a mime of playing trombone or something obscene.

". . . and *then* we say something about him being a prick," he said.

"That's too obvious," Peter replied.

"What about something about letting the dogs out?" Yash countered.

"We made that joke three weeks ago."

"It wasn't that exact joke."

"Close enough."

"So it's a callback," Yash said.

"That's not a callback. That's just a repeated joke."

Yash reached up and rubbed his curly hair in thought.

Someone else was coming down the steps now. Stevie turned to find Nate, dressed in a stretched-out black turtleneck and a worn pair of jeans. His hair was also wet, stuck across his forehead.

"Hey," he said, tapping his fingers on the banister. "What are you doing?"

"Just watching," she said. "I guess that's what writing looks like."

Yash noticed that he and Peter had a small audience and waved Stevie and Nate into the sitting room. It had a strange feel in the morning—the chairs were too low and soft, the drapes too thick, the glasses and trays of drinks not appropriate for the hour.

"This is how jokes get written," Yash explained. "I make offerings and he insults them."

"Edits them," Peter replied.

Yash gestured as if to say, *You see?*

"In this case," Peter said, "we've got a government minister who keeps cheating on his spouse and getting caught. This is the third time this year. And we've got to come up with new jokes about him."

Behind them, Julian was pacing the cavernous hall again, still talking about an upcoming vote.

"Oh, not Julian," Yash said, sensing the direction Stevie was looking. "Not this time. But we've written jokes about Julian for the show too."

"We had *years* of material stored up for that," Peter added. He shut his laptop with finality. "Bugger if I know what to write right now. Let's continue after breakfast."

There was a general movement toward the kitchen, where Sebastian, Theo, and Sooz were all engaged in different activities. Theo was on the phone, talking doctor talk about a patient.

". . . well, I did send a message to neurology, but no one got back to me. Has the bloodwork come back yet?"

Sooz sipped a coffee and paged through the glossy color supplement from the newspaper on the table. Sebastian, meanwhile, ran from stove, to fridge, to sink, to counter, managing all the pans and trays he had going. The air was thick with good smells—frying bacon and sausages, some savory scents that she could not place.

"Have you had a full English?" Sebastian asked cheerfully. "It's a cultural icon. Eggs, bacon, sausage, beans, tomatoes, mushrooms, and the most important . . ."

He held up something that appeared to be dark salami.

"Black pudding," he said.

"Pudding?" Nate asked.

"It's not pudding," Sooz said, wrinkling her nose. "It's made of blood. There are veggie sausages as well, for those of us who don't want to eat congealed pig's blood."

"Pig's blood and *spices*. It's delicious."

"Yum," Nate said grimly. Sooz nodded agreement.

"Don't be put off," Sebastian said. "It's a national classic."

"Yash, grab the bacon from under the broiler, would you? Peter, the mushrooms and tomatoes are in the slow oven down there. Nate, Stevie, would you mind taking those teacups and plates through to the dining room?"

Stevie and Nate each grabbed a stack of crockery and brought it through. As they dropped them off, Stevie picked up an empty wine bottle that was still on the table from the night before. She considered it for a moment.

"It's a bottle," Nate said. "Hold it up to your ear and you can hear the vineyard."

Stevie kept looking at the bottle for a long moment, setting it down when the parade of breakfast foods came through the door. Yash wrangled a platter of still-spitting sausages and bacon. Peter carried the tomatoes and beans and mushrooms. Sooz kept the plant-based food away from the black pudding and animal grease that was going everywhere. Sebastian brought up the rear with platters of eggs and racks of toast.

"Get Theo and Julian, won't you?" he asked Sooz.

Sooz went off, and a moment later her trained voice rang through the entirety of Merryweather, curling through the hall and slipping under doors.

"Would you like to learn something about country house etiquette?" Sebastian asked them. "Meals were always served at table by servants—except for breakfast. One always serves oneself at breakfast from the sideboard. I'm doing it that way because I am lazy and cannot be buggered to serve these layabouts. And everyone likes a buffet."

Theo reappeared, looking harried.

"They're having a nightmare of a morning at A and E," she said. "I had to explain I was out of town. I'm starving."

Janelle and Vi appeared, summoned by a text from Nate. David took a moment longer, and Izzy was last. This was curious, but Stevie shook it off.

Julian still had not appeared.

"Always the last one," Sebastian said.

"Must be off saving the country," Peter said.

"I'll text him," Theo said.

"Anyway! Let's start."

Everyone filled up their plates and took a seat.

"What are your plans?" Sooz asked them.

"We have to go back to London today," Janelle said, with a subtle side-eye at Stevie. "It's our last day in England. We fly home tomorrow."

"Do you have something enjoyable planned for the last night?" Sebastian said.

"Tea," Vi replied. "At a hotel in Soho. And then we're going to see *Richard III* at the Barbican."

"Oh," Sooz said. "I've got three friends in that production. I could text them and let them know you're coming. They could show you around backstage, if you'd like?"

"What about you, Izzy?" Sebastian said gently. "You're welcome to stay here with us, or if you want to go back with your friends . . ."

"I think I'll go back," she said. "I have lecture notes to go over and a project to work on. And I'll go over and clean Angela's flat and feed Doorknob. She left it a mess. I might stay there until she gets back."

"Good idea," Sebastian said.

"I have a stupid question," Stevie said. "I wanted to get something for my dad. He loves whisky, and I can buy it here legally . . ."

This immediately caught the attention of all her friends, who knew that there was basically no way in hell Stevie was bringing her parents home a bottle of whisky. A magnet, maybe.

"And . . . this is weird, but . . . in the statements, I was reading about this amazing bottle of whisky? You drank something, you know . . . and I know you know whisky . . ."

"Oh, that whisky," Sebastian said, nodding. "I don't think you're going to find that one at duty-free, and if you did, you wouldn't buy it."

"Why?"

"Because it cost ten thousand pounds," Sebastian said, slicing himself a large chunk of sausage. "In the nineties. It would probably be about forty thousand pounds today."

"You drank a ten-thousand-pound bottle of whisky?" Stevie said.

"Oh yes. Every drop."

"You were obsessed about that whisky," Peter said.

"*I* wasn't obsessed with it. My father was. He sought rare

361

bottles, and that one was the rarest of the lot. He seemed to value that bottle of whisky more than me. I was determined that we should drink it as a symbolic gesture."

"Except you almost knocked the house over getting it out of the cabinet," Yash said.

"I remember approaching the cabinet elegantly."

"You crawled," Theo said.

"With a candle in your hand," Yash added. "Which I took. Then you banged and scratched that cabinet door until Peter got on his hands and knees and helped you open it."

"I was testing the soundness of the wood."

"It's still got the scratches," Yash said. "I looked. Someone's tried to cover them, but I saw them."

"Must have been the cat."

"You don't have a cat," Sooz said.

"I have *you*," Sebastian replied. "That's close enough."

Julian appeared in the dining room doorway, making an entrance as usual.

"The eggs are cold, darling," Sebastian said. "I hope your constituents know the pains you go to on their behalf."

Julian did not respond. He looked out over the table at his friends and the strangers he had just met. His shy, come-hither glance was more deliberate. He couldn't quite look up. The table came to nervous attention. Stevie stiffened and put down her fork.

"They found her," Julian said quietly.

"Where?" Izzy said. "Where is she?"

"Is she all right?" Yash added.

Mumbled versions of these questions came from almost everyone. But not Theo. Theo looked down at her plate.

"They found her," Julian said with an obvious effort to keep his voice clear and steady. "In the river."

26

SHE HAD SURFACED NEAR A PLACE CALLED LIMEHOUSE, WHICH WAS A section of the Thames on the east side of London, where the river bends. This was all there was to know. The breakfast broke up. Izzy got up and left the room. David went after her. Janelle, Vi, and Nate immediately made quiet exits. Stevie wanted to do the same but found she could not move. Angela had been her case, her charge, her person to protect. She had known something was very wrong, but now it was final.

"Let's go and sit in the other room," Theo said gently, putting her hand on Yash's arm as he wept. "It's more comfortable."

Sooz and Peter supported each other. Sebastian sat at the table, stoic, for several more moments, looking at Julian.

"Thank you," he finally said. "For . . . making the calls."

Julian nodded grimly.

"Come on, Seb," he said. "Let's go with the others."

They all left, and Stevie sat at a long, empty breakfast table, dotted with squares of weak sunlight and bowls of beans and sausages.

Stevie felt the overwhelming need to get out of this house.

It wasn't raining yet, but there was a taste of it in the air. She put in her earbuds and listened to a podcast, mostly to drown out everything around her. She had failed. Failed utterly and totally. She had not saved Angela, not found Angela, not figured out what happened that night in 1995. Sure, she had gotten partway, but to something that wasn't murder, not even close.

Merryweather was a good place to get lost. Its twisting paths and walls of green invited you inside, to wander, to be absorbed and never look back. The house vanished behind the curtain of trees, the walls, the high yew hedges. Here, there were only the calls of birds, the giggle of the slender brook that wriggled through the grounds. She found herself in the room of topiary with the burbling fountain. The meditation spot. When she had first been diagnosed with anxiety, she had to take a meditation class. She kept forgetting to do it, even though she knew it helped and that it worked better as a practice. It changed the brain. She turned off her podcast and closed her eyes, trying to settle herself. She listened to the birds complaining overhead, the sound of the fountain.

Someone was there. She opened her eyes in a flash.

"Sorry to startle you," he said. "I came out for some air and to . . ."

He pulled a pack of cigarettes from his pocket.

"Do you mind?"

She shook her head. What was she going to say to him after what had just happened? That he couldn't have a cigarette outside at his friend's house now that his other friend was dead?

"I'm the only one who still smokes, I think," he said, sitting next to her on the bench. "Don't tell Theo. She'd be livid."

He put a cigarette in his mouth and lit it. Even now, maybe especially now, she saw the allure of Julian. He had an elegant slouch, a way of leaning on one knee. His eyes were so arresting. Double lashes, maybe? What was it about hair around the eye that was so mesmerizing?

"I'd like to speak to you, actually," he said, exhaling a long plume of smoke. "It's clear you're very perceptive. I read up on you last night, in fact. The cases you've solved. Quite remarkable."

Stevie mumbled thanks.

"Last night," he said, "you asked me if they'd traced Angela's phone. I had a bit more detail about that than I let on."

"I could tell," she said.

"The pings indicated that she was walking between Waterloo and Vauxhall—that's along the river. It's about a mile and a half. That time of night, parts of it would be desolate. I had a pretty good idea what that probably meant. I didn't want to upset everyone before we knew for sure."

He took a long drag, examined the cigarette, then stubbed it out carefully on the metal arm of the bench. He pinched the end to make sure it was fully extinguished, then slid it back into the pack. The pack went back into his pocket, and then he withdrew his phone.

"My contact sent me some more information just now. I want your opinion."

He passed his phone over to Stevie. There was an email up on the screen that came from someone at the Metropolitan Police.

Body found at Limehouse at 19.50 in the evening. Pronounced on scene. Time of death unable to be determined but likely over 48 hours. No visible injuries. Purse contained: wallet (containing £40 and credit cards, intact), set of keys, phone, Oyster card, new Oral-B toothbrush in package, box of Strepsils, blister pack of Nytol (can hold seven tablets, six were missing, one remaining), five large rocks. Identification based on cards in wallet, verified through photo match pending formal identification. Postmortem scheduled for tomorrow morning.

"Nytol is sleeping medicine," Julian said. "I'm sure you could gather that by the name. There's little doubt what happened here."

"Where did she get the rocks?" Stevie asked. "Where do you get rocks in London?"

"There are many beachy areas along the Thames. It's not hard to find rocks along the shoreline, especially when the tide is out. I did check. Low tide was at eleven p.m. that night. What I want to ask you . . . these details, do you think knowing this would be easier for Izzy or harder? You're her friend, and you seem to have a head for this sort of thing. Should I tell her about those?"

"I think," Stevie said after a long moment, "she should know, but it would be easier coming from us. Could you share that with me, and we can show it to her when the time is right? Or, David will."

"That's very sensible," Julian agreed. He screenshotted the message and sent it over to Stevie. He thanked her, excused himself for interrupting her privacy, and left her sitting in the calm greenery.

Stevie also had little doubt what had happened here. Six sleeping pills and five large rocks. She was looking at the tools that had led to Angela's murder.

When Stevie stepped back inside Merryweather, the house had an uneasy quiet. The doors to the sitting room were open, but no one was inside. People had dispersed. The great grandfather clock ticked heavily. The house made an occasional conversational creak, but otherwise, all was silent.

She returned to her bedroom, hearing only slight noises from behind some of the doors—muffled sobs and voices. She packed quickly, pressing the fire safe back into the suitcase. Then she walked down the hall on the tips of her toes; it didn't feel like the right time to be heard walking around. She approached David's door and wrapped on it softly. There was no reply. She decided to walk around a bit more, turning the corner and entering a bit of the upstairs she had not been in before. Behind one of the doors, she could just make out David's voice, soft and low. She knocked on this one, and after a moment, she was told to come in. She pushed open the door to a cheerful rose-pink bedroom with a four-poster bed dominating the center of the room. David and Izzy were sitting on the bed. Well, not sitting. Reclining. Izzy was curled up in a near-fetal position, her head resting on David's chest.

Stevie found that a lump of bile had surfaced in her throat, and she was balling her hands into tight, nervous fists.

"Hey," she said.

"One second, Iz," David said, slipping Izzy off his chest gently. She dropped down onto the pillows, all dead weight, and turned her face into their depths. David came over and motioned for Stevie to join him in the hall.

"She doesn't seem . . . good."

"No," David said. "She's not."

"The car is coming in a few minutes," Stevie said. "Do you want me to get your stuff together for you?"

"Izzy needs to stay here for a little while," he said in a low voice. "She wants to be here. I feel like I should . . . stay with her."

"Stay?" Stevie asked.

"Only for a few hours. There's a train later this afternoon. And you have stuff today, right? Tea and a show or something? I can meet you after that."

He was accurate—they did have plans all that afternoon.

And sure, Izzy had suffered a huge loss and needed support. He was doing the right thing. But she had just entered the final twenty-four hours of her trip. Everything counted now. The car ride, sitting together on the train—all these moments she couldn't have again, because she was leaving England.

She forced her face into something that was appropriate for the occasion—something serious, understanding. A heavy sadness started to fall over her limbs.

A few minutes later, a car came crunching up the drive, and then they were on their way back to London. Stevie turned to look at Merryweather as they went. It shrank in the distance before winking away through the trees.

"Have a nice visit?" the driver asked cheerfully.

The train ride back to London was subdued. Janelle and Vi sat on one side of a table and Stevie and Nate on the other. After Stevie recounted what she had learned from Julian, no one said much of anything for some time. Because what could be said? The trip had resulted in nothing but bad news. The weather was dreary. Rain spat at the train windows.

"Tea is at four," Janelle finally said. "We should make it on time."

Of course. Their final day. Tea and theater. Normal tourist things. This was supposed to be the celebration—the cherry on the sundae.

"What were you doing at breakfast?" Nate asked. "With the wine bottle. The whisky. What was that about?"

"I don't know," Stevie said. "I saw the empty wine bottle

on the table, and I thought about how they were drinking that night. There's this point in the night that almost everyone mentions—they come back in and have the fancy bottle of whisky. Everything kind of stops after that."

"You think they were drugged or something?" Janelle asked.

Stevie shook her head noncommittally.

"I don't know what I think. Just . . . *something* about it. It matters somehow."

"Can I say something awkward?" Vi cut in. "You think one of your friends is a murderer. You accidentally say this out loud to your niece while you're on painkillers. Your niece tells a bunch of Americans she's just met, one of whom has solved a murder before. You tell your friends you should meet at the place where the murder happened. And then you leave the house, take a bunch of sleeping pills, and jump into the river."

"And you leave one in the package in your purse," Stevie said, "just in case anyone has any questions."

"She was drugged and dumped in the river," Nate said. "That's what we're all thinking, right?"

"Definitely," Stevie said. "Probably."

"But what can you do about it?" Janelle said. It wasn't meant unkindly—it was a practical question. And the answer seemed to be, not much.

27

THE TEA WAS AT A HOTEL IN SOHO—SOME FANCY BOUTIQUE PLACE known for elaborate afternoon tea. They had all agreed to this, but as they approached the hotel doors, Nate started to backtrack.

"Maybe we could get actual food?" he asked. "It's fifty pounds a person, and it's just tea."

"It's tea, and sandwiches, and desserts," Janelle said. "We have to do a British tea. Come on. We *agreed* to this. This is the last day of our trip, and we have . . . to make something of it."

Instead of a fizzy, fun atmosphere, it was a somewhat grim group around the gaily laid table, with its lush arrangement of fresh flowers and a cheerful set of green-and-white china cups. Before them was placed a three-tiered selection of small sandwiches, cut into delicate, crustless rectangles. The waiter pointed at them in turn, introducing the smoked salmon with the filled cream cheese, the Stilton with apple and mayonnaise, the coronation chicken and celeriac, the Yorkshire ham and mustard. Another tiered dish came laden with scones and

Cornish clotted cream, lemon curd and jam, tiny chocolate cakes, tarts of winter fruits and bramble jelly, spiced carrot cakes with cardamom. More and more things arrived at the table—all the little plates required for the little foods, the dish of brown and white sugar lumps, rough and uneven, the silver utensils and tea strainers and the tea strainer holders and the special knives for spreading the cream . . .

So many *things*.

It only served to remind Stevie of that dinner at Angela's— the many bowls of curry, the rice on the side with the flecks of yellow on top, the half dozen or so chutneys and accompaniments, the breads and the popadams . . .

Angela talking about Anne Boleyn. The swordsman standing there, calling to an imaginary assistant to get the victim to turn their head to better meet the needs of the sword.

A ruse so you could murder them.

"Is anything wrong?" the server asked, concerned by the many untouched sandwiches and cakes. They all made for the food to show that they were fine, just normal tourists being normal at tea. Stevie ate a little chocolate cake. It landed in her stomach like a lump of wet sand. She checked her messages. Nothing from David.

How's it going? she wrote. Do you know when you'll be back?

No dots appeared. It was almost five o'clock. Their show started at seven. *Richard III.* Stevie felt like watching a play about as much as she felt like tipping this pot of scalding-hot tea into her own lap, but what else was there to do? Angela was dead. She'd failed, and she would be leaving England tomorrow.

The show was at the Barbican, which was a complex built of concrete—a fortress, sort of like the Tower of London, it was made of bare concrete lumps instead of stone towers. More brutalism, Janelle told them.

"How did anyone make something this ugly?" Vi asked. "They could have made anything at all, and they decided to make this."

"I kind of love it," Nate said, looking around. "It looks like the moisture farm that Luke Skywalker lives on."

"Me too," Janelle added. "It feels like a machine."

"Two different ways of looking at a big concrete block," Vi replied.

If you'd asked Stevie what *Richard III* was about, she would have said two and a half hours, with a few minutes in the middle to get some expensive M&M's from the lobby and shove them down her face near a concrete pole. There were a lot of people in tunics running on and offstage, seemingly all of them named Richard or Edward or Lord this or that, with the occasional Catesby thrown in to keep things confusing. Stevie had her phone in her lap for the entire performance, checking for texts from David that did not come, much to the annoyance of the woman sitting beside her, who huffed and tutted until Stevie got up and sat in the lobby for the final fifteen minutes. She must have missed the scene where Richard begged for a horse. She could guess that he wasn't going to get one. No horse for you, Richard.

She didn't want to be angry. She didn't want to be wandering around the lobby of a brutalist building with only hours left to go in this country before she would be ripped away from all this, from David, from the case, from the misting rain and the relentless tea drinking.

"Why did you leave?" Janelle said as they exited the theater at the end of the play.

"Sorry," Stevie replied. "I just couldn't sit there anymore."

"I didn't really like it either," Vi said, rubbing the peach fuzz on the back of their head.

The events of the day had gotten the better of them. No amount of tiny cakes and tea and screaming English lords was going to fix it.

On the Tube ride back to Craven House, the group settled into a damp silence. The silence came from the knowledge that the trip was pretty much officially over at this point, and the damp from the invisible rain that had attacked them on the way to the station.

"I'm going to figure it out on the plane," Janelle said out of nowhere. "How many schools. I'm going to pick them on the plane. I'll have eight hours and probably no internet. I just need to get it done."

She turned to Vi, silently asking the question, "Are you in?" Because their project was largely a joint one.

"Maybe," Vi said. "Can we see? I might just want to watch movies. Planes are so . . . I get sad on planes sometimes."

Janelle slid her arm over Vi's shoulder and kissed their forehead. Stevie could tell she was disappointed in the answer, but if planes made Vi sad, there was no way she was going to push it.

"How about you?" she asked Nate. "Want to work lists with me?"

"What?"

"I need to spreadsheet," Janelle said. "Figure this out. We can work on our lists. Want to?"

"I'm good," Nate said.

"Just tell me how many you've gotten down to. I need to figure this out. I need to make *something* work."

Stevie lifted her head from her phone (which wasn't really getting a good signal on the Tube anyway). Something was happening here. Janelle was about as frustrated as Stevie had ever seen her. The fact that this trip hadn't been quite what she'd expected was eating at her, and she had to pull a victory from the rubble.

"How many have you applied to so far?" she asked. "I need something to work with. Data."

Nate looked up like Janelle had pulled a gun on him.

"Come on," Janelle said. "What? Is it a secret?"

Nate's expression suggested that it was very much a secret. He was being evasive in a way that didn't quite make sense. Something bubbled in Stevie's mind. There had been a pattern developing. She'd been clocking it without being entirely aware that she was doing so. Nate had been writing all the time—or, Nate had been doing *something* on his

376

computer. He'd been skipping the occasional meal or coffee, and his credit card wasn't working.

"Oh my God," Stevie said. "You've been applying to schools. *That's* what you've been doing."

Nate's face flushed a faint purple. She'd hit the mark. Janelle and Vi looked to Stevie in confusion.

"How many?" Stevie asked.

Nate looked at her with an expression that said, *I am never letting you use my ace pride drone.*

"Seventy-one," he finally said.

Silence for a moment from the assembled.

"Is that even legal?" Vi finally asked.

"How?" Janelle said. "How did you apply to seventy-one schools? You'd had to have applied somewhere every day for the last two months."

"Not every day," Nate said, his shoulders sagging. "Not every day. There's the Common application, and you can use a lot of the stuff over again. It's not that—"

"How did you even get all the recommendation letters?" Vi asked.

"I didn't use Ellingham," he said in a low voice. "I asked my editor and agent to write letters, and this guy who runs a book festival. They gave me form letters that I could adjust to wherever I was sending them."

"*Seventy-one*," Janelle repeated. "That's . . . how much did that even cost?"

Having admitted this much, Nate was prepared to give his full confession.

"Five thousand seven hundred and forty dollars," he said. "So far. Some of them haven't run my card yet. I don't know where to go, okay? And I thought—if I'm going to have to be in debt for the rest of my life to go to school, I should probably pick the right one. But they're all just . . . brick buildings and people walking around with backpacks and doing presentations in front of whiteboards full of triangles, and I have no fucking idea which one to choose. There are the little weird ones where you can make your own major so you can study the history of teacups or vibes or whatever you want. There are big ones that have buildings with pillars and they offer everything and it's like living in a city. And then there's where—like, they are all in cute little towns where the leaves are always changing, or are in the city. There are some near the beach. There's one where everyone kitesurfs all the time . . ."

"Kitesurfs," Janelle repeated. "You. Kitesurfing."

"I don't know! They don't *make* you kitesurf. I'm just saying."

"Do you even like the beach?" Stevie asked.

"Everyone likes the beach! I'm a swimmer! I'm just saying, I don't know where to go so I figured I'd cast a wide net."

The train arrived at their stop, and they disembarked quietly. At least Stevie had solved one mystery, even if it had raised more questions than it had answered.

When they got back to Craven House, Stevie went directly to David and Izzy's side of the building. She knocked on his door but got no answer. She asked a few people who walked by, and eventually found someone who knew where Izzy's room was—it was at the other end of the hall, through two fire doors and down a pointless set of three steps. Beyond the door, Stevie could hear music playing—low. Something calm. When she knocked, there was the sound of movement, a pause, and then Izzy opened the door. To Stevie's surprise, she immediately caught her in an embrace.

"Come in," she said.

Though Izzy had the same basic room as Stevie occupied, it had none of the plastic quality. The bed was covered in a thick, sunshine-yellow duvet with white dots. The walls were hung with prints and colorful boards on which schedules, reading lists, and little handwritten notes were pinned. Her desk was stacked with books, empty champagne bottles, a pair of engraved wineglasses, a feather boa around a mirror. There was a white shag rug on the floor, along with a pile of fuzzy pillows. David was resting on and against this assortment of plush objects. He nodded to her but didn't move to get up.

"I was wondering if I could talk to David," Stevie said.

"Oh. Of course. Of *course*."

David peeled himself from the carpet with less enthusiasm than she anticipated. Stevie didn't know what was happening, but it appeared that he wasn't particularly eager to speak to her. Tonight. Their last night together. He stepped out into the hall, shutting the door behind him.

"When did you get back?" she asked, trying to act like

she hadn't noticed anything amiss.

"About an hour ago."

An hour? That was so late.

"Do you want to . . . come back? With me?"

"I will," he said. "She's still wrecked. Let me stay with her for a little bit and I'll come over."

"But you've been gone all day," she said. It didn't come out the way she meant it to. It was sharp. Peevish.

"Her aunt just died," he said.

"I know that," Stevie said.

"I just need to make sure she's okay and then I'll come over."

"Are you mad at me?" she asked.

"What?"

"Because I failed," she said. She lowered her voice, conscious of the other people coming in and out of their rooms, and Izzy just beyond the door.

"This isn't *about* you," he said. "It's not about whether or not you solved it, like you always do."

The words were like a slap. Stevie reeled. He'd gotten her feelings, but also her pride. She straightened up.

"It's fine," she said. "Don't worry about it."

She turned and walked away without saying anything else. She expected him to call out, to catch up with her. She lingered for a moment by the one fire door like she was looking for something in her pocket, but he didn't come. The same when she lingered by the next fire door, and the lobby. She almost turned back but realized that would not work.

She had to do this on his schedule now.

She waited with the door cracked halfway open for most of the night, lingering, trying to look ready, but not too ready. Casual. She tried to read, to listen to something, to watch TV. But she had to keep one ear open for any movement in the hall, any sign of a message. Midnight passed. One in the morning. Two.

Her lack of sleep from the night before caught up with her. She fell asleep sitting up, wearing the onesie, the door open a crack all night long.

No one came.

28

STEVIE WOKE TO A STEADY PATTER OF RAIN ON THE WINDOW. A steely London morning. Last night was a waste, and now all she had was . . .

She consulted her phone.

Four hours. That's how much time she had left before they went to the airport.

Also, no texts from David.

That had been a bad scene last night, a weird argument. He'd had a point—she had been focused on herself, on them. Izzy had experienced a terrible loss. But it was still her last day, and now the last hours, and he'd spent the entire day yesterday with Izzy. Was it so much to want to see the boyfriend you'd crossed the ocean to visit?

Maybe no texts was a good sign. This was how they were—they got mad at each other, walked it off, and came back fresh. There was just so little time.

She took a speedy shower, missing the rainfall-style water and the beautiful-smelling soaps of the day before. She dressed before she was fully dry, her jeans clinging to her damp legs as she pulled them on. She stared at her stuff scattered around the room. Dirty clothes, bags, some jam for her mom, some weird tea, a book about murders . . . all these cords and adapters and things to charge and documents to find. She needed to pack. But she also needed to see David immediately. She would bring him over here while she packed. She had to take the fire safe back over to Izzy, anyway. In the confusion of leaving Merryweather without Izzy or David, she had ended up taking it with her.

She hustled down the hall, bypassing the far-too-slow little elevator, and taking the stairs far too quickly. She half ran through the lobby, past the sad Christmas tree, then ran up the steps to David's room. She knocked. Nothing. Tried again. Tried the door. Locked.

She texted him.

Where are you?

Down the street getting a coffee, he answered.

I'll meet you outside, she replied.

She considered running the fire safe up to Izzy, but that would take too much time. She took it outside with her and waited on the front steps of Craven House, shivering in the chill. It took David at least fifteen minutes to come back with his coffee, which was ridiculous. Every second counted now. She tried to compose herself. Look patient. Not desperate. Cool. Like it was no big deal. Just a girl with a fire safe about to catch a plane and leave her boyfriend.

He finally appeared from around a parked van, the coat snapping around his ankles. He was wearing a worn green

T-shirt and jeans, as well as a black knit hat. He had put no effort into this, she knew. He probably hadn't even showered. This kind of effortless bullshit was part of his appeal. She both resented it and felt it tugging at every part of her.

"I got you a coffee," he said quietly.

Already, her ice was starting to melt.

"Thanks," she said, accepting it. She expected him to sit on the step next to her, but he remained standing. He wasn't smiling—which made sense, as they were about to be parted. But his expression was distant. Distracted, almost.

"Do you want to . . . sit?" she asked.

"How about we walk for a minute."

Stevie nodded toward the heavy fire safe.

"I'll carry it," he said. "Let's walk."

"I have to pack," she said.

"Ten minutes. Look at the view."

She could maybe do ten minutes, though her pulse was quickening.

They walked the familiar path in the direction of the river, but David's steps were slow.

"You didn't text last night," she said.

"No. Sorry."

"Or come by."

"You said not to."

"I said whatever," she clarified. "I didn't say . . ."

There was no time for this, much as it irritated her. He had wasted the last night they had together on semantics and pettiness.

"You haven't asked how Izzy is," he said, sipping his coffee.

"How is she?" Stevie asked.

"Pretty bad. But getting English about it again. Stiff upper lip. She's going to speak to the undertaker today to plan the funeral."

This was not something Stevie had considered. Funerals were . . . things that just happened. She didn't know. She had never been to one. But to have to plan one yourself? Call an *undertaker*?

"I'm sorry," she said.

"Not your fault."

"No. I know. But . . . it still feels . . ."

It's not about you, he had said.

David stopped, even though they had not gotten to the riverside yet. They were standing on the street by the bus stop. He drained his coffee in one long final gulp and dropped the cup into the trash.

"Are we . . . crossing the street?" she said. "Because I kind of need to pack, and I thought you could come with me while I do it?"

He rubbed at the tip of his nose.

"I know," he said. "I get it. I . . . I get it."

He had no idea what it was he got, and she had no idea what he got twice. Stevie felt something in the left side of her chest, around her heart. It felt to her like her blood had started running backward in her veins.

"What's happening right now?" she asked.

It was in the way he moved his chin—down, a little to the left. His eyes were focused on a delivery bike chained to a pole. He kept widening his eyes slightly like he was trying to wake up. He pulled the lapels of his coat closed over his chest.

"You and me," he said. "I'm . . ."

A seismic tremor passed over her nervous system. Her muscles went rigid.

"I don't think we should do this anymore," he said, looking down at his hands. "It's not working out."

"What do you mean?" she said, panic rising in her throat. He couldn't be saying this. This *could not* be happening.

"I don't think . . . it's good."

"Is this . . . Izzy?" she asked.

He cocked his head and shook it.

"Izzy? No. Nothing with me and Izzy. It's . . . me. It's . . ." Her phone was ringing.

"You should answer that," he said.

She wanted to throw the phone into the street. Instead, she stared at it. It was Janelle. She didn't answer.

"I'm sorry," he said. He didn't look at her. "You should probably go back. It's easier that way."

"David . . . ," she said, her voice a croak. This seemed to affect him, and he drew his arms closer into himself.

"Let me know you got back okay," he said. "When you land."

And then he turned and walked away, down the street, taking the fire safe with him. She wanted to run after him but found she couldn't move. She was magnetized to the sidewalk. Her brain was free-falling. It was a gentle fall, slow, like a feather on the wind, tacking back and forth toward the ground. It was almost funny. She might laugh, except there was a hollow ringing in her ears.

The phone rang again, and she answered it.

"Where are you?" Janelle said, out of breath. "We're . . ."

"He dumped me," Stevie replied before bursting into tears.

There was not a moment's hesitation.

"We're coming," she said. "Where are you?"

"What the hell happened?" Nate said as Janelle and Vi helped Stevie back to her room a few minutes later. Stevie was crying so hard she was hiccupping violently. Janelle and Vi eased her onto the bed.

"He dumped her," Vi explained.

"What? Just now?"

"Just now," Janelle said. "Because he's an asshole."

This was a crisis, and one that required organization. In other words, this was Janelle's moment to shine. They sat Stevie on the bed, and Janelle surveyed the mess around her. She looked almost pleased, like this was the kind of challenge she had been waiting for.

"Okay," she said. "We have five minutes. Vi. Everything out of the closet and drawers. Just dump it here in a pile. I'll sort and pack. Nate . . ."

Nate was retreating away from the doorway.

"Get her some water."

Nate vanished waterward.

As quick as Vi could throw items, Janelle plucked them up and rolled them. Everything—the dirty underwear and socks, the over-worn T-shirts. She found a nook for everything, from the unused tampons to the spare coat. She wrapped the jam and a coffee mug in clothes, picked through the toiletries, leaving behind anything that was no longer viable or posed a leak risk. Watching her, Stevie found that her crying was slowing. She was out of moisture. Out of energy. Transfixed by movement, like a lizard.

Nate returned with a bottle of water. He approached Stevie cautiously, like she might explode. She accepted it and tried to drink, but it started her hiccups again. Nate sat next to her, keeping an inch or two between them.

"Do you want me to. . ." He searched for something to say. "I don't know, punch him in the dick or something?"

"Leave that for me," Janelle said, maneuvering the last items into the bag. "Where's your passport, Stevie?"

Stevie glanced around and pointed at her backpack. Soon, everything had been accounted for. They gave her a cloth to wipe her face, took a box of tissues, and headed out. Stevie wondered if the elevator door would open and he'd be in the lobby, ready to apologize and call it all off.

But of course he wasn't.

Vi had gathered up their keys and placed them on the front desk. Her room was gone.

"All keys look the same," they said, trying to make conversation while the front desk person checked the keys back in. "You would think there would be more designs of keys . . ."

Janelle gestured that the car had arrived. And that was that. They were back in the car, back on the motorway, going back the way they had come.

Before David, Stevie had never had a boyfriend. That meant that she had never known what it meant to suddenly *not* have one. She had not experienced someone saying, "I don't want to be with you." It made no sense. It was David. Her David. Stevie and David. A giant hole had been ripped in the backdrop of her life, revealing some weird, indistinct vista ahead. England was being wiped away, mile by mile. Looking out the window reinforced her imminent departure, so Stevie closed her eyes. At first, the darkness brought a wild swell of pain—emotion she couldn't control or understand. It was a wave, and she was going under and would not survive. She pressed her eyes tightly, trying to remember the meditation tricks she'd learned to deal with anxiety. She would retreat so far inside herself the world would never see her again. Let the thoughts and feelings come. Just acknowledge them and let them be.

There was no name for this staggering monolith of heartbreak. She tried to note that it was pain—pain, pain, pain, fear, pain, agony, panic, pain, nausea, embarrassment, anger, loss . . .

Under all of that, something was calling to her.

You saw it, said a voice in her head. *You saw it*.

Saw what? Where?

The voice in her head mumbled, cleared its throat. Stevie

could almost hear it shuffling its notecards.

House, it finally replied. *House. You saw it in her house.*

Stevie grabbed this mental lifeline. She would give it every ounce of her being. She tightened her jaw and put in earbuds and blasted Britpop at herself. Get into the feeling of the time. The rhythm. The mindset. The jangling guitars and joking lyrics. She closed her eyes and floated around Angela's house in her mind. She materialized in the living room, staring down at the sofa. What color was it? Emerald. The wall behind it was slate gray. There were crumbs on the coffee table. There was the smell of the curry . . . this was followed by the smell of the curry in the garbage later. The sourness.

What else? Angela kept money in her kitchen. A fire safe under the stairs. Books in every room. Books and beheadings . . .

"We're here," Vi said gently.

They had stopped in front of the massive glass and metal of Heathrow Airport. They were inside, dragging bags, waiting in line. Then the bags were tagged and taken away on a conveyor belt and they were off to security to put their remaining belongings in bins.

Remaining belongings. What were they again? Sleeping pills. Rocks. Keys. Phone. Throat drops. A toothbrush, maybe? Something else.

She followed along behind the others, weaving through the crowds. She cast a dazed and sad eye over the many things the airport offered to her as she left. Surely, she couldn't depart England without a bottle of whisky, a set of china teacups, a Paddington Bear, a biography of some grim-looking sportsdude, an overpriced purse, a shawl, several bottles of perfume . . .

Did people come to the airport just to set their money on fire?

There were more practical offerings as well. Every other shop offered candy, water, luggage tags, and toothbrushes. Stuff you might have forgotten or need on the way.

You saw it, said the voice as Stevie was cleared through security. *You walked right by it.*

"Are you okay?" Janelle said. "You haven't said a word in almost an hour."

"Yeah," she mumbled. "I should get some water."

She spent the last of her English cash on a giant bottle of water and a candy bar. England was going to be over in less than an hour. Every step along the stark white corridors of Heathrow was a step away from everything. It was over. They followed the golden-yellow signs to their gate, where they had to go through one last passport and document check. Stevie was behind her friends, letting her vision go blurry.

If you go, the voice said to her, *you will never know.*

I have to, Stevie replied internally.

Then you'll never know what you saw. Never know what happened.

Nate was beeped through. Janelle. Vi.

Stevie stepped out of the line.

"Where are you going?" Nate said.

"I just need to pee," she said. "I'll be there in a second."

They had already crossed into the lounge. Stevie stepped back into the bathroom that was a few feet away from the line and locked herself into a stall. Her heart began to beat a little faster, and the fluorescent glow of the bathroom made a halo around her view of the world.

It was so close. It was right there. She squeezed her eyes shut. What had she seen?

A buzz. A text.

Are you okay? Janelle wrote.

Fine. Peeing.

Still?

Hurry.

We're getting on.

Stevie, we're on the plane.

WHERE ARE YOU?

Stevie was in the stall. She remained there when she heard, "Final call for flight seventeen to Boston. All passengers must immediately report to gate twenty-seven."

They just closed the boarding door?

WHAT THE HELL IS GOING ON

Stevie stepped out of the stall and gripped the edge of the sink as the announcement came that the gate was closed. She lifted her phone and texted a reply.

I have to finish this, she wrote to the three of them. I will get another flight. Not lying. Not pulling you into it. I will see you at home.

She switched off her phone and turned around to leave the airport.

29

Making her way back into London, by herself, at night, was a different experience. She took the Heathrow Express, back-tracking to Paddington. There was no warm bed waiting for her. No loving boyfriend. No friends at her side. No support of Ellingham Academy backing the trip. Just her and a phone rapidly running out of charge. There was enough to send one text message. As soon as she got the reply, she put her head back and tried to close her eyes. Tried to focus. Tried to keep the grief from pressing on her chest.

There was work to be done.

The train dumped her at Paddington, where she emerged in a crush of commuters. She used the remaining battery power on her phone to navigate the streets, winding her way back to Angela's shiny black door.

Izzy was waiting there, in her blue coat and a big pom hat. Doorknob wound around her. Izzy wore no makeup, and her eyes were puffy from crying.

"You missed your plane," Izzy said in greeting, as Stevie approached the door. "Are you going to be in trouble?"

"Yes," Stevie said simply.

"What are you looking for?" Izzy said, unlocking the door.

"I don't know. But I know I saw something, the thing that makes this all make sense. I just have to look at everything again until I recognize what it is."

Left unattended, even for a few days, houses take on a strange feel. The cold accumulates in the corners. The dark settles down and pools on the furniture. Quiet leaks everywhere. The air sours. Doorknob was fine with all this. He scrabbled inside, ran up the stairs like a bat out of hell, ran down again just as fast, chasing nothing.

It struck her instantly. She'd been too preoccupied to see the obvious. She went right to the little cabinet under the stairs, which was still partway open. She turned on her phone flashlight and shoved her head into the space, digging around until she could put her hand on Doorknob's disgusting little treasures: part of a dead mouse, a used tea bag, a dirty cotton swab, a tissue . . .

Two buttons.

She plucked them out and brought them into the light, setting them on the coffee table. One was bright pink, the other silver. And once they were on display, Stevie instantly began to dismiss them. If Angela had a critical piece of evidence in the form of a button, it seemed like she would lock it up in the secure fire safe rather than let her cat get it. Besides, these buttons were next to the fire safe.

"We think this is evidence?" Izzy said, looking down at

them doubtfully. "From 1995?"

Stevie deflated a bit when she heard the tone.

"They're buttons," she replied. "I just wanted to see them."

"This one," Izzy said, pointing at the bright pink one. "I think this comes off a sweater she has. It's this color and it buttons down the front. I can check upstairs. And this one . . ." Izzy leaned close to look at it. "It says Stella McCartney."

Stevie drew a blank. The name sounded familiar. McCartney.

"I don't think Stella McCartney was designing in the nineties," Izzy said. "Let me check."

Stevie deflated a bit further as Izzy checked her phone.

"2001," she said. "And I think I might know what this is from because I borrowed it once."

"I was just thinking about the button," Stevie said, trying to seem in control of this situation. "I just wanted to check."

"Of course!" Izzy said. Her voice was full of confidence. "Look around. I trust you. Do whatever you have to do."

That landed strangely. Izzy trusted her. For a moment, the gravity of what she had done settled on Stevie. She had gone AWOL in another country, and now she was standing here in the half-light of a dead woman's house, trying to work out a *feeling*.

She pulled off her coat and got to work.

She opened her bag and fished out her phone charger, then she walked up the stairs, touching the gray banister lightly with her fingertips, moving into the shadow at the top. She plugged her phone into the socket in the upstairs hallway, switched it to do not disturb mode, and turned on the mix of Britpop songs. She put in her earbuds and began walking around the upstairs.

She went to the bedroom first. Neat and precise Angela, cashmere sweaters folded and shoes in clear shoeboxes. Just one book on the bedside stand—a biography of Catherine Howard, bookmarked in the middle. One book at a time, not the jumble of books in process that lay splayed by Stevie's beside. She went into the bathroom and took a moment to go through the medicine cabinet. Floss. Deodorant. Extra heads for her electric toothbrush. A tub of skin cream. Nail polish remover. A bottle of bright pink indigestion medicine, birth control pills, and cold medicine.

No sleeping pills.

In the office, she worked her way around the room, staring down the spines of the history books on the shelves. She looked at every framed photograph. There were the formal photos from Cambridge—the group shots, the graduation photographs in the strange, sleeveless dark gowns with the collars that looked like skunk fur. The framed posters from the Nine's shows. Posters from her documentaries. Pictures of Angela with friends and family. With Izzy at different ages.

Stevie sat in the desk chair and spun. What were you thinking, Angela, when you were gathering your box of evidence? Where did you find Samantha Gravis? What made you think of her? What did you remember or see or hear? What sent you looking into the past, at an American pretending to be a Canadian, who hooked up with two of your friends and then fell into a river and died . . .

Just like you.

Who likes rivers, Angela? Who kills with waterways and an *axe*?

There was something in that. The contrast. Samantha had a blow to the head and sank in the shallow waters, and Angela was full of medicine to make her sleepy. She wouldn't have suffered. But Rosie and Noel? They suffered.

"Talk to me," she said to the light fixture on the ceiling. "What did you *know*? Who called you? What did I see here that doesn't make sense?"

Doorknob poked his head into the room. He rubbed his big orange body on the doorframe and purred loudly. He walked up to Stevie and rammed his head into her shins as a greeting. He allowed her to pick him up, going happily limp in her arms.

"What the hell am I missing, Doorknob?" she asked.

Doorknob circled her lap and coiled up into a resting position. She stroked him absently. She spun toward the desk and grabbed a pen to write a list.

> Things that keep coming up:
> A lock
> A button
> Samantha Gravis

This was an equation. These three things somehow added up to the answer. What did they have in common?

Not much. The lock was on the door of the woodshed. Samantha Gravis was in Cambridge. And no one knew where or what the button was. There didn't even seem to *be* a button.

Doorknob yawned and stretched himself, almost rolling off her lap in the process. She grabbed him before he fell.

She felt that sizzling feeling between her eyes. Doorknob's purring sounds powered it. She let him wriggle and drop to the floor. She took the steps two at a time, down to the kitchen, where Izzy was washing the disgusting, curry-stained dishes, which were furry with mold. "The text messages," Stevie said. "Show me her text messages again."

She tried not to scream with impatience as Izzy peeled off the washing gloves to get the tablet from her bag. Stevie clutched it and scanned down the exchange.

9:46 p.m. ANGELA: She had the button
9:47 p.m. THEO: ?
9:48 p.m. SOOZ: What Theo said.
9:48 p.m. YASH: Button?
9:49 p.m. PETER: what?
9:50 p.m. SOOZ: I have to go back onstage. Please someone explain to me what is happening.
9:51 p.m. SEBASTIAN: Can you ring me?
9:55 p.m. THEO: Ange?

"She got the call at 9:53," Stevie said. "That's seven

minutes after her last text. That button got someone's attention. Seven minutes . . ."

Stevie continued saying seven minutes for perhaps seven minutes. She was almost shaking now. She looked around the kitchen in desperation. She had still seen something *in this house*.

"What the hell did I see?" she yelled.

The answer was all about Angela—what Angela had been doing, what Angela said, what happened that night that made her spring into action moments after Stevie and the others had gone. Perhaps recreating the scene would help.

"Come on," Stevie said to Izzy, who was watching Stevie's wild stares and strange proclamations wide-eyed.

"I was sitting here," Stevie said, finding the spot on the floor she had occupied. "You were over there. Sit there. Exactly as you were. Think back. What were we talking about the other night, before we started talking about the murders?"

"Mostly history. The Tower of London. Guy Fawkes. It was a lot about Anne Boleyn, I think. About her execution, how it was different from a lot of other executions. She had a special swordsman from France, and she had to sit up straight because of it. You put your head down if it's an axe, but you have to sit up for a sword, and the swordsman pulled some kind of trick to get her head in the right position . . ."

Stevie looked at the two buttons on the coffee table.

Click, click, click. A sequence of things snapped into place. This was how it happened—all the things she had been collecting, all her ruminations and wandering thoughts, all that she had ever absorbed from mysteries and true crime and puzzles, all those times she read Wikipedia articles about gruesome things until three in the morning, all that she had observed without knowing—it brewed in her head. It bubbled. It seethed. It would not be ready until it was ready, but when it was ready it cascaded over like one of those model volcanoes she built in grade school that spat up baking soda and vinegar lava. It was the great hork of realization.

Stevie looked up at Izzy in a kind of wonder.

"There's no button," she said.

"We haven't found it yet, but . . ."

"No," Stevie said. "There is no button. *That's the point.* And if there's no button . . ."

The thoughts were coming quickly. Stevie had no ability to articulate them. If she tried, she would lose it all.

"Did you take out the trash?" she said.

"It smelled bad," Izzy replied.

"Oh God," Stevie said. "Is it gone?"

"I think it's still in the bins out front."

Stevie tripped over her own feet in her haste to get up, sending Doorknob flying off in fear. She hurried down the steps and leaned over the little black wrought-iron fence to get at the bins. They were still full of pungent garbage. She pulled out the bags and brought them back into the house. This time, she didn't even bother to line the kitchen floor with plastic bags before she upturned the contents. She dug in with her bare hands, pushing aside the food wrappers and napkins. Her eyes fell on a small slip of paper stained with curry and dotted with bits of rice. She lifted this out and studied it in silence for several minutes. Then she ran up the steps, to Angela's bathroom. She examined this for a minute, then slowly returned to the living room and looked at Izzy.

"That friend of your family who works at the London Eye. I need you to call them."

"Why?"

"Because I know what happened," Stevie said, clutching the filthy piece of paper, her eyes glowing. "And now I have to prove it."

30

IT WAS BITTER NOW, WITH AN UNKIND WIND BLOWING OFF THE Thames. It made Stevie's eyes water as she and Izzy made their determined way along the Embankment and over Hungerford Bridge. She did not turn her head to look at Parliament over to her right, with the glowing face of Big Ben. She was not here to think about the view, to recall being here with David and her friends.

This was being a detective in London. Focused. Facing the cold. Alone.

"How long will they give us?" Stevie asked Izzy.

"I think as long as you need. They're doing maintenance on one of the pods so they're keeping it stationary. They'll let us down when we text. They were very nice about it when I said it was for a memorial."

That was how they had set it up and how they drew in the six remaining members of the Nine. Izzy had messaged them to say she had gotten a private pod on the Eye and they could hover over London in peace and pay tribute to Angela over the river in which she had been found. Julian and Sebastian were staying in London for Angela's memorial and to be with their friends. Sooz's understudy was playing her part, and Theo had taken a few days off. They were all together, so it was a relatively easy business to summon them as a group.

Stevie sniffed. Her nose was running in the cold. She felt dirty and scrappy in her well-worn travel clothes, and her red vinyl coat was too thin. It was good to be cold, though. It kept her sharp.

The six were already there when they arrived, sitting on the benches by the empty lines of the Eye. The last passengers disembarked.

"Thank you for coming," Izzy said. "I know this is a bit unusual, but my aunt loved riding this, and since we have a family connection . . ."

"It's a lovely gesture," Theo said. She sounded congested, like she had been crying a lot.

"Stevie," Sooz said. "I thought you were all leaving today."

"I missed my flight," Stevie answered. "Izzy gave me a place to stay, and I wanted to . . . you know."

"It's good of you," Yash said.

"And we brought a hamper," Peter said, holding up a small basket with some bottles and glasses. "Something for a toast."

Izzy stepped up to the person manning the platform and explained who they were. After a moment's discussion, they were all shown to a pod. The door was sealed, and the wheel began to rotate. Stevie looked at the massive spokes. The river fell away, dark and forbidding, and London gleamed around them. Peter and Julian opened the bottles and distributed glasses of whisky to those who wanted alcohol and sparkling elderflower drink to those who did not. Yash had brought a portable speaker and started to play music—some Britpop, of course. Some Blur. Stevie knew the sound of them by now. This was a slow, pensive song called "Best Days."

As the wheel crested, the six put their arms around each other's shoulders, even inviting Izzy and Stevie into the huddle. This was awkward, but Stevie slipped in between Sooz and Julian.

"We love you, Ange," Sooz said. "We're so sorry."

"We love you," Sebastian echoed.

It went around—Julian, Peter, Theo, Yash, Izzy. Stevie tucked her head down.

Just as the pod reached the peak, it slowed, then stopped completely. It wobbled when the wind hit it.

"To Ange," Sebastian said, raising his glass. "A historian. A writer. A thinker. A drinker."

"To Ange," everyone echoed. Stevie lifted her fancy Sprite shyly.

Of course, the Nine, or the Six, had made this into an event. But as the quiet settled over the group and the wind knocked against the pod and Stevie realized just how high up they were inside a metal-and-glass bubble on a windy major river . . . she knew it was time. She looked to Izzy, who was wiping tears from her face with the back of her hand, smearing mascara and black eyeliner in all directions.

She cleared her throat.

"Actually," Izzy said, which is a strange way to begin

anything. "We wanted to bring everyone up here to have a chat. Because . . . Stevie has something she wanted to say. If you wouldn't mind sitting down."

In that moment, Stevie missed her friends so profoundly that she could have cried. Janelle, Vi, and Nate were in the sky, moving toward home. And David was here, but he might as well have been on Mars.

She couldn't think about that now. This was the thing she had to do. She wished she could do it from the stability of the bench in the middle of the pod, but she had to stand at the head of it, where it shook the most, but where everyone could see her.

"I wanted to talk about the button," Stevie said. "The one Angela mentioned in her text."

"Yes," Yash said, tucking himself inside his gray cashmere coat in the chill. "What was that all about?"

"It was a message," Stevie replied. "A message to a friend. She was trying to tell one of you something. I could only figure out what the message meant because I happened to be there on the night she sent the message. People get ideas from things around them. They use examples they know, that make sense to them. And, you know, Angela knew history. She knew all about Henry the Eighth and his wives. When we visited her that night, Angela told us a story about the execution of Anne Boleyn. She was telling us in a lot of detail how Anne was set up to die, and how the king ordered a special, fancy executioner from France. This guy used a sword, not an axe . . ."

The word *axe* was the moment the mood in the pod shifted. Stevie could feel it. Everyone got a little more attentive, more brittle.

". . . so the victim's head had to be in a certain position to do the job in one blow. He used a trick. He would call out to an imaginary assistant to bring the sword, the victim would turn their head in that direction to listen for the sword coming—but the guy already had the sword. Now the neck was in the right position, and he would swing. She said, 'A little bit of fakery does so much.' She gave herself the idea. Make a little bit of fakery. Get someone to turn their head. Angela had grown tired of waiting, tired of not knowing what she knew. She'd just found out that she started talking about the murders when she was on painkillers . . ."

All the pretense was gone. Now they all knew what this was.

". . . and she decided enough was enough. She wanted an answer. She decided to call her assistant to bring her sword. She put something out there. Anne Boleyn gave her part of the idea; her cat gave her the rest. Her cat steals buttons. He tried to take one off my coat while we were there. What if there was a piece of evidence? What's a good piece of evidence? Something small that might come off clothing. She'd just seen that happen. A button. She texts that she has the button. It's just a stab in the dark. If this doesn't work, it doesn't matter. Who cares? It's nothing. It's a typo in a text. But if it does . . ."

She turned to look at the assembled.

"And it does," Stevie said. "Seven minutes later, someone called her. And right after that, Angela put on her coat and left the house to meet this person. The fact that she went tells us something. I don't think she thought she was going to meet the murderer. I think she thought the person she was meeting with had the same suspicions that she did. But she was going to meet the person who killed Samantha Gravis, Rosie, and Noel. She was going to meet the person who unlocked the woodshed. She was going to meet the person who had the key that night in 1995 and was desperate to keep a secret."

She turned to Sebastian, who blanched and leaned back. "I didn't . . ."

"No," Stevie said. "There was something interesting in the witness statements about that night, something that seemed completely insignificant at first. But if you read them back and focused on only one thing, it was instantly obvious what happened. Someone had a key. So where were the keys? Down your pants, apparently. But remember when you tried to get the cabinet open to get the whisky? The cabinet didn't open. It wasn't because you were drunk. It was because *you didn't have the right keys*. But then you got the cabinet open. And when did that happen?"

Stevie turned to the man who was leaning forward, his elbows on his knees, a curious look on his face.

"When you switched them," she said to Peter.

June 23, 1995
11:00 p.m.

IT HAD STARTED WITH THE GIRL THEY MET AT THE PUB. THE CANADIAN.
The American. Samantha. That was her name. Peter should
have realized she was American. She had that head of curly
hair—big American hair. Big American smile. That American confidence. Julian met her first, because he was Julian.
There was nothing monogamous about Julian. He flapped
those long lashes at everyone, flashing those ice-blue eyes,
giving that look that seemed so shy. Everyone fell for it. He
and the American were all over each other within minutes.

Peter had watched this over his pint. Typical. Annoying.
Everything was so *easy* for Julian because he was born looking like a Greek god. He had talent as well—a good singing
voice, a decent guitarist, and a perfectly acceptable actor. If
Julian wanted to go into acting professionally, he could do it
in a heartbeat. Agents had already been sniffing around. But
Julian was going into law and politics, where he would also
succeed on looks and charm.

Peter did want to go into television and comedy. It was
all he ever wanted. It was his life, and he *worked* for it. He

wrote obsessively, studied every show, crafted every joke. He was going to the Edinburgh Festival with Yash and then to London. He knew it would be hard graft, and that they'd be broke. They couldn't afford a flat—they were looking at getting a spare room in a house to share.

As he sipped his pint and watched, his anger grew, his awareness that they were days from going out into the world and that people like Julian would be everywhere. Someone needed to give Julian a kick up the arse.

Peter had had it. He drained his pint and left the pub, claiming exhaustion, which was fair enough. He walked home along the river, his resentment increasing with every step. At the house, he found Rosie furiously revising for her last exam. It was a bad night to tell her this news, but Peter did it anyway. He told her gently, with an apologetic tone— and he did feel bad for her—but he was also pleased by the steely look in Rosie's eyes, even as they filled with tears. She wasn't surprised, but the confirmation hit hard. She didn't cry, really; she turned into a fierce and tiny ball of Irish rage. She thanked Peter, wiped a stray tear away, and then waited in the garden with a bottle of Coke, which she poured over Julian's head on his arrival.

Peter saw this from the upstairs window. It was very satisfying to watch.

"Did *you* tell her?" Yash asked as they sat in their room that night, listening to the yelling coming from the garden below. "She knew by the time we got home. You must have?"

"I thought she should know," Peter replied.

"Bad timing with her exam, but fair enough, I suppose. Anyway, Noel's been circling for ages. I've seen them slipping off together. I expect that's how this ends."

Yash was right. Rosie spent the night folded in Noel's long arms, sobbing. Probably doing other things too, but Peter wasn't privy to that and didn't really care.

The American was back at the pub the next night, and Peter was feeling better about things. Julian was sulking in the corner and didn't want company. She was pretty, the American. Maybe he should have a go and try to talk to her. But before he could approach her, Yash was there, telling her a joke. And she was laughing. Laughing and laughing and laughing. With Julian, they had simply attached themselves to each other's faces and dispensed with the niceties, but it was clear that Yash and this girl were connecting, getting along. Yash was leaning in, pulling faces, trying so hard to entertain, and the girl was giving as good as she got, gesturing and joking back.

Peter watched this over his pint as well. This was less typical, and somehow more annoying.

He was so sick of being with these people all the time. He loved them, sure, but he was finished with it all. The drama. The competition. The never-ending need to impress, to entertain.

The next night, Peter was not at the pub; he was walking home from a long revision session for his last exam. That's when he saw her, wobbling down the slender dirt path along the river. He knew where she was going, of course. No one would have walked this far in the dark from the center of town toward Grantchester Meadows unless they lived there or were visiting someone. The girl was going to their house, to see Yash. Peter caught up with her, introduced himself. She only sort of remembered that he existed, that he had been there with the others.

Of course.

The American was drunk and in a happy mood. It was her last night there, she explained. She wanted to give Yash his CDs back. Maybe, she suggested to Peter, they should steal a boat. Row down the river toward home. It was a stupid idea, but the girl seemed to be flirting with him. Maybe things were turning in his direction after all. So he went along with her to one of the many tiny docks along the river where punts were tied up.

What happened was not his fault. It was a misunderstanding. He honestly couldn't remember all the details anymore—it was fear and confusion. She jumped up and away from him and the boat rocked. He saw her smack her head and she went over into the water. Suddenly she was screaming and saying something about the police, but he hadn't done this, hadn't hurt her—she fell and everything was vanishing in this instant, his whole life if he didn't *do something*.

It takes very little effort or time to hold someone under. That was where it started—an ill-fated walk home.

Rosie knew something.

The morning after, she'd watched him from the kitchen

table, asked when he'd come in. Why did she want to know that? He'd lied, of course. But now he knew—Rosie knew something. Rosie was a strong, passionate person. Once she got into something, she did not let go.

There was no news of the American. Why was there no news? The Cam was maybe six or seven feet deep—it wasn't the *ocean*. How could she not have been found? Surely bodies floated? Maybe she was stuck on something. The Cam was full of shopping trolleys and other things. You heard of people getting their foot stuck when they fell in. The American was in that water somewhere. Days passed, and with each one, it seemed less real. Maybe it had never happened at all.

But of course it did.

Rosie was watching him. He saw her doing it. Peter could see so many things now, things barely visible to him before. He could see everyone's traits and movements and tics. Sooz's attention-seeking. Julian's indecisiveness. Yash's need to be the funniest. Theo's fussy overbearingness. Angela's compulsive apologizing. Sebastian's sham-glam and jokes about being lord of the manor that weren't really jokes. Noel's slyness.

Rosie's stubbornness.

Rosie's willingness to walk into any argument.

Rosie's unwillingness to back down.

Who cared anymore? In a week he would be rid of most of them. All he had to do was get through this last week and they could all move on. They were going to Merryweather, which was good. He needed to get away from Cambridge.

And then, on the morning they were to leave, it was on the front of the newspaper. Her photo and the headline: BODY OF MISSING AMERICAN STUDENT FOUND. Peter read the article at a furious speed and was relieved at what he saw. That was when he discovered she was American, that her name was Samantha Gravis, and that the police were certain she had fallen off a punt while drunk. Relief washed over him. He destroyed the newspaper, then he threw up. They just needed to *go*, get out of this house, finish packing and leave and the whole thing would be over. But everyone was taking so much time. Then Rosie went into town for something before they left and came back quiet and strange. Rosie never went silent.

She must have seen the paper and started to put it together.

That's when he knew for certain that something needed to be done. He'd been mulling it over all week in a distant way, but now it came into sharp focus.

Given her behavior over the past week, Peter was sure Rosie would go for Noel's car, so he headed that way. But as he did so, Rosie turned and joined the group that was going in Sebastian's car. He didn't change what he was doing. He'd already put his bag into the small boot of Noel's car. He had to go with it. He got in with Julian, Noel, and Angela.

This car contained the heaviest smokers, and it was a ride full of cigarettes and Blur and Pulp blasting out of the tinny speakers of Noel's shitty Golf. All during the ride to Merryweather, he smiled and nodded and pretended to be interested in whatever anyone was saying, but his mind was elsewhere. He worked out every step. The first was to get the keys. Surely, when they arrived Sebastian would set them down at some point. This turned out to be exceptionally easy—the keys were still in the door for a moment as everyone pressed inside. Peter removed them, and before tossing them to Sebastian, exchanged them for his own. Had Sebastian looked, he may have noticed the difference. But he didn't. Sebastian took without a thought. The house was already full of commotion.

Peter sprinted up the grand staircase, past the paintings of the Holt-Careys of the past—the viscounts, the ladies, the ones in military uniforms. One of the rooms he wanted was still available. It wasn't one of the better ones. It was a little small and poky, papered in arsenic green, but it had one major advantage—it had the most direct line of potential sight to the woodshed. As he peered out, he saw Noel and Rosie still outside, conferring in the garden. Rosie looked up and saw him. In that moment, when they locked eyes, there was a communication: *I know what you did.*

Peter tried to be casual about it and moved away slowly, but the world wobbled. Only one other room overlooked the kitchen garden and potentially had a view of the woodshed. That room was next door, and he could hear someone moving around inside. He collected himself, pulled his cigarettes from his pocket, and knocked on the door. Angela called out for him to enter. She was standing with the window open.

"Lost my lighter in the car," he said. "Can I use yours?"

"It's in my bag, the blue one, on the bed."

He opened the bag and dug around inside until he found the yellow disposable lighter buried at the bottom.

It was convenient that she was already at the window. Even a few paces away, he could see that Rosie and Noel had left the garden, so it was safe to come to the window and take in the view. The trees utterly obscured the garage and the woodshed from here, as they had almost certainly been planted to do. He silently gave thanks to the wealthy builders of this country pile who worked very hard to make sure they never had to see other people doing work.

For a moment, standing there with Angela, he considered abandoning his entire plan. There was something so lovely about seeing her there. He had always been so fond of her. Angela had shaved her head on a dare. A bit of dark brown fuzz was coming through. It suited her, brought out her freckles, highlighted her deep brown eyes. She looked sad. Angela was loyal and emotional, and he could see that she was taking the fact that this was their last week together as students and roommates hard. In this silver summer night, with the smell of petrichor and climbing roses, nothing terrible could happen. Maybe he could tell Angela, tell everyone, come clean. They would help him. They would understand it had not been his fault. He was one of the Nine, and the Nine stuck together.

There was a tremendous clap of thunder in the distance and the rain came down.

"Do you think we'll still play?" Angela asked.

This snapped him out of any romantic revelry and brought him sharply back to the matter at hand. Of course he couldn't tell them. You can't say to your friends, "I drowned the girl we met at the pub." Even if he claimed it was an accident, Rosie knew it wasn't. They had to play. Otherwise, they would stay inside and drink, and Rosie would tell everyone. He had to make damn sure that the game went on as scheduled. He handed Angela back her lighter and left her by the window looking pensive.

Peter took a quiet turn around the dark upstairs hallway, making mental notes of who had taken which rooms. He was about to go downstairs when he noticed Rosie making her way to Angela's door. He froze and backed up. He stepped into the empty room that was between his and Angela's. This was one of the worst rooms in the house. It didn't even have a window. It was perhaps a dressing room, or perhaps a room for a maid or a personal servant, someone not important enough to deserve fresh air and a view of the outdoors. There was an adjoining door to Angela's room, and he pressed his ear against it to listen, but between the music in the house and the noise of the storm, all he could make out was Julian's name repeated several times.

Typical. Fucking Julian. And that was usually the problem in a nutshell.

Then there was a heavy footfall, someone taking the stairs two at a time. It was Sooz, who was always a bit louder than everyone else, and she had champagne. Good old Sooz. You could always count on her to bring the party. He heard

Sooz directing the other two to go downstairs. He could have kissed her—he *had* kissed her, everyone had—but at this moment, he felt tremendous affection for her. He cracked open the door to leave the room and found that Rosie and Angela had lingered for a moment. This time, he could make out what was being said.

"I'll talk to you after," Rosie said. "Come up and meet me here after the game."

"But what's it about? What's going on?"

"Not now. It's too important."

Sooz ushered them on, but Rosie turned at the last moment.

"I'm desperate for a piss," Rosie said. "Go down. I'll be there in a moment."

Sooz and Angela continued to the stairs, and Rosie made her way toward her bedroom. Peter stepped out from his hiding spot, trying not to startle her, and failing. She backed up against the wall.

"Rose," he said in a low voice, "I need to talk to you about something. I think Yash is in trouble."

That genuinely confused her. He saw her shoulders relax. "What?"

"Yash needs our help. I think you know what I mean. We need to talk. Privately. Go around to the woodshed. I have the key. Meet you there as soon as the game starts."

He nodded confidently and jogged down the stairs, catching the tail end of the preparations for the game. He was sweating already. He had to calm down. He kept an eye on Rosie as the game began. She looked back at him as she went out the front door with Angela. He went to the right, through the library, slipping out the greenhouse side. Best to keep a little distance. Don't stay on her heels. He was fast, though, making a loop of the house, coming around the back to the shed. At first, she did not appear to be there, but then he heard her voice. She was behind one of the trees by the shed.

"What's wrong with Yash?" she asked as he approached.

"Not here. Inside."

The rain was pounding on his head, dripping off the slicker into his face. He fumbled around with the dozen or so keys on Sebastian's key chain before he finally got the one that opened the lock. The two stepped inside. There was no lock inside, and clearly they could not be disturbed. If he tried to secure the door himself, she might panic.

"Help me," he said. "We need to keep this shut. We need to hide while we talk."

After a moment of consideration, Rosie took a rake and secured it just so, enough that the door could not be opened.

"What's this about Yash?" she said. "Are you going to try to tell me that Yash hurt that girl?"

His suspicions were unfortunately correct, and this was already going too fast.

"The girl . . . ," he mumbled, stalling for time. Words failed him. He would always remember how she looked at that moment—the most Rosie she had ever been. So short, yet she seemed about eight feet tall. Her face rigid. Her eyes fixed, arms folded across her chest.

"We saw you," she finally said.

This caught him so unready that he didn't say, "Saw what?" He said, "We?"

Rosie almost smiled. Peter felt the foundations under his feet slipping away.

"That night the girl disappeared, fell into the river, we heard yelling. Two voices. One was North American, sounded like a girl. We came out of the tent to see what was going on. It had all gone quiet. You came down the path not long after. You were wet and agitated. I had no idea what I'd seen until I saw the paper this morning. Her picture was in it—the girl. The Canadian. She wasn't Canadian, she was American. Her name with Samantha. She was the one you told me was snogging Julian the other night, and then she got together with Yash. Yash gave her our address. And now here you are, trying to convince me that Yash did something. Yash would never."

The panic was taking over his body. He had to control it. Had to push back the black-and-white spots that were taking over his vision.

"I've been watching you," Rosie said. "Ever since that night. I've been trying to understand what I saw. Something happened out there, Peter. What happened to her?"

"You must be joking," he said. But his voice was dry.

"I'm not joking. I even asked you the next morning about your night. You lied, Peter. You lied about when you came back. What happened, Peter?"

He had to try harder. Get more conviction in his voice.

"You honestly think I'm capable of hurting someone? And why?"

"I think you're competitive," she said. "I think we all are. I think something happened. I wasn't sure before. I am now."

In that moment, it was decided. Because what else could he do? What choice did he have? What happened next was much like what had happened with the American. He needed to survive. He felt the panic slip away. It was replaced by a warm clarity. A focus unlike any he'd ever felt. Now the lie was easier. It was soft as butter.

The axe was leaning by the door. He'd seen Sebastian use it before to get to the loft space.

"Rosie," he said calmly. He rubbed his hand over his forehead like he was troubled, just trying to make sense of the matter. He was in a sketch, that was all. A sketch about a misunderstanding. He was playing an exasperated man in a shop trying to explain what he wanted. "I think that you . . ."

He moved in the middle of the sentence. Peter had always been an athlete; he was an excellent cricketer and tennis player whenever he could be bothered to play. The axe had a long handle, so as he swung he made a long arc. When the first blow made contact, Rosie made a weird, low noise. Each successive swing got easier. It didn't take many. Axes are effective tools.

When he was sure it was over, and he was heaving and sweating and looking down, the figure on the floor didn't look like Rosie anymore. It was like a sack.

There was a buzzing in his head. A strange euphoria that made no sense because he couldn't be happy about this. The body compensates in times of extreme stress. There were work gloves on the shelf. He put them on and pulled Rosie over to the pile of wood on the far side and covered her gently. He found that he was talking to her even as he did it.

"Sorry, Rose. So sorry, Rose. I had no choice here, Rose. It'll be all right, Rose . . ."

He meant it too. So sorry, Rosie. Didn't mean for this to happen.

The door began to rattle. A sharp stroke of panic whipped through his body.

"Hello?" called a voice. One of the girls. It was a little hard to hear over the pouring rain and the sound of his heartbeat in his ears. He went to the door and listened.

"Hello? Who's in there? I saw your light under the door. Come on, it's awful out here . . . I have champagne!"

Angela. Just playing the game. He forced himself to breathe calmly and waited until he was sure she was gone. As he waited, he had to look at the pile of logs that Rosie was under. That wasn't tolerable. He swung the axe up and smashed the lightbulb, leaving the woodshed in the pitch-dark.

That was better. No light at all. Just the sound of the rain. He leaned against the door and closed his eyes and listened to the sound.

We saw you, Rosie said. *We came out of the tent.* The shag factory. Rosie and Noel in each other's arms and talking by the garden wall when they arrived. It didn't appear that Noel knew the whole story—his demeanor had been far too casual for that—but once Rosie was found, it would all come out. Noel would put it all together. Noel would come after him.

Peter wiped the axe with a rag and set it down by the door, just in case he didn't make it back in time. What time was it? What was time? He checked his watch. Just coming up on midnight. Was that all? Just an hour since they ran out of the house? It could have been seconds. It could have been years.

He peeked outside, found nothing but rain and the night waiting for him. When he left Rosie and the woodshed, he snapped the lock back on the door and took a few bouncing strides to the gravel of the parking area. Nature had provided. The rain washed him clean, made the blood run from his rain slicker, off his hands, off the Wellington boots. He tipped back his face as he ran and allowed himself to be soaked.

He needed to find Noel, which meant the best thing to do was to be found himself. Become a seeker. Get a torch. He heard voices coming from the back of the house, so he moved through the trees and around the tennis courts. Angela and Yash were back there somewhere, in the topiary. He moved toward the sound, then ducked under the first bench he saw. It was Yash who came through the entrance to the topiary area, flashed his torch around, and caught sight of him. Peter made a pretense of running.

"Bastard, bastard!" Yash said, laughing and giving chase. "Ange! Peter's here!"

Peter pretended to trip and allowed Yash to clap a hand

on him. Yash and Angela took him to the folly, where Sebastian gave him a yellow poncho and a torch.

"Go forth," Sebastian said, "and seek for me."

"Who's still out there to be found?" Peter asked.

"Rosie, Julian, Noel, and Sooz. Find them and bring them to me!"

Noel was still out there somewhere.

When you must find someone because your life depends on it, you will find them. The trouble was, Noel was famously good at this game. He was extremely limber and willing to go to great lengths. He also liked to climb things. He would be *up* somewhere. He might have scaled some part of the house, might have gone out a window to the roof.

No. Not on a night like this. Too slick. Too exposed.

In the process of looking for Noel, he discovered Sooz hiding in a wall of topiary. He wasted precious time taking her to Sebastian. After that, he broke away from the others again and began going through the woods. A tree, perhaps. Plenty of them. It would be impossible to search them all, so he would have to be lured.

"Noel," he called gently as he made his way through the tree line that ringed the house. "Noel, she needs you."

For a full half hour, he poked through trees, shining his torch up into the branches. He made his way to a small orchard off the back gardens. These trees were a bit smaller, and thus, more promising. The branches were just as plentiful, but closer to the ground. Easier for Noel to climb up and escape as necessary. He should have started here.

"Rosie," Peter said, making his way through the orchard. "She needs you."

A faint sound from somewhere above.

"Rosie needs you, Noel," Peter said. "She needs your help."

The rustling grew louder. Noel slithered out of a tree just behind him.

"What's wrong with Rosie?" Noel asked, dropping from the lowest branch.

"There you are," Peter said with real relief in his voice. He switched off his torch. "She's asked for you. Come on."

"But what's wrong?" Noel said, allowing himself to be led through the darkness.

"Have to be quiet," Peter replied. "Come on. You'll see."

They almost ran into Sooz on the way, but they managed to stay hidden. Peter found that he was almost looking forward to what was about to happen. It was so terrible and huge that it bred a queasy, wild anticipation. He was aware that something odd was happening in his mind, that he was so swamped with adrenaline and champagne that he had developed an intense focus. The life-or-death moment brought forth the heaviest chemicals the body could produce.

Peter unlocked the shed while Noel hid behind. He had one hand on the axe as he waved Noel into the darkness with the other.

Noel never knew what happened. Of that, Peter was sure. The first swing seemed to land somewhere around his ear, his face, probably. Knocked him sideways. Confused him.

Peter swung and swung again.

He covered Noel with the same care that he had shown to Rosie.

He was back outside at two fifteen. The storm was getting worse. He moved away from the woodshed in the fulsome darkness, crossing around to the opposite side of the house. Then, as if on some celestial cue, the power cut out.

Everyone retreated back inside, shivering, pulling off wet slickers and clothes, wrapping themselves in the woolen throw blankets, opening more champagne. And there was Sebastian, crawling along the floor with a candle in his hand, trying to get to some bottle of whisky that his father loved so much. He would need a key to open the cabinet.

It was like the universe gave him a path, or perhaps it was that life becomes simple when your choices are few. Here was his chance. Peter dropped to the floor and joined Sebastian's little play while fumbling with the set of stolen keys, looking for the one that might open the cabinet door. Triumph. The cabinet was opened, the whisky procured, and the keys put back into Sebastian's hand as if they had never been gone.

Just one more thing to do. This required being seen going to bed. He claimed that he might be sick, which was true enough, and retired to his room. He waited over an hour on his bathroom floor, trying to hold himself together and finding that he was doing all right. Theo would come around with water like she always did after a long night. He wanted to be in the room when she made her rounds. It was a good thing to know your friends so well. Within the hour, he heard Theo enter his room and call out for him. He answered from behind the bathroom door that he was fine.

She left the water.

Once Theo was gone, he did a quiet creep around the upstairs, checking rooms and mentally marking where everyone was. Angela, Yash, and Theo had retired to their rooms. That left Sooz, Julian, and Sebastian. He took the back stairs down to the main floor and lurked by the sitting room door for a moment to count the voices he heard inside. Sooz was having a go at Julian. Good for Sooz. Sebastian sounded bored by the discussion.

Everyone accounted for. He could now complete the cleanup.

First, he would need clothes. The Nine swapped and shared clothes, so it was an easy enough matter to get some from someone else. Noel would have been ideal—he wasn't around to notice—but Noel was very slender and wore vintage clothes, usually from the 70s. It seemed like a bad idea to clean up his murder scene in a tight pair of flares. He needed something less distinctive that wouldn't be missed. Julian, then. He was downstairs, and surely he had a pair of track bottoms and a T-shirt that would do the job. And if the clothes were discovered to be missing? Not a bad thing. Next Peter went back to the mudroom, where he slipped on a pair of wellies and a pair of gardening gloves and grabbed a garden spade from a shelf. He took a careful path to the woodshed, using the house and garden walls for cover. He had to work quickly. The birds were starting their dawn chorus and the sun would soon rise. The reality of what he had done would come down, crashing, falling scenery. It would all be real. He forced himself to carry on. Just a little more and it would all be over. First job: force the door open to make it look like a robbery. It was, after all, an outbuilding full of cannabis. He used the spade for this. It took a few tries and he almost broke it in the process, but the wood finally gave and the door snapped open. While it was partially a relief not to be able to see much inside, he had to check the scene. He swung the torchlight over the piles of wood, the broken bulb, the blood on the floor. He pulled the wheelbarrow out and tipped in on the ground outside the shed, making it look like someone had been disturbed in the process of taking it.

The axe was a more difficult matter. Peter felt a rising nausea as he picked it up. The blade was covered in blood and . . . things he could not force himself to look at. He replaced it where it was usually kept by the door. In a final attempt to literally muddy the evidence, he bucketed some of the rainwater from the barrel outside onto the floor, destroying footprints and washing blood into the cracks and corners. He poured more on the strip of grass and mud that ran between the shed and the gravel drive to confuse any footprints outside of the shed as well. Those wouldn't really matter anyway—all of those would be standard wellie footprints anyway, and the grounds would be littered with them. They'd all been wearing wellies that night.

He was about to return inside when he had a final idea.

427

Why not add one more thing to confuse the timeline? He crept along to the front of the house and saw that there were still lights on in the sitting room. A few people were still awake. He got as close as he dared, turned on the torch, flashed it straight ahead, then turned it off and ran back the way he came. As he entered, he could hear Sooz calling out for Rosie and Noel.

Peter went up the back stairs and into his room. He removed his clothes and shoved them under a curio cabinet to get rid of in the morning. Taking a bath or a shower would be too loud; he washed himself quietly at the sink. Then he threw up in the basin. He got into his bed.

He drank the water Theo had brought for him.

Of course, the police would come in the morning. They'd find evidence of a break-in interrupted. They'd find all that cannabis. Sebastian might go down for that, and he was sorry.

It was over now. Nothing else to be done. He would be a good person to his friends. He would help them through this. Peter felt nothing but goodwill and charity toward everyone and everything. He would make something of himself. None of this would be in vain.

He sank into a deep and dreamless sleep.

31

THE GLASS TOWERS OF THE CITY OF LONDON TWINKLED BEHIND them. The pod juddered. The Nine sat, an attentive if confused audience.

"I'm going to tell you a story," Stevie said. "That's all I've got for you right now is a story. But it's a story that makes a lot of sense. It's a story that fits the evidence. It begins with an American named Samantha Gravis, who was visiting England and pretending to be a Canadian. You all met her. Julian and Yash hooked up with her. She had your address, and she had some of Yash's CDs. She was likely on the way to your house when she died in the early morning of the fifteenth of June, 1995. It seemed to be a case of a tourist who got drunk and was screwing around on a boat on the river in the dark, fell, and drowned. You said your house was on the river, and you said there was something in the backyard—the garden, whatever—a tent?"

"The shag factory," Sooz offered, her face a marble mask of shock.

"Would that be the kind of place that Rosie and Noel might go when they got together?"

"That's what it was for. Shagging. Trysts. Yes."

"So we have a connection. A girl dies in the river. Rosie and Noel are out back near the river. Rosie sees something that night, something she says she can't understand. On the day you left for Merryweather, there's an article in the paper saying Samantha had been found and it printed her picture. According to the statements, you were in Cambridge most of that day—you left late, around eight o'clock at night. Which means there was plenty of time that day for Rosie to see the paper. And she did. And Rosie suddenly knows what she saw. She tries to tell Angela about it when they get to Merryweather, but there's no time. And then Rosie and Noel go out into the storm and never come back. This is the part where you all enter the story. You were witnesses to what came next. You know that Angela said the lock was off the woodshed that night. She said she saw it off the door. She told you, right?"

This was to Theo, who nodded.

"I thought she was drunk, upset about the lie we had to tell."

"She was probably both of those things," Stevie replied. "But she was right. When she went by that woodshed, someone was inside, killing one of her friends."

She let this settle on the group. It was not a calming kind of thing to say, not up at a great height, locked up and alone. But that was part of what Stevie needed to do.

"Some things all look the same," she said. "Like keys, right? Maybe you notice a key ring, but who notices a key? My friend was just saying that as we checked out of student housing. No one pays attention to them. When you realize that, the whole thing begins to make a lot more sense. When you arrived at Merryweather, you unlocked the door. Maybe you set the keys down when you came in? Even for a minute or two? It wouldn't have to be much time."

"I suppose," Sebastian said. "That's normally what happens with keys. I know I had them before the game started."

"You definitely had *some* keys before the game started," Stevie said. "Because everyone saw you put them down your pants. Those were not your keys. You took those . . ."

She finally looked at Peter again. His expression had not changed.

"You met Rosie at the woodshed," she said. "You unlocked the door and barred it from the inside. The police report makes it clear that Rosie and Noel died one at a time—Rosie first. Is that when you found out about Noel? You buried her. You broke the light. Is that because you couldn't look at what you'd done, or because you didn't want Noel to see her body when he came in next?"

Nothing from Peter. Stevie pressed on.

"Maybe it was both," she said, shrugging. "At some point, though, Angela comes by. Angela sees the lock off the door. Angela was primed to know something was wrong. Rosie just *told* her so."

Now she was getting to the part that would be most difficult for them to hear.

"Rosie and Noel were both dead by the time the power went out and you all returned to the house," she went on. "I know this because that is when you gave Sebastian his keys back. You probably just planned on slipping them into his pocket or something, but this story of him crawling across the floor to the cabinet keeps coming up. He kept trying to get it open, and it wouldn't open—until, of course, you got on the floor with him. You opened the cabinet because you had the keys. You handed Sebastian his keys right in front of everyone. You didn't need them anymore. But you had one more thing to do. The stage had to be set. It had to look like a robbery. You said you were sick, and you went upstairs. When the coast was clear, you slipped back down, went outside—there's only about a thousand doors, so this couldn't have been too hard—and you broke open the shed. You pulled out a wheelbarrow and a bucket. You did one more thing, for good measure—you walked around toward the sitting room and you flashed a light. Sooz saw it."

Sooz got up and started circling the pod, looking over at Peter. Yash had retreated into himself. Theo looked reflective, like she was running through the case in her head, checking Stevie's math. Julian concentrated on his hands, stretching out his fingers. Only Sebastian looked directly at Peter, considered him fully.

"It probably would have worked," Stevie said. "It *did* work. You knew that woodshed was filled with weed. The

432

police would immediately think that someone had come to steal it. If anyone got in trouble, it was going to be Sebastian. But then, something happens. Theo steps in to make sure that Sebastian is safe. Everyone takes part in getting rid of the plants. Your friends were *helping* you disrupt the scene, *helping* you bake in all the lies about that night. Lying sucks. It's so lonely. Did that make you feel better, having everyone in on a lie? Not just you?"

This was the one and only time that night that Stevie saw a flicker of something pass Peter's face.

"So," Stevie said. "That was the end of it. Except . . . Angela saw the lock off the door. She lied to the police about it, but she couldn't get it out of her mind. Angela knew something was wrong about that night. She wanted to know what it was Rosie wanted to tell her. I know what it's like when you can't solve something. It takes over your mind. She used her skills as a researcher and she got records and reports. She couldn't tell the rest of you what she was doing, because she had no idea who to trust. She kept her investigation hidden from everyone, but then she had to get an operation, and she's given painkillers. The painkillers made her loopy. On the night she vanished, we had dinner with her. Everything was fine until Izzy mentioned what Angela said while she was on the painkillers. Everything changed in a second. She suddenly had to get back to work and asked us all to call it a night. What happens once we leave the house? She's upset. She knows her thoughts are out there in the world—she's said them out loud. Her fears are real. She knows something is wrong, and now her niece has brought some weird American student detective . . ."

She indicated herself.

". . . to her house. So maybe this thing is going to blow up. She can't take it anymore. She gets out her phone and starts to text her friends. And now we're back to the button and Angela going out the door."

Finally, after all that, Peter stirred. He straightened up, cracking his back accidentally, and looked at Stevie.

"Did you just say all that because you think *keys look alike?*" Peter said. "Because you just told all my best friends that I killed three of our friends, and you are basing this on the fact that keys look alike. I'm not entirely comfortable continuing this. We came here to have a memorial, and this—"

"Oh no," Stevie cut him off calmly. She felt better now that he was talking. She liked having something to work with. Silence was freaky. "There was one more thing. Angela's purse. Julian showed me the list of what they found in it. Here, I'll read it to you."

She had the photo ready to go on her phone, which didn't want to wake up right away and made her do facial recognition three times.

"'Purse contained: wallet (containing £40 and credit cards, intact), set of keys, phone, Oyster card, new Oral-B toothbrush in package, box of Strepsils, blister pack of Nytol (can hold seven tablets, six were missing, one remaining), five large rocks.' Doesn't something stand out there?"

"I'm going to go with five large rocks," Peter said.

Stevie shook her head.

"No. You put those there. What's weird is the *toothbrush*."

She fished around in her backpack, where she had carefully placed the curry-stained receipt she had just fished from the trash.

"I went through her trash the night she vanished," Stevie said, in the same way someone might say, "I went to the beach because it was sunny."

"She bought decongestant, throat drops, body wash, and a toothbrush. She was getting over a cold the night we saw her, so the decongestant and throat drops make sense. The body wash is self-explanatory. But the toothbrush isn't. She had a fancy electric toothbrush. She didn't need a toothbrush. And why, if you were going to drown yourself in the Thames, would you bring a toothbrush? Is that what you would grab?"

"Maybe she just left it in her bag after she bought it?" Izzy said.

Stevie shook her head.

"The cold medicine was in her bathroom," she said. "She unpacked the bag at home. The receipt was in the trash. It makes sense to carry throat drops if you have a sore throat. But she didn't need a toothbrush, and the toothbrush was clearly for something, because it was separately wrapped in a bag. Like she was going to give it to someone. And what does everyone say about Angela? That she's so conscientious. That even though you all borrowed each other's stuff, she was the one who always gave it back. When did everyone last see her? At a party, at Peter's house. Where she stayed over. And may not have had a toothbrush. So she bought one to replace it. When she went out that night, she put it in her bag to give to him. That's not something you do if you think you are meeting a murderer. She went there not knowing. Something happened."

"So," Peter said, "keys and a toothbrush? Really?"

He looked around, but his five friends all regarded him strangely.

"Well," Yash said quietly. "If it's not true, it should be easy enough to disprove, right, Pete? Julian's been able to get information. I'll bet things could be worked backward. Instead of looking for Angela on the CCTV, they could look for you. At your flat. Where your phone was. You could do that, couldn't you, Julian?"

"I could," Julian said. "I will. Tonight. I'll have your life turned inside out."

"It's all right, Pete," Yash went on. "If you didn't do it."

Peter seemed to be churning inside. He was maintaining control, but there was a faint curling at his upper lip.

"You've always been so *annoying*, Julian," he spat. "Everything's always been about you, hasn't it? Who Julian was sleeping with or flirting with or cheating on. It was endless. And now here you are again. The MP. The politician."

"Oh, you think it will just be Julian?" Sooz said, standing up and stepping over to Peter. "We worked together to save Sebastian. We'll do the same again. In fact, how about we pry open this . . ."

Sebastian grabbed Sooz from behind and moved her away

436

from Peter. Izzy had already whipped out her phone and was making a call.

"I think we're ready to come down," Izzy said. "Quick as you can, please. Someone is, um . . . ill."

32

It was just coming up on ten o'clock, and Big Ben bonged out the hours. They were on the ground, which was a relief. The ground didn't sway in the wind.

Sooz had been prevented from throwing Peter out of a glass pod door. She probably wouldn't have succeeded—the pods were made for safety and were designed to withstand any attempts to be opened from the inside—but Sooz had been willing to give it her very best try. The minute they got back to the ground, Peter walked off, his coat flapping behind him in the wind. Sooz was once again prevented from following him and shoving him into the river. Now she was being embraced by both Theo and Sebastian. Julian was on the phone. Yash was leaning against the stone wall by the riverside and taking a moment.

Izzy and Stevie sat by themselves on another bench watching all this.

"So what happens now, to Peter?"

"I don't know," Stevie said. "I think I'm right about what happened, but it's hard to prove. That's why doing it up on the

438

Eye, in a high-pressure situation, was important. He needed to be freaked out. Start making mistakes. And I believe them all when they say they're going to find out."

"But will he go to jail?"

"I think it depends on what they find," Stevie said, looking over at her.

"And we're already looking."

That was Sebastian, who came up and joined them, along with Sooz. Theo went over to minister to Yash.

"What's going to happen," Sebastian said, sitting down, "is that we're going to pursue this to the ends of the earth. There'll be more evidence somewhere—CCTV, or witnesses, something. Whatever it is, we're going to find it. He knows that his life, as he has understood it, is over."

"Julian may be an arse, but he's our arse." Sooz wrapped her arms around herself and considered for a moment. "He's not actually *that* much of an arse, really. Still *has* one, but . . . he's turned out all right." She turned her attention to Yash and Theo. "It will be hard for him. They've been writing partners for years. But we'll make sure he's all right. And . . ."

Theo had taken Yash's hand in hers as they spoke.

"Look at that," Sooz said, mostly to Sebastian. "About time. Maybe some good will come of this."

"Yes," Sebastian replied thoughtfully. "Perhaps it's finally going to happen."

Julian strode over, slipping his phone into his pocket.

"Just talked to my contact at the Met. They'll have someone pull all the CCTV footage and look at Peter's cell phone records. We'll use whatever we have to—social media, whatever—we'll find someone who saw him with Ange that night. We'll sort it."

The five were united.

"You missed your flight," Julian said to Stevie. "For this."

Stevie nodded.

"Is that going to go badly for you?"

Stevie nodded again.

"We'll sort that. For what you did here. There's a prominent doctor . . ."

He nodded in Theo's direction.

". . . who's been treating you tonight for . . . what would you like? A stomach bug? And there's a Minister of Parliament who would be happy to phone your school to explain it all."

"You threw up on me," Sooz offered. "It was in my hair. I'd be happy to describe it in detail."

"We're good at lying," Sebastian said, leaning over and managing a smile. "We've been doing it for years."

When the five had been assured that Stevie would stay with Izzy for the night, and when they had walked the pair to a taxi that would take them directly to Craven House, the group parted ways. London black cabs were massive on the inside—practically a small, moving room with a plastic wall between them and the driver, and an intercom system to communicate between the two.

"Do you think Peter might come after us?" Izzy said. "They seem worried about it."

In truth, Stevie did not know. Desperate people did strange and terrible things.

"Peter acted out of fear," Stevie said. "He killed four people to try to keep himself out of trouble. That's what motivates him. He's afraid. And now he knows he's being watched. You can't discount it, but . . . I feel like he's going to play innocent, or he'll run."

They fell into silence for a moment as London rolled past. At night, it was lit up like a theater, bright lights on white facades and monuments, glowing advertisements, blue-and-purple neon tracing lines through the dark. Now Stevie had time to let it all sink in. She was alone, her luggage gone and only her small backpack with her. Her friends were on their way home, far out of reach.

David was gone. The wave of emotion hit her with the sudden fury of a freak wave. She had to turn quickly toward the window as her eyes filled up. She squeezed her hands into fists. London was blurry through her tears. She hoped Izzy was too lost in her own thoughts to notice, but apparently not.

"Are you all right?" she asked quietly. "I . . . I know what happened. David mentioned it. I'm sorry."

Stevie opened the window halfway and took a huff of the cold, minerally air to try to steady herself. It didn't work.

"I was stupid," she said, her voice cracking a bit.

"You?"

"I was jealous," Stevie said. "Of you."

"Me?"

It seemed this conversation might be one of identifying who was who.

"You thought— David? And me? Stevie, I have my own complicated romance going on with someone at home. It's a mess. No, David and I never . . . it's never come up."

This caught Stevie off guard.

"You do?" she said. "You never said."

"There's been no time this week," Izzy replied. "I've barely thought about it."

The idea that Izzy had a full life that didn't revolve around David had somehow never occurred to Stevie. Love made her stupid.

"Last night," Stevie said. "I waited for him. He never came over. It was our last night and I left the door open, and he never came. I thought he was with you."

"No," Izzy said. "He left about an hour after you came to the door. He was talking about you the whole time. I was too much of a mess to really listen. I wanted to go to sleep—I was so tired—but he was sitting there on the floor going on and on. He does that a lot—goes on and on about you."

"So he was sitting with you telling you he was going to break up with me," Stevie said.

"No," Izzy said. "He wasn't saying that. Actually, last night, he was talking about himself. I don't want to sound unappreciative—he was very kind to me all day—but by the evening he was having some kind of personal crisis and I didn't have the energy to help."

"Wait," Stevie said, turning to face Izzy. She no longer cared about her wet face or the fact that snot was going to run out of her nose at any second. "*What* was happening?"

"All he ever talks about is you. He's intimidated by you. Stevie this and Stevie that, and Stevie figured this out, and Stevie ran into the woods. . . . Last night he was talking about what you did at Merryweather, and how he has no direction in his life, and how you're special and he's not. That kind of thing. He does this. I was almost prepared not to like you, just because he's always banging on about his amazing girlfriend, Stevie, but then I met you."

This utterly foreign idea swept through Stevie's mind, erasing other concepts and realities as if they had been written in sand. David was *intimidated*. By her? David wasn't afraid of anything.

"Then this afternoon he had this strange look on his face when he brought me the fire safe and he told me what he did," Izzy went on. "I can see why you would think it had something to do with me, given that you found him in my room. You've helped me. You helped my aunt. And I need to do something for you. Something has to come out of this."

This seemed to rouse Izzy. A light came back into her eyes, and she sat up a bit straighter. There was something she could do to distract from the pain.

"What?" Stevie asked. "I don't know what to do."

"David," Izzy said, "is an idiot. He's lovely, but he is an idiot. He's impulsive. He didn't break up with you because he doesn't care about you—he did it because he's panicking about losing you. I'm sure of it. He's probably back at the house now regretting it and losing his mind. Have you told him you're here? Texted him?"

Stevie shook her head.

"Right." Izzy pulled out her phone and began to type. She held it up so Stevie could see the message.

You made a mistake with Stevie, didn't you? You're an idiot. What were you thinking?

A pause. Three dots appeared, retreated, appeared again.

I know.

Another set of dots.

At pub. Vodka sodass ar twi pounds

I screwed upp

gonna drink everything all the vofka sodas

"Do you *see*?" Izzy said. "Let's go make it right before he drinks that place dry. Excuse me!"

This was to the driver, who switched on the intercom. She redirected the cab to the Seven Bishops. And with that, the entire world spun around. The tears stopped. The streets of London propelled them toward David. It was all going to be all right.

They reached the Seven Bishops within minutes. The smell of beer hit Stevie as soon as they entered, along with the warmth of so many people packed into a small space. Izzy scanned, then guided Stevie deeper into the crowd that gathered along the bar and filled the floor space. In seconds she would be with him.

Then Izzy whirled around, a lopsided smile on her face.

"Oh," she said. "He just texted. He's not here. He's at the house. We should . . ."

Izzy had not looked at her phone or watch.

"What?"

"This way!" Izzy said, a forced brightness in her voice. She grabbed Stevie's arm and tried to guide her back through the crowd, but Stevie shook her off. Izzy was not a good liar. David was not back at the student house. Something weird was happening.

"Pizza!" Izzy said. "I'm starving. We need food. I haven't eaten since . . ."

Stevie looked over Izzy's shoulder, despite Izzy's attempts to block the view. There, in the same booth that they had sat in together just a week ago, was David. She could see the back of his coat. His head. But his face was missing.

That was because it was pressed into another.

Acknowledgments

I did it. I finally wrote an English country house mystery. This has been a goal of my life. Little Maureen spent many afternoons with her head in a mystery, dreaming of finding the body in the library. I was bad at kickball, but I was good at finding the murderer. Many people helped me to realize this dream, and all deserve thanks.

Nothing happens without my agent, Kate Schafer Testerman, of KT Literary. We've been roommates. We've been partners in publishing. We've been inseparable friends. She has agented from the hospital bed while in labor (I didn't ask her to—she said she was bored), on horseback, while being an amazing mom every day. She's everywhere at once. I don't know how she does it. You're the best, baby. See you in Vegas.

I am lucky beyond words to have Katherine Tegen as an editor. She has supported me (and Stevie) through all our adventures. Without her, these books would not be possible. My gratefulness has no bounds. Sara Schonfeld has been there every step of the way, for all my late-night emails and questions. So many thanks to everyone at HarperCollins who worked on this book, including: Alexandra Rakaczki, Vanessa Nuttry, Jessica White, David DeWitt, Joel Tippie, Leo Nickolls, Taylan Salvati, and Michael D'Angelo. My publicist, Megan Beatie of Megan Beatie Communications, is always there, helping bring Stevie to the world.

My friends and writing partners fill my life with happiness and my brain with ideas. Cassie Clare provided refuge and a place to write during the pandemic, as well as much support. Many things in the book started to make sense after a long conversation with Holly Black (most things in life start to make sense after talking to Holly Black). Robin Wasserman, as usual, provided much insight, because Robin is a bright beacon of pure wisdom. Kelly Link has devious ideas about romance. Additional thanks to Roosevelt Sinker for his comments, and Dan Sinker for keeping me going.

Thanks to Alexandra Padfield Young, for taking me to the gardens of Hidcote, and to Marion and Dom Young for walking me through the plant life of the English forest. Alexander Newman filled me in on the art of sitting exams. (At Oxford, not Cambridge. He'd be furious at me if I didn't mention this.) Simon Cole provided much-needed assistance on procedure and a lot of enthusiasm for the Manic Street Preachers.

All the thanks and love in the world to my husband, who spent a lot of time mentally walking around his alma mater with me, planning murders. He wants you to know you should not swim in the River Cam. It is full of Weil's disease and shopping carts.

And to you, of course, for reading. You are the most important part. I hope you enjoyed your time at the manor.

A riddle. A disappearance. A murder. Can you solve the mystery?

 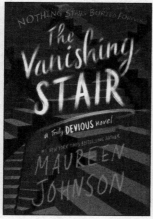 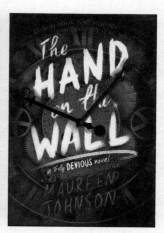

"Remember the first time reading Harry Potter and knowing it was special? There's that same sense of magic in the introduction of teen Sherlock-in-training Stevie Bell."
—*USA Today* ★★★★